The First Wives Club

The First Wives Club

OLIVIA GOLDSMITH

POCKET BOOKS

New York   London   Toronto   Sydney

Pocket Books
A Division of Simon & Schuster, Inc.
1230 Avenue of the Americas
New York, NY 10020

First Pocket Books trade paperback edition April 2008

POCKET and colophon are registered trademarks of Simon & Schuster, Inc.

For information about special discounts for bulk purchases, please contact Simon & Schuster Special Sales at 1-800-456-6798 or business@simonandschuster.com.

Designed by Mary Austin Speaker

Manufactured in the United States of America

10 9 8 7 6 5 4 3 2 1

ISBN-13: 978-1-4165-6283-2
ISBN-10:   1-4165-6283-4

ACKNOWLEDGMENTS

Never having won an award or a grant or a prize, I am especially aware of the generosity of others when I am the recipient. I am particularly grateful to those who assisted me during the long process of researching and writing this book. Sincerest thanks to:

Sherry Lansing, who understood everything and gave me the freedom and courage to do the book my way.

Justine Kryven, who typed and retyped and always had something positive to say, despite the dirty words.

Brendan Gunning, who gave superb editorial assistance, and so much of his time.

Barbara Turner, who lent me a cottage.

Louise Edwards Smith, who lent me grocery money.

Rosemary Sandberg, who insisted I do it.

Jan Villano and the staff at Elovitz and Partners, who photocopied, collated, typed, and mailed it for me.

Rob and Suzi Mascitelli, who laughed at all my jokes.

Acknowledgments

Rob and Suzi Mascitelli, who laughed at all my jokes.

Lenny Gartner, a great accountant and a great friend.

Lastly, deepest thanks to Paul Eugene Smith for the endless readings and rereadings, as well as all the brave encouragement during difficult times.

To Curtis Pickford Laupheimer

Contents

BOOK ONE:
The Wives: Getting Mad

Contents

BOOK TWO:
The Husbands: Getting Scared

BOOK THREE:
The Wives: Getting Even

Contents

EPILOGUE:
The Wives: Getting It Together

The First Wives Club

BOOK ONE

The Wives
Getting Mad

I

Annie

Manhattan, island of glittering dreams, slept in the predawn darkness. It was an island where dreams came true, where dreams were outgrown and discarded and sometimes turned to nightmares. Right then, in the darkness of a May night in the late 1980s, it was an island where many women slept alone.

Annie MacDuggan Paradise's bedroom had the simplicity that took a great deal of both taste and money to achieve. The floor was finished in an unfashionably dark chestnut color, gleaming with a dull richness, perfectly setting off the satiny Chinese rug that rested upon it. Other than the stunning exception of the mauve and cream and sapphire of the rug and the deep green of Annie's carefully tended bonsai trees, the room was a quiet oyster white, from the upholstered walls to the raw-silk curtains to the damask bedclothes. Everything about the room was immaculate; even the fire in the beige marble hearth had burned down neatly to a fine white ash. Only the bed itself was disheveled, the duvet rucked up, pillows on the floor, under the sheets.

Everything in the room was in exquisite taste, and calming, with one exception: beside the bed a pile of books towered up from the marble-topped nightstand. *Buddhism and*

Ecology: A Way to Save the Planet; The Wounded Woman; Women Who Love Too Much; Jung's Symbols and the Collective Unconscious; The Dance of Anger; and *Women of Japan.* Juxtaposed incongruously beside the garishly dust-jacketed pile was a tiny crystal vase with three delicate sprays of miniature *Cymbidium* orchids, the exact oyster white of the room. The serene tiny blooms seemed to float against the lurid backdrop of the book jackets. Then the phone beside the vase trilled.

A thin, tanned arm snaked out from under the blankets, reaching expertly for the receiver without upsetting the flowers or the books. The hand at the end of the arm was also brown and thin but, though a closer look revealed the thousand tiny lines of a certain age, was shaped much like a child's hand, the fingers small, the nails blunt and unpainted. The hand clutched the phone before it trilled again and pulled the receiver under the untidy mound of bedclothes.

"Hello." Her voice was a croak. She cleared her throat. "Hello."

"Anne? This is Gil." In the pause that followed, while Annie cleared her mind and came to full consciousness, he elaborated. "Gil Griffin." She had been dreaming, deep in another world, a place she didn't want to leave. With reluctance, however, she let it go. Gil Griffin.

"Gil. Hello." This couldn't be a social call, she thought. Annie couldn't remember the last time she had spoken to Gil Griffin. Certainly not in years, not since long before his divorce from Cynthia. And never on the phone at—she looked at her wristwatch—half past five in the morning. Something must be very wrong.

"I need your help. It's Cynthia. She's dead, Anne."

Annie couldn't quite take it in. Something wasn't jibing; the words and the tone were so at odds. No emotion at all. A weather report. A cold front sweeping south from Canada. Then it hit her.

"Oh, my God. What happened?" It wasn't possible. Cynthia wasn't sick. At least Annie didn't think so, hadn't seen any signs. And Cynthia was only a year older than she was. Maybe it was an accident. Had Cynthia been drinking too much? No, she reminded herself, it was her friend Elise who was the drinker.

"It was suicide," Gil said, and for a moment Annie couldn't speak. In the silence, dryly, he gave a few dreadful details. Bathtub. Wrists. Almost two days dead. "I'd rather not discuss it." His voice was bland, uninvolved. Intermittent rain across the Midwest, she thought. He's reporting the weather. Then, "I need you to do something."

"Of course. How can I help?" It was her automatic good-girl reaction. My God. Cynthia is dead. Cynthia is dead and I'm being polite. Annie shivered under the blankets, though it was the end of May. "What can I do?"

"The funeral is tomorrow morning."

"Tomorrow morning, Gil? So soon? But people will need time—"

He cut her off. "Could you call some of her friends and let them know? I've been out of touch with her circle for a while."

"Certainly, I'd like to help, but it's almost Memorial Day. People are leaving town early. And . . ." She thought of her own trip to Boston to see her son graduate. And Sylvie. The packing. These were their last few days together. Oh, no. Not now. The week had been so very hard already. Now this. Then she felt a wash of shame at her thoughts. She cleared her throat. "With so little notice I'm not sure that . . ."

"Do the best you can. I'm absolutely flooded myself," he reported tonelessly. Flood warnings in New York, Annie thought, an unpleasant joke. She sat up. Why the rush? Why so awfully quick?

"But are all the arrangements made? No one will know about flowers and things. I mean . . ." She felt herself begin to choke up, tears rushing to her eyes. She tried to calm herself. "And what about the eulogy, Gil?"

"I've handled it, Anne. Just call her friends. So, Campbell's, tomorrow at ten."

"At ten?" She shook her head, as if that would clear it. "So quickly? I—"

"Do the best you can. And thank you." He hung up. She was dismissed. Annie continued to hold the dead phone in her hand. She could hardly breathe. You bastard, she thought. You cold bastard. Slowly she replaced the receiver.

Cynthia has taken her own life. Cynthia is dead. Annie huddled in bed, shivering, despite the duvet. She would just lie here for a minute, in the safe darkness under the bedclothes and try to take this in. Feel my feelings, as Dr. Rosen, her ex-therapist, told her to do. She stretched out under the quilt. Her Siamese cat, Pangor, silently crossed the room and jumped onto the bed beside her. Cynthia, dear, sweet, funny Cynthia, was dead. It was awful. But surprisingly, the tears didn't come.

Just the memories. Cynthia, her friend at Miss Porter's. Her roommate. Cynthia had been so kind to her. On their first night at school, when Annie, ashamed, stripped down to her undershirt, Cynthia hadn't mocked her. Silently, she'd handed her a bra, turned away, and said, "You'll probably want to wear that, or the other girls might tease you."

She and Cyn had double-dated together. Cynthia's brother had introduced Annie to Aaron, and when they married, Cynthia had been her maid of honor. Then Cynthia had married Gil. And they'd each had a daughter at the same time.

Cynthia's daughter, her only child, had come late in life. She would have been the same age as my Sylvie, Annie thought. They had gone through their pregnancies together. Cynthia's daughter, Carla, had been a beautiful, perfect baby. It was ugly to admit it, but it had hurt Annie to see Carla grow and develop, while Sylvie was so slow. Then, one March day, Carla had been hit by a car while getting off the school bus. Annie felt doubly guilty over her secret envy. She had gone to sit the week-long vigil at the hospital in White Plains where the child lingered in a coma, brain-dead. Eventually most of Cynthia's other friends had stopped going, but Annie kept it up: she knew she couldn't do any good, but couldn't bear to think of Cynthia alone.

Then, one morning at the end of May, Cynthia had come into the sunny room paler even than usual, her eyes deep in their shadowed sockets. From across the room she spoke to Annie in a loud, flat voice. "He wants her off the respirator," she said. "Gil wants it finished."

Annie stood up and opened her arms. Cynthia walked into the embrace and bent her head low to reach the comfort of Annie's shoulder. Then she cried completely silently, but her tall body shook, and her tears were so hot that even Annie, always cold, was too warm. Still, she stood there and held Cynthia for what seemed like a long time. When at last Cynthia stopped crying, she took a deep breath, looked directly at Annie, and said, "My mother never loved me." Annie had nodded at the non sequitur. Then Cynthia shrugged, took out a handkerchief, and wiped her eyes.

They took the child off the life support system that afternoon, and she died early that evening. Soon after the funeral the Griffins had left for Europe. Shortly after they returned, they sold their house and bought another, grander one in Greenwich.

Meanwhile, Annie's two boys had gone off to school, and she and Aaron and Sylvie had moved to Manhattan. Of course she saw Cynthia for lunches, and occasionally for shopping in town, but Cynthia seemed to freeze, somehow. She spoke less and less. And after the divorce from Gil she was even quieter. Silent Cynthia.

Now Cynthia was dead. And by her own hand. It wasn't a coincidence that Carla had also died at the end of May.

Oh, God, she realized, it was the anniversary of Carla's death! She should have remembered! How could she let herself get so distant from a friend? How could she not know? Why was it that the deepest pain, the despair, was so shameful even good friends kept it secret? She turned over in bed and groaned.

Annie was forty-three. She was five foot four, exactly average height for an American woman, but she weighed only 109 pounds, not any more than she had weighed at Miss Porter's School more than twenty-five years before. She was compulsive about her weight, as she was about a lot of things: clothes, apartment, cottage, bonsai trees, writing, therapy. Now, as her therapist had instructed her, she let the waves of grief roll over her. Oh, God, it hurt. Cynthia, dead. If only she had called, Annie thought. I haven't seen her much lately. I should have . . .

Tears began to roll out of her eyes, down her cheeks. She began to sob, the noise tearing out of her. She pulled the comforter over her face, hoping to muffle the ugly cries. It wasn't only out of concern for her daughter, asleep down the hall. Annie herself couldn't bear to hear the sound.

The pain seemed unbearable, she thought as she wept. Images came to her mind. The flick of steel on skin. Blood snaking through bathwater. It was too awful. Why hadn't I called her? Oh, Cynthia, why didn't *you* call *me?* Lying on her back, crying, the blanket pulled over her face. Annie's tears moved down her cheeks, following the fine lines at the sides of her eyes, and rolled into her ears. They itched. She had to put a finger in each one to stop the tickle. At last her sobbing slowed, the tears stopped, and she slowly sat up.

She looked across her immaculate room toward the tall windows, where the early light was just beginning to tint the sky. She was exhausted, and the day hadn't yet started. "Fuck," she said as she threw off the comforter, and got out of bed.

Below her, the city was just beginning to awaken. Lights were still twinkling across the gray river over in Queens, making it look like a fairyland. In reality, much of Queens was a grim little borough that Annie had only been through on her way to the airport, so she knew how deceptive that view was. Things weren't always what they seemed. From her penthouse window, Annie could see the few predawn joggers making their lonely way along the rainy promenade. The whole previous week had been miserable, wet and chilly. Gray as death. She hugged herself and turned away.

How do you get through your oldest friend's suicide? she wondered as she padded across the soft carpet to the bathroom. Well, she'd do her usual routine. She'd keep busy. There was so much to do. She'd have to call Brenda and Elise and as many of Cynthia's friends as she could think of.

Who were Cynthia's friends? Annie admitted to herself that she rarely saw any of that old Greenwich crowd now. Just Brenda Cushman, who had never fit in up there, and Elise Elliot Atchison, who also had a place in town. But she'd had the most history with Cynthia. Cynthia was a real friend in a city where friendship was based on whom you knew, whom you married, what you had, and what you could give or get. Annie wished—well, it didn't matter what she wished now. Cynthia was dead.

When Annie emerged from the bathroom, swathed in beige terry cloth, her hair curled from the humidity, she looked drawn, her skin blotchy, her eyes red. She shook her head at her own reflection, but didn't pause. She walked down the long hallway that led from the master suite to the rest of the penthouse. She passed the closed door of Sylvie's bedroom, where she still slept. In just a few days she'd be gone. Annie knew she would have to mourn not only Cynthia's death but also the loss of her daughter.

But now there was no time. There wasn't even time to think any more about Cynthia. Only things to do. Annie told herself she had better get moving. In the immaculate tiled kitchen she went to the built-in desk in the corner beside the window. Here was where she did her writing, stuff that didn't amount to much. She'd published only two books of short stories, one just before her marriage, the other after, and both long, long before her children. But Aaron and her growing family had made her quit. The third book wasn't good enough for publication, he had said. Probably he was right. Still, she kept it up and the manuscripts piled up in the desk drawers.

She reached into the second desk drawer and found her large phone book. A reproduction of a Mary Cassatt was on the cover, a painting of a mother and her little girl. Annie sighed. All at once she longed for a cup of coffee, good and strong, with a lot of sugar. She'd given up both, but she could use the jolt now. No. Bad idea. Instead, she put some water on for tea and then sat down at the desk.

First, of course, she'd dial Brenda, her best friend in New York. Brenda was funny, solid, honest. But sometimes, well, not sensitive. Still, Annie wanted to call her, to be reassured and grounded. She looked at her watch, the gold Cartier Panther that she never took off. She liked always to know the time. It was almost a quarter to seven. She hated to do it to Brenda. While Annie was naturally an early riser, she knew Brenda sometimes slept till noon, and they had an agreement that Annie wasn't to call before eleven. Well, that rule wasn't in force now. Annie punched one digit and her automatic dialer beeped the familiar tones into her ear. Not surprisingly, it rang quite a few times before it was answered.

"Who the fuck is this?" Brenda's voice was always husky, but at this hour it was a virtual growl.

"It's me. I'm sorry to wake you but—"

"Not as sorry as you're going to be. What the fuck time is it, anyway? Jesus Christ, Annie, it's not even seven o'clock. Your only hope is that it's seven at night and I slept through the whole goddamned day."

"Brenda, I wouldn't call if it weren't serious."

"Are you upset about Sylvie leaving? I'll wake up. Is that it?"

"No. No. It's not that. Cynthia Griffin died."

"Who?"

"Cynthia Griffin. You know, Carla's mother." Brenda's son, Tony, had briefly been in a class with Carla at Country Day.

"Shit. Well, it's a damn shame when anyone dies, but what are you calling me for? At six A.M.?"

"The funeral's tomorrow morning."

"Jesus, what did she die of, the plague? Why are they sinking her so fast?"

"Brenda, she killed herself. She did it a couple of nights ago. They didn't find her until yesterday. A very bad scene, apparently."

"Jesus." Brenda was silent for a few moments. "Christ, she had the balls to check out, huh? I'm surprised. She was such a cold, snotty WASP." Annie thought of Cynthia's hot tears on her shoulder at the hospital. Sometimes Brenda was completely impossible. A reverse snob, and always hiding her feelings with wisecracks.

"Are you going or not?"

"Of course I'm going. Where and when?"

"Ten o'clock at Campbell's."

Brenda groaned again. "Gil couldn't wait to bury her, huh? What a *strunz*."

"I'm going to call Hudson and have him drive me. If you want, I'll pick you up at nine."

Another groan. "Jesus, Annie, it doesn't take an hour to drive ten blocks, even in Manhattan. Anyway, this week the city is a ghost town. Everyone's pushing Memorial Day. They're out at the Hamptons, or up in Connecticut. And there's no airport check-in at Campbell's. Make it ten. We'll be fashionably late."

Annie sighed. "I'll pick you up at nine-thirty. Don't keep me waiting. Now I've got to go. I've got calls to make."

"What calls?"

"Gil asked me to help, to let some people know."

"Nothing like short notice to help keep down the turnout."

"Oh, it's not as if he planned it that way."

"Wanna bet?"

"With a thing like this I suppose it's best to make it as discreet as possible."

"You gonna call Aaron?"

Annie felt something in her chest flutter. "I hadn't thought of it." She paused. He should be told. He'd want to come. He always considered Cynthia flaky, but he had liked her. Annie was going to see her ex-husband the day after tomorrow, at their elder son's graduation from Harvard. She'd hoped it would be a happy time, that maybe . . . She thought of calling him now, of the possibility of another woman answering the phone.

"I'll call him for you," Brenda offered, sensing Annie's hesitation.

"Would you?"

"Sure. It would be a pleasure to wake that dickweed up early."

Brenda blamed Aaron for leaving Annie, but Annie herself still couldn't go that far. And secretly, she still hoped. Well, perhaps Cynthia's tragedy would bring them together again.

"Thanks, Brenda. See you tomorrow at half-past nine. Go back to sleep."

She hung up and crossed to the range, turning off the flame under the kettle. She'd have to call Elise next, but she wasn't looking forward to it. And then all the other phone numbers she'd have to track down. Plus there was packing to finish for Sylvie, and tranquilizers for the cat to be picked up from the vet. She had to select her clothes for the graduation and have Ernesta pack her overnight bag. Then she'd think about the funeral. She'd have to dress. Aaron would see her. She felt the flutter in her chest again. Vanity, vanity. As if it mattered what she wore or how she looked. Cynthia was dead. But still. She would see Aaron. Maybe talk to him. Maybe even cry together. Oh, Aaron. I could use comfort now. But Aaron was still angry at her, over Sylvie. Over sending Sylvie away to school. Although he himself didn't visit their daughter much since he'd moved out, and wasn't participating in her care, he didn't want her sent away to school.

Annie looked over at the neat breakfast setting that waited for her and Sylvie on the table. She'd set it last night, in another universe, before she'd heard the news about Cynthia.

Annie realized she was still holding the kettle. Suddenly she turned, roughly shoving it back on the range. With renewed energy she reached for the refrigerator and began rooting through the freezer. Somewhere in there was a pound of French-roast Brazilian coffee, and she was going to have a cup. After all, she was alone now and no one would see her fall from grace. One of the few comforts of the deserted wife.

All at once a wave of loneliness hit her so hard that she had to clutch the side of the refrigerator until her knuckles whitened. She thought of the day she had stood in the same spot, watching, as Aaron walked through the kitchen with his clothes packed, ready to leave them at the service door. "I'll just bring these two with me and have the porter hold the rest downstairs," he had said.

Annie had nodded silently.

"I'm going to stay at the Carlyle for a while. And you can reach me at the office during the day."

She had nodded again, mute, stupid with sorrow and confusion.

"Let's just try to give each other some space, okay?"

"Space is the last thing I need," Annie had said. She knew the moment she said it how forlorn it sounded.

He looked at her kindly. At heart, Aaron was kind. "Don't look so tragic, Annie. This too shall pass," he said. Then he was gone.

He had said it was a temporary separation, but he had lied. Aaron—her college sweetheart, her love, the good father to her sons, the man she believed in above all others—he had walked out. She clutched the refrigerator handle, dizzy from the memory.

She stood alone in her shining, immaculate, empty kitchen until the feeling passed. Annie thought again of Dr. Rosen, her therapist for over three years, who had so abruptly terminated her. Perhaps she should call her, just for help to get through this latest episode. But Dr. Rosen had hurt her, had called her a "dependent personality" and a "martyr," and though a part of Annie agreed with the diagnosis, she wanted to prove Dr. Rosen wrong.

Annie knelt and stroked Pangor. "Are you hungry, baby?" she said, opening a can of Ocean Feast, his favorite cat food, grateful for the activity, grateful for the cat's affection, even if it was tied to his stomach. Maybe, if she took pains with her makeup, if she got to the funeral early, maybe she'd see Aaron. The divorce was so recent. Despite this separation, the fight over Sylvie, maybe he was as unhappy without her as she was without him. Though he hadn't seemed unhappy two nights ago when he called about the graduation plans. But this news would rock him. Perhaps now they'd talk. He'd look at her and remember that once, once, it had been so very good. Maybe the funeral would bring back some of the past, the past worth saving, worth cherishing. Maybe.

Annie was the kind of woman who believed in taking actions, and to some extent it worked for her. She was healthy and attractive and had managed to marry well, bear and raise three children, nurture strong friendships, do a great deal of charity work, survive a separation, create this perfect home and a life of some elegance and comfort in the costliest and perhaps most beautiful square in Manhattan's Upper East Side. She could still turn men's heads, though she knew she was subtle rather than stunning. But she was alone, and her husband had abandoned her. The trouble was that, like Cynthia, Annie was only the first wife.

2

Campbell's Soup

Probably half of the wealthy WASPs in the so-called silk stocking district of Manhattan and virtually all of its celebrities are buried out of Campbell's Funeral Home. It is also a second home to paparazzi, who snap pictures of the bereaved family and friends (when it is a noteworthy death) and are then served coffee and doughnuts (charged to the funeral) at the side entrance.

Ashes to ashes, dust to dust. Here we go again, Larry Cochran thought, loading his camera. The people who buy the tabloids eat up those haggard faces in the photos.

Today's, however, was not a noteworthy death. When Larry Cochran showed up, it was simply because he had nothing better to do and also because he could use the free breakfast. He quickly checked out the scene and immediately gave up hope of a score. Some matron from Connecticut. No one anyone ever heard of. Typical. He'd been running low on luck for weeks.

He spent a little while bullshitting with Bob Collechio, who ran the catering. He didn't want it to be too obvious that he was scarfing up the pastries like an animal and trying to stay in out of the rain. His press pass expired at the end of June, and if he didn't get some shots soon, he'd not only be penniless but undocumented. It never ceased to amaze him that things really could always get worse, and usually did.

"So, anything new?" he asked Bob.

"Well, this one was a cute job. She offed herself. A cutter. The spic maid found her a couple of nights later, emptied out in the bathtub. Didn't need to drain her before they embalmed her, but I hope the big shot bastid ex-husband don't expect no discount. It was a rush job. Brought her in yesterday and they're sinkin' her today."

. Larry internally winced at *spic* and at his own image of the sanguine bathtub. Larry was visual. He *saw* things that other people described. Which helped him make his living as a photographer and film editor, he admitted, but made his internal world almost too graphic. He needed cooperation from Bob, but felt like a worm dealing with him.

"So why the rush?"

"Ah, she's the first wife of some big deal Wall Street guy, ya know, and now he's got the new one stashed on Park Avenue, so I guess he don't want no muss, no fuss, know what I mean?" He winked at Larry. "It ain't good for business when you lose the ladies' sympathy vote, ya know." He laughed, a tinny sound that seesawed unpleasantly.

"So what's her name?" Okay, it was a long shot, but maybe there was something in it.

"Griffin."

"As in *Gil* Griffin? Gil Griffin's first wife?" This could be news. Everyone knew Gilbert Griffin. He was the barracuda of hostile takeovers, one of the big players at the big players' table. And he was class. Not like Boesky or Milken. Discreet. Well, he had been until the scandal broke over his office romance with that blond MBA he was mentoring, the one with the slightly horsey face and the unbelievable body. He'd denied it for months in the press, talked about his home and wife, but then when the pressure was off him, he divorced the first one and married the MBA. After a brief new flare-up the Boardroom Sex Scandal headlines had died down. Now Larry couldn't even remember the MBA's name, or the name of Gil's first wife either. He was real bad with names, but great with faces. What do you expect from a photographer? He looked up on the bulletin board over Bob's head. Cynthia. Cynthia Griffin. "Listen, thanks for the tip. I think I'll stick around."

The tip paid off when, a few minutes later, a big black Mercedes limo pulled up and Elise Elliot Atchison stepped out. Of course, Larry recognized *her* immediately. He'd know those bones anywhere, the shape of her unforgettable face. She was wearing a deep navy suit with a creamy white blouse, and her long, long legs were sheathed in silky stockings that matched her simple beige high-heeled pumps. Her hair, a dozen shades of blond, was pulled back into a French braid, and her eyes were hidden by enormous sunglasses, her head swathed in a dark blue chiffon scarf.

Only last week, Larry had seen one of her old films, a favorite of his, *Walking in the Dark.* Now he lifted his camera for a shot, but he had taken so long to make his move that he missed her. *That* hadn't happened in a long time. He realized he was actually excited. And it wasn't because he could sell the photograph, which he was sure he could do. It was because he actually was impressed. He, Larry Cochran, New York newshound and filmmaker-to-be was impressed. She must be, what, fifty-five? Sixty? She'd come along right after Grace Kelly, had been promoted as her successor. Well, however old Elise Elliot must be, she still looked beautiful. Larry wondered briefly how she knew this Cynthia Griffin, but immediately flashed on the scene in *Nobody's Fool,* when the Elise Elliot character had attended her sister's funeral. This could have been a replay, but thirty years later. Too bad he'd missed the shot, but he'd hang around and get her coming out.

Elise Elliot had really been something. If the studio system hadn't broken down, she'd have been a big Hollywood star instead of an interesting footnote. She'd been an intelligent actress during a period of floozies, but her elegance had contrasted with her sexuality. She'd had both, and when she left Hollywood and went to France to work with unknown directors in tiny-budget foreign films, everyone thought she was crazy. She showed them. She'd made some beautiful movies, classics, and then she'd retired almost two decades ago. She'd just disappeared, gotten married to some big business type. Christ, what was the guy's name? Atkins or something. A nobody. And she'd worked with Chabrol, Gerard Artaud, all the great ones. Larry had seen every one of her films at least a dozen times, but he'd never seen her in person before. It actually took him a few minutes to recover and start keeping an eye out again. Hey, who knows who might show up next? he thought.

Two women were walking down Madison toward him. He tried to check them out. Maybe this was going to be a bonanza of stars of a certain age. One of the women was obese, dressed in an enormous black poncho with some kind of fluffy trim, fringes or something. Hey, some of them let themselves go and had taste in their toes. Look at La Liz. But no, this was no one. Neither was the other, a thin, attractive brunette. Well, that was okay. He was used to waiting. And a picture of a grieving Gil Griffin could possibly bring in something. He could wait. That was his business.

Inside the funeral home, Annie Paradise and Brenda Cushman surrendered their coats and walked down the carpeted gray hall to Salon D. Chandeliers gleamed above them, but despite the somber colors, the multiple rooms and the announcement boards outside each door created the effect of a catering hall.

"It always reminds me of a great place to have an Episcopal bar mitzvah," Brenda whispered to Annie. "That is, if there was such a thing."

Her husky voice carried, and Annie told her to be quiet. Annie felt drained, empty of tears, but still so sad and angry.

"Oh, c'mon. Who'm I gonna upset? Cynthia? That rotten scumbag Gil? He could give two shits."

"Brenda, if you don't behave, I swear, I'm going to sit separately."

"Okay, okay. But I'm no hypocrite. I never was friends with Cynthia. She snubbed me, like all the other women up there in Greenwich. Annie, you were the only one who was nice to me. You're the only thin woman I can stand, and if you were blond, too, you could forget about it." She paused and raised her eyebrows. "Speaking of thin, rich, blond bitches, look who's coming."

Annie turned to see her other good friend, Elise Atchison, striding toward them.

"Annie," Elise said, bending to kiss the air beside Annie's cheek. "Just dreadful. Isn't it?" Elise looked paler than usual, her exquisite features blurred, a hint of darkness under her eyes. "I couldn't reach Bill this morning, so he won't make it."

"Hello," Brenda said loudly, extending her hand. "Brenda Cushman," she reminded Elise, who nodded in acknowledgment.

"They're about to start," Elise told Annie, and the three women moved forward together.

They reached the door of Salon D and Annie opened it. Elise entered first, but Annie stood aside for Brenda to pass through, which she only just managed without scraping her wide hips on the doorjamb. For about the seven thousandth time, Annie wished she could get Brenda into Overeaters Anonymous or therapy of some kind so she could lose the weight. She'd given her a copy of *Starving for Love: Women and Compulsive Eating Disorders.* Brenda had said nothing, then sent her a copy of *Fat Is a Feminist Issue* in return.

Salon D was not well lit, and it was very nearly empty. "I told you we'd be early," Brenda hissed, but it was already five after ten.

Annie had brought a bonsai boxtree with her, one she had developed herself and Cynthia had admired, but now she was too uncomfortable to put it anywhere: certainly not the casket. The place was so empty, any noise or movement would attract attention. She and Brenda followed Elise to a row and took seats.

Through her skin, in the way people can sense the presence of someone they love, Annie knew Aaron was already there. She cautiously looked around. Yes, there he was, at the other side of the chapel, near the front. She knew he would come. She felt her heartbeat accelerate. So wasteful. She could spot the back of his neck among a million others: the dark, dark hair that always gleamed, as if it had been brushed a thousand times; the neck, with that healthy pink-brown glow. Aaron, even from the back, looked more vital, more alive, than other people.

It didn't matter that he had left her. It didn't even matter that he'd asked to finalize the divorce. Love was not like water in a faucet, something you could simply turn off. She could learn—she had learned—to live without him, but she couldn't stop loving him. She still hoped. It was shameful, her secret, but it was true.

She looked at Brenda on her right and Elise on her left, the first divorced by her husband, the second virtually abandoned by hers. And I, too, am a woman alone, Annie thought. Just like Cynthia. She sighed.

Several other women sat scattered about the room. Annie recognized one or two. At the front was a Hispanic woman, crying quietly, the only woman with a man beside her. Other than he and Aaron, there were only females in the room. Dreadful for Cynthia to end her life without masculine attention. Then an older man entered briskly, followed by a younger one, but Annie recognized the elder as an attorney from Cromwell Reed, the old-money law firm that had represented Cynthia and her family for generations. Just business.

Altogether, there were perhaps a dozen people scattered about Salon D.

"Where's the scumbag?" Brenda whispered, and for a moment Annie thought she meant Aaron. She inclined her head toward him.

"Not that one. I meant *Cynthia's* scumbag."

Annie saw Elise's eyelids flicker, but Annie was wondering the same thing. Where *was* Gil? Well, perhaps he was waiting in the wings to give the eulogy. The coffin lay on a draped bier at the front of the room. There was only one floral arrangement, red roses. How awful, Annie thought. Cynthia hated red roses. God, I could at least have seen to that. She laid her bonsai tree on the empty seat beside her. Cynthia's family should have done better than this.

But then, who *was* the family? she asked herself. No surviving parents, no surviving children, no surviving marriage. But there was Stuart Swann, Cynthia's brother. Where was he? Even though he and Cynthia hadn't been on speaking terms for some time, surely Stuart would want to say goodbye. Annie knew him well enough to believe he would want to do the right thing. And wasn't there a doddering aunt somewhere? Aunt Esme. But I don't know if she's even alive anymore, Annie realized. She remembered Cynthia's whisper at the hospital: "My mother never loved me." Perhaps no one had. Annie's eyes suddenly filled. It was a tragic, tragic waste.

Once again, Annie felt that wash of loneliness. She missed Cynthia, she missed her two sons, she missed Aaron. And soon she would miss Sylvie. She thought she had gotten over the pain of separation and had begun acceptance, but Cynthia's death had opened all the wounds.

Annie looked up as a cadaverous white-haired man in a dark clerical robe entered from a side door and stepped onto the platform. He looked like the generic "very reverend" to Annie, and he immediately launched into a generic memorial address. Man's days are like sand in the hourglass, and God's salvation and our good works live after us. No mention of Cynthia's life, of the spectacular garden she had created, of her generosity, of Carla. In fact, he only mentioned Cynthia by name once. The rest of the time she was "the departed." It was as if he might forget, or get it wrong, if he tried to say her name again. Well, surely Gil would say something personal in his eulogy. The divorce had been bitter, humiliating, and public, but he would manage something.

It wasn't until the "very reverend" began the Lord's Prayer to close the service that Annie realized that Gil wasn't "in the wings," wasn't even making an appearance. It must have been like this for Cynthia, too, she thought, never quite believing Gil was really as cold and insensitive as he obviously was.

Then for a terrible moment Annie wondered whether when she died Aaron would skip her funeral. She *was* the mother of his children. God, she was becoming morbid. She shook her head, trying to clear it. At least she had her children, and her friends. And Aaron? Annie looked over at the back of her husband's head. He must still care *something* for her. He had never been mean, never humiliated her. Poor

Cynthia. How could Gil treat her so badly? Such a sad, shabby ending. And Annie had helped. Gil had used her to gather a few people, and then he had washed his hands. Cynthia was disposed of. Refuse.

As the service ended, the director from Campbell's made an announcement. "The deceased will be taken to City of Angels Cemetery in Greenwich. Those who wish to attend, please see me for transportation." Elise shook her head. Annie looked over at Brenda. "No way!" Brenda whispered. Annie crumpled the wet tissues in her hand nervously. She had so much yet to do to finalize Sylvie's departure. Every moment she had left with her daughter was so precious. Worse, she hated burials, but who would go to see poor Cynthia put in the ground? How lonely, if she was buried without a single witness. Annie, along with everyone else, rose. She wiped her eyes quickly and began to move toward the back of the room, walking slowly, hoping not to be too obvious in wanting to wind up beside Aaron. Elise, with her long strides, glided quickly up the aisle. Brenda stayed beside Annie, then gave her a nod.

"He's gone. First out," she said.

But in the hallway, Aaron stood waiting. "Hello, Annie. It's terrible news, isn't it?" He looked white, stricken.

"Terrible." She wished he'd take her hand, hold her, but he only shook his head. They stood facing each other for a time, wordless. Annie remembered how badly Aaron handled loss.

"She was never really happy," Aaron said.

For a moment, Annie felt anger wash over her. For God's sake, why did people feel that lives could be summed up in a sentence, one so trite at that?

"Who is?" she asked tartly, and silently prayed that Aaron wouldn't next tell her it was "better this way."

"Well, Alex seems happy. He's finished his last final."

"You spoke to him?" Alex, her eldest son, hadn't called her last weekend. He had asked that Sylvie not come for his graduation, and Annie had been hurt by his decision. Aaron, she knew, had been relieved. Only Chris, her middle boy, understood just how special Sylvie was.

"He called last night. He's looking forward to tomorrow."

"So am I." Annie managed to smile at Aaron. They would be in Boston together for it. Maybe in Boston . . . If only they could have a few pleasant words now; if only she saw some sign that he still cared.

"When does Sylvie leave?"

"In three more days."

"You won't reconsider? Those places," he said. "They're degrading. They beat the children. They abuse them. She'll wind up a complete vegetable."

"Aaron, please. We're not talking about a state institution. We're talking about a private, sheltered community. We've been through this before."

"Look, we'll get you some more help. Ernesta isn't enough."

"That's not it. I don't need more help. It's Sylvie, Aaron. She needs to be with other people like her. She's too lonely, Aaron. She's too isolated."

"Don't be ridiculous. She's with you all the time." He sounded bitter.

Annie sighed. "That's the problem. She's too dependent. She on me." And maybe I on her, she thought to herself. How will I fill my days without Sylvie? "Aaron, please. We've been through this a hundred times. Not now."

"Fine." He was brusque.

She knew that tone. She had hurt him. Oh, God, this wasn't what she wanted.

"I've got to get back to the office," he said. Then he turned away. Turned away and walked out the doors of Campbell's without a kind word for Cynthia or any comfort for herself. These men! she thought. Emotional cripples.

Annie looked away from Aaron's retreating back to see a receiving line of sorts with Gil Griffin standing there, shaking hands and accepting condolences. Annie felt herself begin to tremble. "How could he?" she asked, meaning both Aaron and Gil. How could they?

She had not directed the question to anyone, but Brenda, who had come up behind her, answered it: "Easy, when you're a hypocritical reptile."

Dazed, Annie moved along with the others. God, the last thing she wanted to do was talk to Gil right now. No, the last thing she wanted was to go to the cemetery; seeing Gil now was bad, but not as bad as that. What possible excuse could he have for missing the service? And now, showing up for this farce. It was an insult; no, worse than an insult. Well, surely he'd see Cynthia to her grave.

When Annie reached Gil, she didn't extend her hand, but Gil took it anyway.

"Thank you, Anne," he said. Her fingers were cold, his hand surprisingly warm. She withdrew her hand; Elise, who was beside her, folded her own hands behind her back. "Hello, Gil," she said coolly.

Annie, as always, was embarrassed by the contretemps. "Do you want me to ride with you to the cemetery?" she heard herself ask. Here I go again, the ultimate good girl, she thought. And it was the ultimate sacrifice, but she could stand it.

"Oh, I can't make it out to Greenwich, now."

"What?" Brenda asked. Even tough Brenda sounded shocked.

"I can't make it. I'm double-booked as it is. It was very difficult getting here at all."

"Obviously," Annie said coldly. "You didn't make it in time for the service and now you're not going to the burial?"

"It's none of your business, really," said Gil calmly. He began to turn away from the three of them.

"Gil, please come to the cemetery. It would matter to Cynthia."

Gil paused and looked down at her, his head tilted, bird-like, quizzical. Then he smiled grimly. "It matters very little. She's dead, you know." He walked away.

Annie stood silently in the hall between her two friends, breathing heavily. Then she began to tremble.

When Brenda and Elise left, Annie was still trembling. All the other funeral guests had gone, and Annie found she was the only one going to the graveside. She said good-bye to Elise and watched Brenda walk up Madison Avenue in the light rain that was beginning to fall. She told Hudson to get directions in case they were separated from the hearse. As he returned with an umbrella and helped her into the limo, Stuart Swann, Cynthia's brother, approached. Annie hadn't seen him in years, but she recognized him immediately. He's still nice looking, she thought, but dissipated. She noted his red-rimmed eyes and flaccid skin.

"Hello, Stuart." She extended her hand politely, although she didn't feel like it. Why hadn't *he* made it to the service on time? She wanted to demand an explanation, but his distraught look stopped her. After all, what could be done now?

"I should have known that you would come, Annie. Loyal to the end." His eyes filled with tears, and he patted her shoulder. Much as he might a well-behaved dog, she thought, which was what she felt like right now.

"I'm so very sorry."

"Me, too. I just found out. I was in Japan. I can hardly

believe it." He stopped, and tears began to spill out of his eyes. "Oh, God. I'm sorry."

Annie didn't know if he meant he was sorry he was crying or sorry about Cynthia, or both. There was nothing to say, so she took his hand and squeezed it. He pressed back, desperately.

"Annie, can I go with you?"

"Yes, of course, Stuart."

"Thank you. Thank you."

Together they rode through the rain along the dripping Hutchinson River Parkway, past the New York–bound traffic. Stuart cried for most of the trip, then was silent. By the time they reached City of Angels the rain had turned into a downpour.

Cynthia was gone. Annie looked at the small bonsai box-tree she had been holding all morning. She placed it gently on the lowering casket and cried for her friend. *I won't let him get away with this, Cynthia. I don't know what I can do, but I'll try, Cyn.*

She stood at the graveside and watched as the shoveled mud slid onto Cynthia's coffin.

3

Elise

Elise walked through the drizzle as she headed downtown to Madison Avenue. It was only a quarter to eleven. She nodded at Cynthia's brother as he emerged from a taxi outside the funeral home. A bit late, wasn't he? she thought. The whole affair was a travesty. Cynthia Griffin's life had been summed up and disposed of in less than half an hour. And while Elise hadn't been close to Cynthia for years, she had known her and her family well at one time. The Swanns were a part of the old guard, the Greenwich crowd, a privileged world to which Elise, also, belonged. She had always believed that Cynthia had married beneath her, and the way Gil Griffin had behaved today proved it. Poor Cynthia.

Elise had told her driver to meet her at one at the Carlyle—who could have predicted a twenty-minute funeral?—and after the service she had no stomach to do anything other than head in the direction of the hotel where her car would eventually be waiting. At one time she could have distracted herself with shopping, but that had become boring. Besides, she couldn't bear looking at herself in the mirror anymore. There was never any good news there. She actually avoided her reflection in the windows of the stores. That and her pain prevented her from noticing she was being followed.

Larry Cochran tried to keep a discreet distance away. He knew his quarry was elusive and self-protective: there were few candid pictures of her, which was what would make these valuable. He walked on the opposite side of the street from her; using a zoom lens, he had already shot a whole roll of film. When they came to Seventy-ninth Street, he caught a real break when she crossed over to him, and he realized he might be able to squeeze off full-face shots. Maybe, if it clouded over more, she might take off her dark glasses. That would be a real coup.

Looking through his lens, he saw her do just that. And there it was—her face in clear close-up! It was such a perfect face, but contorted now by so much pain that it literally took his breath away. He touched the shutter and found his hand was shaking. What an astonishing face! A face of desolation, a soul in the desert.

He squeezed off two shots before she passed him and turned. She seemed not to notice. He was right behind her now, and he watched the smooth mechanism of her hips and legs as she moved. She was tall, maybe five ten and a half, but she didn't stoop. She glided with a strong pelvic lead: like a model, her hips seemed to arrive before the rest of her. Larry felt a stirring in his own pelvic region. Well, she was still beautiful and had been the stuff of intelligent men's lustful dreams for two decades. Still, he was surprised and embarrassed by his own reaction. He wasn't the kind of animal who walked around with a hard-on and pursued strange women. Jesus, this was a legend he was walking behind, and she'd obviously just suffered a great loss. Who was Cynthia Griffin to her anyway, and why did she have to bear this alone? He felt moved to pity, and ashamed of his spying. Still, he followed her.

On Seventy-sixth she turned left. Of course, he should have guessed. The Carlyle Hotel, a favorite watering hole and trysting place of the very, very wealthy. Reportedly John Kennedy had had assignations here when he was president, and only last year Sid and Mercedes Bass had holed up in a suite on the tenth floor when their affair was at its peak and they were still very married to other people. He'd made a few bucks on a shot of them he caught.

She was turning in at the hotel entrance. Well, he had enough shots. The pictures would be beautiful. Perhaps he should just take off. Yet her face haunted him. He started to think crazy, like maybe he'd follow her inside. There was so little in life that was beautiful, truly beautiful. It was no surprise that he was drawn to what was. Maybe he'd talk to her.

But Jesus, he was a professional, and a broke one at that. What was he thinking of? He wasn't even sure he had enough cash on him to buy her a drink. This was no time to get weird, risk having some burly security guard expose his film or dump his ass on the sidewalk. Still, he followed Elise in through the gilded revolving doors. Luckily he had put on a blazer and tie this morning, but he wasn't sure it would pass muster. Probably they wouldn't eject him if he kept a low profile. He saw Elise slip up the low, elegantly carpeted stairs and decided to follow. He didn't think she had spotted him yet. This was ridiculous, but he couldn't walk away.

Elise entered Bemelman's Bar and took a seat on a banquette in the corner. It was dimly lit, which was the way she wanted it. Then no one could watch her fall apart. Because she was falling apart, no doubt about it.

It was too early for a drink, of course, but she'd have one anyway. Today she needed it, anything to calm her. She desperately didn't want to go all the way back to Greenwich or East Hampton, but she also wanted to avoid the New York apartment and a possible encounter with Bill.

So perhaps she would stay right here, in Bemelman's Bar.

She'd always liked this place, and so many good things had happened to her here. She'd been brought here after her coming out party, and it was here she met with Howard, her agent, and heard the news that she was being signed by MGM. She'd been here on Oscar night, 1961, when she was the dark-horse winner. She'd met Gerard here for the first time. Only good things had happened in this place.

And there hadn't been good things in her life for some time. Of course, things were different for her than they were for other people. Being one of the three wealthiest women in America didn't help one fit in. She knew that, had accepted it long ago. But surely *some* things had to be the same. So what were they, and how could she tell? Was this sense of dislocation normal for everyone, or was it just her?

Growing up so very different had been difficult, although her mother's direction had helped Elise learn to deflect much of the envy and resentment of others. Of course, there was a price: she could never be completely natural, never completely herself with outsiders. Even her mother couldn't save her from the loneliness. Because it wasn't just the money that set her apart—as she grew up, her beauty and intelligence became more evident, and for many, the powerful combination of looks, money, and brains was too much. Elise was also thoughtful, pleasant, generous; as a result, she was popular and well liked. But lonely. Always lonely.

Lonely in spite of the fact that everyone seemed to know who she was, her life having been made public through the press coverage of her father's death, her huge inheritance, and her New York City debut. Still, she continued to be thoughtful, pleasant, and to make a conscious effort to play down her wealth. In college, she took buses instead of limos, always paid in cash, and joined her classmates at the cheap restaurants they prized. Still, she was not a normal coed and she made no real friends.

She cut short her stay in college to try Hollywood, a place that at first seemed to be ideal for her. Here, finally, it didn't make a difference that she was one of the richest women in the world. She settled into a life as normal as she ever had.

Except, of course, for the men. They were all over her. Attractive, young, talented, clever, monied. They were wonderful, and she fell in love again and again. Frightened by her own hunger for affection, and for sex, she made a foolish, disastrous first marriage to a young Adonis. And when it crumbled, Uncle Bob and the studio bailed her out quickly.

Then the studio system itself began to crumble. By the time she saw that the American market was more youth oriented, she knew her popularity was waning. She was too formal, old-fashioned. Her calls were not returned. Her agent dumped her. For once, her money couldn't protect her or buy her acceptance. It was at the Cannes Film Festival that she met French film director François Truffaut, who encouraged her to work in the European movie industry. She found it a surprisingly difficult decision to make, but once it was made, she adjusted to her new world beautifully. Truffaut saw to it that Elise met the most brilliant, avant-garde thinkers of the day. Gentle and brotherly, his nurturing affected her deeply. Finally finding a man who wanted nothing from her, only wanted for her to be the best she could be, she bloomed as an actress under his tutelage. Her only trouble came when an affair with one of her costars, and one of France's top sex symbols, got out of hand.

She'd escaped that trouble by turning to Bill Atchison. And now Bill was the trouble. She sighed. They had been married now for almost twenty years, but it was all too obvious he had tired of her long ago. For years she had turned a blind eye to Bill's ever more frequent infidelities, even when they were too obvious to ignore—the calls from women "clients," the late "working" nights—because she wanted this marriage. Their home was in East Hampton, and he spent weeknights in the city. Lately, however, he hadn't come out even on the weekends. Then yesterday she couldn't reach him with the news of Cynthia's death, so she had no idea where he was sleeping. So far her humiliations had been private, but they were threatening to explode publicly. Now she was afraid Bill was going to leave her.

The truth was, she loved Bill, and their life together. She'd tried so hard for years, but it had all been a waste. Now she saw that she shouldn't have given up the career, shouldn't have buried herself in his life. He took her for granted, he ignored her. He hadn't touched her for how long now? Since Acapulco? She tried to count backward. Eleven months. And how long had it been before that?

Perhaps it was just a new phase in the marriage, she reasoned. Perhaps. But she was more frightened than she had ever been. And she had been drinking even more than usual to keep that fear down. It churned in her stomach, it made her hands shake.

Maurice, Bemelman's day bartender, someone she had known for a dozen years, approached the table. She ordered a Courvoisier, hoping it wouldn't make her sick. She'd only have one, she promised herself, as she always did. Only one. But when Maurice brought the brandy, she drank it straight off and ordered another. As she always did.

She hoped that, if Bill left, she would not be as publicly humiliated as Cynthia had been by Gil. God, does Bill have to leave me? Don't let me end up like Cynthia. She took a deep breath, trying to get a grip on herself. He wouldn't dare. But for the first time, he had actually threatened to. Important men can get away with it now. It's acceptable. For God's sake, even Ron Reagan got a second wife and he got to be president.

Finally warmed by the liquor, Elise smiled. I must remember, she told herself, that I'm merely a demographic statistic in a changing culture. Welcome to the nineties, Elise, a decade in which you bid your sexuality good-bye and become irrevocably old.

God, she thought, what is less appealing than a fifty-year-old divorced woman? A sixty-year-old one.

She waved to Maurice, who was at the table of the only other patron in the bar. He turned and approached her. "Madame, excuse me, but the gentleman insists he knows you and asked me to bring you a drink. Is it all right?"

She looked across the room. Without her glasses on, she hadn't a clue. Was it someone she knew? She picked up her glasses and, without unfolding them, peered through the lenses. He was a young man, and he didn't look familiar. Was he the son of some Greenwich friend? He wasn't smiling, but only looking levelly past the empty tables to her seat at the banquette. What the hell. After all, this was Bemelman's Bar. Only good things had happened here, and she felt that she could barely tolerate being alone another moment. "Certainly, Maurice," she said, and looking across the room, she did her best to smile.

Larry helped Elise as she almost staggered down the hall. He was taller than she, but not by too much, and she was surprisingly heavy for a thin woman. She was letting her head hang forward, and she kept saying, "Please don't let anyone see me." Over and over, quietly, in that lovely but frightened voice. "Please don't let anyone see me."

It was all right now. He'd spoken to them at the desk, handled it. Thank God his credit card hadn't been revoked. He had his right arm around Elise, supporting her. He stopped in front of Room 705 and fumbled with the key. Sometimes he had trouble with locks. Today, thank God, it opened easily.

He felt as if he were in a dream as they crossed the room together and Elise sank onto the bed. Once there, her crying began in earnest. She clutched at the pillow under the perfectly folded spread and pulled it to her stomach. He stood over her, helpless, as she cried like a little child.

She lifted her head from the bed. "I'm going to be sick," she told him, and moaned. Larry reached under her shoulders and helped her stand. They got to the basin just in time, and he held her head as she vomited into the sink. In between the retching, she moaned. Then, "Oh, don't look!" she cried, but she was so ill he couldn't leave her. After a time she stopped, and he helped her stand, turning her from the mirror, gently wiping her face with a damp cloth. When he was certain she could stand alone, he filled a glass with water and handed it to her. She rinsed her mouth, then picked up the courtesy toothbrush and began to brush her teeth. "Would you get me my bag?" she asked.

She let him stand in the doorway as she fixed her face. Expertly, she quickly reapplied lipstick and eyeliner, then highlighted her cheekbones. When she was done, she saw his reflection in the mirror and looked at him for the first time. She said nothing and walked past him back into the bedroom. He followed her.

"I hope you're okay," he said, very unsure of himself.

"Well, I'm not, but thank you. I'm miserable, and very embarrassed."

"Oh, don't be. I'm Irish, with five sisters. All of them threw up when they drank." He was an only child, but he could improvise.

She looked away. "Well, then I'm lucky I ran into you, unfortunate as this may be."

"My great pleasure." She looked up, surprised to see that there wasn't a hint of sarcasm on his rather long, intelligent face. Her eyes filled with tears again, and she turned away.

"I'll just get my things," she said, moving toward her scarf and jacket on the bed. She picked them up, then turned to find he was beside her, his arms around her. He pressed his cheek to hers, and she felt its surprising smoothness and great warmth. It burned against her cool one. Then he put a hand, carefully, on either side of her face and he was kissing her, softly, on the mouth. His lips were smooth, too, and he simply held her face up to his, his mouth on hers. It was a very long moment, and Elise felt herself tremble against him.

Then he let go and turned away. "Now *I'm* embarrassed," he said, and she saw that he was. "I didn't mean to. I'm very sorry."

She had never, in almost twenty years, cheated on Bill. She hadn't been brought up that way, and she was always smart enough to distrust the men who had made passes at her. This man was half her age, probably, and God knows what his background was. His shirt cuff was frayed, and his hair was badly cut. Still, she moved toward him. If he didn't hold her, she would die. It was that simple. She had to be held. Nothing else mattered.

Larry wasn't sure what was happening. She was near him and then she kissed him and then they were on the bed, and she was beside him and in his arms, her lovely face against his, her long body pressed to him. She must have felt his erection now, against her thigh. Still he held her, and she began to stroke his face, so very gently. The tips of her fingers were cool, and she ran them into his hair. He couldn't suppress a moan of pleasure. She was so beautiful, and now she was stroking his forehead. He didn't know what she wanted, but he tightened his hold around her, and then she, too, moaned. It was a small sound from deep in her throat. I made her do that, Larry thought, and the feeling of power surged into his loins. Yet he made no move.

Elise was luxuriating in the circle of his arms. She hadn't felt this good in years. She couldn't think. She wouldn't think. She ran her hand over his chest, then down along his thigh. He was hard, aroused for her. She was so grateful she felt she might cry. She mustn't. She moved her hand away and began to unbutton his shirt. "Please," was all she said.

"Yes," he answered, and sat up and stripped in a few graceful moves. She felt awkward and frightened for a moment, lying there. But he turned to her and carefully began to undress her. She averted her face until he was done, then felt him lie beside her. He was long and smooth, and his erection pressed firmly against her leg. He turned her to him. "You're so lovely," he whispered.

Then he was kissing her again, small, dry kisses of great tenderness, covering her face. She was almost shocked by the tenderness; she hadn't experienced it in such a long time and hadn't expected it now. For a moment she didn't know what to do. Then he moved his mouth down to her breasts and covered them with the same kisses. She felt a flood of wetness between her legs and gasped at the pleasure of it. Oh, it had been so long, so very long. The goodness of the feeling.

"May I come inside you?" he asked, his voice blurred. She was startled by the question, wasn't used to it, and then felt another rush of pleasure at being able to grant permission.

"Yes," and he was inside her, moving so very slowly. There was none of Bill's thrusting and sawing. She had forgotten, completely forgotten, what this could be like. Oh, the pleasure of it, the relief! She was being held, and his smooth, young-smelling flesh covered her and entered her. This was slow, and he was so long that he could almost withdraw completely and then move back inside her when she felt she couldn't bear the separation. She strained against him, and there was no pain, no boredom, no cessation of feeling. She was alive to every nuance, every change in him. He shifted subtly, moving on his arms, merging his hips with her own. She felt hungrier, needier than she ever had before, but her shame and anger were gone. All that was left was the pleasure, the benison of his body pressed into hers.

"Who are you?" she asked. He was looking down at her, watching her face, and then moving his eyes lower, watching himself enter her. He bent his head to kiss her—again those hot, dry, sweet kisses. "Who are you?" she asked again, nearly out of her mind with the pleasure.

"I'm the man who wants to make you feel better than anyone ever has," he said, holding her tightly as she came.

4

Cynthia Swann's Song

The first thing Annie heard when she opened the door to her apartment was Sylvie murmuring to Ernesta, and Ernesta's gentle, lilting voice in response. Annie paused for a moment, taking in the sounds, knowing they were to become her happy memories. Letting the door close with a clack, she tried to shake off the sadness, calling out with a lightness she didn't feel, "Hi, ladies, guess who's home."

"Mom-Pom," Sylvie called as she came bounding from the kitchen, a colorful napkin still tied around her neck. "Mom-Pom. Ernesta made me a grilled cheese sandwich and she let me make tomato soup and I didn't burn myself 'cause I'm a good cook."

Sylvie's round face was bright with the joy of accomplishment, her almond eyes opened wide at its wonder. The face that had been so cute and beguiling on a five-year-old now seemed oddly out of proportion on a girl of sixteen. Not for the first time Annie tried to reconcile the teenage body of her Down's syndrome child to the five-year-old's mentality.

"Come back in here, Sylvie, and finish your lunch. That's the good girl," Ernesta called out.

Annie kissed Sylvie and patted her cheek. "Go on, honey. I'll be there in a minute." She watched as Sylvie skipped back to Ernesta.

Annie walked through the living room to the glassed-in conservatory where she kept and nurtured her small collection of bonsai trees. She sat back against the soft pillows of the antique chaise longue and took a deep breath, kicking off her damp, mud-stained pumps. She was so very, very tired. She didn't know how she was going to do it. The funeral and burial and Stuart Swann had drained every ounce of vitality out of her, but she still had to lay out clothes for Ernesta to pack for the trip to Boston tomorrow. And there was still the packing for Sylvie to be finished.

Annie closed her eyes, wishing she could succumb to the sleep she needed so badly. Maybe things in Boston will go well, she thought. Maybe things will get better. Then, sighing, she stood up and walked back to Sylvie.

Later, she was labeling some of Sylvie's boxes when she heard the porter drop her mail on the mat outside the apartment door.

It was the usual collection. A bill from Bergdorf's, a card from Alex up in Cambridge, half a dozen catalogues. And then there was the letter.

It was unmistakable. The Old Greenwich postmark. The weight of it. With a sick feeling in her stomach Annie turned it over. There, in perfect engraved script, was the return address: *Mrs. Gilbert Griffin*.

Annie didn't want to open it. She knew that what she would find inside Cynthia's envelope would be shattering. And Annie already felt shattered. Somehow she got down the hall to her bedroom and stretched out like a corpse on the bed, the letter lying on her lap like a piece of white shrapnel. As she opened the envelope, Pangor jumped up beside her and nuzzled his nose under her chin. Usually she found it comforting, but now it was distracting. She looked down at the spidery, shaky handwriting.

Dear Annie,

Please forgive me for asking you to hear what I have to say. I'm afraid to die without letting the one person who loves me know why.

First let me say that everything—everything—was my own fault. My father had objected to my marriage, but I wouldn't listen to him. Then my lawyers didn't want me to sign the power of attorney, but I did. And I never should have let him take Carla off the respirator. It was all my doing, my fault.

You see, I've never felt important to my family. Stuart was always the favorite. I was a good girl, quiet in school, like you, but not smart like you. No one ever noticed me much. Then I got rather pretty and then there was Gil.

Gil wasn't always the way he is now. When we first met, he was handsome and ambitious, not hard. He had energy that was irresistible. And he loved me. Of course, he loved my money and connections and his Jaguar more, I used to think, but never could allow myself to believe.

Dad didn't really want to take him into the firm, but he did. We gave him his start. Without the Swann family there would be no Gil Griffin, but perhaps I am wrong about that. Men like Gil will always find someone to help them.

At first things were perfect. Gil loved me, and I loved him, and it was all I ever wanted. Then, one day, I accidentally scratched Gil's Jaguar while I was shopping in town. When he found out, he was furious. He hit me without even speaking, and when I fell on the floor, he stood over me, screaming about what I had done to his car.

Then Carla was born and things began to get worse. Gil had hated me pregnant. I was hurt and upset, but I did look so big, so distended, that I just waited until after the baby. Even then, Gil seemed distant. He was distant to Carla, too, from the very beginning. Some men just don't like infants, I thought. I should have done something, but I didn't know what. So I put off doing anything. I'm great at that.

And then, when Carla was three, I got pregnant again. I was afraid to tell Gil, but I finally did. He went insane. He smacked me, hard, across the face. Not once, but several times. But then again, we both just tried to ignore it. And I did, for a while.

After that, he was nicer than he'd ever been to me, nicer than I imagined anyone could be. And so, when he asked me, almost a month later, to abort, I was shocked. I was three and a half months gone by then, and I wanted the baby. I had no idea that he wanted no more children. I refused. But he begged me, and then he threatened me and then he begged again. He was relentless. And in the end I gave in. Nobody knew. We just said I had miscarried.

And there were many more beatings after that. Here's the strangest part: I didn't leave and I didn't tell anyone. I was too ashamed. And I am to blame, because whenever he came back and said he was sorry, we made up. He'd say he'd been drinking too much, or the pressure of the firm or the pressure of the family had been unbearable. And I chose to believe him every time. As my daughter used to say, that was then and this is now. I said it, too.

And when Gil was made a partner, I thought everything would finally be all right.

But I was wrong. Once he was partner, he was unstoppable. He'd been managing my money, and then most of my family's, and made them fortunes, but it wasn't enough. He started those big takeovers, then got into all kinds of deals to finance them. My father and brother fought him. But the money was irresistible, and Gil got the other partners to turn against my dad. And the worst thing was, when my father came to me to ask me to vote with the family, I turned against him, too.

It broke my father when that happened. The stroke was just the finishing touch. Stuart hasn't spoken to me since then.

I think you know the rest: Gil moved up to president and sold the firm out three years later to Federated Funds, and it became Federated Funds Douglas Witter. The Swanns were obliterated. He came to me first and asked for a power of attorney. By then I really didn't want to put all my shares and my portfolio in his hands, but when I said no, he made my life impossible. There was only Gil. I chose him again.

And there was Carla's coma. Once again, it was a choice. And once again, against every instinct, I chose him.

And when he had taken everything—my family name, my money, my contacts, my children—he then began that disgusting public affair with the Birmingham woman. It was even in the business magazines, and I heard about every tiny thing from one "friend" or another. I begged Gil not to leave me, but of course he did.

Perhaps you think that a child's death and a husband's betrayal aren't enough reasons to take my own life, but I simply can't bear another day. We only have one life, and I did mine all wrong. Weak and stupid to the end, I simply can't take the pain any longer.

I CHOSE HIM, ANNIE. I WAS SELFISH AND STUPID AND MUST PAY FOR MY MISTAKE. I killed my baby for him, I ruined my father for him, I gave myself for him, and now there is nothing left. It is too awful to go on this way. God forgive me. I'm sorry.

The letter ended there. Cynthia had not even signed it. "Oh, my God." Annie had spoken out loud.

She laid her head forward onto her chest. Her hands were cold, and they trembled, shaking the letter she held. She walked to the window and looked out at the gray velvet clouds against the darkening sky. She was dizzy again, nauseous, and for a moment she was afraid she might vomit.

Gil was a monster. Here were all his dirty little secrets. He had killed Cynthia. A day at a time, Annie now knew, Gil had killed Cynthia.

In all their years of friendship, Cynthia had never breathed a word of this. And Annie had never imagined it.

Then she thought of Gil's call. He had tricked her and used her, too, just as he had Cynthia. She had already helped him make the funeral today look okay. She had fallen for it, too. He had made her a fool, when all she wanted was to do one last kindness for Cynthia.

Annie felt she couldn't bear the weight of Gil's brutality alone. She had to show someone this letter. No more secrets, damn it, she thought. She felt nausea wash over her again, followed by a chill. How alone Cynthia had been. Annie's chest tightened. It was unbearable.

We are a generation of masochists, she thought. Brenda, Cynthia, me, Elise. What a pathetic bunch of losers we are. Anger suddenly surged through her, momentarily overwhelming the sadness. I'm sick of it, she said to herself. Sick of being a lady and a mother and a good girl. Stupid, passive. It's got to stop.

I could wring Gil's neck with my bare hands, she thought, gritting her teeth. He robbed Cynthia of everything: her child, her money, her family, her dignity. He beat her, and all he left her with was shame. And the shame killed her. Gil killed her.

Brenda, too. Morty tricked her, shamed her, and she fell for it. She built his business, then he threw her out, cheating her of her rightful share in the bargain. Brenda's behind on her maintenance payments at her co-op and is dunned in the elevator by her neighbors. What humiliation! *He's* late with *his* alimony payments month after month, so *she* winds up begging for what is rightfully hers.

Even Elise, who looks so cool, so powerful, so immune. She's been brought low by an empty suit like Bill Atchison. He shouldn't get away with humiliating Elise, flaunting his affairs. There isn't a person in Greenwich who doesn't know that Bill chases every secretary and maid he comes across. Elise is a beautiful, talented woman, but Bill hardly ever seems to notice or to care. But she, like Brenda, just accepts whatever crumbs are thrown her way.

And not just them, Annie, she told herself. Be honest for a change. Aaron left you and his daughter. He abandoned you, left you alone to care for Sylvie, as if his responsibility ended when he moved out. All right, maybe he wasn't as bad as the others; he wasn't a monster, or a lech; he didn't beat you, but he's treated you badly. Admit it. He said he loved you, but he left when things got hard.

Annie had to talk to someone, to have someone else hear the horror of what she had just read, what she had thought. Whom could she call? She thought of Brenda: a good friend, big-hearted, but sometimes a little insensitive. Well, Brenda would have to do.

When there was no answer at Brenda's apartment, she next tried Elise, whom Annie knew to be exquisitely sensitive, but not warm, not in the way Brenda could be.

Again, there was no answer. Hanging up the phone, Annie felt her anger give way to sadness. Only one person in her life, she thought, had all the characteristics she would like to find in a friend: her son Chris. But with all Chris's warmth and gentleness, this would be too much to ask him to share. It's too much for anyone to bear alone, Annie thought. Cynthia proved that.

5

Brenda Isn't Upset

After the funeral Brenda left Annie and Elise and walked uptown along Madison. Of course she could have gotten a cab, but she preferred to walk. Actually, she wanted to eat. It was barely noon, but she was starving. She rooted around in her handbag and dug out half a Heath bar. In two bites it was gone and she was still starving. Thank God Greenberg's cookies were just up ahead. She hoped they were open.

They weren't. Well, she'd find something. She had nothing to do today, and she'd been up since seven, so she'd take a long lunch. Screw it, she was in no mood for jokes *or* diets today. It wasn't that she cared about Cyntha Griffin, because she didn't. The woman was a cold bitch, and she deserved whatever she got. She remembered when her Tony had been the only child in their class not invited to Carla Griffin's birthday party. Nothing hurt you in your life like the hurt that was done to your child. That had been the year they had moved to Greenwich, which was also the year before they moved out. In fact, in that whole time, no one was kind except Annie, but then Annie was always so good. She and Aaron, fighting it out for the Martyr of the Month medal.

Who needed that Greenwich high WASP shit anyway?

Brenda reflected. It wasn't like she was a golfer or anything, and they certainly hadn't moved there for Tony or Angela, though that's what her husband had said. He said it was for them, but it was for Morty, like everything had been.

"For you, babe," he would say, and give her the mink or the jewelry or the new dress (always a size too small, as if that would make her lose weight). First the business was for her, then the house in Greenwich was for her, then the Park Avenue duplex, the paintings, the boat. As if she gave a shit, which she didn't.

But it had taken a long time to catch on. Much too long. For years he had snowed her with all that bullshit. Bullshit that didn't quit. Morty could bullshit almost anyone, at least for a while. And now he was Morty Cushman, Morty the Madman, his face on billboards and TV commercials all the time. The most successful, fastest growing retail operation in the world. Two hundred stores selling name-brand appliances at discount all across the country.

And now *he* had the Park Avenue duplex, the boat, the paintings, the whole shit thing. Of course, he was always screaming that he was cash poor and overextended. But it was Morty who kept doing the extending. Old "boom and bust" Morty. Was he rich, was he poor? Would his check clear or would it bounce? Who knew? She couldn't count the number of times she'd been late with her co-op maintenance check. She couldn't meet the eyes of the neighbors she met on the elevator. And the bounced checks at Tony's school. And at Gristede's. She was sick of it. When they divorced, Morty whined about the children and cash flow and mortgages, and she settled when he bought her the crummy place on Fifth and Ninety-sixth, paid the kids' school bills, and gave her some alimony. *Strunz*. Like an idiot she bought it. Even bimbos like Roxanne Pulitzer make a buck on their divorces, one way or another, and she, Brenda Morrelli Cushman, wound up with *bubkes*. Nice work, Morty, you cheap fuck.

So she bought a bag of Pepperidge Farm Milano cookies at the overpriced Korean on Eighty-fourth, then turned east on Eighty-sixth Street. She'd have lunch at Summerhouse, if they were open yet. Ladies who lunch and all that crap, but good curried chicken with grapes and *crème brûlée* to die for. Then she'd see. Maybe she'd pick up something for Angela, her daughter. If her cards weren't declined.

When she got to the restaurant, she was thrilled by signs of life. They were just opening, and when she asked for a table, the skinny bitch at the desk lifted her eyebrows. "Are you only one?" she asked.

"Yes, but I'm eating for two," Brenda snapped. Out of spite the bitch seated her in the back at a table beside the waiters' station when the place was completely empty. Of course, because she was a middle-aged woman alone. A *fat* middle-aged woman alone. But Brenda all at once was too tired to make a big stink. Sometimes she just lost all her spirit.

Like over the divorce. She should have hung in there. Christ, it wasn't that she loved Morty. She couldn't even remember when she had. But she should have hung in there and made a better deal. That fuck lawyer Leo Gilman had been too much for her, playing the family friend and all. And she was represented by little Barry Marlowe because Morty paid for it all. They were in collusion. They had to be. More bullshit. What was the difference between a laboratory rat and a lawyer? You could get attached to a laboratory rat.

It wasn't that she cared about money. She didn't really; she never had. She was Vinny Morrelli's daughter and she grew up with everything she needed. But because she was Vinny Morrelli's daughter, she didn't like it that she'd been made a fool of, and she especially hated that Morty still had power over her. If he was slow with his alimony or support, she and Tony and Angela sweated it. And Morty was so goddamn cheap, or at least he had been to her and the kids.

It was hard now to think of Morty with that socialite bitch. Shelby Symington. A little blond Southern *shiksa*. Jesus. And now she was opening an art gallery. She was written up in the magazines. A Southern Mary Boone. Dragging Morty up from the depths of social anonymity. Brenda couldn't pick up a copy of the *Post* or the *News* without seeing their pictures on the gossip pages. She shook her head. Christ, what was he paying his publicist? A hell of a lot more than he was sending her every month. Bet *those* checks didn't bounce.

Yes, she admitted, Morty should be punished. But by who? My father is dead. My brother is a failed stand-up comic out in LA. What could I do? Sue Morty? Big deal. Maybe I should see my cousin Nunzio. Christ, she hadn't seen him in years. Was he still in the shoe business? Cement ones, that is. The thought of Morty planted inside one of the Bruckner Expressway support columns made her smile. Her father had once told her the Expressway construction was never finished because there was always more "planting" to be done. Maybe we could have a Morty Cushman Memorial Off-Ramp. She smiled to herself again.

The thing about Morty was that he only liked to spend money on things that showed: fancy boats and jazzy cars and suits from Bijan, where they were so snotty you needed an appointment to get into the store. But his underwear he got from some close-out place like Job Lot. That was how she knew when he started cheating on her: he bought silk boxers from Sulka. When they'd moved into the duplex, he'd called in that *faygeleh* Duarto to do the living room, library, dining room, and guest room, but their bedrooms were left alone. "After all," he said, "nobody sees them but us." Not that *she* gave a shit. She couldn't stand all those goddamn cabbage roses and fakola English crap. After all, who were they kidding? Certainly not Duarto, who knew they had taste in their ass. He had looked around at their old place and looked as if he needed CPR. He gulped and asked, "And what do chou do, Mrs. Cushman?" in his charming accent.

"About what?" she asked. Actually, he was a great guy, if you ignored his society-faggot routine. When the two of them were alone, they'd dish a little, and eventually they'd become great friends. He was relieved to learn that Brenda wasn't interested in taking credit for the job ("Dey always try to, chou know. Dey say dey deed eet with some help, as eef dey could select a goddamn trim color by demselves. Puhleeze!") nor did she expect him to provide her with social introductions. ("Somehow I don't see chou and Anne Bass ever getteen really close.") He had made her laugh, and she had made him laugh, and he'd gouged wads out of Morty, as he did with all his clients.

He was actually just a poor Cuban kid who made good originally by sleeping with his boss, but he had put out the story that he was Spanish, from Barcelona, and a cousin of Gaudi, and Brenda promised she'd never tell. "Dey don't know that ees where we get de word *gaudy* from," he said, laughing in his charming accent. Of course, Duarto was very, very big time now. His style—what Brenda called wretched excess— was the hot look. He draped thousands of yards of flowing fabric over everything, creating a sort of updated Arabian nights feeling, and the chic shelter magazines were calling him the Sultan of Silk.

But she and he had become really close only in the last six months. Duarto's lover, Richard, had gotten sick. Duarto had broken down, cried in her arms like one of her kids when he told her. So, every day, Brenda made the pilgrimage to Lenox Hill hospital, sometimes bringing something she had cooked but more usually takeout, and sat for a while with Richard. They'd play gin, or she'd read him the gossip columns from the papers, or feed him. She watched him waste away, until he couldn't speak, or even follow her with his eyes, and she watched Duarto's agony and helplessness.

She wished he were here now to cheer her up. The funeral had been terrible. It isn't like I give a shit about Cynthia one way or the other, she told herself fiercely. Our husbands did business together once upon a time. We had them on the boat. She invited us to Greenwich because Gil made her do it. She thought I was vulgar and I though she was boring and repressed. And we were both right.

Brenda focused on the menu. The waiter approached with a basket that Brenda knew held the tiny hot biscuits and strawberry butter the place was famous for. She opened the napkin folded in the basket. Two lonely biscuits, each the size of a shot glass, rolled about in the otherwise empty basket. "Hey, where is the rest of the litter?" she asked him. "Bring out the whole family of these puppies. And I'll have the curried-chicken salad, a side order of the carrot and raisin slaw, plus *crème brûlée* for dessert."

"Wouldn't you like to hear the specials?"

"Thanks but no thanks." He looked at her, annoyed that he had missed his chance to perform. Just one more out-of-work actor in a bad mood. Well, she wasn't in a bad mood. She wouldn't let herself be. The funeral was okay with her. Everything was okay with her. She'd eat lunch and then she'd walk up past Sweets for the Sweet, pick up a few éclairs, and then be home in time for Angela, who was coming to dinner. They'd have a salad tonight and she'd watch herself tomorrow. She knew she shouldn't do this. She knew she'd be sorry later. But right now Brenda was hungry. In fact, Brenda was starving. But Brenda was *not* upset.

As Brenda stepped out of the elevator to her apartment, juggling the bakery box and fumbling for the keys in her bag, she almost tripped over her neighbor's copy of the *Times*, inadvertently left in front of Brenda's door. She looked down at it as she swung in her door, then kicked the paper into her apartment and closed the door behind her. Fuck her, she said to herself. She never liked that bitch anyhow, the co-op's president, a nosy-body.

She did it just for spite, she knew, because Brenda rarely looked at the *Times*. It was too ponderous, and too big to handle easily. Despite her weight, Brenda was a small woman, with small hands. The *Times* always wrinkled and tore when she attempted to go through it. Secretly, she preferred the *Post*. A guilty pleasure.

She went into the kitchen and deposited the box of éclairs in the refrigerator, after taking a furtive lick of chocolate from one. She walked back into the living room, kicked off her shoes, and dropped ungracefully onto the downy sofa. Picking up the newspaper, she began to flip through the pages, not really reading.

And then she saw it: an ad announcing the underwriting of Morty the Madman stock. Morty the Madman was going public.

Brenda couldn't believe it! Her hands were shaking, rippling the big pages of the *New York Times* spread out before her. She had almost missed it, but there it was. A whole page. How much did that cost? Brenda wondered. Just like Morty: if it showed, spend big bucks. But maybe this wasn't even paid for by Morty. Brenda, who was shrewd, and gifted with cartloads of common sense, knew that she hadn't a clue about how big business worked. But neither did Morty. Christ, the little *pisher* was in the big time now. She began to study the page more carefully.

The offering was enormous, handled by Federated Funds Douglas Witter. That was Gil Griffin's firm, she knew. *So now that he's divorced and bought me off for a few shekels and this crummy apartment, Morty goes public. I signed over my stock to him for nothing. After he cried poverty and complained about loans and mortgages eating him up alive. And I got bubkes for alimony and child support. Nice. And strangers are getting rich off this right now, while I'm sitting on my big fat ass, waiting for the puny maintenance check to come in, hoping it won't bounce.*

Brenda moved quickly. She put on her shoes and, not bothering to lock the door, ran out to the newsstand at the corner and came back with the *Wall Street Journal.* Now, sitting on the edge of the sofa, she began to look through it carefully, page by page. There on page nine she found a four-column story.

It appeared that Morty's offering was regarded as an event as important as the Second Coming. That a household name, a retailer, could expand so rapidly by offering the consumer what he wanted at a price he could afford was apparently considered a miracle of modern business. *What am I missing here?* Brenda thought. *His giant leverage allowed him to buy low and sell only slightly higher, and his genius lay in passing on such a large share of his savings to customers, gaining him both huge volume and an enormously loyal customer base. His inspired Morty the Madman commercials, albeit masterminded by Paradise/Loest Advertising, made him and his stores an American icon. Genius? Inspired?* Was that really Morty the *Journal* was writing about? What bullshit! The man could *handel,* she'd give him that, but most of the time Morty didn't know whether to shit or go blind. What was wrong with this picture? She looked at the byline. Asa Ewell, whoever the fuck that was. His mother actually named him that?

Yeah, I should tell old Asa baby about how Morty managed such low prices before he had all that leverage. Morty had sold TVs, stereos, and VCRs hot off her daddy's trucks for years. She'd been his bookkeeper, so she ought to know. *Passing on such a large share of his savings* my sweet ass. He laundered the money for the mob. What would Asa Ewell say to that? She shook her head. What a moron.

She looked back over the piece. *Expansion brought with it state-of-the-art inventory control and high-tech market analysis, using the most advanced point-of-sale MIS technology yet installed in this country.* Were they talking about Morty's operation, the debacle with the computerized cash registers? They couldn't know the real story. She shrugged. Why be surprised? she asked herself. She always suspected that this big business crap was a gigantic jerk-off.

But now *she* was the jerk. Maybe Morty was only a bullshitter, but he bullshitted the *Wall Street Journal* and Federated Funds Douglas Witter. And he bullshitted me. Morty must have known his company was going public at the time of the divorce settlement, Brenda now realized. No wonder he was in such a rush to get it finalized. And she had thought he was just accommodating her. The balls.

You make a very pretty picture she thought. She looked down and saw her big stomach and, for the first time, the ink that grayed her hands. Tears sprang to her eyes. I'm a mess. I'm forty-one, fat, and stupid. And my hands are filthy.

Brenda stood as tears ran down her cheeks. He made a fool of me, she thought. Christ, what a moron I am. She couldn't remember the last time she had cried.

After a while she stopped, and she wiped her face with her hands, unaware that she smeared ink around her eyes as she did so. Okay, so now what? She thought of calling the *New York Times* and that stupid Asa Ewell at the *Journal*, but she knew better. What she'd like to do was call one of her father's old friends and have Morty's knees broken. She found the thought of Morty in a hospital bed with his legs in traction very satisfying. But no. That wouldn't help her pay her apartment maintenance. She could just forget about it and try to get a job as a bookkeeper again. Yeah, she told herself, and make four twenty-five an hour. Christ, everything now was computerized anyway. She probably couldn't get arrested. And anyway, then Morty would get off scot-free. Shit.

It was unbearable. Brenda, on her father's side, came from a long line of Sicilians who had made vendetta a way of life. But her mother had been middle-class Jewish. Ashamed of the gangster side of the family. And Brenda's family had so much to hide, even now after the death of her capo father, that she could never go through the courts.

She lifted the phone and dialed her brother Neil in L.A. but got a busy signal. She tried Annie, but there was no answer. So she tried Duarto, but his service picked up. Giving up, Brenda walked into the kitchen, took out the box of éclairs, and ate each and every one.

6

Greenwich Time

The next morning, Elise had that awful, needlelike pain at her left temple, right behind her eye. She wasn't certain how she'd gotten through the night. Actually, she wasn't sure of much—how long it had taken her to fall asleep, how long she'd slept, or even what time it was now. Something had gone wrong, her sense of time perhaps. Sometimes when she woke up, she could remember her dreams, but not where she had been the night before. Sometimes she awoke and thought her dreams had really happened. Or occasionally, she woke up with the horrifying feeling of not knowing where she was. Those times she would lie very still, terrified, not daring to move or make a sound, hardly daring to breathe, until the windows defined themselves and the room became familiar. In the city it wasn't so bad, but here it was tricky. Here it was Greenwich time, with a capriciousness that frightened her.

Yes, today she knew where she was. She just wasn't sure how she'd gotten there. Or where she'd been. Last thing, last thing, last thing. Yes, the funeral. Oh, of course. Cynthia Griffin. Oh, God. The stabbing needle felt sharper than ever, making her eyes water. A tear dripped slowly, slowly down her cheek toward her ear. She longed to wipe it away, but knew the price she'd pay if she so much as trembled. The needle was merciless. She breathed carefully, shallowly, afraid to alter her precarious position. Soon enough Chessie would sail in and help her begin her day.

Then it came back all at once. Bemelman's. Elise jerked her shoulders, sending a searing pain through her eye and up to her forehead. She groaned with pain, and with the shame of the memory. Oh, God.

It hadn't been the first time one of those little filmies had recognized and complimented her. And she was always gracious. Gracious but not familiar, just as her mother had directed her. She smiled, thanked them, but never stooped to autographing or picture-taking. Not until yesterday. She groaned again. Oh, God; oh, God. It was coming back more clearly.

Tall, thin, wearing that costume of jeans and tweed jacket that young men seemed to prefer, rather like the black pullovers that Gerard and their friends had favored back in the early sixties. What had they talked about? Her films, the good ones. Yes, he had understood about them. About Truffaut, and Godard. She had looked at his hands. Big, with long fingers. Young hands, and strong. She had had another Courvoisier, or maybe two, and then he had begun to stand up. "Thank you," he had said. "I won't take up any more of your time. I've always admired you, but now I adore you." It was the line from *Walking in the Dark*, when Pierre was about to leave her. "*Je t'adore*," he finished.

And she had fallen apart. Publicly. Noisily. Oh, God. In front of Maurice. In front of the help. She remembered her mother's frosty look, her slightly elevated brow: "*Pas avant les domestiques.*"

Oh, she'd been pathetic, her behavior shameful. "Please, don't leave me. Don't let them see me like this." What then? Through the hall, to the lobby bench. Then upstairs. Then . . . oh, my God. She'd been ill. Oh. He'd helped her. And then?

And the rest of what had happened in Room 705 broke over her like a wave. Images returned to her, and feelings. His hand curved around her breast, his soft cheek against hers, his face looking down as he entered her. A man she didn't know, a boy almost, less than half her age.

How could she have done this? It must have been the Courvoisier. On an empty stomach. She remembered the young man offering to take her home. The thought of going to the New York apartment and maybe encountering Bill in her state had appalled and humiliated her. No, she had said, she was going to Greenwich. Then the agonizing ride through the early-evening traffic, home to Chessie.

It was unbearable. What if Bill . . . but that was unthinkable. The pain was now intolerable. Her eye was watering uncontrollably. Involuntary tears. If only she could have a drink. Horrified at the thought, a drink at nine A.M., she prayed that Chessie would soon come.

What could she do? Talk to Uncle Bob? But he'd be so disappointed in her. How could she tell him she was a drunk? Check into a clinic? She closed her eyes at the thought. Twenty-eight days, to listen to them whine over their problems, to lie to herself, pretend she was like them, that she'd be better now, that she would go for therapy and never drink again. But it wouldn't work. She wasn't like anyone. She was smarter, more beautiful, better educated. When she was born, she'd been the wealthiest baby in America. Now she was a drunk. And a whore.

Once again, despite herself, she remembered the feel of the young man's cheek against hers. Tears, real ones this time, sprang up in her eyes. It had felt so very good, but now she felt so very bad. And oh, God, hadn't he had a camera? What exactly had happened to the camera? She couldn't even remember what had happened after the sex, or when they had parted or how she got home. With a horrible feeling in her stomach, Elise realized she didn't even know his name.

Mother had once told her to find a man who would not be competitive with her, who would bask in her glory. Bill had seemed to be such a man. She recognized it the moment she had met him at the cocktail party. She heard his name and realized that he must be one of the Atchisons who went so far back they were probably part Indian. Old family, old money, although not very much of it anymore. He had noticed her looking at him from across the room. When he started toward her, she had dropped her eyes, pretending to be deeply engrossed in conversation with a very small woman with very large jewels.

Bill had waited for the woman to leave before he made his move. "You can do me a very big favor. You could take me away from all this," he said with a boyish grin.

"Oh, could I now?" she asked. "And where would I take you away to?"

It was his answer that did it. "To the model-sailboat lake in Central Park. I've had a boat in the storehouse there ever since I was a kid. I'd much prefer watching it sail across the lake in the moonlight with you by my side to standing in this very overdone room with very overdone people."

She hadn't said anything, just laughed, real, spontaneous laughter. He understood this as an answer, took her hand, and led her through the crowd, away from the party. It wasn't until they were in the elevator that either one of them spoke, when they both said together, "My name's . . . ," and then started laughing at the timing.

"Bill Atchison," he had said, "and I know your name."

There had been so many times like that. Spontaneous, fun, and childlike. He was so normal, so natural. It had filled her with joy. She felt alive. She'd found herself enchanted by ordinary things: tennis dates with friends, dinners at sweet little restaurants, walks in the Village, in Central Park, through Chinatown.

He had helped her to be like other people. Not an heiress, not a movie star. Just a woman, and a wife. And it seemed so perfect for so long. They had settled into a happy routine, the first normalcy she had ever known. They agreed to basics about how money was to be handled and, from the beginning, it seemed there would be no problems. He accepted the fact that they would be living in her homes, and that she would pay her own bills. He was on the partner track at the law firm of Cromwell Reed, so was able to pay his own expenses and sometimes pick up imaginative presents, with which he was always able to delight her. He never ceased to compliment her looks, her clothes, her taste. She was a catch, and she took delight in his pleasure at showing her off. It seemed that he was so perfect for her.

She had helped him enormously with his career. He handled all her business, and she had brought him the Van Gelders' business and that of other friends. Being able to entertain the partners of the firm in any one of three homes in the area hadn't hurt his chances for a partnership, either. She had accepted his late nights, delighting in a man with enough drive to do his job, but without an all-consuming competitive ambition. He had lots of time for her, so she rarely questioned him on those nights, accepting his broad explanation of work.

She first found out that Bill was cheating on her when she overheard one of the maids at her mother's camp in the Adirondacks telling another the gossip about a cheating husband. She had been chilled to the bone when she understood they were talking about Bill, her Bill. He was involved with a chambermaid. She was nauseous with humiliation and panicked enough to tell her mother.

They had had another of their talks. After her mother had let her get it all out, she had settled Elise down and asked her what she was going to do.

"I don't know, but I can't stay with him. He betrayed me. And with the help, Mother. He could have spared me that."

"Of course he did, my dear," her mother said, "but why would you punish yourself for what he has done? It's a man's nature to betray women. So why would you give up your very comfortable life just because of that? As I see it, you've gotten a better deal with Bill than most women have with their husbands. He still sleeps with you, doesn't he?"

"Mother, of course, that's why I didn't suspect anything."

"There, that's settled then. Go to New York, take him out for a wonderful steak dinner at Christ Cella's, and then home to bed. Tomorrow, go to Harry Winston's and buy yourself the most extravagant piece of jewelry you have ever bought. These things happen. Be glad it isn't worse. And be thankful. You do have a good life, after all."

And so she began to live the lie. Mother is so knowing, she thought as she folded the truth away and tucked it in the back of her mind like an unwanted winter blanket. But the blanket wouldn't stay folded and put away. The infidelities got more frequent and then more flagrant, became harder and harder to ignore. Each time with younger, ever younger, women.

Little by little, day after day, her ordinary life eroded, until now all that was left was the order, the shell of a life. The emptiness closed in on her, the only fullness she now felt coming from the extra drink before dinner, then the wine, and the brandy before going to bed. And yes, the occasional morning bracer, but only if she had a luncheon date that she wasn't looking forward to.

Not a very pretty picture, she thought as she came back to the present. Poor me. Poor Cynthia. And Poor Annie. And yes, even poor Brenda. We made bad deals.

Of course, Annie has that awful situation with Aaron dating her own psychiatrist. Or former psychiatrist, I guess it is at this point. Never trust them, Mother told me, and I never have. So Annie goes to one to help her marriage, and the psychiatrist steals her husband. And when Lally Snow told me, I couldn't say anything to Annie. After all, she and Aaron were already separated. But what a betrayal. Elise shuddered at the thought. Yet Annie continued to live her life with dignity.

And Brenda bore the humiliation of being fat, rejected, and penniless, if not with dignity, at least with a defiance that carried her forward from day to day.

Chessie rapped softly at the door before entering. Well, she, Elise, had humiliations of her own to deal with, she thought as the pain behind her eye or something else made it water, the tears rolling slowly down her once-perfect face.

7

Putting on the Ritz

As the taxi pulled up to the marquee of the Ritz Carlton, Annie took out her mirror and primped for a moment. The ordeal of the funeral and of the shuttle flight to Boston were over; now the ordeal of seeing Aaron and watching Alex graduate would begin. She'd decided to put Cynthia's letter and her whole overreaction to it behind her—for now at least.

Annie tried to be calm, not sad or angry. Alex, not Aaron, had asked that Sylvie not attend the graduation, and though it almost broke her heart, Annie could understand his resentment of the sister who took up so much of his mother's time, who brought so much unwanted attention to the family. It was foolish of her to expect anything else, she thought. Still, she was disappointed. She sighed, then shrugged, paid the driver, and slid out of the cab. The doorman helped her, and as she smiled her thanks, someone ran up from behind her, covered her eyes, and kissed the top of her head. She felt her heart jump in her chest and turned, only to find Chris towering over her and grinning. He was wearing a soft cashmere turtleneck and a well-cut tweed jacket. She managed another smile.

"Mom! Wow, you look like a million bucks!" Chris cried. He hugged her again and as always she felt so grateful for his warmth, his open affection, so different from his father's and older brother's restraint.

"Have you seen your brother yet?" she asked. She wanted to ask about Aaron but controlled herself.

"Oh, sure," he said, adding quickly, "Me and Al went out to the Plough and Stars and got loaded last night. Then we hit the Combat Zone. It was great. It's a good thing I'll never graduate, because I don't think either of us could survive another night like that. It certainly wouldn't help my career in advertising."

Annie smiled again. Though Aaron fumed over Chris's dropping out of school, Annie knew he was secretly proud to have his son join the firm. Chris was working under Jerry Loest, Aaron's partner, and he was thriving. "So, where are the other guys?" Annie tried to sound casual.

"Dad's working on some kind of surprise or something, and Alex is up in the whirlpool, trying to get unbent. We're all meeting in the lobby at seven. Dad's got a party set up tonight, and Al's invited his friends, and Grandma and Grandpa Paradise are coming. They're in Suite 502." Chris rolled his eyes.

Annie shook her head at him. Aaron's parents were difficult, formal people. She was surprised to hear they were at the hotel, since they so rarely left Newport during the season. She sighed. Well, there goes any real hope of a pleasant dinner, she thought.

"Is this your bag?" Chris asked, hoisting her Vuitton case. "Hey, Mom, what's in here? Planning to move in permanently, or you just carrying gold bullion for exercise?"

They crossed the marble floor of the lobby, and Annie quickly signed in. She started to hand the clerk her credit card, but he waved it away. "It's been taken care of, ma'am. Mr. Paradise asked for the bill to be charged to him."

Annie nodded. How nice of Aaron. She felt hope move

through her once again, light and ephemeral, like a mist through a valley. A bellman took the bag from Chris. "Hey, Mom. I'm going to go round up Al and get dressed. Meet you here in an hour. Okay?" As he strode off, Annie marveled at his height, his long lope, and his broad shoulders. As she turned to follow the bellman into the elegant, gilded elevator, she heard Chris call, "Mom," and come running back to her.

"I almost forgot," he said as he came to a stop in front of her. "I wanted to ask you if it's okay with you . . ." He faltered.

Annie laughed. "Chris, ask me."

"I know it's her last day home and everything, but could I take Sylvie out Monday? I mean, you get to see her every day, and I've been promising her for a while."

Annie herself had been looking forward to this time alone with Sylvie, but Sylvie did love being with Chris. "Of course you can. She'll be delighted," Annie said.

"Great." And off he went again. "See you in an hour," he called back over his shoulder.

Annie shook her head. Even a few moments with him revived her spirits. It was hard to believe that delicious young man was her son.

Her room was lovely, and soothing, as were all the rooms in this truly fine hotel. The window overlooked the Boston Common on the front, and Newbury Street on the side. And on the low table beside the settee sat a breathtaking arrangement of blue delphiniums and pink roses. A card was perched in the midst of the foliage. Annie approached the table slowly, pausing for a moment before reaching out for the card. She stared at it for a moment, then tore open the envelope in a single eager movement. *Congratulations, and best love on the occasion of Alex's graduation,* it said. It was signed, *Mother and Father Paradise.* Well, what did you expect? she asked herself, but she knew what she had hoped for.

Annie quickly unpacked and shook out her dresses. The Gaultier black silk for tonight looked fine.

Reclining finally in the huge white marble bathtub, she took a few deep breaths and felt her tight back muscles loosen. She stretched out her toes, trying to touch the far end of the tub, then she took a deep breath and submerged herself. Delightfully, the tub was big enough to float in, and Annie floated, her eyes closed. I'm going to relax, she told herself. Really relax. For the first time in weeks.

She settled into the foam. Dr. Rosen, her ex-therapist, had taught her relaxation techniques, which she used now. Fragments of memories came to her, and she let them. Aaron, standing next to Stuart Swann and staring at her on the day they first met. Chris and Alex wrestling on the lawn of the summer house in Amagansett. Then Sylvie's face when Annie left her this morning, followed by Cynthia's face, Cynthia at fourteen, singing a song as they biked along the Fairfield Common. The Dixie Cups' song—something about going to the chapel of love and getting married and never being lonely anymore.

She sat up, the water rolling off her. Though she hadn't said a prayer in more than a decade, she said a small one now. *God, let this happen. Let Aaron love me again.*

Dinner went surprisingly well. Aaron looked elegant, and he and his father both behaved, the boys joked easily, though as usual, Annie saw, Alex got all his father's attention. But it was, after all, his celebration. Chris smiled a lot, spoke only a little, and told Alex, when he asked, that Uncle Jerry was great to work for. No one mentioned Cynthia's death or Sylvie's absence.

Alex was proud and relieved to be graduating, and he looked more relaxed than he had in years, Annie thought. She was surprised to find that she was actually happy. It felt odd. It had been so long since she had had that happy fullness in her chest. She looked around the table. Aaron and the two boys, so healthy, so right. She felt warm, glowing. This was how the family would have been without Sylvie. Annie sighed. Several times she caught Aaron looking at her. Each time he smiled.

After dinner, his parents excused themselves and went up to their room, but Aaron, his eyes snapping with excitement, hustled the rest of them out to a waiting car and they drove to the Hancock Center. There they were joined by a dozen of Alex's friends. They all boarded an elevator, and Aaron led them to a suite of offices on the fifty-third floor. "It's showtime, folks," he said, and the group moved into a small screening room and took seats. Annie sat at the back, Chris on one side, but she carefully kept an empty seat beside her. A young woman handed her a program and a bag of popcorn, then went on to the others.

"Come on, Dad, what's this all about?" Alex asked.

The room went dark. The giggling and teasing stopped, and as the screen lit up, Aaron slid into the seat beside Annie. "This ought to be good," he said, and, delighted, she smiled in the dark.

And then credits began to roll. *An Annie and Aaron Paradise Production.* There was a trumpet fanfare. *Alexander the Great.* There were groans and catcalls from the audience as Alex's face appeared. A smarmy, typical announcer's voice began. "From the time that he was very young, Alexander MacDuggan Paradise was a man with a mission." A long shot of Alex, aged about two and a half, chasing a kitten, Pangor's predecessor, flashed on the screen.

"Oh, Dad," Alex groaned.

"Oh, Aaron," Annie murmured. In the dark, he took her hand.

"I'll walk you to your room," Aaron said, and Annie's heart jumped. Alex had remained behind with his friends, but Chris was still with them. He smiled. "I think I'll go get mugged on the Common," he said, grinning at both of them. As she watched her son saunter across the Ritz lobby, Annie felt Aaron take her hand again. Oh, did he mean to come in? Did he mean more? She smiled at him, then bowed her head for a minute to collect herself. Here she was, over forty, and on a date with her soon-to-be-ex-husband, yet she didn't know how to behave.

In the elevator she could feel his warmth under the sleeve of his blazer as his arm just touched hers. She shivered. "Cold?" Aaron asked, and without waiting for an answer, he moved his arm around her shoulder. How could he be so cool, so smooth? Annie wondered. Was it because he felt nothing, or was he just better at masking his feelings? It was one of the riddles about him she had never satisfactorily answered for herself: Did he feel things less deeply than she did? She shook her head, in the characteristic way she had of trying to shake a thought away. Aaron looked at her and grinned. "Same old Annie," he said.

"It was a wonderful film, Aaron," she said. "Alex loved it. So did I."

"Yeah. I finally finished a screenplay."

They were to her door. She fumbled for her key, then fumbled at the lock. He took the key from her and quickly, smoothly, fitted it into the keyhole, easily twisting the door open. She hesitated for a moment, took a step in, and turned to him, about to say good-night. But Aaron had his hands up, cupping her face. He was tilting her head up, he was kissing her! Oh, the softness of his mouth on hers. His smell, his taste. Annie wanted time to stop. Just let her melt into this moment, be lost in him.

He stopped kissing her. She opened her eyes to find him looking at her face. "Same old Annie," he said again, and adroitly closed the door behind them. "You looked beautiful tonight." He hugged her. Then he took her by the hand and led her to the bed. He reached around her, to the back of her neck, and began to unbutton the Gaultier. He pulled down the top of her dress, revealing her neck, her shoulders. He bent forward, laying his head there, breathing against her.

"God, Annie. Cynthia's death did something to me. It shook me up." He paused. "Time is so precious," he said, his voice thick.

Annie reached up to his head, caressing his smooth hair. It felt so good, so right to have him pressed against her. It was all she wanted. And for now, at least, she had it. Thank God, thank God.

He undressed her, quickly stripped off his own clothes, and lay beside her. Then he made love to her. It was perfect, having him against her, holding her. It had been so long. The pain of Cynthia's death, of Sylvie, of losing Dr. Rosen, all floated away. There was only the warmth of his body, his arms, the comfort of his smell, his breath.

He moved inside her, and then, before he came, he gasped, "I love you."

"Oh, Aaron, I love you, too." Tears poured out of her eyes. Maybe the nightmare was over. Maybe they could be a family again. "I love you, too."

Keeping busy was the answer. That was what Annie told herself, and of course, there were plenty of things to do instead of sitting around waiting for his call. After their night at the Ritz Aaron had said he couldn't ride to the airport with her and the boys yesterday because he had to drive to New Hampshire on business. She hoped there hadn't been an accident. Don't be such a worry-wart! she told herself. He just got caught up with business. You know how Aaron gets, she thought, and smiled.

Today she had planned to do some pruning and shaping of her bonsai trees. Two of them desperately needed her attention; they made her feel guilty. She knew most of her friends didn't bother with plants or flowers; Elise had told her about a service that actually picked up your orchid plants after they had bloomed and didn't return them until they were ready to bloom again. Somehow, Annie felt that was unfair. Maybe even unwholesome, and certainly unnatural. You had to pay for the loveliness of plants by nursing them through the unattractive, ungainly times. Her Protestant work ethic was amazingly strong for a girl who had grown up Catholic.

The doorman's phone buzzed from the lobby, and Annie heard Sylvie running to answer it. "Hello. This is Sylvie Paradise."

"Who is it, Sylvie?" Annie asked, joining her daughter in the foyer.

Sylvie's face lit up. "Nestor said Chris is coming up to see me," she squealed with delight.

Annie remembered Chris's asking in Boston if he could take Sylvie out alone on her last day at home. From the moment Sylvie had come into their lives, Chris had bonded with her. Alex, so like Aaron, had been more emotionally removed from the baby, and when after time Sylvie's limitations became obvious, Alex distanced himself further. But Chris never stopped seeing Sylvie as a joy. And that joy was evident now as he helped Sylvie on with her cardigan.

"Where are you kids going today?" Annie asked, feeling Sylvie's excitement.

"Should we tell her, kiddo, or keep it our little secret?" Chris asked Sylvie, tousling her hair.

Sylvie paused for a moment, struggling with her loyalties, but couldn't keep the secret. "We're going to do three things," she said, holding up the corresponding number of fingers.

"We're going to the zoo to see the black-and-white birds that walk funny."

"That's right, the penguins," Chris encouraged. "Then what?"

Sylvie thought for a moment, then said, "Then Chris is going to let me row a boat."

"And what else, kiddo?"

"And then . . ." She hesitated while watching Chris's face intently, trying to remember. Chris smiled and waited patiently.

Sylvie remembered, "Lunch. I'm going to eat pasghetti for lunch." Sylvie beamed, proud of her accomplishment.

Chris smiled broadly. "Hey, right. Spaghetti. Now tell Mom-Pom good-bye till later," Chris urged, his hand on the door handle. Annie kissed them both, her eyes meeting Chris's. "You have a good day," Chris said. "And thanks, Mom." Then they were gone.

Annie closed the apartment door and returned to the conservatory and her task, feeling suddenly unneeded. Keep busy, she told herself as she considered the shape of the tree on the table, preparing herself mentally before beginning the pruning.

Later that morning she would have her regular exercise class with Roy and Bernie at their gym. She was meeting Brenda there. At last Brenda had agreed to start exercising. Then they'd lunch. In the late afternoon she had an Italian class, and then there was the dangerous hour when she used to see Dr. Rosen at half past five. She missed her therapist, but she'd get through it. She'd get through whatever she had to. Because soon Aaron would call.

She looked out over the landscaped terrace to the playground where she used to take Sylvie, until the other children became too cruel. Please, God, let this new place be a true home for her, Annie prayed. She looked to the east, beyond the East River, and beyond that the Triborough and Whitestone bridges. She could see a plane thrusting into the air from its takeoff at LaGuardia, and a train crossing the railroad trestle from Queens, a ship passing on its way to the harbor, and cars moving along the FDR Drive. Yet up here, suspended above the city's movement and frenzy, there was perfect silence and perfect calm. Sometimes Annie felt that this was her perfect place as well. But today, as she anticipated Aaron's call, was not one of those times. Everything seemed flat—except for those champagne bubbles of anticipation, arising from somewhere deep inside her. Aaron, each one said. Aaron. Aaron.

Without Aaron, her life seemed to stretch in front of her, an empty calendar. Fill up the month, fill up the week, fill up the day. Fill up the next five minutes. There was nothing to look forward to, nothing to feel excited about. She would miss Pangor, she would miss Sylvie, she missed her sons. She missed Dr. Rosen. She missed Aaron. And she needed Aaron. She longed to hold him.

For a moment, Annie felt guilty, thinking how hopeless Cynthia must have felt. I should be sorrier Cynthia is dead. But how sorry should I be? she thought. She didn't want the sadness of Cynthia's death and Sylvie's leaving to intrude on her newfound hope. I am among the living, Annie thought, and hope keeps me going. Aaron will call and I hope we'll be together. But poor Cynthia will always be in the ground alone. What had Cynthia said in the hospital that awful day?

Her mother never loved her and, like a curse, no one else seemed to have either.

Please, God, let Aaron love me, Annie prayed, and then went into the bedroom to dress for her exercise class.

Why did I agree to this? Brenda thought as she rode up in the elevator with Annie to the aerobics class in the Carnegie

Hall Rehearsal Building. But she knew the answer. She looked like shit and she felt like shit. Even Angela had mentioned it. Soon, they'd have Field Day at Tony's fancy prep school, and she didn't want to embarrass the kid. She winced as she remembered the kids at her own school teasing her about her father. She had to do something. Also, she was curious about the exercise styles of the rich and famous. Brenda knew that Bernie and Roy were the most exclusive personal trainers in town. But if they were anything like Siegfried and Roy, she didn't want to be one of their trainees.

They entered a room that reminded Brenda of the Julia Richman high school gym but without the smell. She followed Annie to the lockers.

"Can't I just have periodontal surgery today? It hurts less and it's cheaper," Brenda begged, not leaving but not undressing either. Annie ignored Brenda's protest.

"You have five minutes. Get to it, Brenda. Anyhow, it's my treat. And you'll feel better after it, I promise." Annie smiled.

She certainly is cheerful today, Brenda thought resentfully. Next to her, Annie smoothly stripped out of her skirt and sweater, exposing her thin, flat little body. Brenda watched as Annie put her skirt and sweater on a hanger and reached into her gym bag for her spandex workout suit. Brenda still didn't move. "Get going, Brenda, we don't have all day. And Bernie and Roy don't like it when we're late." For a moment, Brenda hated the bitch.

"Fuck 'em. I have to call in the Army Corps of Engineers to help me put on my panty hose, and you want me to take an exercise class where I'm expected to raise my legs higher than ankle height?" Brenda flashed on the image of dancing hippos in *Fantasia*, then she shrugged. Oh, well, what the hell, she thought, and began to undress.

"You'll see, Brenda, you're going to love it. You'll become positively addicted. If I miss even a single class, I feel guilty. You know, Catholic guilt?"

Why is she being so fuckin' cheery? Brenda wondered. She seems distracted, not all here. "Listen," Brenda said. "I'm half Catholic, half Jewish, and as I see it, Jews own guilt. Catholics only rent."

"Well, if I miss more than a couple of classes, I can't keep up, and then I feel humiliated."

"Hey, humiliation is Bernie and Roy's business, and it looks like business is good."

With as little enthusiasm as possible, Brenda changed into the exercise clothes she'd bought at the Forgotten Woman boutique. Turning from the locker, she looked at herself in the cruel full-length mirror and understood how the store got its name. She followed Annie into the workout room. She immediately recognized two of the other three women there. One was the leading soap opera star of the previous year, the one Luke almost married, and the other was Lally Snow, the old society bitch. She and Duarto were working with Lally on the AIDS benefit being held next weekend. She hated the old snake. The youngish girl was Khymer Mallison, some nouveau riche kid who wanted to break into New York society. Duarto was doing her new town house.

"Annie," she hissed, "look who's here. I can't do this." Annie shrugged. Just then Melanie Kemp ran in, perfectly togged out in matching leotards, leg warmers, and sweatband. Melanie was one of those society women who decorated, first their husbands' houses, then their friends'. Duarto hated them.

Then a door opened at the other end of the room and Bernie and Roy came bouncing in. They were both muscular and had short-cropped blond hair. Jesus Christ, Brenda thought, they're twins. Identical fucking twins. Athletic. Military. And cheerful. Ridiculously fucking cheerful.

"Okay, girls, let's dance to the music." Roy, or maybe it was Bernie, started it up. As Marvin Gaye's "Sexual Healing" began to blare out of the speakers, Bernie, or maybe it was Roy, began the choreographed exercise steps. His twin moved among them, adjusting stance, correcting posture.

"And I would like to welcome the latest member to our group, Brenda. Brenda, you know Khymer, Melanie, Barbara, Lally, and Annie. Now don't be shy, just follow the leader." Each of the women stretched into a warm-up split.

Through her breathlessness, Brenda muttered to herself, "I'm not a fuckin' Rockette, Slim. Give me a break." Brenda saw Annie stifle a laugh and try to concentrate on her workout. Why was that woman laughing? The tempo of the taped music began to increase. Left kick, right kick, step, step, step, step. Left kick, right kick, step, step, step, step. Brenda puffed as she struggled to keep up with them.

Bernie came over to her. "I know you can kick higher than that, Brenda," he said with a professional smile.

"Only to crotch level," she warned him, baring her teeth.

In only minutes Brenda had been pushed beyond her limit. Christ, isn't this the shit that killed Bob Fosse? she thought. Her face was glistening with sweat, and her forehead was knitted tightly in a scowl. But she saw that the old viper Lally kept up. Jesus, she has to be twice my age, even if she's half my weight, Brenda thought. She was mortified, and she sure as hell wouldn't quit in front of Lally. For forty murderous, agonizing minutes she kept it up. At last the class came to an end.

The twins came over to her for consultation. Well, they could fuck that shit, Brenda thought as she collapsed onto the floor, gasping for breath.

"Are you premenstrual, by any chance?" Roy asked, peering down at the fat, wet heap on the floor.

"Yeah, and I've got a bad case of PMS," Brenda growled. "It makes me cranky and erratic, so for two days a month, I behave the way men always do. Care for some sumo wrestling?" The two backed off.

Dragging herself off the floor, Brenda was joined by Annie, and they made their way to the changing room and showers. What does Annie have to be so fucking happy about? Brenda wondered again.

Puffing slightly, Annie said, "This really picks me up . . . makes me feel alive . . . and you have to admit, they're very attractive. Did they turn you on, Brenda?"

That, too, is unlike Annie, Brenda thought. She never talks about sex. What's with her? "Marat and Sade? You gotta be kidding!" Brenda exclaimed. "I feel like a James Bond martini: shaken, not stirred."

Lally Snow, thin as she was, didn't strip before the others. She went into one of the curtained booths and emerged immaculately dressed, if just a tiny bit overdone. She was the kind of woman, Brenda thought, who had never heard the old rule—get dressed, put on your jewelry, then take one piece off. Now, glittering, she waltzed over to the two friends.

"Sold another table!" she sang out to Brenda. The AIDS benefit, a relatively new charity, had been stuck with a tough date—the second Friday in June. Everyone left town in June, and tables were a little difficult to unload. But Brenda had done her part and impressed Annie, who'd gotten Elise to help, and in the end Brenda had done well. Not as well as Lally, though, who had the goods on *everyone*.

"You'll never guess who bought a whole table," Lally cooed to Annie. "Aaron. Isn't that lovely of him?"

Annie looked stunned, but only for a minute. Brenda

knew she had asked Aaron herself, but he'd said he'd be away, though his partner, Jerry, had bought two seats. Brenda watched as Annie recovered, looked at Lally, and smiled.

"Aaron always supports worthy causes."

"Yes," Lally agreed. "He seems very into psychology right now." She smiled, turned, and waltzed away.

What the fuck was that supposed to mean? Brenda wondered. She looked over at Annie, first so happy, now upset. "What's with you, Annie? Is it Sylvie? Do you want me to come with you tomorrow?"

Annie sighed. "No. No, we'll be fine."

Was it Aaron, Brenda wondered, going to the benefit? "You know, if you don't want to go to the AIDS thing, you don't have to."

"Oh, no. Chris is taking me. He's bought his first tux and he'd be disappointed not to go."

Brenda tried another tack. "How was Alex's graduation? You haven't told me anything about it. Who was there?" Brenda noticed Annie tighten up just a bit. Getting warmer.

"Just the family—you know, Chris and Alex, the grandparents, and Aaron, of course." Annie's eyes didn't meet Brenda's.

"And?" Brenda said.

"And what? That's it. We all went out to dinner together and had a perfectly nice time. Alex was delighted."

Brenda was relentless. The trail was getting hotter. "And after dinner?"

"Brenda, now really, you're such a snoop," Annie said, but she had a guilty smile on that good-girl face of hers. "Let's just go to lunch."

Bingo! Brenda turned to Annie and looked at her, suddenly understanding. "You fucked him, didn't you?"

Annie eyed Brenda with a look of shock. "Brenda! I did not!" she said, but she blushed.

"Oh, yes, you did! You fucked him!"

Annie shrugged, giving up her pretense. "I prefer to say we made love." She shook her head, dropping her haughty pose. "It was after the graduation party. Oh, things went so well, Brenda. It was so good to be with him again."

Brenda winced, disturbed, but she saw Annie didn't notice. For a moment she wished she hadn't pried this information out of her friend. As far as Brenda was concerned, it was not good news.

"So what does this mean, Annie? Has Aaron changed his mind since the divorce?"

Annie's face froze. "Well, we haven't talked since then." Brenda nodded slightly, but Annie quickly went on before her friend could speak. "He had to go to New Hampshire on business. Right after the graduation."

"Did he call yet?"

"No," Annie admitted, "but it's only been two days. I think he's still out of town."

"They have phones in New Hampshire."

Neither of them mentioned Lally Snow or the table Aaron had bought for the benefit. Obviously the bastard hadn't invited Annie. Brenda busied herself for a moment, applying lipstick. Then she turned and looked directly at her friend.

"You were used, Annie," Brenda said, as gently as such harsh words could be spoken. "He had the warm and friendlies from the graduation. Just one for old times' sake. He's used you again."

Annie picked up her towel, patted the moisture from her forehead, and crammed the towel into her gym bag. Brenda saw that her eyes looked frightened. "He'll call, Brenda. I know he will."

"Oh, yeah. Expect fair treatment. What a laugh. Like Morty treated me fair. An amicable divorce. What an oxymoron. Well, I guess I'm the oxymoron." She sat down heavily on the bench beside the locker and told Annie about the stock, about how stupid she'd been, about how Morty had robbed her.

"Oh, Brenda! I'm so sorry. But you have to do something. You have to sue."

"Yeah? With what? Lawyers cost money." Brenda paused. She couldn't tell Annie about her father, about all that. "I'm afraid of the courts. Morty knows it."

"Brenda, you can't let him take advantage of that. I'll lend you money. Or we can find a lawyer who will work on contingency."

"You think so?"

"Yes, because you have to do something, Brenda. This is dreadful."

Brenda was surprised and touched to see tears fill Annie's eyes. What a good friend. But boy, she was taking this hard.

Then Annie sat down on the bench beside her. She reached into her purse and pulled out a note.

"Brenda, I want you to read this," Annie said, handing her Cynthia's letter. Brenda's brow furrowed as she unfolded the pale notepaper, began to read it, then searched for a signature. "It's from Cynthia," Annie told her.

"But Cynthia's dead!"

"She wrote it just before she died."

Brenda read it through again, slowly shaking her head.

"A suicide note?"

"Oh, Brenda, it's more than that. It's about us all."

8

Upset Upstate

It was only a few minutes past seven A.M. and Annie was already exhausted. After Cynthia's suicide, the weekend in Boston with Aaron, and Sylvie's tearful good-bye to Chris yesterday, this day would surely be the roughest to get through yet.

She had already packed all of Sylvie's necessities—plus lots of things that weren't—and arranged for the porter to take down the baggage. She put a bag of buttered rolls and fruit out, ready for the trip. She called the garage to be sure that Hudson and the car would be downstairs at eight. She no longer kept a driver, but Hudson had been one of those limo owners who catered to a few of "his ladies." Discreet and courteous, he had ferried Annie to Saks, Mortimer's, Kenneth's, and other exclusive daytime destinations. But this trip was different.

Annie had wanted to savor this time before she had to disturb Sylvie. It was impossible, of course, she knew that already. Yet she shrank from waking her, and so she sat in the comfortable kitchen, taking in the last few moments of having her daughter in the house. Everything normal, for the last time.

When she looked back, Annie could clearly see that her

life was divided into two parts: the twenty-seven years before Sylvie was born, and the sixteen years after. Real demarcations weren't the shallow events—graduations, parties, relocations—but the bone-deep markings of birth, death, love, loss. And those only if they marked you forever.

Alex's and Chris's births had been wonderful, miraculous, of course, but they occurred during that long period when Annie was in the dream of her life, not her life itself. With Sylvie's birth, Annie woke up. Sylvie was a problem that prayers or patience or time would not heal. And in the fire storm of rage and pain and blame and guilt, Annie woke up—and finally grew up. She wished she'd done it years earlier. Except in growing up, she'd left a husband and a son behind.

She worried about Alex sometimes, her beautiful, gifted golden son. Did he really want to study medicine? She sighed. Most mothers would be grateful for a boy who was drug free, dean's list, and about to go to med school. But Annie worried that he might be in that obscuring fog of ambition and social pressure that she had once lived in.

And Chris—she wondered, would he be all right? He was the middle child, the problem-free sunny one, but hadn't Aaron always favored Alex and hadn't she become immersed with Sylvie? Chris had dropped out of Princeton and was working with his father at the ad agency. Was it just his way of getting Aaron's attention at last? Chris was working hard, and Alex was working hard, and both seemed headed for success. But did they know joy? Were they *really* okay? Because the rest just didn't matter.

And it was Sylvie who had made her see all this. Sylvie, without trying, had juggled Annie's values, thrown the givens out the window. It wasn't what you earned, how you looked, what you achieved, whom you knew, how much you had. It wasn't even how smart you were. Those were not important.

Every precept Annie had been carefully taught, every value she had swallowed, they all amounted to nothing. Catholicism. Being nice. Staying attractive. Ignoring the unpleasant. Denial. Wrong, wrong. All wrong. But once you realized all this, once these precepts were abandoned, the world sometimes became a painfully ridiculous place.

Annie looked out the kitchen window, over the East River, watching the sunrise this last morning with Sylvie at home as it spread a blush across the man-made landscape below. *"The earth is the Lord's, and the fullness thereof, the world and they that dwell therein,"* she murmured. She was no longer religious, having left the Catholic Church years ago, but she felt the truth and beauty of some of the psalms, and they comforted her. Today she needed comfort.

Today Sylvie will leave me, she thought. Even before Cynthia's funeral, Annie had cried, secretly, most nights that previous week. She had to do it privately. Sylvie became so very upset when Annie cried. Annie, of course, had known the separation would be hard for Sylvie. But Annie also knew that Sylvie lived in the moment, and if her moments away were filled with sunshine, a pet, good food, and some friends, Sylvie would be all right. But what about me? Aaron thinks I'm doing this for me, but he's so wrong. This is my gift to her, Annie thought. And it's the hardest thing I've ever done. She wiped her eyes again, then took a shuddering breath. Maybe this is the start of the third period in my life: life without Sylvie.

Maybe it would also be a new start for Sylvie. She needs this school, despite what Aaron and Alex say. Annie had seen what was happening to her. Day by day, week by week, year by year, surrounded by others who were smarter, faster, quicker, Sylvie had grown more and more frustrated, more and more alone. Annie saw that she hadn't given her daughter what she needed, just as her own mother hadn't given Annie her birthright.

But unlike her own mother, Annie wouldn't run from the problem. She was fighting for Sylvie. She'd researched the schools and sheltered communities out there and found Sylvan Glades. Though it would cost her everything to give up her little girl to strangers, she knew she had to do it. And Chris, bless his heart, had seen Sylvie's need and agreed.

The irony was that for years Aaron had accused her of being too close to Sylvie, of being too protective, of "spoiling" her. He had tried to present the issue as his selfless concern, but Annie knew it was otherwise. *I don't think he could love anything, anyone, so imperfect. He's just like that,* Annie thought. Having a child with Down's syndrome had not fit in with Aaron's image of himself. It had hurt him, somewhere deep, deep inside, and as time passed and Sylvie grew, it became harder, not easier for him. She wasn't as cute at ten as she had been at six, and at thirteen she wasn't cute at all. To him she was simply imperfect.

And much else became imperfect as well. Certainly, after Sylvie, things between them had changed. It had been a difficult birth; Annie had healed slowly and had then been depressed. And Aaron had not been good at comforting her. Thrown against adversity, he ran from it. He wanted her to "get over it." At last, when their intimacy resumed, she had not achieved orgasm. Ever. From then till now.

Aaron had tried, at first, to be patient. She'd had minor surgery, started therapy, had been prescribed tranquilizers. For a long time they had simply lived with it. But by now Annie, too, in his eyes was imperfect. It was too much for him. Aaron had read about Dr. Leslie Rosen, the sex specialist, and finally insisted that Annie consult with her.

To be sure, Dr. Rosen had helped her tear away many of the

veils that had hidden the truths of her life. Dr. Rosen helped Annie see how poorly she had been mothered, how sad, how angry, she was. Annie had even brought Aaron to her. Then Dr. Rosen helped Annie see the problems in her marriage. She helped her decide to find a school for Sylvie. Then Aaron had left, and the doctor had terminated therapy when Annie refused to give up on her marriage. And now, now with all this happening, Annie felt abandoned by Dr. Rosen, dropped just when she needed support the most. "You're still in a dream-world. You refuse to see reality," Dr. Rosen had said. "There is nothing more I can do."

Annie felt dizzy again. She would just have to take this day slowly. She thought of calling Brenda. Brenda had offered to come with her to take Sylvie to school, but Annie had declined. She wanted all the time alone with Sylvie that she could get. Now, however, she realized she needed to talk to someone. She looked at her watch and realized it was only a quarter after seven. She couldn't call; Brenda would kill her. After all, no one had died, she thought to herself dryly. I just feel as if *I* might, she thought. Well, I can survive without the call. I've done most of this alone up till now. Surely I can get through this, too.

She walked down the hallway to Sylvie's room. It was almost empty of Sylvie's treasures. Only Pangor, the Siamese cat, and Sylvie herself waited to be readied for the trip. Quietly, Annie opened the curtains and turned to look at her sleeping child. Sylvie's white-gold curls lay across the pillow, her face relaxed in sleep. She had the distorted eye structure that had once labeled such children "mongoloids," but in sleep she looked younger and the blankness that was so telling when she was awake was more appropriate.

"Sylvie." Annie touched her shoulder gently. So far as she knew, Sylvie had only been touched with gentleness and love her whole life, just like Pangor, their cat. And like Pangor, Sylvie stretched, arched, and rolled onto her back. She opened her arms to her mother. As Annie hugged her, she hoped that Sylvie would always be protected so that she could stay open and loving.

"Hi, Mom-Pom." Sylvie's speech was slightly slurred, but easily understandable if anyone tried. Many didn't.

"Hi, Sylvie."

"Hi, Pangor." The cat gave another stretch and rolled onto its side. Annie gently stroked its soft, soft belly.

"Time to get up, both of you." Annie sat down at the side of the bed. "You remember what we do today, don't you?"

"Go to school," Sylvie whispered. There was a fear deep in her eyes, one that all of Annie's talks had not dispelled. "But I will like it, after a while." She parroted what Annie had told her, over and over. Annie nodded. "And Pangor can come, too, right, Mom-Pom?"

"Absolutely."

"Good." Sylvie threw off the blankets and got to her feet. She was awkward in her movements, a little clumsy. And so very, very trusting.

"Get washed up and dressed. Hudson will be here right after breakfast." Sylvie smiled. She liked Hudson, and he liked Sylvie. Annie watched her daughter as she struggled out of her pink pajamas. Then she turned and walked back to the kitchen. She felt tears sting her eyes.

The school wasn't far away, she reminded herself, only one hundred and seventeen miles north in a quiet part of New York State. Annie sighed. She looked at the boxes and the trunk packed and waiting in the hall. She remembered when she had gone off, younger than Sylvie was now, to Miss Porter's School. Like Sylvie, she'd been confused and upset. But unlike Sylvie, she'd had no mother to take her. Her mother had run away. Run away and never come back. She never said good-bye to either Annie or Annie's father. And he, bewildered, had sent his only child off to school.

It seemed that she had always fought loneliness. Did other people feel it? she wondered. Did others spend their lives outrunning the loneliness? She had suffered it, but decided she would never let her children twist in its grip, if she could help it.

Well, Sylvan Glades was her insurance against loneliness for Sylvie. Despite what Aaron said, Sylvan Glades was actually a residential community where Sylvie would be happy to be with other retarded people. She would have a job, eventually, and friends, and help with all the things she needed help with in daily life. And she wouldn't be the slightest bit different. She'd be just the same.

It was costly, very costly, but they had planned for long-term care eventually, and Annie had added most of her trust fund to the money that Aaron had put aside. It was more than enough. All that was necessary then had been for Annie to let go, to free her child of the loneliness, and then to wait for the same loneliness to come hunting her.

And now, it was here.

She got the travel box for Pangor and slipped a tranquilizer wrapped in a ball of cream cheese down the cat's throat. Without it, he'd yowl the whole way. She wished she had one for herself.

At eight, exactly, Hudson rang up. Sylvie, dressed in a white linen blouse and a pretty blue jumper from Saks, danced with excitement. "We're going to school. School. School," she sang, and Annie tried to smile.

"Sleep-away school," she reminded her.

"Sleep-away school." Sylvie nodded. "Like Chris. Like Alex." And she reached out and held Annie's hand. "Let's go. Let's go."

Sylvie was too excited to sleep in the car, so they played I Spy and colored. Sylvie ate a roll and butter and half a banana. To Annie, the ride seemed endless, but it also ended too soon.

"Is this your new school?" Hudson asked as they pulled into the drive that lead to the elegant converted mansion. He whistled. "Some place."

Sylvie, squirming on the seat, giggled. "Some place!" she echoed, her eyes widening. Annie loved her daughter's eyes. To outsiders, they were one of the marks of Down's syndrome, but to Annie, Sylvie's slightly tipped, Asian-looking eyes were mysterious and poignantly sweet. Cat's eyes. Now frightened eyes. Sylvie had once surprised Annie when she had pointed at a picture of a geisha in one of Annie's books on Japan and said, "Like my eyes, Mommie."

As they pulled up to the main building, the big front door opened, and Dr. Gancher stepped out. A big woman. No-nonsense, but warm. Hudson opened the limo door for Sylvie and Annie and began to unpack the car while they were greeted by the doctor.

"Hello, Sylvie. Nice to see you again." Though Dr. Gancher was large, she was not intimidating. Still, Sylvie hung back.

"Hello, Mrs. Paradise." Annie took Dr. Gancher's hand.

"Say hello, Sylvie," Annie coaxed, and Sylvie mumbled a greeting. Then she looked up.

"I have a cat," she said. "It has eyes like mine."

Annie looked at Sylvie, startled. Sylvie had never compared herself to Pangor before. Once again, Annie was struck by how often the child seemed to know some of what she, Annie, had been thinking.

Now Dr. Gancher smiled. "And I understand your cat is going to stay here with you." Sylvie nodded.

Hudson turned to them. He had already lined up Sylvie's

boxes and trunk neatly beside the car. "All here and ready to go. Where should I put them?"

"I think it's best to just leave them for the present." Dr. Gancher looked at Sylvie. "Are you ready to see your new school?"

"Yes."

They toured the main building, the cafeteria, and the group house where Sylvie would have her own room. All of the "students" that Annie saw seemed well cared for and occupied. After more than an hour, they ended the tour on the front steps where they had begun.

"And are you ready to say good-bye to your mother?"

Sylvie nodded. "Bye, Mom-Pom," she said casually.

"Then I think it's time for you to go, Mrs. Paradise. May I call you this evening?"

Annie was startled. "Now?" she asked, and then realized that, of course, this would be easiest on Sylvie. "Yes, certainly."

She turned to her daughter. "Good-bye for now, darling. I'll talk to you soon."

Sylvie kept smiling. "Don't go, Mom-Pom. Don't go." But she seemed calm.

"I have to go now, darling. That's the rule at sleep-away school. Remember?"

The smile started to dissolve. Sylvie's broad face distorted, one side of her mouth crumpling. "Don't go!" she repeated, her voice beginning to rise.

"But you're here at your new school. Here with Pangor and Dr. Gancher. Just as we said."

Sylvie jerked her hand out of Dr. Gancher's.

"No. No," she screamed, and ran to Annie. She flung her arms around her neck. "No," she shrieked, and buried her head under Annie's arm.

"It's best to get in the car," Dr. Gancher said calmly, taking Sylvie's hand again. Sylvie shrieked as the doctor pulled her gently but firmly away. Annie stood rooted. Dr. Gancher gave her the gentlest push.

Annie backed to the car. Her daughter tried to pull out of the stranger's grasp. "Mommy, no. No, Mommy, no!" she cried again. Annie struggled to keep her own tears back, to hide her pain from Sylvie. Hudson, behind her, opened the door for her. She got in.

"Don't go. Don't go. Don't go." Hysterical, screaming, her face red, tear-streaked. Sylvie fell to her knees. "Please, Mommy, don't go."

Hudson rounded the car, got into the driver's seat, and started the engine. On the steps, two attendants came out and stood beside Dr. Gancher, who was now crouched beside Sylvie, holding her firmly by her shoulders. But Sylvie's arms, pleading, reached out to Annie.

"Is it time to go?" Hudson asked in a low voice.

"Yes," Annie managed to gasp, and they drove down the alley beneath the maples. Annie could hear Sylvie's screams until they got to the gates.

9

Morty, You Fuck!

Annie is right, Brenda thought. Her own life might be totally fucked, but when it comes to advice for me, she's right on. Brenda entered her apartment and walked down the narrow, dark hallway that led to the living room. She began searching through the drawer of the credenza. Somewhere in there she had stuffed her divorce papers, check stubs, and withdrawal slips. She scrabbled through the empty wrappers, unmailed warranty cards, and crumpled Kleenex. At last she found the business card that Duarto had given her: *Diana La Gravenesse, Esq. Practice limited to women's issues and matrimonial law.* Annie was right. "Get a good lawyer," she had said. Very good advice, Brenda thought. She'd thought about it a lot since their conversation after the exercise class Monday, and now she was going to act on it. She crossed the room to the phone and dialed the number.

It wasn't easy to get an appointment. La Gravenesse's male secretary had tried to stick her with one three weeks later, but Brenda had stood firm. "It's an emergency, and it has to be today," she told the little lisper. She had bullied him. Usually she liked gays, and her buddy Duarto was a riot, but this guy raised her hackles. Too prissy.

Okay, she had her appointment. So now what? She couldn't go alone. And she couldn't ask Annie. Annie was already a total wreck.

Duarto was the answer. He was always supportive, and better than that, he was funny. She'd ask him to go with her. Because, to be honest, she was scared. She'd been stupid, and now, if it was too late to fix the stupid, she'd be very unhappy for a very long time. And that scared her. She couldn't do this alone, she realized. So maybe Duarto would go with her. She dialed his number.

"*Principessa, cara!*" Duarto sounded so alive over the phone. "*Va bene?*"

"I feel like dog meat, if you wanna know. What's with this *principessa* shit?"

"Eet eempresses the peasants, eef you want to know," Duarto explained sotto voce. "De happy hooker ees een. I'm sitten' here, up to my teets in samples, and dees beetch keeps looken' for more. Two hundred an' twenty deeferent turquoise ees not enough. Che joost got up to take a whizz, but the heard me call you 'princess,' and now che'll suck up for another hour." He sighed. Brenda knew he was working for Gayfrieda Schiff, a slut who got lucky and married her john. And now John Schiff was spending more than ten million bucks on their new forty-three-room Park Avenue co-op. "Happy hooker" was the code name Duarto invented for Gayfrieda. "When I theenk of how my light ees spent. What a way to earn a liveen'. So what ees wit' chou?"

Brenda's chest tightened. She couldn't ask him to come. He was busy. She'd have to go alone. "Morty went public. I thought I'd go see that lawyer that you recommended."

"Fabulous! Choost what chou should do. But of course I'll come wit' chou."

"You can't. You have the happy hooker there."

"Ees notheen. I'll tell her I have my period." Duarto's voice changed. "Dees ees dreadful news, *principessa*. Eef dey are all seek, how weell chou feel de table at chour dinner?" He paused, and Brenda knew Gayfrieda had returned to the room and he was performing for her. "Oh, of course I weel. Certainly, *principessa*."

"If Gayfrieda Schiff thinks that you can get her invited to some princess's soiree, she's on drugs."

"But ees worth a try, *cara*. I weel be over een haf an hour."

Brenda's eyes filled with tears. She wouldn't have to go alone. "Duarto, you're a prince."

"No, *cara*. Buatta ees de prince. I'm de *sultan*. Ciao."

Then she had no choice but to stuff her divorce decree, the contract, the transcripts from the partial examination before trial, all of it, into a D'Agostino shopping bag. And she added the clippings from the *Times* and the *Journal*. Next came dressing. It was always difficult and she avoided the mirror. She put on black slacks that she couldn't manage to button at the waist, but she covered that up with an Issey Miyake cashmere sweater set in black and gray, which covered a multitude of sins. She'd bought it on sale, long before the divorce.

"Oh, *cara*, chou look like Elizabeth Taylor. Maybe to loose a few pounds, but steel, ees not bad, eh?" Duarto said when he arrived.

Later, in the taxi, after Duarto had tsked over the clippings, Brenda still felt frightened. It was a long ride, all the way downtown, and the taxi smelled almost unbearably of body odor. Duarto rolled his eyes, then rolled down the windows.

"Duarto, I don't know how I'm going to pay this lawyer."

Brenda sighed. "Morty is three months behind in his payments to me, and I owe everyone and his brother."

Duarto began to rummage in his attaché case. "That reminds me," he said. "Chou now got a job." He pulled out a check made out to Brenda and added, "Thees ees chour first paycheck."

Brenda looked at the check in Duarto's outstretched hand, then raised her eyes to meet his.

"Take eet, *cara*," he said, pushing the check forward.

"But Duarto, I don't work for you."

"You do now, *cara*. I need an asseestant. Eet's getten harder and harder to keep the business end going while doeen the decorating work. I'm goeen nuts weethout Richard's help. And I have to hustle more now that those two reech beetches are een the business." Brenda knew he meant Melanie Kemp and Susan Carstairs.

"So," he continued, "chou are my asseestant."

Brenda took the check, folded it, and put it in her purse. With her head down so Duarto couldn't see the tears brimming in her eyes, she said, "Thank you, Duarto. You've been very good to me."

"No, no, *cara*. Chou have been very good to me. And to Richard. He say to me at the hospital, 'Duarto, make that woman go out and get a job and get her out of the kitchen, for everyone's sake.'"

Brenda leaned across the seat and kissed Duarto on the cheek. "Thank you, Duarto, and thank you for coming with me."

"Ees nothing. Eet make me happy."

Brenda sighed. "I wish I didn't have to go do this. And I hate that part of town. I hate it."

"Chou have to do dees ting," Duarto told her. "Ees dees-gusting, what he do. How come chou take so leetle, anyway? Chou aren't so stupid like dat."

"I know, but I hate courts and lawyers and all of it. I just wanted it over with." Even to Duarto, Brenda wouldn't talk about why, wouldn't talk about her father's "business." Though he'd been dead for years, the legacy her father left her was a terror of the courts. Morty knew that, and he had used it against her. They'd settled out of court. "Money just isn't that important to me," she added, as though trying to convince herself.

"Chure, not eef chou always had eet. But getteen old ees no fun, and getteen old when you aren't rich ees deesgusteen. Look at dis cab. Chou should have a car and driver, *cara*."

Brenda looked out the window. They had arrived. Duarto paid the driver over Brenda's protests and they walked into 125 Broadway. The directory was long, and it took Brenda a while to find the listing. The office was on the fourteenth floor, which really meant the thirteenth. Great. Off to a great fucking start.

"She's really good?" Brenda asked Duarto as they stood in the elevator, waiting what seemed to Brenda an endless time for the doors to close. There was a sour smell, and a faint whiff of sardines. The elevator cab had once been paneled in mahogany. Now what was left of the wood was covered with gouges. Initials and vulgarities covered every dark inch.

"Duarto, she is really, really good?"

"Of course, *cara*. Che ees fabulous."

"Who else has she handled?" Brenda felt that a man, a really aggressive man, was probably what she needed, but she did trust Duarto. On financial issues he was realistic, even hard-boiled.

"No one chou know, but believe me, I have seen her do

some real numbers. Che has been up against Raoul Felder and Melvin Belli and made them both look like cheet. Che's a mad dog."

They stepped out of the elevator at fourteen and found themselves in a narrow hall lined with dozens of doors. "I don't remember the room number," Brenda moaned. Another ride in the elevator would undo her completely.

"Fourteen twelve," Duarto told her, but the hall branched and split several times, and only a few of the old, brown-painted metal doors had names or numbers. The hall smelled dusty and stale, and the doors were dented, as if they had been kicked or hammered on. Brenda felt worse and worse. She thought of her Jewish mother's single bit of useful advice: "Only get the best. Otherwise you'll regret it." Too bad she never taught me where it was found or how to recognize it, Brenda thought, clutching the slippery plastic shopping bag. One thing she did know: this was not the place where the best would ever be found.

"Ta-dah!" trumpeted Duarto. They had come to another of the ubiquitous brown metal doors, this one with a pebbled-glass window with *Law Office of Diana La Gravenesse* painted in black and gold. Duarto opened the door, and Brenda walked into a drab, beige, unwindowed waiting room with a few old leather armchairs, a coffee table with some ragged magazines, and a window in a wall behind which sat a redheaded male receptionist.

"Seet down. I weel take care of eet." Brenda watched from a chair as Duarto spoke to the receptionist. They went on for some time. Duarto returned to her, his lips tight.

"I love dees self-important leetle nellies. T'inks who de fuck he ees." He raised his brows. "Diana will come soon, *cara*."

And she did. The brown-painted door opened to reveal an amazing sight. She was tall, well over six foot, with broad shoulders and long arms and legs. Her hair was short, an indeterminate color between blond and brown, parted in the middle and slicked back in almost a parody of the Wall Street–banker look. Her pumps, stockings, suit, and silk shirt were all a gray-brown-taupe color, as were her eyes, and her glasses were rimless with gold ear-wires. Big, classy, austere, tough. She looked formidable.

"Duarto! I didn't know you were coming today." Her voice was deep but not unfeminine. She smiled, and her broad lips revealed the most perfect natural teeth that Brenda had ever seen. And if they weren't her own, Brenda wanted the dentist's name. Angela needed some caps.

"You're Brenda Cushman?" The statement had an interrogative lift at the end of the sentence, but the big woman didn't wait for an answer. She held out her hand, a big, flat one with long fingers, and took Brenda's small, chubby one for a moment. And for the first time all day, the anxiety stopped. Just for a minute, as Diana La Gravenesse took her hand, Brenda felt fine.

"Let's go into my office," Diana suggested, and they did.

Nervous, perspiring, Brenda told the lawyer about her case. When she began, she was almost stammering, but she gradually began to relax. Maybe it was stupid, but she trusted this woman. So much so that she even explained about her father and his connections to "the Family." "I don't want to be asked about that stuff. I'm afraid, and my husband knows it."

Diana was soothing. "I can understand. But he's used your fear. And he's certainly hidden marital assets. We have enough to reopen the case." She paused. "Tell me, Mrs. Cushman, did you ever help your husband in his business?"

"Help?" Brenda asked. "I used to run the place. Why? Does it matter?"

"A great deal. Tell me about it."

What a creep Morty had been, Brenda thought. Morty had lost his job—the third one that year—two weeks before the wedding, but she had buried the significance of that event in her excitement at her new life. Her father and mother had given them the down payment for their first house, a little semi-attached in the Bronx.

Each of her aunts had bought a room of furniture for them, so they moved into a completely furnished house, compliments of her family. Morty walked into the marriage with only his salesman's personality and the promise of a good life. She'd left the darkness of her family behind. No more crooks, no more phone calls from Peewee and Lefty, no more visits from men in limousines in the middle of the night.

But things weren't good. Morty couldn't hold a job; he was always mouthing off to his bosses. He couldn't hold on to money, either—when he had it, which was rarely. So Brenda swallowed her pride and hid her disappointment; she went to her father to ask for his help in getting Morty another job. That was when she knew she would have to be the one to steer their futures. And it scared her. She was raised by her Italian father and Jewish mother to marry comfortably, stay at home, and depend on her man. But now she knew that that formula wasn't going to work, not if she was ever going to have anything without her family's help.

Brenda's father knew the score as well. He saw that unless he gave Brenda a hand, she was doomed to life with a loser.

So he had set Morty up in an appliance store on Fordham Road in the Bronx, and Brenda adapted immediately to her role as bookkeeper, since Morty couldn't be trusted to handle the money. The business prospered, she remembered, not because her husband was such a hotshot businessman—as he tried to convince people—but because Brenda's father was providing the stock through the back door. With his connections, appliances that had "fallen off the back of a truck" were delivered each day and, because the overhead was so low, sold the next.

There was no one she could explain this to, except her much younger brother, Neil. But he was a stand-up comic, a nut bag who was living on the West Coast and had nothing to do with the family.

Brenda sat in Diana's soft leather chair, remembering those early years, finally talking about them. She had hated being involved with the dirt again, but she had to admit it proved to be the perfect setup, with the business growing so fast that they had been forced to go legit and enlarge. Again, it was Brenda's father who got those wheels rolling, and Brenda who kept them greased.

That prick, she thought, as she remembered how each night Morty came striding into the office, being his usual officious self. On-the-job training was how she picked up her knowledge of bookkeeping, along with the principles of business, and she was trying to teach him all she was learning as quickly as possible, so that eventually she could stay home. Her mom was watching Angela, her baby, grow up.

But Morty was not a man who stooped to learn from a woman. "Take care of it!" he would growl. He was only interested in being the front man, playing proprietor. She paid the bills, dealt with deliveries, did the firing. Morty, of course, did the hiring. He was strictly fun stuff. And when they outgrew the store, he wanted another, and then another. Be a bigger man. Brenda was stuck negotiating the leases, getting credit extended. At last, after Tony was born, it was too much, and they hired Sy, who took over the back office. Brenda gratefully retreated to the house in

Greenwich, only to find it was all wrong for her. The neighbors were snobs. Her parents were far away. The kids were unhappy. She was unhappy. She sighed. Nothing turned out the way you planned.

Now, she looked up at Diana La Gravenesse's interested, attentive face. "Let me explain how it was," she began.

10

The Unpleasantness
at the Carlyle

The weekend stretched before Annie, empty and end-less. Aaron still hadn't called. She felt frightened by the thought. Why hadn't she accepted Elise's East Hampton invitation? Well, because she couldn't bear the effort of being social. But she couldn't bear the loneli-ness either. Summer weekends in the city were awful. But she had no choice. She was a prisoner—imprisoned, waiting for Aaron's call.

She managed to get through Saturday by reading a bit, watering the plants, eating a little yogurt, then, exhausted by the fruitless waiting, she fell into bed at eight-thirty. She slept until almost one, then woke, dreaming she was in Aaron's arms. When she realized it was only a dream, she knew she wouldn't sleep again that night. She wished, desperate for a moment, that she had some pills. Tomorrow she'd call Brenda and borrow a few Seconals. She disapproved of them, but she couldn't face another sleepless night.

She got up, drank a glass of water, and walked down the hall to Sylvie's room. Perhaps there was something she had overlooked, something she could pack and send to her daugh-ter. She turned on the light and opened the closet. Sylvie's old coat, her outgrown sneakers, and some odds and ends were all that were there. Annie closed the door. Television. Annie rarely watched television, almost never the one in the living room. Now, she turned it on.

A made-for-television movie, an evangelist, a rerun of *Mannix*. She was on the cable channels now. A woman, nude, appeared on the screen. "Want to suck these tits?" she asked, holding up her breasts. "Want to do it to me doggy style? Want to give me your hard cock? Call Elite Escort Service. We're young, we're hot, and we want *you*. Lonely? Call Elite." Annie snapped the set off, repulsed. Channel J. Public Access. It should be stopped. Who was so desperate that they called those numbers? Who was that lonely? For a moment, despite her disgust, she felt compassion for whoever they might be.

She walked out to the kitchen. It was 1:18 in the morning. How would she get through the night?

Sunday. Yes, *Sunday* was the loneliest day of the week. Standing at the kitchen sink, Annie forced herself to take two high-potency vitamin pills, one at a time, following each with a sip of orange juice. She fought the urge to retch, waited a moment for the feeling to pass, then looked at the kitchen clock. Two-fifteen in the afternoon. Then she double-checked against her wristwatch. For a moment Annie was surprised at how late it had become. She was disoriented. Her insomnia had affected her thinking, she knew. But then it wasn't really thinking. It was only yearning for Aaron, for her old life.

Her sleeplessness and loneliness were closing in on her. Perhaps, she thought, I should call Dr. Rosen for a prescription. No, she would not be dependent. She'd handle this.

I made mistakes, Aaron. I should have been more attentive to you. I shouldn't have blamed you for not accepting Sylvie as she is. You needed more attention. I'm sorry I grew away from you. I'm sorry I didn't have orgasms. I'm so very, very sorry. But Aaron, why did you make love to me in Boston? Why did you say you loved me? And why, oh, why, haven't you called me?

He was the only man for her, the only one. She knew that now. Without Aaron, she'd spend her life wandering through purgatories like this one, alone. Alone, she couldn't take New York in June. Alone, she couldn't escape to their cottage on Long Island. She couldn't bear to be alone, unloved. Since the separation she'd fooled herself. Only temporary. Not permanent. So she'd hoped. And then graduation, and her night with Aaron, had confirmed her hope. But she'd been foolish.

What will I do without him? she thought for the hundredth time. Get out and get some fresh air, she told herself. But the heat on the street stunned her, adding to her confusion, her disorientation. As she walked west on Eighty-fourth Street, she passed a storefront and looked at her reflection in the window. Someone I used to know, she thought. Annie stopped and studied the image in the glass: forest-green polo shirt, beige chino skirt, loafers. She hadn't realized as she was dressing in these castoffs that this was the way she used to dress at Smith.

As she continued her walk, she remembered her college days, and before that Miss Porter's School, and Sacred Heart. Cynthia. She thought of Cynthia. But that was too much. Suddenly aware of her surroundings, she looked across Park Avenue at the massive church on the southwest corner of Eighty-fourth Street. St. Ignatius Loyola. The nuns at Sacred Heart in Philadelphia used to take the girls to a Jesuit church for Sunday vespers at four. Annie used to love that service. She'd go into the church. She'd light a candle for Cynthia, for Sylvie, and for herself. She looked at her watch. Ten to four.

Annie crossed the avenue and entered the large Romanesque church. She didn't know if vespers was still sung, what with all the change in the Church since the sixties. She hadn't been to church for years, aside from the inevitable weddings and funerals, and these mostly in Episcopal churches. She didn't approve of the Church or the Pope, but she was drawn to this church today. Annie stood in the rear, looking down the main aisle toward the huge mosaics behind the altar, moved by their beauty and the sense of timelessness they gave her. She slipped into a pew near the rear. The church was almost empty, except for a sprinkling of old Irish ladies mumbling their rosaries. How little has changed. She sat back in the pew and let her mind wander between memories and prayers. Bless Cynthia. Poor Cynthia. Help my daughter, Sylvie. And Aaron. Aaron, his name became a litany. Please, God, let him love me. Let this be a worthy prayer.

She'd guessed correctly that the Jesuits wouldn't give up vespers. The service began and the chanting and incense transported her, weaving its simple cloak of peace around her. For a moment, she lost sense of time and place. Then suddenly, like an answered prayer, she knew what had to be done. *I'll* call *him!* I've been too cold. I'll tell him how I feel. I'll show him. Perhaps he doesn't know. But he *must* know. I'll tell him. Yes, this was right. Feeling inspired, empowered, she genuflected beside the pew and whispered, "Thank you," to the echoing emptiness and quickly left the church.

Annie found a pay phone on Madison Avenue. Of course, she thought, he's waiting for *me* to call *him*. He is unsure. He's afraid it will be like it was. He doesn't know how I've changed. How I've grown. How different things will be now that Sylvie is gone. Why didn't I think of this before?

There was no shaking in her hand as she dialed Aaron's number at the Carlyle, no tremor in her voice as she asked for him. What if he was away for the weekend? What if he was out on a shoot or at the office? Not until she heard his voice did she feel the panic. He did love her, didn't he? He'd said so.

"Aaron, it's Annie. I've got to see you."

"Annie. Is something wrong?"

"No. No. But it's very important, Aaron. I have something to tell you. May I come over to see you?"

"Now? Today? Is it necessary?"

She pushed against the reluctance in his voice. "Now," she said firmly. After he agreed, Annie put the phone back on the hook and wiped her moist hands on her skirt. Too bad she wasn't well dressed. Well, this couldn't wait. She walked the few short blocks down Madison Avenue, her eyes looking straight ahead. When she got to the Carlyle, she realized she was breathing rapidly and willed herself to slow.

Quietly, as calmly as she could, she crossed the small lobby. No one stopped her. Even in her casual clothes she looked as if she belonged. She took the elevator up to his floor.

She rang Aaron's bell and waited. Oh, God, no answer. She rang again and waited. When Aaron finally opened the door, Annie sucked in her breath at the sight of him.

"Annie, I didn't expect you so quickly. Come in," he said, closing the door behind her as she entered the sitting room. He continued, "You must have been at the corner when you called. I didn't realize."

She looked around the small but elegant room. Who paid for this? she wondered idly. She supposed his firm did. "I talked to Sylvie," Aaron said, almost defensively.

"Oh?"

"Yes, I talked to her yesterday. She says she likes school. We had a good talk. Maybe the place is okay." He paused, running out of words.

Annie walked to the window and looked down onto Madison Avenue. She saw couples walking arm in arm, and at this moment it seemed to her like an omen. Yes, people should be in couples. Aaron and she would be reunited. Thank God.

"This is an amazing view. So different from ours." Then, for the first time, she lost her composure and blushed. "I mean, of Gracie Square." She stopped for a moment, disconcerted. This was going to be harder than she'd thought. "One could look out this window for hours, or days even."

"Would you believe I haven't looked out it once since I'm here." Aaron laughed, averting his face. This was going nowhere. She felt the pressure to do something.

Annie walked around the room, feeling suddenly self-conscious. Her skirt was ridiculous, and Aaron noticed these things. She sat on the sofa, while Aaron walked over to the small bar. "Would you like a sherry?" he asked. She accepted, then held her glass while he poured himself a Scotch and took two quick sips. He looked over at her as he sat down in the club chair. She could see the strain on his face.

"Is there something wrong, Annie? If it isn't Sylvie, is it one of the boys?" He sat forward in his chair.

"Oh, no, nothing like that. They're all fine, Aaron," she assured him quickly. He looked so handsome, his warm skin so smooth, his black hair so very shiny. And he loved her. He'd said so. But she couldn't help but notice that he had taken off his wedding band. She'd never removed hers.

She took a sip of sherry to bolster her resolve and placed the glass on the coffee table between them. At that moment, her love for him was so strong, she was certain that he would feel it, would know and return it. "Aaron, I'm going to be very direct," she said. "I think I can be that with you, after all. I've done a lot of thinking since Alex's graduation, and I've made a decision." With surprise, she watched Aaron get up and walk to the half-opened door to the next room. Why did he always move away from strong feelings? "No, please, Aaron. Let me say what I've come to say." She motioned him back to his chair. Reluctantly he returned. "I've been waiting for your call since then. I was beginning to think you didn't call me because you didn't want to. It wasn't until sitting in church today that I realized why you hadn't called."

"Church?" Aaron asked irrelevantly. "Since when do you go to church?"

Annie clasped her hands together on her lap and sat straighter, as if to give emphasis to her words. "You were afraid of hurting me again. You needed me to call you. And I think you need to know just how much I love you. So, here I am, Aaron. To let you know I'd like us to try again."

She looked around the elegant but anonymous room and said, "Come home, Aaron. This isn't the place for you. We'll start over, without the strain of Sylvie. She's doing well now, Aaron. And for us the good things we shared could get better. I know that now." Annie smiled and opened her hands, palms up. But Aaron slumped down into his chair. Annie looked at him and blinked. "You do want this as much as I do, don't you?" she asked.

"But you don't understand, Annie," he blurted. "It's over."

"Over?"

"Annie, we're divorced. Remember? Our marriage is over."

"Well, that was started a year ago. But things changed. How could it be over, Aaron? Up in Boston—"

"Nothing happened in Boston, Annie," Aaron interrupted. "We just had a good time at our son's graduation." His eyes flickered toward the bedroom door. What was he so nervous about? Annie wondered for a moment. Then, the force of what he had said began to break through the wall of hope and magic and crazy, childish religion she had conjured up to buttress her obsession. Her face reddened with the humiliation and her body began to shake. It couldn't hurt more if he had hit her. But no, it couldn't be. It couldn't be that it was all over. Not when he had told her he loved her. Not when he'd taken her to bed. Not when he sat there now, just across from her, so warm, his flesh so good, so healthy, so male.

"Annie," he said gently, "I'm getting married."

Annie's hand went to her throat, as if to choke the scream she was hearing in her head. "Getting married, Aaron? What do you mean?"

"Just that, Annie. We're divorced, and now I'm getting married."

"Just like that?" Was she going crazy? Perhaps he didn't love her. But he certainly couldn't love anyone else. This wasn't possible . . . it couldn't be. It left her breathless.

"Not just like that. Believe me. Not just like that," Aaron sighed.

Still she couldn't believe it. He was making it up. It was insane. He'd have to prove it. Like a child, she had to demand proof. "To whom? Whom are you marrying?" Annie heard her voice and realized it was almost shrill.

"Leslie Rosen."

"Who?" The name seemed familiar.

"Dr. Rosen. I'm marrying Leslie Rosen."

For a moment she paused. It wasn't true. This was a joke. Unbelievable. Not *her* Dr. Rosen. Then she laughed, confused. "Aaron, you can't. She was my therapist. My sex therapist. You didn't even like her. You only consulted with her twice, and you didn't even like her."

"Annie, that was almost two years ago. Things have changed since then."

"Yes. You've left me and Dr. Rosen terminated me." Annie felt her heart begin to pound, her face flush with blood. "Is this what that was about?" She gasped. "Oh, my God, Aaron. How long has this been happening?" She covered her face with her hands. And then she thought again of the Ritz.

"You made love to me, Aaron. You came into my bed and

came inside me. It was like it used to be, Aaron. You even said so."

The door to the bedroom swung open and Leslie Rosen walked into the room. "That was all a long time ago, Anne. Come on now. This daydreaming, this living in the past *must* stop." She strolled over to Aaron's side of the room and placed her hand on his shoulder. "You're still playing the victim, Anne."

Annie's mouth opened. Her face burned. Oh, God. They had betrayed her. Aaron. Dr. Rosen. Both of them. And now to have the two of them witness her humiliation was more than she could tolerate. She jumped to her feet, her hands clutched in fists at her sides, her wedding ring cutting into the tender flesh of her ring finger.

"I'm the only one in this room who isn't crazy," she said, spitting the words out in tight little gasps. She was absolutely breathless, so she paused for a moment. They must be able to hear my heart pounding. Aaron sat there, staring at her, Dr. Rosen stood behind him. Silent. United. She looked at them and for a moment the room actually seemed to swim around her. Dr. Rosen's hand remained on Aaron's shoulder, as if she claimed him as her property.

"I didn't understand," Annie muttered. "I didn't know you hated me so much." Tears filled her eyes, but she refused to cry in front of them. She focused on Aaron. "I can only believe that you've gone insane."

She would not cry, but the pain was intolerable. She averted her face. She felt like a small child in the presence of two cruel and sadistic older children. She must get away from these people before they could hurt her more. She breathed deliberately and tried to move.

"I am going," she said quietly. "Don't speak to me. I hate you both. You are demented, both of you. I am going."

As she took her first step, a rush of dizziness nearly felled her again, but she managed to rise, groping for something, a chair, anything, to help her get out of there. Shaking, she turned her back on them and walked to the door. Her feet felt leaden, weighted to the floor. It seemed to take a very long time to cross the room. Finally, with her hand on the knob, she looked over her shoulder.

"Oh. By the way. I might be living in the past. Daydreaming, as you said. But Aaron did fuck me in Boston. The past in this case is less than a week ago," she said. "And he fucked me in all senses of the word." She opened the door, and with as much dignity as she could muster, she left them there.

II

Elise Is Not Amused

Bill had asked Elise to have lunch with him. That was unusual, but of course having any meal with Bill lately was unusual. She spent a lot of time alone in Greenwich, or in East Hampton during the summers. Manhattan made her feel claustrophobic. Let's face it, Elise, New York belongs to all those women who work. Like Linda Robinson, Tina Brown, Alice Mason, and that dreadful Mary Birmingham, who'd taken Gil Griffin from Cynthia. Even that poor flake Mary McFadden managed to work. Yes, New York was for the shining workers. So what if she got the best tables at Mortimer's, Le Cirque, and the other spots for ladies who lunch, she always felt disposable and onstage, window dressing for the people who really mattered.

Again her mind flashed back to Room 705 and her indiscretion last week. Oh, God. Well, I won't think about it. But he had a camera. I distinctly remember a camera, she thought. Then she pushed the whole episode out of her mind. I'll first stop off at Martha's to see what they might have, then lunch with Bill. She felt comfortable at Martha's, the most exclusive shop in the city. There she would pull herself together without having to worry about being watched, without having to endure presumptuous salesgirls.

—

As Elise rode to Manhattan, she became aware of how uncomfortable—physically uncomfortable—she felt in her skin. She avoided the urge to pour a vodka from the console in front of her and fidgeted instead at her hemline, her hair, then her skirt again. I'm dressed like a Greenwich matron going to the city for lunch, she thought. I can't even shop in these clothes. The image frightened her, so she pushed the button of the intercom to her driver and said, "I want to stop at the apartment first." I have to get out of this outfit, she told herself.

Riding up in the elevator, she wished she had thought to have Chessie come back to the city with her. She longed for Chessie's tender, discreet ministrations and her impeccable taste, but here in Manhattan they only had the butler, cook, and cleaning woman. Elise, like Oscar Wilde, was easily satisfied by the best, but it was getting harder and harder to find. How would she get along if Chessie ever left her? Chessie looked after her wardrobe and her hair and her calendar. Well, Chessie would never leave, so don't let's worry about it, she told herself.

Yes, don't let's worry. The worry was poisoning her life, increasing her drinking, telling on her looks. She looked at herself in the elevator mirror and managed a smile. She'd dress and make up even more carefully than usual. She'd stun them when she met Bill for lunch.

Entering the apartment, she went directly to her bedroom, which was large and high ceilinged, with an Austrian crystal chandelier that Elise absolutely never turned on. Overhead lights were decimating. Her rooms were lit by table lamps that all had sixty-watt pink-toned bulbs, and the shades were all lined with pink silk. The walls were also pink, a shade that helped reflect color kindly. Detailed

Adams plaster moldings graced the walls as well, and there were two recessed niches with shell-like arches at the top. Each niche held a priceless porcelain vase that Elise had inherited from her mother's vast collection, now housed in its own wing at the Metropolitan. Otherwise, the room was surprisingly ordinary, furnished in slightly dated (and slightly tatty) upholstered furniture.

Elise quickly shrugged off the suit she was wearing while trying to decide on what to change into. Maybe a Blass, or an Armani. They had been right for a long time. Perhaps too long. She reconsidered. I don't want to look like Nancy Reagan visiting the Big Apple, she thought, smiling. A jazz pianist she knew in her Paris days had once told her New York was called the Big Apple because it held all the temptations of the flesh. She thought of Room 705 again and sighed. No. She'd wear something European. Maybe that lavender leather Claude Montana with the big shoulders and the peplum; it was outrageous, but it suited her long frame, and the color was good with her hair. And it definitely was not Greenwich matron. She'd only worn it once and left it here somewhere. Besides, it had cost the earth, so she'd better wear it again.

Elise had grown up believing in having the best and making it last. She still had her first Chanel suits from the fifties, Halston hats from the sixties. Mackies from the seventies, and Lacroixs from the eighties. Her homes were decorated by McMillan and looked undecorated—and the furniture and fabrics were a bit frayed. They were never redone. She had grown up in an enormous town house in New York, a mansion in Palm Beach, and the even larger "cottage" in East Hampton, and in all there were holes worn in the carpets, and silk lampshades that were shredded. But the carpets were Aubusson and the shades Italian silk. Generations of wealth and social standing had eliminated the need to prove anything to anyone.

Now, stripped down to her lingerie and stockinged feet, she walked across the threadbare carpet to her dressing room and began to search for the Montana. It wasn't there, but it could be in several places. Though the dressing room was as large as the bedrooms in a normal apartment, Elise's clothes overflowed into guestroom closets, hall armoires, and even into Bill's much smaller dressing room. Now she looked in her spare places, but couldn't find the distinctive lavender outfit.

She crossed her bedroom again and opened the door to Bill's bathing and dressing area. She stopped short on the threshold, her eyes widening. The room was empty. There wasn't a single bottle or jar on the counter, not a shirt on the shelves, no shoes in the specially constructed shoe racks made for Bill's size-ten feet. Elise ran to a drawer and opened it. No underwear, no socks, no sweaters. Her breathing seemed to stop, then it started up again in uncomfortable gasps. He was gone. She had known it all the time. He was going to leave her. Oh, God. He had left her already.

She sat down hard, almost collapsing, on the side of the tub. What had he said on the phone? Think, think. She tried hard to remember. He had offered to take her to lunch and insisted he would meet her at the restaurant. He hadn't wanted her to know, that was it. But it couldn't be. It couldn't.

But it couldn't be anything else. Bill had a full wardrobe in all three of their houses and in their London flat. He rarely had to pack more than an overnight bag. Now, everything was gone. He had left her, and she hadn't even realized it.

Without hope, she stood and opened the door to his suit

closet. Perhaps, somehow . . . The door pulled open smoothly, revealing the dark interior, barren but for the lavender leather Claude Montana dress, which swung back and forth gently, gently in the emptiness.

"Drive down Fifth Avenue," Elise told her driver through the open partition. But where to? she thought. What am I going to do? Where can I go? "To Martha," she added, saying the first thing that popped into her head.

Elise let her head fall back on the creamy leather head-rest as her limousine inched its way through midday traf-fic. She was still too shaken to feel the effects of the double vodka she had downed before she left the apartment. Clos-ing her eyes, the emptiness overwhelmed her. She placed the fingertips of her right hand on her throat, the rapid pulse reassuring her that she really was alive. The gentleness of her own touch on her skin caused her to release a long, low, almost primal moan. Feeling the tears at the corners of her eyes about to bubble out, she quickly pressed the button at her fingertips, closing the opaque partition between her and the driver. *Pas devant les domestiques.*

Slowly, as if a mantra, she said the word in a soft whisper: empty. She didn't know if she was referring to the closets or to herself. But the emptiness felt old, very old. And she felt old. Now her worst fear had been realized. She was alone. No matter what she had done to ensure that she would never have to feel that aloneness, no matter how much she had compromised her life to avoid it, she was now alone. All her money, her connections, her looks, her talent— none of it could hold off this onslaught. She reached into her handbag and took out a handkerchief. What am I going to do? she thought again as her tears slowed. What am I going to do?

She pictured Bill's dressing room, mentally going through each closet, each drawer, one more time, to be sure she had not been wrong. No. They were all empty. Everything, gone. There was no misinterpreting that. She shook her head suddenly, almost violently, to shake off the awful image of all those opened closet doors, the open drawers, empty of every trace of the man she had been married to for almost twenty years. She clasped her hands together and squeezed, as if the effort would wring the tension from her body.

As her tears ended, and her silent sobs quieted, she realized that she hadn't even asked herself the classic inevitable question and was immediately heartened by that fact. She hadn't asked herself the question that comes to all abandoned women first—what did I do wrong? Elise blew her nose and savored that fact for a moment, accepting it as a small gift. I am not responsible, she thought. And without a scintilla of doubt, she realized that she had done everything she could to preserve their marriage. It was Bill who had continued to have affairs, to betray her time and again, while he enjoyed all the benefits of her wealth and social position.

Elise sat erect, holding her head up. She dabbed at her eyes once more, then snapped open the console mirror to survey the damage. Mechanically, she reapplied her makeup, then her lipstick, rolling her lips to even out the coat. Bill didn't know that Elise had gone to the apartment, believing that she was coming straight down from Greenwich to keep their lunch date. Was he going to tell me over lunch, in a public restaurant? she thought. That was it, of course. He'd asked her to lunch to tell her he had left her. And he had relied on Elise's breeding and her natural repugnance for public scenes to allow him to say what he had to say and walk away without having to deal with her feelings.

Her head rolled listlessly to the side, and she caught sight of the Guggenheim Museum. The tinted-gray glass of the car window leant an eerie, otherworldly aura to the building, causing Elise to squeeze her eyes shut once again. When she opened them again, she saw the grandeur of the Metropolitan Museum looming on her right, its size overpowering her. Not until she spied the manageable stateliness of the Frick was she able to think again. She remembered the lovely May afternoon she had spent there with Annie, slowly moving from room to room. Afterward, they sat on the stone bench in the garden amongst the exuberant pink azaleas. What was it that Annie had said that day? Men have it so easy.

She realized then that she couldn't face the midday crowd around Martha. Nor the swarm of tourists in Rockefeller Center. "Mosely, I've changed my mind. Go *up* Madison Avenue." Maybe I could go to that lovely out-of-print bookstore in the brownstone on Ninety-third Street, she thought. I could sit by myself in the stacks, figure out what to do next.

Annie was right, of course. Men just pack a bag and walk away. How was it that men didn't see the abandonment of a woman as the act of cowardice it really was? Elise, like most women of her generation, she supposed, had grown up believing that real men were both brave and responsible, despite evidence to the contrary. Bill, she now had to admit, was neither. Nor were any of those empty suits that passed as appropriate partners for the women she knew and admired. Like Annie's Aaron.

Elise picked up the car's phone and punched in Annie's number, praying she would be there, relieved that it was answered on the second ring. "Annie, it's Elise." She cleared her throat. "I need you."

"Elise, what's the matter?"

"Annie, I . . . Bill's left me." Elise heard her voice grow tiny.

But Annie's voice was even, soothing in Elise's ear. "Where are you, Elise? Do you want me to come to you?"

"Thanks, Annie," Elise managed with a laugh she knew sounded ghastly. "Actually, I'm in my car about ten minutes away. Could I come to you? Could you meet me downstairs, out front?"

"I'll be waiting," Annie said, and hung up.

Good, thought Elise. Now she had someplace to go. She would pick up Annie. She took the first deep breath she had taken in an hour. "Mosely, take me to Gracie Square."

While the attendant held the door, Annie climbed into the car, taking the seat facing Elise instead of beside her.

"Where should we go?" Annie asked.

"I don't know. I've just been driving around."

"Mosely," Annie said, pushing a button and speaking into the intercom. "We're going to Sutton Place." To Elise, she added, "We can get out and walk in that little park. It's always empty."

As the car turned downtown on York Avenue, Elise popped open the door to the bar and reached for the bottle of Stoli. "Care for something, Annie?" Elise dropped two cubes into a cut-crystal glass and poured a large double. She stirred it briskly with her index finger, then swallowed hard.

"I'll just have a club soda. I'll get it myself." After Annie poured the carbonated drink, she looked at Elise and said, "Now tell me, what happened?"

Elise turned to look out the car window, holding her own drink in one hand, and the gnarled handkerchief in the other, then turned back to Annie. "Bill's left me. He's packed his bags and he's gone."

Annie paused for a minute. "Well, it's about time. So what are you crying about?"

"What? Don't you understand? Annie, I'm all alone. We're not married anymore," Elise said. "I'm all alone," she repeated, saying each word slowly.

"You've been married in name only for a long time, Elise. And it's killing you. You've also been alone for a long time, so what's different? What are you afraid of?"

Elise paused, trying to absorb Annie's calm reasoning. She gulped from her drink again. Too much drinking, too much fear, too much loneliness. "Annie," she stammered, searching for the words. "I'm afraid I'm going to end up like Cynthia."

Annie picked up her handbag from beside her on the floor, snapped it open, and took out an envelope. Handing it to Elise, she said, "Read this."

Elise placed her drink in the indentation on the armrest and took the note from Annie. "What is it?" she asked.

"It's Cynthia's suicide note. I've wanted to show it to you, and now I think is the perfect time."

Elise dropped the envelope back into Annie's lap as if the note had suddenly caught fire. "Annie, don't be macabre."

Annie returned the envelope to Elise. "Read it," she said, "if you don't want to end up like Cynthia."

Elise tapped the envelope, reluctantly opened it. Cynthia's message crawled out of the grave and turned her skin to gooseflesh.

Annie waited until Elise had finished, folded, and silently returned it. "So, Elise, no regrets. You got out just in time. I want you to go home and write in lipstick on your bathroom mirror. 'He was not good enough for me.'"

Elise felt a tentative smile at the corners of her mouth.

"He wasn't, you know. And Aaron isn't good enough for you."

"So it would appear. He's only good enough for my therapist." Dryly, Annie briefed Elise about the scene at the Carlyle.

"Oh, Annie."

Annie smiled back. "So what are your plans for the rest of the day?"

Elise shrugged. "I'm to visit Mother later this afternoon. And I was supposed to meet Bill for lunch, but . . ."

Annie sat up straight. "He doesn't know yet that you found out he's left?"

"No, I came down from Greenwich to have lunch with him and only stopped by the apartment on a whim. He was probably going to tell me at lunch . . . in a public place, of course, so I wouldn't make a scene."

"Make a scene, Elise," Annie urged.

"Annie, I couldn't even sit at the same table with him now. I'm too . . ." She faltered, searching for the word.

"Too what?"

"Too angry. I'm afraid if I set eyes on him, I'd wipe the floor with him."

"Do it, Elise, but not in a restaurant where he can get away. Go to his office. Corner him."

"Like a rat?" Elise asked. "Right. Like the rat he is." she answered herself. Elise snickered at the thought of humiliating Bill at his office. "Annie, he'd drop dead on the spot if I confronted him there. I'd love to, but I couldn't."

"I'll go with you and wait in the car," Annie offered.

Sitting back in the deep upholstery of the limousine, Elise paused, considered, and then gave her driver Bill's office address. She turned to Annie. "I'm nervous," Elise admitted.

"I'll be waiting for you. I'll be here. And afterwards, you'll be glad."

Elise looked at her friend and tried to shrug gracefully. "What the hell," she said. "I've got nothing to lose."

You prick, she thought, and laughed a throaty laugh. Surprise, Bill. You're in for a *big* surprise. I'm not rolling over on this, she thought. Oh, no. No matter what Mother would have said, I am not going to slither away quietly like a beaten animal. Annie did, and Aaron rubbed her nose in his betrayal like a cruel master rubs the nose of his dog in its excrement. Annie's right. I won't let him slither away.

And Brenda, for all her glib, earthy language, and blustery talk, let Morty walk away from her, leaving her practically broke and completely alone, while he ended up sitting on millions of dollars. He, like Bill, had used his wife's weakness to his own benefit. Except, surprise, Bill. I'm not as predictable as you assumed.

She pictured Bill in his office, preparing to take compliant suburban Elise to lunch, secure in the belief that he had gotten away free and clear. She imagined him there, in the office she had decorated discreetly in muted tones of blue, with *William Taft Atchison—Partner* etched on the door in gilt. Thanks to *her*, he had been named a partner, albeit a lesser one, in the distinguished law firm of Cromwell Reed. Today, she could see him hiding behind the paneled door, surrounded by the little, comforting totems of his hobbies and power, those clichés of WASP old family he held on to so dearly. But the hand-carved duck decoys, the leather golf bag, the polo mallets, wouldn't help him today. Nor would his enormous mahogany desk, his array of crystal paperweights, or his collection of antique Japanese china; no, not even the sterling silver picture frame with her picture she had given him that sat at the corner of his desk.

As the car pulled up to the front entrance of the imposing skyscraper on Wall Street, Elise had the door open before her driver got out. Annie leaned out the window as Elise turned to face her. "He wasn't good enough for you, Elise. And Gil wasn't good enough for Cynthia. So go in there and let him have it. For all of us."

"This one's my pleasure. Don't go 'way, it's not going to take very long." Then Elise walked resolutely through the revolving doors, hearing them swoosh behind her from the force of her push. Once in the elevator, she jabbed the button for the forty-fifth floor.

Elise saw Bill jump as she threw open the door to his office, crashing it into the cherrywood paneling. She stood in the doorway, taller than he, while she watched his face turn white, bloodless. "You dickless excuse for a man. Of all the contemptible things you have done to me, this is the lowest."

She took two hard strides toward his desk, arms akimbo. Bill's secretary was hovering near the door, not knowing what to do. Elise gestured to her without turning around, so she stepped back over the threshold, but continued to watch.

Elise blew a wisp of her usually perfectly coiffed hair off her face and said, "Not man enough to face me to tell me you were leaving? I had to see your empty closets to find out? Where's the note, Bill? Even Nelson Rockefeller left a note, you worm."

She saw the moisture break out on Bill's upper lip. He struggled with a cottony mouth, then finally managed to speak, his voice strained, high-pitched. "Calm down, Elise. Let's not have a scene. I was going to talk with you over lunch."

The lock on the door must have broken, because the secretary couldn't get it to stay closed. Elise could see out of the corner of her eye the knot of secretaries gathering in the hall. Bill noticed them, too. "Let's just talk about this like mature adults," he pleaded.

"Mature," she yelled, "You want to be mature?" He gestured to the door. Ignoring his signal, she continued, "Almost twenty years, Bill. Two decades of lies and infidelities and

—

humiliation. I loved you. I gave you a home, I gave you my body, I gave up my career for you. All I wanted was to be normal, and maybe to be loved. We could have had so much more, too. I never asked for your gratitude, I never threw my money in your face, not even when it bought you this partnership. I was a good wife to you. I deserve better."

Bill edged around the desk, but Elise followed. "Just tell me this, Bill, and then I'll go. I just need to know. Why now? Why now, after years of your affairs and one-night stands and mistresses and women calling our home in the middle of the night. After all the secretaries and maids and waitresses. Why now?" She noticed him try to head her off, but she continued around the desk, and he backed away. Then her eye fell to the silver picture frame. She paused. Her picture had been removed, and in its place, the smiling face of another woman—a much younger woman—someone vaguely familiar.

"This time I'm in love," he said.

Elise stared at him for a moment. She strode around his desk to the credenza. She picked up a hand-carved duck decoy, turned, and smashed it into the picture of her replacement. Bill jumped at her sudden move, at the shattering noise. She saw his face go ashen, his mouth drop open.

At that, Don Reed, the firm's senior partner, stepped through the doorway with a placating smile on his face. Before he could get a word out, Elise turned to him and in a voice as deep as Mercedes McCambridge's in *The Exorcist*, growled, "Get out!" He immediately did just that.

Bill leaned forward to touch his fingertips to the desk, as if to balance himself, to keep from falling. "Elise, please, this is neither the time nor the place. Let's talk about this later, at home."

She detested the imploring tone in his voice. "Home?

Whose home, Bill? You moved out. We don't have a home together, remember?" She whipped a golf club from the bag leaning against the wall and, with a swing worthy of Babe Didrikson, shattered the Lalique shade on the desk lamp.

Bill just stared.

Another swing shattered the glass case of his beloved Imari. "You used me and discarded me." Tossing the golf club to the floor, she walked to the door, crunching over the broken glass, and pushed her way through the mob of partners and secretaries that were now blocking it.

"You're not going to get away with this, Bill. I can't let you. Not this time."

As she sauntered to the elevator, Elise heard Don Reed, the head of the executive committee of the firm, say, "Bill, we'd like to have a word with you in my office."

Elise tapped gently on the door of her mother's bedroom, then opened it softly. Her mother's nurse stood up from the bedside chair and turned and smiled.

"Hello, Mrs. Atchison. We were just talking about you." The nurse came closer to Elise and said in a low voice, "I'm afraid she couldn't remember you were coming. I had to remind her." Patting Elise's arm she added, "She's been in and out all day, poor thing." Then she stepped out through the door and said, "Call me if you need me. I'll be right next door."

Elise walked over to her mother and placed her hand on the satin comforter, avoiding the plastic drip that snaked down into her mother's painfully thin arm. Elise never knew, week to week, if she would find her mother fully aware or floating in a world of dreams and the past.

Elise saw her mother's eyes open when she stroked her cheek. "Mother, it's Elise."

"Well, of course it is. It's Monday, isn't it?"

Elise released the breath she realized she was holding and sat down. "That's right," she said with a smile. "It's Monday, so it must be Elise." Elise leaned forward, kissed her on her forehead, and said, "So, how are you, Mother?"

"Old and tired. And how are you, my dear?" she asked, searching Elise's face. Old and tired, too, Elise thought. And so alone. I hope I don't look too awful. I hope she can't see the loneliness in my eyes.

"Just fine, Mother. And I've brought you something." The last time Elise was here, her mother had become agitated when Elise identified herself. Her mother had cried, "No, my Elise is just a little girl." Elise reached into her bag and brought out a flat package wrapped in brown paper. She undid the string and took out a silver-framed photograph. She hoped that a current picture of herself would help her mother remember; it was too painful to have her mother not recognize her. "Can you see it without your glasses?"

"Of course." Her mother squinted as she tried to discern the figure in the picture, Elise sitting on the lawn of her house in East Hampton. "It's you. How lovely."

"Yes, it was taken out at the beach last summer. I think I look rather good, don't you, Mother?"

"Is that for a movie?"

Elise looked up suddenly. "Movie?" she asked.

"You're still going out to Hollywood, Elise? What a dreadful place. You must be very careful."

"I haven't been to Hollywood for years. That was when I was very young, remember? I live here now. In New York. I'm not going anywhere."

Elise's mother closed her eyes and shook her head slowly from side to side. "They'll be after your money, Elise. They'll want you to put your money in your pictures. You mustn't do that, darling. That would be too humiliating."

Elise felt a chill run down her back. She knew it wouldn't do any good, that these lapses in her mother's memory came and went with a will of their own, but Elise had to try. "Mother, darling, I went to Hollywood a long time ago, and I'm back now. I'm here to stay. I'm older now, Mother."

"Men live off beautiful women in Hollywood," her mother continued, not hearing Elise. "A rich, beautiful woman wouldn't have a chance. They'll use you, my dear, and tell you they love you. But it's the money. Always the money."

Elise caught her breath, stifling a sudden sob. She swallowed, then said, "I'm careful, Mother, but sometimes I feel I'm too careful. I have to take a chance."

"You'll never get over it, Elise. They'll humiliate you, take your money, then cast you aside. Look what they did to your cousin Barbara. The poor darling, living over there in Africa, strange men swarming all around her. They feed her drugs, and take her money." Her mother's voice became louder, and she opened her eyes and stared intently at Elise. "Don't let them drag you down, my dear. Keep your dignity. That's all you'll ever have, after all, your honor. Always do the proper thing."

Elise felt her throat tighten and hoped that her mother didn't notice. She would be very disappointed in me now, Elise thought, if she knew. And as much as Elise ached for her mother's kindness and understanding, she could never let her mother know of Bill's betrayal and of her terrible indiscretion at the Carlyle. And how living honorably was no insurance against loneliness.

She looked over at her mother, who was now beginning to nod off, her tissue-thin eyelids fluttering closed. Very softly, Elise said, "Mother, it's late and you should get some rest."

Elise placed her framed picture on her mother's night table, next to the array of pills and potions that took up most of the surface. "I'll see you next week, darling. Is there anything I can do for you before I leave?"

Her mother didn't open her eyes but muttered, "Tell Grandpere I want to ride my pony."

Elise rose and kissed her on the cheek, tears now filling her eyes, feeling more alone at that moment than she had ever felt in her life. . . . "Yes, I will. I'll tell him."

12

The First Wives Club

Annie had been surprised when Elise telephoned to ask her to lunch at Le Cirque. Why lunch? And why Le Cirque? Though Elise had more money than any woman Annie knew, she also knew that Elise wasn't eager to spend it. Le Cirque charged six dollars for a half a *pamplemousse*, making it surely the only twelve-dollar grapefruit in Manhattan. Maybe they did it just for effect, since no one was going to order *that* as an appetizer when there were all those marvelous other starters.

If Annie was surprised by the invitation, she was truly shocked when Brenda called to tell her *she* was invited, too. Annie had been sitting at her desk, trying to put a few of her thoughts on paper. She wasn't even sure if she was trying to write a story or a poem or just keep a journal. In fact almost nothing had transferred from her mind to the paper. She had committed herself to sitting down every day for one hour, even though she simply stared at a blank page for most of that time. But thank God, at least she was trying. The problem was, the minute she sat down a fierce tide of depression had swept over her, leaving her blank, empty. When the phone rang, breaking the numbing silence, she jumped, then sighed with relief.

"What gives, Annie? Elise has invited me to lunch at Le Cirque. Has she decided to slum?"

"I don't have a clue," Annie replied.

"I wonder if it has anything to do with Bill. Did I tell you that Angela told me that he's had three secretaries in the last year? He absolutely harasses them. She says that one girl, a summer intern, swore he wagged his weenie at her."

"Come on, Brenda. Is that what the new summer interns at Cromwell Reed talk about? Bill may be a compulsive, but he's an attractive man. I can't imagine he's been reduced to exposing himself to get laid."

"You never know what turns 'em on. As far as I'm concerned, all men are dogs."

Annie felt the emptiness in her chest, the silence that her life was now.

Brenda must have heard it because she asked, "How's it going, without Sylvie home? How are you filling the time?"

"I'm fine. I was thinking of starting a novel."

"Great! I started one back in college."

"Really?"

"Sure. It was *War and Peace*, but I got bored reading it."

Annie laughed. Brenda always got her to fall for it.

"So, about lunch," Brenda prompted. "Why would she invite *me*?"

"Who knows? I guess we'll soon find out."

"Angela also told me that Elise showed up at Cromwell Reed the other day, that there was a huge scene."

Annie tried to picture the scene again as Elise had described it to her in the car ride home. She couldn't help but smile. "And?" she simply asked.

"In Bill's office at Cromwell Reed. And in the hall. In a purple leather dress, no less. Angela says that the marriage is *finito*."

"Well, that's a relief," Annie told her. And a relief that Brenda had found out from someone else.

"God, she ate dirt for so many years. What could have made her break now?" Brenda wondered.

Annie felt the anger move into the empty space in her chest. She sighed, trying to expel it. It was outrageous, the way these men behaved. It was beyond bearing.

"Who knows? Maybe it was Cynthia's death," Brenda postulated. "Maybe it was Bill's latest. Apparently he took the little babe to the firm's Partner Dinner the other night. And she's a Van Gelder, Phoebe Van Gelder, so maybe Bill figures to turn one heiress in for a newer model. Except this newer model is running on cocaine."

"Brenda, how do you know all this?" Annie asked, partly irritated, partly amused.

"Today's *Post*," Brenda admitted. "There was a blind item in Suzy. You know: 'What beautiful conceptual artist from one of the gilt-edged families played wife at the Cromwell Reed sock hop? And they played footsie, too.' I figured it out all by myself. And Duarto gave me the tip about the nose candy."

"Poor Elise."

"So, Annie, on a more important note, what are you going to wear? I'm even too big for my fat pants."

"Oh, come on, Brenda. What kind of a question is that?"

"A Jewish one. It's one of the Four Questions from Passover: What are you going to wear? Where did you get it? How much was it? And do they have it in my size?"

"Very funny."

"So, should I buy something?"

"You know what Emerson said."

"I seem to have momentarily forgotten."

"'Beware of all enterprises that require new clothes.'"

"Yeah, and never date a guy named Spike. What the fuck

does a guy named Ralph Waldo know about fat pants, or anything? Do you know that the whole time he lived at Walden Pond he ate lunch each day at his mother's? *And* he brought his laundry home? Honest."

"Brenda, it was *Thoreau* at Walden Pond, not Emerson," Annie said, but she was laughing. It felt good to laugh, and she knew Brenda liked to hear it.

"Come on, Brenda," she remonstrated. "Cold as you like to think she is, Elise is actually a very good person, and I'm sure she's in pain. Maybe she just needs some friends. So get serious."

"I am serious. I was thinking of going real bizarre. I call it my 'Elizabeth Taylor attends a Hawaiian bar mitzvah' look. Wouldn't Elise just *plotz*? Why is it that being around her makes me want to speak Yiddish and wear caftans? But I can't even fit into my fat pants. I'm hitting my weight ceiling. You know what that means, don't you?"

"I'm not sure."

"Of course not, you anorectic. For those of you out there in the studio audience, I will explain: When you grow out of your fat pants, you either have to lose weight or buy a new wardrobe that's even bigger. Expensive and demoralizing, to say the least, so I eat. But if I keep trying to fit in things I don't fit in, I'm also demoralized, and then I eat. Of course, if I buy new fat clothes, I'm rewarding myself for bad behavior, reinforcing it, and then I eat. I've never been over a size eighteen before. So, the question is, do I establish a new weight ceiling? Should I buy something even bigger for Le Cirque or look like shit?"

"Brenda, you're giving me a headache. Would you please let up on yourself?"

"Yeah, yeah. Next you'll be telling me that there's a thin person inside me longing to get out. I wish to God she would—then I'd only weigh half."

They agreed, at last, that Brenda wouldn't buy anything and that they'd both wear conservative clothes, which was just as well, since Annie didn't have any other kind.

As Annie walked over to Le Cirque on Park Avenue, she accidentally walked along East Seventy-sixth Street. Ever since her Carlyle encounter she had hated that street and had taken to going out of her way to avoid it. She'd been out that morning since eight and hadn't even been home to change. It was her morning for work at the hospital, always exhausting, and yet she hated to leave the patients there. So she stayed late. Elise and Brenda would forgive her. But because she was late, she'd been hurrying without thinking. And now, by accident, she had walked onto the block where Aaron's hotel was located. She shivered.

It was a clear day in New York, complete with blue, blue sky, and though it was still cool, that undefinable something had changed in the air. It smelled of autumn, hinted at winter. At Le Cirque, Annie was greeted at the door by Sirio, the social genius behind the place. He knew the standing of every wealthy woman who lunched in the city and seated them accordingly. Now, he smiled cordially and led her to Elise, who was already seated in one of the banquette tables, those in the narrow entrance foyer that, surprisingly, were considered the most desirable. Elise obviously still pulled weight. Annie had never liked the room, thought the crystal and ice blue decor too formal for lunch, but she had to admit, it suited Elise, who sat, beautiful and perfectly groomed, poised and relaxed, posed as though onstage. And it was a stage. Across from them, Brooke Astor sat with two women whom Annie didn't know, and the new "young set"—Blaine Trump busily talking to another lovely looking woman—were ensconced nearby. Elise waved when she saw Annie and air-kissed her cheek as she was seated next to her. Elise picked up her glass and smiled. "A martini? Or would you prefer some carbonated French benzine?" Her voice sounded strange, almost mechanical.

"White wine," Annie told the waiter. "Elise, are you all right?"

"As well as can be expected. I think hospitals call it 'serious but stable.'" She lifted her glass. "I'm taking medication."

Some commotion at the door heralded Brenda's entrance. She was wearing something very big and very red, with a neckline bordered with feathers of some type. I'm glad I convinced her to go conservative, Annie thought wryly.

"I hope that's an endangered species, because it deserves to die," Elise murmured. Annie herself hated fur and feathers, but was only somewhat relieved to see these were synthetic. What the hell *was* Brenda wearing? Annie glanced covertly at Elise, but she seemed unruffled. Elise would never publicly acknowledge any imperfection in one of her guests.

"Brenda, hello." Elise smiled broadly and made sure that everyone heard her greet her guest. Only generations of savoir faire and self-assurance could produce that kind of confidence, Annie thought. She often had to will herself not to be embarrassed by Brenda.

"Well, the gang's all here," Brenda said, smiling brightly. "What the fuck is up?"

Elise didn't even wince. "The jig. The jig is up," she answered, and Annie noticed again how harsh her voice sounded.

Annie and Brenda looked at Elise, waiting for her to continue. "It seems to me that something is very wrong with the balance of things, and that needs to be corrected." Elise looked from one to the other. "I propose we do something about it."

"What are you talking about?" Annie asked.

"As you know, Bill has left me, and you also know what they say about a woman scorned." Elise's smile was as brittle as her voice.

"Elise, I'm so sorry."

"Brenda, I don't want any damned sympathy now. I picked a very public place to do this, so there will be no crying. If I want a husband later, I'll buy another one. Meanwhile, right now I simply crave a little justice."

"Way to go, Elise," Brenda breathed. "Let's get that little Van Gelder bitch."

Elise gave Brenda a look that would have withered anyone else. "I asked you here because I thought you weren't stupid," she said deliberately. "I think you've missed the point. It isn't the women, the new trophies, I care about. It's the men—Gil Griffin, and Morty and Aaron and Bill. Certainly Bill. There ought to be some kind of retribution, some way to even the score. We have to show society that we can't simply be discarded. We have to *do* something. We have the resources, the brains, the connections, *and* the imaginations. Let's make sure they pay a price."

Annie thought again of Cynthia's letter, still in her purse. She hadn't been able to put it away, just as she couldn't seem to get it out of her mind. Maybe, if she did do something to even the score with Gil, maybe then she could put it away.

"I'm in," said Brenda, picking up her menu. "But can we order lunch first?"

They did, and as soon as the waiter left, Brenda asked, "Are we talking about revenge, I mean *Death Wish III* here, or what?"

"Not exactly revenge. Something more sophisticated, I thought. Like justice," Elise said.

"Gee, I personally always liked Hammurabi's code. 'An eye for an eye' has a nice ring to it. So how about a little ritual cas-

tration? We get them, tie them up, wear war paint and masks;
I've always looked good in feathers." Brenda preened. "And
one by one we ruin 'em. It's like fixing dogs—it'll keep them
out of trouble in the future. It's actually a humane solution.
An end to testosterone poisoning."

"Castration. Hmmm." Elise paused as if really considering
it. "Tempting, but messy," she decided. "No, just too messy."

"There you go, always criticizing. So, what's *your* big idea,
Elise?"

Listening to her friends' remarks, Annie's mind began to
race. Revenge? Justice? They couldn't mean it, she thought.
We need to stick together, sure, but what Elise was proposing
was violent, drastic. No, she thought, this wasn't what she
wanted.

Suddenly a vision began to form in Annie's head. Maybe
they could form a club, an action committee of first wives who
could come to terms with themselves and their anger. Who
could support one another. And who would finally do something about Gil. We wouldn't be so alone, Annie thought. All
three of us have plenty to be angry about.

She studied Elise and Brenda. Two such different friends,
but both of them, at the core, so similar. Both honest. Both
reliable. Both with real values. Too bad they didn't like each
other. Annie smiled to herself. Who but she would believe
that Brenda, a fat girl raised in the Bronx, product of an Italian father and Jewish mother, and Elise, the stunning heiress
to two vast fortunes, had anything in common.

But Annie felt they did. They were both in such pain, dis-
guising their anger with self-destructiveness—Brenda's eating, Elise's drinking. But if they couldn't face their own pain
and their rage, maybe they could find a release for it through
Cynthia. The three of them could unite in their compassion
for Cynthia and in their rage at Gil. Maybe they'd take some

action on Cynthia's behalf, such as confront Gil. Just to let him know that they knew what he had done to her.

And then, maybe, just maybe, they could confront their own situations. Brenda's eating her rage at Morty, Annie thought. And she's now driving both her children away with her constant phone calls and interference. Then there's Elise, who looks sadder and more frozen, month by month. Elise has got to see what effect Bill's abandoning her is having on her, on her drinking.

And what about me? Annie thought. What about my anger at Aaron? But a little voice inside her said, "He's not as bad as the others." Still, she needed a group's support. Because to live with such pain over him was suicidal.

Well, perhaps some good could come out of Cynthia's suicide. Annie knew she tried too hard to turn bad into good, to see the bright side, but maybe this time it really would work. This idea was too good not to try. They could form themselves into a kind of support group, like the one she had joined for mothers of Down's syndrome children.

Elise leaned forward and smiled at the other two. "Well, maybe we can castrate them without shedding one drop of blood." She raised her brows devilishly as Annie and Brenda leaned forward, their attention focused on her. "Let's find each man's soft spot. They're certainly not invulnerable. And then let's go for it. Make the punishment fit the crime. Bill, for example. He *must* have an issue about his masculinity. That, or he hates his mother."

Brenda said, "You don't have to be Freud to figure that out."

"Well, let's help him strike out. Get blown off by a woman or two. Maybe hire some girls to jilt him. Something like that," Elise said.

Brenda loved the idea, Annie could see, but she was having trouble with it. God, this was worse than Annie could have imagined. Her vision of warmth and friendship, a loving support group, dissolved into thin air. "I don't think so, Elise," she began to demur.

Elise started again. "Listen to what I'm trying to say. A generation or two ago the deal was different. A couple married. Okay, maybe the husband was the bread earner, and maybe he made most of the rules. But the rules that society made said that if he was a decent man, if he wanted the approval of society, he stayed married. It gave a woman a certain position that she could count on. And if the man broke that rule, his own career was over. Society called him a cad. And anyone who married him after he broke the rule was excluded and punished, too. So you couldn't use up a decent woman like a tube of toothpaste and discard her when she was empty, the way Gil discarded Cynthia and Bill discarded me."

"Or the way Morty discarded me," Brenda agreed. "Not that I wanted the *putz*."

"Listen to this," Elise continued. She reached into her purse and pulled out a photocopy of a magazine article.

"Oh, God, not a self-help clipping! Have mercy," Brenda pleaded.

"This isn't a self-helper. It's from last month's issue of *Fortune* for God's sake." Elise held up the issue and showed them the picture of Carolyne Roehm. "It's happening all over, successful men trading in their wives for newer, better models. Listen to this: *'These trophy wives make the fifty- and sixty-year-old CEOs feel they can compete sexually with younger men, the kind of ego boost that doesn't hurt when going up against Young Turks at the office.'*" She looked at Brenda and Annie. "Sound appropriate?" She continued, "*'Free from the stigma of divorce, these men are looking to be remade.'* And listen to this; I got it from *Forbes*." She cleared her throat. "*'The new CEO is not complete without the newer, taller, blonder second wife. She is the trophy of his success. Rather than having a stigma attached to a second marriage, corporate culture has advanced to the point where a glamorous second wife is more than an asset. She is almost a necessity.'* " Elise paused and looked over the top of her glasses at the other two women. She waited.

"Was this written before or after Malcolm discarded Libby?" Brenda asked dryly. Elise's mother was close friends with the first Mrs. Forbes. "Oh, come on," Brenda added. "This is not news. The deck was always stacked against women. Nothing has changed."

"That isn't the point!" exclaimed Elise, impassioned. "Look how far it's gone when a *business* magazine recognizes the trend and states it as the norm. This isn't *Spy* that I'm quoting here. For Christ's sake, *Doonesbury* is doing cartoons about it." She angrily threw another clipping on the table.

"So what do you want us to do? Wear vigilante outfits and start patrolling the streets? Go out and kill Georgette Mosbacher and Carolyne Roehm? It would be a pleasure, but I'm not sure it's worth a lifetime of rooming with Jean Harris." Brenda smiled. "Of course, I could be wrong about that."

Annie knew Elise, who had gone to Madeira, didn't like the scandal of the headmistress and the Scarsdale diet doctor to be mentioned. Brenda smiled at Annie. Did she know that, too?

"Do you think Jean Harris could help me lose weight?" Brenda inquired innocently. "Maybe it *would* be worth it."

Annie watched Elise lose her patience. The three of them were falling apart, losing their focus. Elise was right, but the approach, perhaps, needed some alteration. "Stop this. Cynthia is dead. Don't you see how serious this is?" Annie bit her lips to keep them from trembling. "What does it take for you to say 'enough'? Don't you see? This isn't just about Cynthia! It's about all of us. Don't you see it?" she cried. "We're leaking.

They've punctured us, and we're leaking and dwindling down to nothing. Society says that's just fine and we aren't even standing up for ourselves."

Annie couldn't help it. "I have less reason than either of you for getting angry. Aaron wasn't as bad as Morty or Bill."

"Yeah, that's what *you* think," Brenda said.

"No, that's what *he* thinks," added Elise.

Elise paused. "I'd like to put a motion on the floor. I think that it's time for what goes around to come around. Let's talk about the total destruction of these men. Emotional, financial, social. We make sure their marriages fail, their businesses go sour, their friends desert them. They did it to us. We can do it to them. We've got the leverage. That's the plan. I say we wipe these dickweeds out."

"I like it," said Brenda. "But perhaps it's not quite strong enough." She turned to Annie. "What do you think?"

"I'm not sure," Annie said, her tone puzzled, ambivalent. "You're kidding, right? You're either crazy, or joking." Annie looked at Elise, but Elise didn't smile. "Elise, Brenda. Do I understand this correctly? Vengeance? You're proposing that we're in this together, out to get our respective exes?"

"Yes," Elise said, adjusting herself to sit even taller in her chair. "Who was it I heard say, 'Only the weak seek revenge. The strong seek justice'? I propose to convene the charter meeting of the First Wives Club." Elise picked up her coffee spoon and, using it like a gavel, tapped the table. She looked at Annie. "Are you in?"

Annie sat very quietly.

"Come on, Annie. Don't be a pussy," Brenda urged.

"I'm in," Annie said grimly, nodding her head.

"The motion on the floor is that the charter meeting of 'The First Wives Club' has been convened. This motion has been seconded and thirded, and passed," Elise said.

"Yippee!" exclaimed Brenda. The three women lifted their glasses and in mock solemnity, clinked them together in a toast.

"Now," continued Elise in her new role as madame chairwoman, "someone has to place a motion on the floor outlining the goals of the club. Brenda?"

"I make a motion that we wipe the floor with the jerks." With a knowing look at Annie, she added, "*All* of them. I want to see Morty broke, dead broke. That would be the one thing in this life he couldn't bear."

Madame chairwoman turned to Annie, "Annie?"

"I want Gil powerless. No power. No status."

Elise quickly spoke up, "And Bill put to pasture. *Finito* as a lover boy. Symbolically, of course."

Annie struggled with her next thought—the struggle of a good girl. Then Annie sighed with acceptance and said, "And I want to see Aaron abandoned; betrayed and abandoned."

Elise smiled, her pleasure deep and real. "Good girl," she said. "And tomorrow night, we get to see all our targets together in one room at the AIDS benefit. Like ducks in a row. It will be the beginning of their ends."

"Or, to put it another way, the end of their new beginnings," Brenda said.

They clinked their glasses in another binding toast. "To us," Elise said. "To the First Wives."

"Here, here," Annie said, and smiled. "Can our motto be 'We don't get mad, we just get even'?"

"Oh, please," begged Brenda, "can't we do both?"

13

Balling the Jack

"Tout New York, *tout* New York, dear," cooed Gunilla Goldberg as she stood in the entrance to the Pierre's ballroom, looking over the crowd and allowing them a good look at her. Gunilla was, as the French would say, "of a certain age," but in her case, there was no way of determining what that "certain age" was, thanks to surgery, cosmetics, diet, and exercise. Her champagne blond hair was combed in the society pageboy, held in the back by a bow-shaped diamond clip that had become her trademark. As usual, she wore a flamboyant dress, tonight's a Lacroix of silk chartreuse moiré, with a full ruffled black velvet skirt that ended at knee length. Her brown eyes were enhanced by dyed eyelashes, and the carefully waxed arch of her eyebrows gave the impression that Gunilla was always surprised.

Her husband, Sol Goldberg, the financier, had already entered the glittering room, but Gunilla waited a moment for her new young friend Khymer Mallison to look about while Gunilla drank in the scene. The Pierre ballroom had three large crystal chandeliers suspended down the center, their Austrian crystal lit like frozen waterfalls. Flowers, white spray roses and delphiniums, were centered on each table, bursting upward like great floral fountains. Wall sconces cast just the right over-the-shoulder light illuminating the perfect tans, perfect makeup, perfect jewels, of the assembled. Glasses tinkled, waiters undulated through the crowd. The dance floor was just beginning to fill up. It was, Gunilla knew, perfect timing for an entrance.

It was the fourth annual benefit party for AIDS relief, and anyone who mattered in New York was there. The women's society mafia had succeeded in selling out all the tables. AIDS relief was becoming too fashionable to miss, Gunilla thought. Always on the cutting edge, she had seen it coming.

The three endless weeks in Vevey had been worth it, she decided. She was glowing, and her strapless Lacroix showed off her perfect creamy skin, her new freshness. She turned to Khymer, her decades-younger protégé, and smiled, her perfect, even teeth glinting. "Now I'll show you how it's done," she purred, and sashayed across the ballroom floor, nodding and smiling to everyone that mattered.

"Look what *le chat* dragged in," Melanie Kemp, society interior decorator, murmured, sotto voce, to her friend and business partner, Susan. Many such women who had been born into New York society continued to mock Gunilla's affected French, her overdone apartment, and her over-the-top couture. Behind her back they even called her Gummy Bear because of the story, surely apocryphal, that she met her first husband when she was still a call girl, and when she took out her dentures and serviced him, he fell in love. Since then she'd remarried twice, always to shorter, richer men. Now she was important on the charity board social circuit, where "scene and be seen" was a way of life. No one now dared call her Gummy Bear to her face. She had worked hard, become almost a fixture in New York society. If there were rumors that her husband Sol had a new interest, well, society would wait and see if he did anything to cement his ties to the new young thing.

"Yes, she *has* arrived," admitted Susan, a rather horsey-looking but chic society blond. "And she's with that Khymer Mallison."

"Don't you mean 'Climber' Mallison?" Melanie asked cattily. Melanie and Susan had their hair blonded at the same salon that Gunilla patronized. Khymer now went there, too. In fact, Khymer followed every one of Gunilla's suggestions, from her hairstyle to working out with Bernie and Roy. The girl was everywhere. "Climber." That's what they called her on Page Six last week. Everyone in New York read the gossip columns, but only the very socially secure admitted it. And both Susan and Melanie were that: they had family money, society husbands, and fun careers. It was *too* wonderful to be paid to spend other people's money.

"Oh, you're just bitter because Duarto got her job," chided Susan's husband, Charles. It was true that the girls had tried to get the contract to decorate the Mallisons' new town house, but had been scooped. "I think Khymer's very nice, very energetic."

"Oh, *please*," said Susan, rolling her eyes. "So has Gunilla finished her work on Shelby Cushman and gone on to Khymer?" Gunilla was famous for adopting social wannabes as they appeared on the scene and helping with their launch. The uncharitable said it expanded her power base, since the new money who made it—that is, found acceptance in the New York social scene—owed her favors. Everyone knew her most recent "adoptee" was Shelby Cushman, the wife of Morty Cushman, the Morty the Madman retailer on TV. In fact, as Susan watched, Gunilla waved Khymer off to social Siberia, a table under the Pierre's balcony, while she herself climbed to the dais and sat beside Shelby Cushman, the very picture of Southern gentility, who was ensconced there with her heavyset husband.

"Gunilla looks good," Melanie admitted.

"She ought to. A thousand monkeys gave up their glands for her."

"Is that where she's been? I thought she was at a Zen retreat."

"Yes, and the Easter Bunny is coming to your house next week. Grow up, Melanie. Wake up and smell the Shalimar." Susan turned and looked across the dance floor to another table. "Speaking of Zen, here comes the avatar himself. Now *he's* what I call 'young and energetic,' Charles," she cooed to her husband.

Kevin Lear was handsome, tall, and well built, famous as both an actor and a Zen Buddhist. In a town like New York, where everyone was blasé about the movies, he had the superstar gleam that was strong enough to turn heads. He crossed the floor to the head table, propelling before him his fiancée, a model twenty-one years his junior. His hand was lodged below the small of her beautiful back, exposed by her puce bias-cut gown all the way down to well below the start of the vertical crease of her buttocks. Many eyes were drawn to the attractive couple. Annie, seated at a table near the front, turned to follow their progress. As she watched, two of the star's fingers dipped and then disappeared into the girl's crease.

Very appealing, Annie thought dryly. Very Zen. She thought of a variation of the Zen *koan*: What is the sound of one hand, slipping? Would he now shake hands with that hand? She averted her eyes and surveyed the table. Chris, she was relieved to see, was busy talking to Jerry Loest about one of the complicated shoots that the agency was about to attempt. Silly to try to protect him, anyway. He was almost twenty, not a little boy anymore, she reminded herself.

Across from her, Brenda Cushman sat fanning herself with the party program, looking overweight and overheated, both of which she was. Jerry Loest had leaned over to Brenda and was talking about the agency. Brenda was listening intently as Jerry explained how costly it was to bring in new business. Although she kept fanning, Annie heard Brenda say, "Morty made a bundle in spite of his overhead." And Brenda should know if anyone does, thought Annie.

Perhaps it had been a mistake for the First Wives to attend the gala. Annie could hardly bear it. Would Aaron appear? And would he be with Leslie? Did everyone in the room know how stupid and blind she'd been?

Well, after all, she couldn't hide forever, and it was a good cause, Annie thought, though she had come to despise these affairs. All gossip and boredom. It depressed her that this crowd of talented, monied people couldn't do any better than this at entertaining themselves. No one really enjoyed this preening and gossiping, did they? What was the point?

She looked around the room for the dozenth time. Where was Aaron? She looked out across the ballroom. Some couples were dancing, but most stood in chattering groups round their assigned tables. The first course had already been served and cleared, and now the waiters, laden with heavy trays, were making their way back to tables. The meals at these affairs were always lackluster. People didn't come to feed, except in the jungle sense. And it *is* a jungle out there, she thought.

Then she looked past Chris, past Jerry and his wife, past Elise and the senator, to the two empty seats at their table. Who hasn't yet arrived? she wondered. Then she remembered.

Cynthia had bought these seats. Annie had urged—begged—Cynthia to come. And in the rush since the funeral, she had forgotten. So, apparently, had Brenda and Elise. Until now. Annie met Brenda's eyes, then Brenda bit her lip, her face paling. Gone but not forgotten, Annie thought, her irony cutting deeply at herself. Only two weeks and I'm so wrapped up in my own life, I practically forgot Cynthia ever existed. She looked away from the ghostly chairs, and her eyes filmed with tears.

"Oh, look," cried Duarto, who was seated next to Brenda. He seemed to be drinking more than usual tonight, Annie thought, but she knew that his lover had died only a few months ago, and to her he seemed desperate in his gaiety. More misery, she thought. She watched Duarto as he eyed a newcomer and whistled his appreciation. "Eet's the cowboy," he said in his thick Spanish accent. Annie turned to see Oscar Lawrence, the designer noted for his luxurious western wear, move up to the dais and take a seat with his wife. Across his forehead was a garish new scar, complete with stitches.

"I hear he was in a polo accident," Brenda said.

"Well," said Duarto, licking his lips. "*He* say he fell off a horse when he was riding eet, down een Virgeenia at the Wolverton Hunt, but *I* hear eet wasn't polo and eet wasn't hunting."

"Dressage?" asked Annie.

"No, *cara*. Fellatio. He was working on a stallion een hees own stables and eet seems the brute deedn't like hees technique."

"Oh, Duarto!" Annie looked over at Chris, but he was still engrossed in comparing close-ups to long shots with his "uncle" Jerry. Eunice, Jerry's wife, giggled.

"I swear I heard eet from one of hees grooms." Duarto tsked. "Such excitement! But they've always said Oscar loves rough trade."

"Duarto," sighed Brenda Cushman, "sometimes I'm afraid life is passing me by."

"Better than running you over," he told her, taking another long sip of his drink. "Look at those steetches!"

Annie couldn't laugh. In fact, she could hardly sit still for the cynicism. The evening had two purposes: to raise money for AIDS hospice care and to honor Gil Griffin, of all people. His funding, rumored to be $100,000, had underwritten part of the evening. The program listed all the attendees, and their contributions, but from experience Annie knew that much of what was published was untrue: Khymer Mallison, for instance, was listed as giving $25,000, but Duarto had told them she had simply sent her old, déclassé furniture to the AIDS hospice and put that overrated value on the castoffs. Still, *some* money would be raised, and Annie supposed that was better than none. As for Gil Griffin, whatever he had donated hadn't been given out of charity. It was simply a good buy. Annie did enough benefit work to know that one hundred grand wasn't enough to buy him a prestige table at some of the more established charity balls, but the annual AIDS ball was a relatively new benefit arena—only in its fourth year—and he'd invested where it showed.

Gil Griffin was elegant and composed, she admitted, ensconced in the center of the head table, his new young wife, Mary Birmingham, on one side, Gunilla Goldberg, the ball's chairlady, on the other. He sat there, his head tilted in the birdlike way he had, and accepted well-wishers' congratulations. This would be an evening of congratulations and self-congratulations, Annie knew. But the real purpose of the evening for most of the attendees was to play the New York game: to show off what they had and to compare it with others who had as much or more. Cynthia's empty place at the table seemed a mute rebuke.

New York society had grown since the days of The Four Hundred, but not by too much. You saw the same people at every soiree: the old money, the new money, the Eurotrash and minor royalty, the bicoastals. Sometimes the lines blurred or merged, but the faces remained the same. When a society marriage blew up, it was difficult starting over in front of this audience. Annie knew that. Once again she scanned the room and wondered where Aaron was.

Duarto bent forward from his seat and leaned across the table. He was eyeing Kevin Lear and his beautiful companion. They had been clients of his. And part of every society decorator's job was entertaining his clients, inviting them to parties and introducing them to the right people. "When they stay weeth me een Connecteecut one weekend, che forgot her diaphragm," he confided. "Che tole heem they could only have anal eentercourse, but he refuse. He say tha's how lawyers are conceived." Duarto laughed, then turned to greet Lally Snow, another of his clients.

She was sheathed in a skintight, poison green, clinging silk jersey, with a puff of organdy ruffles at the neck. *"Ciao, cara,"* Duarto enthused as each air-kissed the other. As she waltzed on, hobbled by the dress, he whispered, "The original serpent een the garden. They say the liposuction was flubbed. Che can never wear a short dress or a bathing suit again. The scars."

"A small price to pay," sighed Brenda Cushman. She looked down at her pendulous breasts and spreading stomach. "How much do you think they can Hoover out?" she asked. Annie knew Brenda was on a new diet and could only eat tropical fruits. She was also taking special new pills made of crushed garlic and papaya enzyme. "I've lost eleven pounds, but I smell like a Sicilian pineapple," she confided to Annie.

Across the table, Annie could see Elise with the senior senator from Maryland, Roland Walker. Elise's uncle Bob Bloogee had arranged this last-minute date for her with his old widower friend. Elise looked slim and regal and cool as ever; Senator Walker, however, wore an ancient dinner jacket that had kept up with neither the times nor his weight. A sprinkling of dandruff covered his shoulders. Elise, for just a moment, allowed herself to think of Room 705, of that young man's delicious kisses, of the feeling of his arms around her. Elise caught Annie's eye, raised an eyebrow, then indicated the next table with a slight flip of her head.

Bill Atchison was seated there, with Phoebe Van Gelder and the Van Gelder family, along with some other people, among them Celia Reed, the dried-up old wife of Bill Atchison's senior partner at Cromwell Reed. Annie looked back at Elise and smiled. For years that frumpy woman had bored Elise at these obligatory functions. Now Annie was pleased to see Celia blithering on about something into Bill's captive ear. She was one of the few people who could manage to render boring even the spiciest gossip. Annie didn't have to strain to hear Celia's annoying, strident voice.

"Well, they announced the engagement, even though everyone knew that he was a blatant homosexual. Just blatant. It was the title, of course. Lally wanted her daughter to be Princess Guliano. The whole thing was about to start, I mean the guests were already seated, when they found out that he'd run off with the best man. Can you believe it?" she questioned Bill and the rest of the table. The Van Gelders seemed bored; Bill only nodded.

"Lally should have recognized a phony, anyway. There aren't any Venetian princes. Only counts. *Everyone* knows that," sniffed Celia Reed. Elise and Annie stifled their smiles.

Elise had told Annie that Celia was originally a barkeep's daughter from Cincinnati, and whatever social graces she possessed had been learned after she married Donald Reed, a member of an old New York family. Annie wondered if *everyone* in Cincinnati knew the vagaries of Venetian nobility.

Elise grimaced, shot Annie a look, then raised her eyes toward heaven. Then they both laughed.

Brenda, however, wasn't laughing. Her eyes were focused on Shelby sitting next to Morty at the head table. And I look like a Sicilian matzo ball, she thought. Even seated, Brenda could see how thin Shelby was. Brenda released a small sigh. When Brenda first met Morty, she had been thinner, but never as thin as Shelby. And time had taken its deadly toll. But how do all these other women do it? she wondered.

But wait a minute. It was only the women who were thin. The men—most of them over thirty-five—were overweight. Brenda considered that fact for a moment. Even in this respect, the men had the power. It didn't matter that they were balding and out of shape. They had the money, they had the power. It didn't matter how they looked.

But the women. They were all whittled down to matchsticks. She looked over at Elise, who, she guessed, weighed little more now than she had at her debutante party. But of course, Brenda thought, I've never seen Elise eat more than three or four forkfuls at a meal, and never dessert. And Annie, always counting calories and exercising. What a way to live! Surveying the room, however, she had to admit that none of the other women of any age seemed to be losing the fat fight as obviously as she was.

Again she eyed her full bosom and large stomach. What I wouldn't give to be able to walk into a dress shop and not be humiliated by bitchy saleswomen. To be able to come out of the ocean without running to cover up with a wrap. Yeah, and to be able to lift my leg parallel to the floor. But I can't, so what's the big deal? she tried to tell herself.

Your husband left a fat woman for a thin one, that's the big deal. Brenda cared little for the opinions of the people who surrounded her in the ballroom. But she knew that when their eyes shifted from Shelby to her, and back again to Shelby, all they could know was that Morty Cushman had left his fat wife for a thin one. Knowing that mortified and upset her. And when Brenda was upset . . . Where's the next fucking course? she thought, scanning the room for the waiters.

Across the table, Elise closed her eyes for a moment and wondered if she'd make it through the evening. She was already through the single bottle of mediocre champagne that had been provided. Perhaps if she danced. But the senator wouldn't budge, so she'd have to have a drink. A double.

Elise knew Bill was capable of almost anything, but Phoebe Van Gelder was not exactly his type. She was sitting at Bill's side, young, pretty, and bored. But a bit too outré for Bill. The outlandish outerspace jewelry, and that plastic or rubber dress. Was that what they wore downtown? Phoebe looked as sick of the evening as Elise herself was.

She heard Bill say, as he turned from Celia to Phoebe, "I suppose you wouldn't consider a waltz with me?" He added, "That is, if you do waltz."

"I do, but only with the right partner," she told him.

"And who is the right partner?" he asked.

"A man who sweeps me off my feet."

Elise watched them as their eyes met, locked. People from other tables were watching as well. In nightmarish slow motion, Bill extended his right hand, grasping Phoebe around her tiny waist; he drew her up to him, then led her onto the dance floor.

"Well, isn't that perfectly romantic?" Elise heard Celia gush.

"Perfectly," Celia's husband agreed.

Elise finished her last gulp of champagne. Without a real drink, Elise thought, I'll die. Well, she'd go to the powder room, just to move, to get away from that deadly little table. The main course was over. Now there was nothing but dessert to wait for. She excused herself from the senator and swept toward the door.

As she walked down the curving staircase of the rotunda, Annie Paradise called softly from behind her, "Elise, wait for me."

"I was just going to the ladies'," Elise said, hooking her arm through Annie's. "Then I'm going to the bar if you'll come with me. I've got to have a moment's respite from the barbarians at the next table. And the senator. He might hold the record for filibustering in the Senate, but he hasn't said one word at the dinner table."

After the necessaries, and the dollar left for the ladies' room attendant, they crossed the rotunda and swept into the Cafe Pierre bar, past the highly polished mahogany trimmed in glistening brass to the stools at the end. Annie scanned the trompe l'oeil sky on the ceiling and glanced at the small faux windows, marveling as she always did at this touch of whimsy. Elise was at once both authoritative and coaxing, impossible to resist. Her years as a film star had given her a patina that time hadn't dulled. Heads turned. Elise is still very beautiful, Annie thought. She projects an air of importance or mystery or something that hovers around her like a cloud.

At the bar, Elise ordered a double vodka; Annie had white wine. "Well," Elise said, "I'm not sorry poor Cynthia missed this. It must be horrendous to have your husband not only deceive you, the press, and his firm, but then turn around and marry the girl. Well, at least Aaron didn't show up with his doctor." Elise shuddered. She was too humiliated to mention Bill and Phoebe. "And now Gil and Mary Birmingham are ensconced up there, as if he's a prince." Elise shook her head. "Just out of curiosity, who had Cynthia asked to escort her?"

"Roger Trento," Annie said.

"Who's he? I think I know his name."

"The tennis pro at the club," Annie admitted. She saw Elise wince.

"No wonder she killed herself," Elise muttered, and ordered another drink. For a moment Annie considered Elise's comment. Aside from Chris, Annie herself had had only one other option for an escort for tonight: Maurice Dingman, a friend of Jerry Loest's, who was twenty years her senior, plus being fat and dull. What would *she* do for an escort if she didn't have Chris to fall back on?

"I better get back to my son." She sighed, kissed Elise, and got up, ready to leave the bar. She stopped suddenly, her hands clutching the bar behind her.

There, sitting together on one of the tiny divans that lined the wall, were Aaron and Leslie Rosen. He was dressed in a tuxedo, a white silk, fringed scarf thrown carelessly around his neck. His dark hair gleamed, his skin shone, his teeth flashed as he smiled. Annie allowed herself a moment to take in the tête-à-tête, then turned from it, as her father had taught her to turn from the scene of any disaster. She walked up the two shallow steps of the Cafe Pierre and across the rotunda. Holding tightly to the banister, she ran up the stairs to the ballroom.

Control yourself, she thought. You know that he is living his own life. Stop it. You had to see them out together like this sometime. Better sooner than later. Act normally, she commanded as she crossed the ballroom floor.

As Annie sat down at the table, Duarto was still talking. "We're all balling the jack, man," he was saying. "Thees eesn't honoring Gil Griffin. Eet's honoring hees jack."

"His what?" Chris asked.

"Hees jack, hees cash, hees *dinero*, hees money. Eet's all about money. No one gives a sheet for the AIDS victims, for the sick, for the homeless. Not these people. Not een thees city. These parties are all about jack. Who got eet, who gives eet." Tears filled his eyes. "No one cares that Richard died.

No one even visited heem." He turned to Brenda. "No one but you, *cara*. I weel never forget you for that." Duarto lifted Brenda's hand and kissed it. Then he held it up to Annie. "She came to see heem every day. She brought heem fruit, and meat loaf and lasagna." He wiped his eyes and turned to Brenda. "You're a terrible cook," he told her.

"I know, but I give good takeout." She patted Duarto's hand.

Now those who were on the dance floor were being asked to leave, to finish their dessert, stop their chatter, and take their seats. It was time for the serious talk. From the dais, Robert Hazzenfus took the microphone. On the board of several of the city's hospitals, half a dozen clinics and medical wings bore his name. There was another benefit of his philanthropy: it was widely rumored that one of the rooms in his enormous penthouse was fitted out as a complete ob-gyn office. Several people swore that each week he had two prostitutes come up, and one dressed as a nurse and assisted while he examined the other. Annie doubted that the story was true, but it had certainly persisted.

Elise caught Annie's and Brenda's eyes as the others in the room turned their attention to those seated at the head table, and with a sweep of her graceful hand encompassing Bill, Morty, Aaron, and Gil, she said in a deep, throaty whisper, "To First Wives." Simultaneously, as if rehearsed, both of the others lifted their glasses in silent agreement.

"Ladies and gentlemen, please," Hazzenfus boomed. "I'm glad you are enjoying yourselves, but let us remember the reason we are here tonight."

The buzz of conversation began to die down, except at the head table where Gunilla Goldberg continued to whisper to Shelby Cushman. "Do you see Perseus Daglevi?" she asked.

Shelby followed Gunilla's stare. "Is she the skinny woman in black?"

"They're *all* skinny women in black, dear. This is New York. I mean the one who is sitting next to Pat Buckley."

"Do you mean the one who looks like some kind of Arab or Iranian?" Shelby asked in her soft southern drawl.

"Never, but *jamais*, call a Persian an Arab, dear." Gunilla shook her glossy head. "Awfully bad taste. Remember, they're the ones who *invented* Aryan."

Shelby, chastised, nodded. There was still so much to learn. "What about her?"

"She had a breast reduction. Well, really, it was her third. For the future, remember the rule: twice is the limit for any body part. Otherwise you wind up with Michael Jackson syndrome. Anyway, there was a foul-up with Perseus's procedure and now she has no nipples on her breasts at all. Oddest thing you've ever seen. She lost one, and they decided it was more symmetrical to remove the other. Now she glues on latex prostheses to show under her clothes. I used to use the same adhesive for false eyelashes. Messy stuff. I wonder if it stains her dresses? I'm so glad those lashes went out of style. My husband—not Sol—my second husband, hated them." She paused, as if considering. "Of course, he hated me, too."

Shelby giggled. Gunilla arched a brow, narrowed her eyes, and continued, "Listen, dear. You may be Southern, but you're not stupid and I know it. After all, you snagged Morty Cushman, and don't tell me it was easy to land the fat bastard. I like you. I want to help you. So remember this: *all* men hate *all* women. There are no exceptions. When you meet one you think is an exception, and you fall in love, it's time to check into a spa for a week till your blood sugar stabilizes."

She turned from Shelby. Robert Hazzenfus was still droning on. Gil Griffin this, Gil Griffin that. God, Gunilla thought, everyone knew he was an exceptional bastard in a world full of ordinary ones. She looked over at her husband, Sol, and wondered if it was true that his latest affair was a threat. The children were getting too old to protect her now: she'd have to try to protect herself. She turned back to Shelby and continued her lesson.

"Of course, all women hate all men back. This is the basis for civilization as we know it." She picked up her evening bag, snapped it open, took out her red Paloma lipstick, and reapplied it carefully, just slightly over the lip line. Despite her care, the deep red bled into the hundreds of tiny lines, like a spider's web radiating from her mouth. That she could do this in front of a room full of five hundred socialites astounded Shelby. She watched, mesmerized, until Gunilla was done and looked up at her and then at the large, glittering crowd.

"We all hate one another, dear. Never forget it."

BOOK TWO

The Husbands

Getting Scared

I

The Sweetheart Deal

Three of the four husband-targets of the First Wives Club were congregated in a celebratory tea. Tea! thought Morty Cushman. Fucking elegant. Just like this joint. Yeah, the Federated Funds Douglas Witter boardroom was impressive. No denying that. Of course, Morty thought, they spent plenty to make it impressive. These guys know what to do, and do it well. They've been in the business of robbing widows and orphans since the Revolutionary War. He looked at Gil Griffin and Bill Atchison. Definitely sons of bitches of the American Revolution.

In fact, the goddamn room looked as if it were built back then. It was paneled with some kind of dark, shiny wood halfway up the walls, and then striped-cream-and-blue wallpaper went up to the high ceiling. The center of the room was completely filled by a gleaming, long table lit overhead by a huge brass chandelier with about twenty arms holding goddamn candles, real candles! It was some kind of special antique out of fucking Washington's headquarters or something, Gil had said. Of course, discreetly placed electrical lights were also sunken in the ornate plaster ceiling. The floors were dark, shiny wood, too, like in a real house. The goddamnedest thing was that the whole *megillah* sat on the sixty-eighth floor of

120 Wall Street, its windows looking out on the spectacular view of New York Harbor. That is, if you could see through the goddamn authentic windows, which you couldn't because of the wavy glass and the bubbles. That was class: having the resources to create colonial fucking Williamsburg on the top of a skyscraper and then ignoring the view. You had to hand it to these *alte goyim*.

The whole team was assembled to celebrate the offering. Morty the Madman stock was now—this very minute—being traded on the Big Board. It was unbelievable. Morty had had his share of success, and as a streetfighter he'd put himself up against anyone, but these guys were something else. They were goddamn animals. Morty had heard enough about their tactics to know. These guys originated "go for the throat," and they did it with so much class. That was the paradox that fascinated Morty.

He surveyed the room. Gil was at the head of the table, looking for the world like a fucking emperor, his head inclined slightly, listening to his wife, Mary Birmingham, who sat beside him, whispering in his ear. How does he get his suit to fit like that? Morty wondered. He knew it took more than money. No, it hadda be in the genes. Like the perfect shape of Gil's head, the blond hair that improves with age when it mixes with gray. And a neck. Morty envied that. Gil's neck held his jaw up and out, giving him the appearance of integrity. Morty noticed Gil's steel blue eyes flicker for a moment as he placed a long, thin index finger to his upper lip and nodded at Mary. Morty continued to gaze around the table.

A dozen Young Turks, all in immaculate white shirt collars and pressed gray or navy suits, were seated around the table. The hair, of those that had any, was slicked back, the glasses, of those that wore them, gleamed. The ties were those boring little patterns on pink or red or light yellow silk. Fucking "power ties" they called them. They all looked rich and clean. Rich and clean. Morty admitted to himself that he looked neither. He was overweight, his five-o'clock shadow showed up daily at noon, and he had only to put on a suit to wrinkle it. Still, he thought as he leaned back and took a pull on his cigar, he was here.

He was here because he deserved to be; because he'd worked hard; because he was smart; and because—he would admit to himself—he'd gotten lucky. He was riding the wave of the eighties, and for him, the wave had just peaked. He was sitting at this table with $61 million in his pocket, and that made for a hell of a bulge in your pants. Christ, he thought with exultation, I'm probably the richest one of these fuckers.

Being so goddamn rich was better than anything Morty had ever known—better than eating, better than a great game of ball, better even than sex.

These people fascinated him. He had to admit that. Fascinated and infuriated him. Yeah, he resented them. He had to admit that, too. They were *shtarkers*, really powerful men who could make things happen. When the idea of going public came along, he had sat down with a few investment banks. They took one look at the figures and walked away without a glance back. But Gil had seen the potential. He hadn't seemed to mind the poor cash flow, or the overexpansion. He'd said he liked the picture. Then Gil Griffin, who had never built a store from a hole-in-the-wall to a chain, who had never dirtied his hands making anything or selling anything, had sat at a table with Morty and told him, *told him*, that he'd take him public. It would cost him—of course—42 million shares. And Bill's law firm would get another 5 million. It almost doubled the nut they had to raise in the offering, money raised on Morty's sweat, on Morty's name, but he had to admit that these guys had floated the shares. What a racket! Were they geniuses or *gonifs* or both?

"I wanted to mark this successful close of the offering," Gil was saying, "with something that would reflect both the delicacy that was necessary to achieve it and the beauty of an offering that can only be called a sweetheart deal for everyone." The handpicked audience of thirty lawyers, brokers, and numbers crunchers smiled appreciatively. Gil had their full attention, and in his hand, a small remote-control unit allowed him to open doors, lower the movie screen, dim the lights, contact security, or buzz the administrative or housekeeping staff to enter and serve them. "I don't think I have to remind you that our management of the deal resulted in a record-setting fee for Federated Funds Douglas Witter, and that means a pleasant Christmas for us all." There was a murmur of appreciation.

Morty knew that bonuses were distributed at Christmas, often doubling these guys' already huge salaries. "And a token of appreciation for all the hard work and long hours is being distributed now," Gil said. Discreetly, two men moved through the group with madonna-blue Tiffany boxes, leaving one at each place. Morty reached for the white satin ribbon, until he noticed that no one else reached for theirs. He dropped his hand to his lap.

Well, he remembered, coming back to earth, Gil is richer than me. How many of these deals had *he* done?

After the speech, Gil turned, hit his remote, and the connecting door to his office suite opened. Two Japanese women, wearing traditional kimono and obi, were poised in the doorway. They bowed low to the room, to Gil, and then entered, immediately beginning some kind of elaborate ceremony. They were washing out bowls and filling them again, moving as if they were in slow motion. The whole thing was abso-

lutely the most boring bullshit Morty had ever seen. He sur-
reptitiously glanced at his gold Rolex with the diamond trim
around the face. He was hungry and he had to piss. He hoped
this would be over soon.

He looked across the table to Bill Atchison. The guy
looked fascinated, but he was such a pussy hound, he'd watch
women do anything. Morty knew he was involved with some
crazy artist girl now, and God knows what he watched her do.
Morty himself knew there was a lot more to life than good
poontang. In fact, he'd rather go to a Knicks game with some
neighborhood guys any day. He wasn't saying that women
didn't have their place. You needed a wife to break into these
circles, no doubt about it. But she had to be the right wife.
And he had the right wife now. Shelby would know what
these goddamn Nips were doing.

He had met her in a SoHo art gallery when that faggot
decorator Duarto had taken him and Brenda around to buy
something for the walls. Shelby had helped him, and then,
when something else had come in she thought they might
like, it was Morty she called, not Duarto or Brenda. And they
had had a drink, and then dinner, and she had talked about
what she wanted to do, her own gallery and the kind of shows
she wanted to put together. She was working on a show with
Ed Schlossberg, the Jew who had married JFK's daughter, and
she knew everyone and everything.

Now she did have her own gallery, Morty's gallery really,
and she was preparing a show of crazy Phoebe Van Gelder's
work. Morty knew it would help him if he could get into that
world, a world that both fascinated and confused him. If he
was going to play with the big boys, it would help if he polished his image. Like this bullshit with the oriental ladies.
What was going on, for chrissake?

At last they were finished. Gil stood up and bowed to the

slants, and then, at last, waiters rolled in carts of food. Fabulous. Morty had never been much of a drinker, but he liked to *fress*, no doubt about it.

But when the cart was rolled up to him, he was confronted with nasty bits of *trayf*. He wasn't religious, but he knew what he liked, and this array of raw fish and whale droppings was not it. Christ, he hated sushi. Fucking faggot food. Shelby knew better than to try to make him eat this shit. He didn't even eat pussy, for chrissake.

He turned to the impressive, bright-looking guy beside him, who had already selected a plateful. "Good, huh?" Morty asked.

"The best," the jerk told him. So much for *his* judgment.

He turned to the guy on his other side. It was Stuart Swann, one of those classy but ineffective types from the old guard. He was the only person who looked less than thrilled with the proceedings. In fact, he looked disgusted. Well, good for him. Behind them an old grandfather clock began to chime.

"That was my family's clock," Stuart said. Morty knew the whole goddamn company had been his family's once. Big deal. So where were you now, *putz?* Morty hated old money gone to seed. Gil Griffin had taken old money and piled new on top. That was the way to go.

People had gotten up and were moving around, so Morty waved the waiter off and stood. Bill, of course, was talking to one of the geishas. Morty had already figured the guy was a lightweight, but he was connected to one of the heaviest law firms in the city, and that made him a heavy. And it made Gil's deals look real solid. Plus Gil could push him around. A pet lawyer. Real convenient.

Meanwhile, Gil Griffin and Mary Birmingham were beside the other geisha, surrounded by a cadre of the anointed. Morty moved toward them as did most of the others in the room.

They were like a pack of dogs, he thought, with Gil the lead. And Morty knew that in the trip through life, unless you were the lead dog, the scenery never changes. He made his way over to them.

"Nice party," Morty told Gil. He nodded to Mary, who stood there, as always, hanging on Gil's every word. But they all did. "Very nice," Morty repeated.

"Thank you. Did you enjoy the tea ceremony?" Gil asked. So that's what it was. Morty saw Mary shoot Gil a look. Why did the son of a bitch always seem to be mocking him?

"Yeah, it was great. Very unique."

"In my work with the Japanese, I saw how much attention they give to detail. Their precision has a Zen rightness to it. It's what I like about the tea ceremony: each action is pre-scribed and perfectly executed. Just as our offering was."

Morty just nodded. Zen, shmen.

But there was a lot of talk now about Gil's interest in the Japanese, and not their goddamn tea ceremony, either. He'd been quoted in *BusinessWeek* recently saying that several of the Japanese firms looked right for takeovers, sparking all kinds of rumors of Pearl Harbor revenge. The guy had a hel-luva pair of nuts. Morty wondered if it was all a smoke screen. You could never tell with this guy.

It was like the scandal before he married Mary. When the press picked it up, he denied it. He said it was male preju-dice against a talented young woman. That there was nothing between them. He said he was only her mentor. That he'd been happily married for over twenty years. The women's magazines picked it up, and the National Association of Women, or one of those dyke groups, had Mary Birmingham speak on the subject at their annual conference.

What cracked Morty up was that then Gil went out and *did* get divorced, and three months later, he announces that *now* he's started a relationship with Mary. So he'd faked 'em all out. *And* he got what he wanted. Mary stood beside him now, while the other dogs sniffed them both. Morty approved. After all, he had traded up, too.

And like Gil, he'd faked 'em out. Brenda hadn't a clue to his net worth, and he'd bought her off for a song. Christ, his lawyer, Leo Gilman, collected more than Brenda did each month!

Yes, Morty thought, I could play in Gil's league. Maybe I could play as well as Gil himself.

Bill Atchison, abandoned by the geisha, joined them. Good—now Morty could mention Shelby and her gallery and not fear getting the cold shoulder. Money changes things. Not like when he was with Brenda. He could take Shelby anywhere and be accepted.

"So, I hear that Phoebe's show is shaping up."

Bill smiled. "So it would seem."

Phoebe Van Gelder was a terminal nut job in Morty's opinion, but she was a Van Gelder, knew everyone, and got loads of the right kind of press. She was a skinny, bizarrely dressed piece of ass, but there was no denying that her credentials were impressive. And her conceptual art, or whatever the hell it was, was big in SoHo, but had never been shown in an uptown gallery. Until now. Neither Bill nor the Griffins had ever socialized with Morty, but he figured he could parlay Phoebe's show into a few dinners and invitations. And then maybe he could get in on some of the action as a regular thing. These guys on the inside always helped each other out. Whenever there was a new stock offering, the inner circle, like Gil and Bill, always got early warning. If he got in with them, he could make money over and over again. Serious money.

Morty had made his first serious money with this deal. Now, instead of having all his assets tied up in his business, instead of being overextended, stretched to the limit, he'd got his hands on $61 million at once. And he wasn't going to part with a nickel of it. He'd got out from under Brenda just in time. She was tied up with the settlement she'd made at the time of the divorce, so this was all his. Good thing Brenda falls apart whenever you mention lawyers or courts. It made it that much easier to get her to settle quickly and cheaply and *before* he went public. Morty had already put a lot of it away in Switzerland. But oddly enough, rather than filling him it had made him hungrier. Gil pulled that kind of money in every year, not once in a lifetime. Morty wanted more. A lot more.

If he had *that* kind of money, really big money, he'd have them name things for him. The Morty Cushman Center for Cancer Research. The Morton Cushman Library. The Cushman Building. The M. R. Cushman Home for Wayward Girls. He reflected for a moment. Ah, fuck the hospitals and wayward girls. He'd buy a team. Maybe the Giants, maybe the Knicks. Who knows, maybe even the Yankees. Steinbrenner, that total asshole, might sell. You never know. And he could build the team, make them something again. And then he'd be famous. He'd have a real image behind him. Not just as the screaming nut on TV, but as a real person. Someone who had done something.

Right now, however, he had to find a toilet. These people probably don't piss, he thought. He hated to have to ask. A weak bladder was a sign of weakness. He continued to stand at the window, squinting, trying to make out the Statue of Liberty through the wavy, bubbly glass. The door to Gil's office was still opened. Morty remembered there was a private toilet and shower off there, as there were in most executive suites. He'd duck in and no one would be the wiser.

No one noticed as he sidled through to Gil's office. He was standing with his back to the bathroom door, emptying his bladder and almost groaning with relief, when he heard someone enter the office outside. He finished and stood silent. Christ, how bad would it be to be caught? He heard Gil's voice, and the voice of Gil's secretary, Nancy Rodgers.

"No, it's important, and I'll call him from here," Morty heard clearly. "No one is to interrupt me." Mrs. Rodgers murmured something. "Well, give me the number, then," Gil said. Morty held his breath. Gil had crossed the office and was at his desk, just on the other side of the lavatory door. Morty stood motionless, staring down at the frothy, urine-filled bowl. He heard Gil begin to speak.

"Hello, Asa? What is it?" There was a pause. "I told you all that, Asa. We've been through it all before." There was another pause. "No, I don't want it to run until October. Wait a month." Morty heard Gil sigh. "Of course we won't be caught, Asa. I have a lot more to lose than you. Remember that. And remember that all the information about Morty the Madman stock is dead true. Absolutely. So you got a scoop. All I'm asking for in return is timing." Gil sighed again. "Asa, don't be an ass. And don't call me anymore. Now that the offering's been made, I don't want these calls. All right? . . . All right."

Morty stood there, virtually frozen in position. He heard Gil hang up the phone and cross the room. He heard a door close. His mind raced. What about his stock and October? Who had Gil been talking to? Wasn't the guy who'd written about the offering in the *Journal* named Asa something? It was a weird name.

Carefully, slowly and quietly, Morty Cushman opened the door and peered out into Gil Griffin's now deserted office. There, on the immaculate marble-topped desk, lay a small pink paper phone message slip. Morty walked over to it and picked it up. Swiftly, he read and dialed the number.

"Asa Ewell," answered a voice at the other end. Morty

replaced the phone silently. He shook his head. Gil Griffin, big dealer. The guy was a *gonif*. He was going to run something to jack up the stock price. Unbelievable. Morty grinned. This was the way the big boys played, but this time Morty Cushman was playing, too. If they wouldn't cut him in, he'd cut himself in. Something gets published, everyone jumps on the bandwagon, the stock price goes up. Good all around. After all, everybody loves a sweetheart deal.

He left the desk and walked out of the office, leaving the door to the lavatory open, his urine still gleaming yellow in the bowl.

2

Uh-Oh in SoHo

In Aaron Paradise's opinion, SoHo—the portion of Manhattan that was once only commercial and manufacturing lofts—was the most exciting part of New York. In only a decade the area had gone from decaying, half-abandoned cast-iron-fronted factories to trendy galleries, hip boutiques, and artsy bars, all topped by fabulous apartments carved out of the big empty spaces of old sweatshops, tool and die plants, and the like.

Someone—a shrewd real estate developer no doubt—had named it, not after London's Soho, but because the area was south of Houston Street (which only out-of-towners pronounced like the Texas city; to New Yorkers it was "Howston.") Like London's Soho, however, this area became a haven for young, developing artists, the buildings' fabulously large windows and great open spaces perfect for their work. *Très avant-garde* and very attractive to New Yorkers always on the lookout for something new. Ironically, the avant garde had driven up the prices and driven out most of the artists and nouveau bohemia who had pioneered the place. Aaron shrugged. So be it. He had no patience for artsy-fartsy whiners. If they couldn't pay the rent, out they'd have to go. He himself had had to give up artistic pretensions to earn a living.

It was all a part of the maturing process. Still, he was glad he had once had them. It gave him the *je ne sais quoi* that so many in business lacked.

Now Aaron strode purposely down lower Broadway, passing the huge plate-glass windows at O. K. Harris without even his customary glance at his reflection. Unlike most of the jean-clad kids around him on the street, Aaron wore a brown tweed Armani suit jacket over a luscious soft cashmere turtleneck. Too uptown for this meeting, but he hadn't expected to be called down to it. Sure, he thought to himself, three thousand dollars worth of clothes and I'm still dressed wrong for the occasion.

He was irritated, no doubt about it. In the advertising game—and rest assured it *was* a game—he was the best, the Canseco of commercials, the Agassi of ads. So he knew that *dressing for success* was not an empty phrase. Well, he wasn't dressed for success at this unraveling. In fact, he wasn't even supposed to be here. United Foods was Jerry's account now, goddamnit. What was all this crisis about? Just another stupid tempest in a teapot. Aaron sighed. He knew he was expected to bring in the bacon, be the rainmaker, lasso new clients, but couldn't Jerry even manage to keep a satisfied one happy? If the two of them expected to stay in the big time, Jerry would have to do a better job pulling his weight.

Aaron turned left on Spring Street, nearing the address of the loft where Anton, the photographer on this shoot, lived and worked. A young girl dressed in typical downtown fashion—black tight-legged pants, baggy sweater, and some kind of outrageous African-looking cap on her gorgeous, unruly hair—ran out from an industrial doorway and flashed him a smile, the afternoon sun glinting off the tiny nose ring in her right nostril. Aaron smiled back. Christ, he liked it down here! Years ago he'd begged Annie to move here, back when the industrial lofts were dirt cheap and only a few AIRs—artists in residence—were visible among the hidden, illegal conversions to living places that impoverished photographers, dancers, artists, and those who liked to live among them had created. But Annie had objected to the lack of grocery stores, schools, libraries. Practical Annie. She'd said it would be hard on Sylvie. Sylvie, always Sylvie. Aaron shook his head. Well, he supposed it didn't matter—he would have had to give up everything to her when he moved out, so it was just as well. Now he and Leslie were looking for a place, one larger than the loft she already owned on West Broadway. It was just too bad he was so financially stretched—by this divorce, by Sylvie, by Alex's tuition.

Aaron wasn't used to doing without. He had never had to budget, never had to worry about money, except for that ghastly time when Annie and he were first married. Success had come fairly early, and soon after, some of the family money—trusts—had kicked in. He supposed, after his father died, he'd get much of the rest. Typical. They only give you the money after you succeed or they die. Aaron sighed.

Yes, he was a Paradise from the Newport branch of the family. A Bennet on his mother's side. He'd grown up going to the right prep school, a member of the Knickerbocker Grays, a student at Mrs. Stafford's School of Dance. He had gone to Yale, married a Main Line girl, and only stepped out of the mold when he tried to write screenplays.

But that hadn't worked. The life of a writer had nearly driven him nuts. He realized that he craved excitement, being with people, taking charge. Despite his soft upbringing, he was savvy. He took pride in that. He was a regular guy. So he settled for writing the mini-screenplays of advertising. And he was a genius at it. He knew how to bring in clients, and how to handle 'em once he brought them in. Advertising was perfect for him. And with his social background, he felt superior to most of the other guys in the industry. It was comforting always to be the most secure guy in the room. His partner, Jerry Loest, on the other hand, was probably the most insecure guy in any room.

Aaron speeded up his pace, wondering how much longer he could stand to work with Jerry. The partnership had seemed perfect when they founded the agency. Even their names combined into a clever joke. Jerry the wunderkind, with those remarkable concepts and a brilliant visual aesthetic, coupled with Aaron, the clever wordsmith with the knack of bringing in the business and keeping the clients happy. And now there were five other partners, all creative and exciting people. Paradise/Loest was thriving, with the kind of excitement that only happens to an agency when it's very, very hot. All the bright young talent wanted to get on staff, despite the slightly lower pay and the much longer hours. People loved to work there. And they worked their balls off. Aaron was proud of the joke around the office that was a variation of the old sweatshop warning: "If you didn't come in on Saturday, don't come in on Sunday." That was how they'd keep their edge.

Aaron didn't like to feel he was losing his edge. He never wanted to become old hat, stodgy, to play it safe. He'd been the bad, bad boy at Darcy, McManus, but his copy had been new, fresh, and it brought in the clients. He had style, and he'd gone out on his own with it.

But now, Aaron admitted, there were all these kids, real kids, nipping at his heels. Duetsch, Kirshenbaum and Bond. They had done the classy clothes ad that showed a Ralph Lauren–type WASP under the headline *Dress British. Think Yiddish.* What a ruckus that caused! Aaron had to admit it was great copy. Then there was Goldsmith/Jeffrey; Aaron felt they'd stolen their name slash from Paradise/Loest. He was equally resentful of Buckley DeCerchio Cavalier, where even the president was under thirty—and a girl. *They'd* gotten the Snapple account that Jerry had been following up on for two years and had run the billings up to 5 million bucks. Aaron sighed. All the new blood made him feel tired.

He thought of his father. The tight-ass. He had once called Aaron lazy. Too lazy to work. Well, he'd told his father to shove it, and look what he'd done. He'd built his own business and was on his way to building a fucking empire. And now his own son was watching him do it.

It was nice having Chris working with him. Aaron's dad and Annie had both been upset when Chris dropped out of Princeton to work for Aaron at the agency. Aaron pretended to be upset, too, but secretly he was proud. Chris wasn't like his brother, Alex—he wouldn't set the world on fire—but it was nice he had chosen to work with Aaron, to learn the business. It would be nice to have someone at his back, someone whom he was building the firm for, someone who could take it over one day. Aaron slowed his steps for a moment. Aging, slowing down, bowing out—all of those ideas upset him deeply. Christ, what was he thinking of? He was young, in the prime of his life. He would soon have a new, younger wife, a whole life ahead of him. Chris was a baby, hardly dry behind the ears. There was no way the kid could take over. Not now, probably not ever. He had no real flash, no pizzazz. No guts.

Aaron arrived at the loft and pressed Anton's buzzer. The grim hallway, just a vestibule really, was littered, graffiti scrawled on the wall beside the ugly, caged elevator. Particularly prominent was "Eat Pussy or Die." Aaron wondered how Herb Brubaker had liked that. Herb was not a man whom Aaron could imagine eating pussy. He was one of those Midwestern, middle-aged middle managers whom Aaron despised, but totally typical for United Foods. Amazing that they had bought Aaron's concept, but after all, it *had* been brilliant.

They had purchased Sandrine cosmetics and then hadn't known what the hell to do with a line of moderately priced makeup aimed at the young, hip market. United Foods knew nothing of young, hip, exciting. Aaron had proposed a stunning visual—a slender nude with makeup scribbled, powdered, smeared, on various parts of her body by various hands—one of them obviously male. The commercials would have to avoid a full frontal, of course, but the print ads, which were being shot today, could go pretty far.

And then, they'd convinced La Doll, the new young singer with typical acting aspirations, to pose. What a coup. United fell hook, line, and large checkbook.

So what the fuck had gone wrong? Aaron wondered as he pushed back the clanking gate and entered the self-service elevator. Apparently Herb had watched them play around with La Doll's body and decided to give it a try himself. Didn't Jerry and the gang have enough sense to keep the moron busy? Clients on a shoot were as annoying as herpes in a whorehouse. They always had to be baby-sat.

At last the elevator groaned to a stop on the fifth floor. The loft was huge and white, with enormous windows down two long sides. Large white umbrellas were poised to catch and reflect the light on the set, a gray roll of horizonless paper and a plain wooden chair, now deserted. Instead of the usual noisy chaos of a shoot, there were silent knots of people: his staff, over in one corner, Herb Brubaker and his in another. Christ, Aaron thought. This was perfect!

He looked over at Paul Block, who shrugged. It was his hand, his masculine hand, that was to legitimately touch La Doll; he and Pat Tilley, Jon Carthay, and a few other hand models earned over half a million a year at jobs like this one. Now Paul sat, uninvolved in all the flap going on around him, his hands absolutely still in his lap. They were insured with Lloyd's, but Aaron knew how careful these guys were.

It was *Herb's* hands that had gotten them into trouble. Jerry, his baggy corduroy trousers bunched at his waist, his sweater all wrong, immediately ran up to Aaron, his face that of a concerned, morally correct beagle. Here was a guy, a Jew no less, who dressed Yiddish and thought British, Aaron told himself, exasperated. Christ, he was impossible!

"Where's La Doll?" Aaron snapped.

"In the rear dressing room."

"Great. What's she doing, calling her lawyer?"

Jerry shrugged. "I think she's crying. Aaron, we gotta call United and get Herb thrown off the set."

Julie, the account rep, joined them. "He's right, Aaron. The guy's a pig."

"Yes, but he's the *client* pig," Aaron reminded them. Jesus, he had no intention of letting word of this leak back to Macready at United. It would look bad for everyone and make an enemy out of Herb. Aaron didn't need someone running a vendetta back in Milwaukee. If he could turn it around, on the other hand, and cover it up for Herb, then Herb would owe him. Big time.

"I'm sure it was misunderstood. Taken out of context," he began.

"Christ, Aaron, he pinched her nipple!" Julie retorted. "What context should that be taken in?"

Chris came up behind him. "He did, Dad. It was unbelievable."

Oh, perfect! Aaron thought. Now his son was lining up on the wrong side. "When I want your opinion, I'll ask for it," he snapped, turning his back on his son's wince.

"Jerry, could I speak to you privately for a minute?" he asked mildly.

Jerry nodded and followed him to a window in the corner. Aaron kept the smile on his face—he knew they were being watched, but his voice sank to a bitter whisper.

"Now listen to me and listen good. I didn't break my ass getting the United account only to lose it because of some silly incident with a client who's had a three-martini lunch. Christ knows, this little bitch isn't a virgin, and it's probably not the first time her nipple's been tweaked for money." He stopped, rubbed his chin, and freshened his smile. "Now, I'll go into her dressing room and promise her anything. Meanwhile, you go make nice to Brubaker."

"Aaron, she won't continue, and I won't work with Brubaker under any circumstances."

"*She* will and *you* will, Jerry. Do you hear me? I bailed you out of all that trouble with your father-in-law, and I guaranteed your mortgage and I got your daughter into Princeton. Now, do what I tell you, goddamnit. I will not have you lose me this account!"

He was breathing hard but the smile hadn't left his face for a moment. "And Jerry," he added, "make it look *easy*."

He turned and strode across the loft, past the hairdresser, past the makeup man, past the prop bench with the products all spread out, ready to be artistically scribbled onto La Doll's perfect body.

It would be an innovative series. Lipstick scrawled across the girl's back, blusher sponged onto her thighs, eyeliner drawn all down a leg, around an ankle. All photographed in beautiful colors, in lush light. It would break ground, it would sell, it would be new. Let those kids at the new agencies try to keep up with him. He could still lead the way.

Yes, he was ready to ring out the old and bring in the new. No more old guilts and burdens. He was still young. He was at the top of his form. He and Leslie would enter a brave new world together. For a moment, inexplicably, as he walked to La Doll in her dressing room, he thought of Annie. It had been a bad scene at the Carlyle. Christ, he was sorry. He shouldn't have had that little slip with her in Boston. He shook his head. It had been difficult getting Leslie to overlook that one. Leslie was a tigress in bed and in life. She, like him, got out there and got what she wanted. And she'd gotten him. Annie . . . well, Annie simply tried to be good. Eternally sorting garbage for recycling, volunteering, being conscientious. But she was no tigress. And certainly not in bed. Sex felt like an accommodation with Annie. It had to be love, not sex! And she still didn't come. It was as if, no matter what he did, his performance wasn't good enough. He could never compete with her relentless goodness. He sighed.

Also, he admitted to himself, Leslie should have terminated Annie as a patient sooner, so the thing between them would have been cleaner. But Leslie had felt Annie needed the help with Sylvie. And maybe she was right. Now *he'd* have to deal with Sylvie. Soon he'd have to visit that place. He winced at the thought. He'd deal with that later.

Now, if he could just cajole La Doll into a forgiving mood. Perhaps a small gift. Jesus, perhaps a big gift. Well, whatever it took, he'd get her to come around.

His hand was on her dressing room door when he saw a girl at the phone waving to him anxiously. Good Christ, it was endless! An endless chipping away at him.

"Mr. Paradise, an urgent call . . ."

They were always urgent. The office with some more childish bullshit that only he could handle. "Take a message," Aaron called over his shoulder.

"But the man says to tell you he's Mr. Cushman and that it's an emergency!"

Aaron turned from the dressing room door and began

moving swiftly toward the kid. Norma, his secretary, knew better than to give a location number direct to a client. Why wasn't she screening this? He thought of La Doll. Well, a few more minutes wouldn't hurt, he guessed.

"Morty, how the hell did you track me down?"

"With radar, kiddo, with radar," Morty said, laughing at his own little joke. "Don't blame your girl. She did her best to keep the secret. But this had to go direct from me to you. No goddamn middlemen. Listen up, Aaron. As soon as we hang up, I want you to call your stockbroker and buy as much Morty the Madman stock as you possibly can, and then buy some more."

Interesting, Aaron thought. But was it legal? He'd already helped Morty Cushman realize his dreams. What next? "What are you asking me to do, Morty?"

"Not asking, telling. You're buying for you and you're buying for me, so bet the farm, pal, and we're both going to make a lot of money. I never would have gotten the Wall Street crowd interested without your help. Now it's payback time, baby. Morty doesn't forget his friends."

Aaron had introduced Morty to Gil Griffin, and Aaron's ads had made Morty king of the retailers. Well, maybe this was a favor. "Is this illegal?"

"Only if we're caught. Anyway, it's small time. Just a little inside edge, you know. Hold the shit for a month, make a million dollars. That kind of thing."

Christ, he could use the money. Buy out Jerry. Eliminate problems like the one he was dealing with now. "So what kind of figures are you talking, Morty?"

"I want a million. Can you do that on margin?"

Jesus. A million. No way. "What's going on, Morty?"

"Let's just say that it's going to make a move."

Aaron thought quickly. He appreciated a stock tip, who

wouldn't, but didn't like the idea of being a beard for Morty's purchase. And then there was the issue of not having any-where near that kind of money. The divorce had not come cheap.

"How safe is this?"

"Aaron, it might as well be FDIC insured. I swear it. But have you got an account in another name, or one that you can use? A friend, or an old aunt or something?"

Sylvie. His daughter's trust fund was the only answer. "Not one that I could easily get a million from, Mort. Nowhere near it."

"Shit. You know what they say: it takes money to make money. Well, I won't be a *chozzer*. Can you do me four hun-dred thou?"

"Yes. I think so."

"And have enough left so you can do a little something for yourself."

"Yeah."

"Good. Then do it."

Morty clicked off. Aaron stood there for a moment while visions of sugar plums danced through his head. It had taken years and a lot of sweat to build the trust fund that insured Sylvie's future. It was a waste when you thought how limited her future would be. But it guaranteed that the poor girl would never be in a state home. Now, perhaps he could double that money. And make some for himself all the while doing a favor for Morty. That would cement the Madman account forever. Still, it was dangerous. But he was a risk taker. He depressed the plunger and began to dial his stockbroker.

Then he remembered. Goddamn it. The trust had joint supervision. Since Annie had added the capital from the trust that her father had left, she, too, had to authorize any purchases or sales within the portfolio. And she would never gamble. Not Annie. Not with Sylvie's money. Aaron sighed. If he could pull this off, Sylvie would be taken care of, and he'd be set. He deserved this chance. He'd been kissing Cushman's ass for years, and now it was about to pay off big. Why should Annie stand in his way now? Why should he be punished? She'd gotten hers in the divorce settlement, and now it was his turn. If he hadn't had to pay off Annie, he would have used that money to ax Jerry long ago.

He thought for just a moment, about the weekend in Boston. He should never have slept with her. It had been a mistake. But she'd looked so sweet and the movie for Alex had been so great, and it had seemed so pleasant, so easy. Too bad Annie had misunderstood. Since that day at the Carlyle he'd been out of touch with Annie. He certainly couldn't call her about this.

He stood by the phone and thought for a moment, the pressure of the confrontation with La Doll building up. There *had* to be a way. He could call Gil Griffin. He was certain that Gil could put through a trade. Federated Funds handled their accounts, and though he normally traded through his small-time broker there, he knew John Reamer was a stickler with this sort of thing. But if the trade came down through Gil . . .

Aaron shrugged. He knew Gil well enough. It was a favor, but just a small one. And it would humiliate him to have to call back Morty to tell him that he couldn't do it because his ex-wife said no. After the trade he'd explain it to Annie and leave extra in the fund. It was a one-shot deal.

He lifted the phone and dialed 411. "Operator, get me the number of Federated Funds Douglas Witter. Executive Offices, please."

3

Masters of the Universe

T he few rays of late-afternoon sun that managed to penetrate the two-hundred-year-old glass of the boardroom windows fell across Gil Griffin's face as he sat alone at the head of the huge table. He was not a handsome man, he knew: his neck was too long and his head was too small. With his hair slicked back in the approved Wall Street shark coif and his patrician but beaklike nose, he had something of the sleek look of an egret. Yet he also knew he was undeniably attractive. And to those who found power erotic, he was irresistible.

For a man over fifty, he was in good, even great, shape. His relentless competitiveness had him on the squash court every day, where he almost invariably decimated the competition. He was territorial to such a degree that he felt personally offended when a player moved onto the court to begin the game. He always won. And if the victories were one part skill, one part intimidation, and one part his younger partners' fear of the repercussions their wins might have, so be it. Winning and having were what it was about, and Gil smiled at the thought of the Hobson's choice he presented to his squash opponents.

He felt powerful, and he knew he *was* powerful. The Cushman offering had flown well, and he was ready now to make an extra hiccup out of it, although he'd wait until October. After his little flirtation with Asa Ewell, he was sure he could use the kid creatively in the future. Bill Atchison, the empty suit, was on line, rubber-stamping whatever he wanted. Gil had needed someone at Cromwell Reed to bend, and Bill bent over backward. The Morty the Madman offering had been a bit dicey, but the name recognition made it a natural. The little people bought it up. And with a Cromwell Reed seal of approval, so did the big boys. He could well afford to throw a bone to Bill, fool though he was.

Now he impatiently waited for Mary, his wife. He had surprised himself and Mrs. Rodgers, his secretary of more than a decade, by arranging this meeting, since his calendar, as always, was already filled with meticulously scheduled meetings and appointments. That, however, was a perk of power, and he had both Mrs. Rodgers and a personal computer committed to nothing but arranging and rearranging his time. Gil Griffin could do anything he wanted, and he wanted to see Mary *now*.

Watching her earlier, during the two-thirty meeting, at which she conquered the twits from Smith Barney, his dick had swollen in direct proportion to his pride in her. He also had her working on the Japanese takeover, and while it was difficult and risky, he let her manage it. He had taught her a great deal, and she was an apt pupil. Plus she was brilliant. An incredible turn-on. He knew he had to have her. Soon. Before the end of the day. Now.

There was an incredible eroticism in working with Mary in their mentor-protégée role. Their work was demanding, and serious. Mary looked the part, dressed conservatively, wore her blond hair in a neat chignon. That was her very allure. As she led the meeting and pointed out both the flaws and merits of each of her team's comments, she was all business, all power, masculine power. Everyone could see that. But only Gil could see her naked, only he knew the noise she made, deep in her throat, when he brought her to orgasm. Only he knew how it felt to possess her.

At the stroke of four-thirty, as the Queen Anne grandfather clock that had belonged to the Swann family for generations chimed once, Mary entered. She walked without the slightest girlish hip movement, projecting an almost tangible confidence. Everything about her was direct, the model of brisk efficiency. And yet, in the few seconds it took her to see his expression and close the door behind her, he watched her transform herself from business prodigy to welcoming vessel. The narrowing of her eyes, the slight bending of a knee, a shift in her hips—subtle adjustments, but to him they were clear, unmistakable. Gil watched silently, unmoving, his eyes gleaming. She was incredibly intuitive, and it benefited him in business as well as in bed. But of course there was no bed here.

Mary put her attaché case down at the end of the mahogany table and walked toward Gil, slipping out of the jacket of her suit as she approached, running her tongue over her already glossy lips. She was broad shouldered with a narrow waist, and now that contrast was emphasized by her plain white silk blouse and dark skirt. She walked to him, and he placed his hands around her waist, his long fingers almost meeting. Without speaking, she began to unbutton her blouse, revealing a pink satin *bustier* that lifted her small breasts high. Their smallness was her one imperfection, but now they were presented to him beautifully, plums on a plate.

Yearning, tight to the point of discomfort, Gil absorbed the white glow of her beauty.

She was a porcelain doll whose pink lips, nipples, and

sex studded her creamy blondness like forbidden candies. He could never get over the contradictions of her. She was tough as a man, independent, yet she was dominated so completely by him. As always, she knew what he wanted just by looking into his eyes.

She knelt, unzipped him, and swallowed his cock whole, just as Gil's lust reached the very moment where ache and pleasure meet. He was rough with her, but she liked it that way. They both liked it that way. It was part of the turn-on. And the sight of her there, kneeling on the boardroom floor, her rosebud mouth crammed full of his dick, the sight was as good as the feel of it. And that was another part of the turn-on. The thrill of fucking her in places where the danger of discovery was ever-present, that was the ultimate turn-on. He had put it to her in the backseat of their limo, in other people's bedrooms during society parties, and on beaches around the world. The first time he had taken her in the bathroom of his corporate jet, initiating her into a sexual relationship with him and the "mile high" club with one thrust. Whispers and scandal had always surrounded their relationship, and that was a turn-on, too. Gil wanted all men to envy, as well as fear, him.

Mary's lips had performed their magic. She now rose as he put his hands around her waist again, lifting her up to the boardroom table, hiking her skirt up over her hips. Gil looked at her long legs, encased in black stockings. He had banished her panty hose long ago, and now she wore a black, lacy garter belt. As he watched, she climbed onto the boardroom table, positioning herself on her hands and knees, turning so that she faced the Swann grandfather clock, her delicious ass pink naked in front of Gil. He stood up. Mary looked over her shoulder, once again licking her lips with her pink tongue. Gil reached out, his hands grabbing the soft mounds of her buttocks as he found his place inside her welcoming flesh. He clutched her tightly, almost viciously. All of Gil's feelings crystallized here, in the cockpit of control, the boardroom of the most powerful firm on the Street, in the most powerful country on earth. He leaned forward over her back.

"You want it?" His voice was hoarse. It was the first time either of them had spoken.

"Yes, oh, yes."

"Right here, on the table? The table we meet at with Jamison, and McMurdo, and the board members?"

Mary groaned. "Yes, Gil, I want it."

"And is it good?"

"Yes."

"Yes, what?"

"Yes, Gil. It's very good." Her knees were slipping against the glossy surface of the tabletop, so he pulled her back onto his cock and pinioned her, clutching her thighs with his strong hands. He rocked into her until she moaned. Then he stopped for a moment and covered her mouth with one hand, gently, yet firmly.

"No noise," he warned her. With the other hand he picked up the remote control. "Do you know what I'm going to do now?" he asked. Mutely she shook her head. "I'm going to ring for security, and in three minutes the guards will be in here." Mary moaned again and he pressed into her. She braced herself against her arms to accommodate his brutal thrusts. Not bad for a fifty-year-old man, he thought, his breathing only slightly labored.

"They'll knock on the door in a minute," he told her. "They'll come in and see me fucking you like this."

She came then, as he knew she would, arching her back to meet Gil's frantic strokes, squeezing him tightly on the downswing, releasing up, squeezing down again. Gil shuddered and groaned as he came inside her. Then he pressed the remote to cancel the security call.

Whenever Gil compared his two wives, there was no contest. In every way, Mary always took first prize. Where Cynthia had been repressed (God, in all their years of marriage, she had never once given him head!), Mary was uninhibited. Whereas Cynthia knew nothing about business, Mary was at the top of the class. He never felt alone when Mary was with him. And while Cynthia was disgustingly domestic, Mary understood all his needs. She knew how he felt about his Jaguar XKE. She even enjoyed his preoccupation with it. And you would never hear Mary whine about children. She realized Gil was her baby, and that he was entitled to all her attention.

Mary slipped out from under him and slid off the table, then wordlessly smoothed down her skirt and buttoned up her disheveled blouse. "You are wonderful," was all she said.

Gil smiled to himself as he watched Mary rearrange her clothes, concealing herself from all the others. He felt a moment of jealous rage at any other man who might ever have possessed her. He wanted to be her one and only, now and forever. It was adolescent, even primal, he knew, but it was undeniable. It amazed him how strongly the feeling came: he had not felt this way in years, not since the early days with Cynthia. But he had actually felt that once for Cynthia, he remembered with a chill. Back in the days when he respected her, when he feared and respected her family, the Swanns and the Witters. But the feeling had passed, dead so long ago. Would this feeling for Mary pass, too?

Seeing the shadow cross his face, Mary ran her fingers lightly over Gil's temples and gave him the smile of adoration that she reserved exclusively for him. Gil felt both the fear and anger subside.

Now Mary was before him, dressed. It was hard to believe

this woman, the one he had just taken on the table, was going to help him with the biggest coup of his career. Together they would find the perfect Japanese company for takeover. And it wouldn't be just the money he would make. It would be knowing, and having all of Wall Street know, that he, Gil Griffin, had turned the tables on the little yellow bastards who had begun to poach on his territory. How he despised other races. It was his natural, rightful heritage to rule, and it offended him, even shocked him, to see blacks or Hispanics or Asians in superior positions. Or—worse yet—involved with white women. He knew, in this respect, he was like many men of his class.

All the wrongs would be righted by this deal. "How about Mitsui Shipping?" he asked Mary. She smiled.

"Well, we've planted the . . ." She paused, searching for *le mot juste*. "Disinformation," she finished.

"Well, that should cause some surprises." Gil smiled slyly. There were leaks even in his carefully controlled organization. And Gil hated leaks. It enabled others to ride his wave, the wave he worked so hard to create. But no one else would ride *this* wave. And maybe *then* he'd even plug the leak, though now it would be useful. The market had to be played like a great actor plays an audience. It had to be manipulated with all available tools: by leaking information, truth or lies, and controlling rumors. Or even starting them.

"And what's our real target?" he asked.

"Too soon to tell, but Dotsoi or Maibeibi look good."

Gil pursed his lips. It was possible. And if it was, no one would do their homework and fine-tooth-comb the numbers as Mary would. But now Mary frowned.

"Gil, you've got to do something about Stuart Swann. I can't stand having him around. He gives me the creeps when I catch the way he looks at me sometimes."

Gil nodded. "Don't worry about Stuart. I'll take care of him."

Then Mary took something from her attaché case. "And Gil, I got another envelope."

Gil sighed and held out his hand. These anonymous notes were nothing. Successful, wealthy, good-looking people were always targets. He had explained that to Mary. Her one character flaw was her concern with her public image, with what people thought. She'd ridden the scandal of their corporate romance to national prominence, but since then she seemed disconcerted by the bad press that followed their marriage. Gil felt she should rise above that kind of concern. Instead, she'd stopped giving speeches at professional women's organizations and was concentrating more on social networking.

She handed him the interoffice mail envelope. Gil opened it and pulled out a clipping from *People* or one of those rags. It featured a somber picture of Elise Atchison, Bill's soon-to-be-ex-wife. Bill seemed completely besotted with the Van Gelder girl. Ridiculous, really. The man was obsessed. Gil would never let himself feel that for any woman, even Mary. He looked down at the page. The caption below Elise's photo read: *The elusive Elise Elliot leaving a friend's funeral.* Scrawled across it were the words: *Ask your husband whose funeral it was. Ask him why the friend is dead.*

Gil looked directly into Mary's blue eyes. She's waiting for my reaction, he thought. But there was none. Gil felt neither guilt nor remorse over Cynthia, and certainly he felt no responsibility for her suicide. That was her choice. The choice of a jellyfish. Contemptible. It came as no surprise to Gil, who knew all of her weaknesses intimately. She had always been the first to give in, often without even a struggle.

"We've been through it all before, Mary."

"I know. But it makes me so uncomfortable . . . someone in the firm sending this stuff."

"Oh, for God's sake. It's nonsense. Go on, we have a lot more important things to do. But if you'll feel better, I'll have security look into it."

Looking back at the photo of Elise again, he hoped, for Bill's sake, that she would show more character in the face of adversity than Cynthia had. He put his arm around Mary's shoulders, and together they walked out of the boardroom to their next appointments.

At their backs, the Swann clock chimed the hour.

4

Some Suit!

Brenda wandered through the decorated rooms of furniture in Bloomingdale's, trying to keep her mind off food and the meeting this afternoon with Morty and his lawyer. She used to shop till she dropped, distracting herself from the emptiness of her marriage, but she couldn't afford that anymore. And she'd already bought something today, a sweater for Angie, which would give her a good excuse to drop by and see her daughter, who was about to return to school after her internship. Now, she could only look. And pretend.

Annie had offered to come with her today knowing how anxious Brenda was, but Brenda had declined. She would have liked the support, but she was too frightened about the things that might be said. Morty was sure to make a scene. And he might even bring up her father's imprisonment. If this was going to get dirty, and chances were it might, best not to expose Annie. Unlike Elise and Annie, she hadn't grown up in a chintz-ruffled country home where feelings were never expressed, let alone at the top of the lungs.

Coming upon a particularly lovely display room done like an English manor house bedroom, Brenda checked the price tags on each item and suddenly smiled to herself. Nothing like Romano's Furniture Store in the Bronx, she thought. There, where her mother and her aunts bought their furniture, everything was sold in sets, bedroom sets, living room sets, dining room sets. Her aunt Sally had called them "suites," but then, she *had* gone to Hunter College for a year.

Now, looking at the Bloomingdale's price tags, Brenda remembered when she and Morty were first married and living in the semi-attached house her father bought her off Arthur Avenue in the Bronx. Her favorite aunt, Rose, her father's sister, had taken her to Romano's. Aunt Rose waddled her way past the salesman to the manager's office in the back, greeting him like long-lost family, which he probably was.

"Anything she wants, Sonny. The best," Aunt Rose had said. Brenda knew exactly what bedroom set she wanted, the one displayed on the raised platform in the center of the store. She had, in fact, picked it long before she and Morty got engaged. She was so excited about her home, her first home. She pored through magazines and agonized over color schemes and swatches.

But weeks later, when the matching off-white and gold furniture arrived, it was a disappointment. It didn't look like the pictures in the magazines. Something was wrong, but Brenda didn't know what. In the magazines, she noticed, things weren't in sets. But where did you get the stuff that they showed in those beautiful pictures? Disappointed, she decided that the right sheets might do it. Armed with an ad from a bride's magazine, she went to Bloomingdale's for the first time and found her way to the linen department. The set of Porthault sheets for her wedding bed had cost almost as much as the bed itself, but Brenda felt delicious as she carried them home. Her dad her given her plenty of money. For the first time she felt that not only had she spent a lot of money but also, at last, had got quality. She was so proud, she showed them to Morty.

Morty had almost swallowed his cigar when he found out how much the sheets had cost. "Are you fucking crazy? You spent that kind of money for bedsheets that no one will ever see? No way, take them back."

She should have known. What else could she expect from Morty, who had his shirts custom-made, but bought his underwear cheap at Job Lot? Cheap underwear because "nobody sees them but you, baby." Ha ha.

Right. Cheap was good enough because it was only for her. Brenda had gritted her teeth to hold back the anger. But she never forgot that lesson, nor the pain of returning the sheets. For the rest of their married life, she had decided, she would never again tell him the true cost of anything she had bought. And she never did.

Fruit of the Loom irregulars might be good enough for him, but not for her. And not for her kids. So the struggle began. And continues, she observed wryly to herself. Morty had paid Angie's tuition, but instead of letting her go to Europe for the summer, he'd gotten her a job at that Park Avenue law firm. Cheap bastard. Well, she'd keep fighting him. She better get her fat ass over to Leo Gilman's office. Today she and Diana were meeting with him and Morty to try to adjust her settlement.

Morty stepped off the elevator at the forty-ninth floor of his lawyer's office building on Central Park South. He stood, damp from the rain, the end-of-August heat, and his own nervous sweat, facing the receptionist. He shrugged his suit jacket up snugly on his shoulders, giving himself a moment to control his nervousness, and walked to her desk. The receptionist sat in front of a window wall that, on a clear day, offered an unparalleled view of Central Park. They pay through the nose for that, Morty thought, and then corrected himself. I pay for it, he realized angrily. And because of today's misting rain, the window was only a gray phosphorescent backdrop, despite the trees, lake, and lawns in the park below. Views! Christ, he wondered at what people paid for. Well, he paid plenty for Leo Gilman, the rat bastid, and even so, it wasn't Park Avenue prices. Plus, he watched those hours. Leo better not bury him with them, not at a hundred and seventy-five bucks per. Bet Bill Atchison, that stiff, got two hundred or more.

At the thought of Bill Atchison, he turned away bitterly from the grayed glass. He and Gil still hadn't cut him in on any other deals. Hadn't even given him a nibble. You work your whole life, you build nothing into something, and then all those weaseling accountants and lawyers and brokers and *momzers* in general took their cuts, leaving you bleeding. He didn't trust one of them. He smiled. He'd put it over on them. His money was safe in Switzerland. He just wished he could get in on another big deal, a Gil Griffin kind of deal. Those two, Bill and Gil, had made almost as much from his offering as he had. And that should count as dues, but he still wasn't in the club. Like the time he called Gil about the Nabisco deal. "Too late, Morty. Everything's committed." Morty almost smiled to himself, remembering the conversation he had overheard between Gil and the guy at the *Wall Street Journal*. Gil wouldn't even cut Morty in on *that* deal, so Morty would cut himself in. I can play their game, he thought.

Now Leo had better not fuck him. He'd handled the divorce real well, Morty had to hand that to him. Of course, Morty had known that Brenda wouldn't want to go to trial. She got hives just passing a cop car. But what was this new business? Brenda wanting to reopen discussions on her settlement? And she got herself a lawyer? Sure, she was greedy like all the other maggots.

It had been easy to keep most of the financials from her.

But he couldn't keep the public offering a secret. Still, he'd put it over on her. It wasn't that she wasn't smart: she was. It was just that he was cagey and had been preparing for the move for a long, long time. His accountant had been the one who had first given Morty the idea of going public. Of course, Morty never gave his accountant credit, just like he never gave Brenda any. And he didn't give her anything else either. Just the lousy, cheesy co-op, in return for which she had signed over all her shares. So if she wanted something more now, it was just too goddamn bad. She could forget about it. I don't care how good this La Gravenesse dame is supposed to be.

"Mr. Cushman?" a secretary asked. Morty nodded. "Mr. Gilman will see you now."

As he followed the secretary down the hall to Leo Gilman's office, Mort began picking nervously at the seat of his pants. His underwear always crawled up his crack. Brenda hated that habit, he remembered suddenly, and stopped. He wondered if Brenda and her new lawyer had yet arrived. He began to feel the rush of adrenaline that always came when he geared up for a fight over money.

Since Leo's call on Monday arranging this meeting, Morty had gone over and over in his mind the terms of the divorce settlement with Brenda. No matter how many times he considered it, he still believed that he'd done just fine by the fat bitch. She couldn't deny that she was better off for having married him. And lucky. After all, he was Morty the Madman. He'd done that. So maybe her father, that little Mafia wop, had helped at first, but it had been his sweat that made it work. Brenda had done well enough. After all, she had maybe been a beauty, but she'd never been thin.

He and the secretary walked to the glass door in the glass-brick walls. The place was trendy. More of my money, Morty thought. Maybe Shelby can sell them something for their walls. It shouldn't be a total loss. When he walked into the office, Leo got up from behind the glass-topped table that served as his desk and came, smiling, toward Morty, his hand outstretched. Morty was never so aware of how unlike himself Leo was as now. Salt-and-pepper hair fastidiously cut at La Coupe, Giorgio Armani suit, handmade Italian shoes. He's going to cost me a bundle, but it's cheaper to pay him to blow Brenda off than it would be to give her more money, Morty figured.

"Morty, good to see you. You're looking great. You've been working out?"

"Hey, Leo, don't grease me up before you stick it in. What does Brenda want? How much is it going to cost me to get rid of her? And who is this La Gravenesse lawyer? What are we dealing with here?"

Leo did what he did best and began reassuring Morty.

"It's taken care of, Mort, I promise you. The agreement is airtight, not to worry about a thing. I'll take care of La Gravenesse, you just sit tight."

"Yeah, that's what they told Donald Trump. I paid you plenty, Leo. I thought this was over."

"Look, Morty, anyone with twenty-five bucks and a resentment can file a suit. We expected this. Your ex-wife saw the offering, she got mad, she got greedy, she found a greedy lawyer."

"Aren't they all?"

"Hey, Mort, I may have cost you, but I saved you plenty. Right?"

Morty reluctantly nodded. "Just make sure the deal holds."

"We'll hang tough while her lawyer makes noises and sees we mean business. You say Brenda doesn't like courts. And she's got no bucks for fees. They'll back down." Leo patted Morty's shoulder. "And Mort"—he paused—"no scenes, okay? Whatever she says, just stay cool. It's all talk."

Morty nodded.

"So let's go. They're waiting for us."

Morty and Leo walked across the hall to a conference room. Brenda and the woman lawyer—a big woman lawyer, Morty noticed immediately—sat together on a sofa at the far side of the smooth lacquer table placed in the center of the room. Morty gave Diana a quick look, trying to size her up. Their eyes met for a moment and Morty felt a brief chill run down his spine. He shrugged it off as Leo greeted them. Morty just grunted and sat down. He stretched his legs out, crossed them at the ankles, and lit a cigar. Finally, he looked over at Brenda, seeing her through the haze of smoke.

She sat on the sofa, her legs pushed apart by the fat on her thighs, both hands clutching her pocketbook on her lap. Her eyebrows were slightly raised, and Morty could see a glistening of moisture on her upper lip. Twenty-one years of marriage was enough to tell him she was nervous. Good. That's how he liked her. But there was something else there he couldn't quite put his finger on. Something new. The same subtle unreadable energy he caught on Diana's face. She has too much, that's what wrong with her, he thought. Never enough.

"You cheap fuck," he heard her growl, startling him. So this is how it's going to be, he thought. Pick up right where we left off?

Brenda had dropped her purse. Seeing Morty sitting there, smoking his goddamn eighteen-dollar cigar and acting like a *shtarker* while Angela had sweated all summer long, was too much. Who the fuck does he think he is? Well, he wasn't. Brenda thought she'd been angry before. Forget about it. Just thinking about it now made her want to kill him with her bare hands.

"So, how many boxes of cigars did you buy this month while your daughter was working for four bucks an hour?" Brenda spat.

Turning to Diana, she continued, as if for the first time, "He always had more money than he knew what to do with, but he wanted to take Angela and Anthony out of private school to save money. That's the year he wanted to buy a boat instead."

"That public school on Madison Avenue was only two blocks from our apartment. It was good enough for those UN chinks and Arabs. Why shouldn't it be good enough for two Jewish wops? You went to Julia Richman High School for chrissake." Morty always knew how to hurt Brenda most—through the kids. They were always the last ammunition he would use, but he would use them if necessary.

"Because I *had* to, not because I *wanted* to. Our kids didn't have to so why should they? Because *you* grew up with nothing? Because my parents didn't know any better? It's good enough? Well, it's not. Not for our kids, not for mine."

Leo Gilman gave Morty a look. "Okay, folks, let's all take a deep breath and start again." The shit, thought Brenda. He's the one who helped Morty screw me the first time. Well, never again. She looked at the two self-satisfied men. She hated them. She hated all of them. Her anger felt good, empowering. And Diana would get them. She just knew it.

Diana leaned slightly forward, giving Brenda's knee a single calming pat, and said directly to Leo Gilman, "We're here because my client would like her financial needs and those of your client's children reassessed. In light of the huge windfall Mr. Cushman received when his company went public so soon after the settlement was signed, we would like you and your client to put aside that agreement and offer a more equitable distribution."

Morty snorted. "If it were equitable, she'd get nothing. She's worth nothing."

"If settlements were based on worth, Mr. Cushman, you'd be bankrupt."

"Who the fuck do you think you are?" Morty shouted at Diana, his face flushed with rage.

Good, Brenda thought, Let *him* get nuts. I hope he has a stroke. Does little Shelby remind you to take your pressure pills?

Leo Gilman quieted Mort down again, then coldly turned to Diana. "Ms. La Gravenesse, the settlement agreement was duly signed and notarized, and subsequently entered into the judge's divorce decision. That was more than three years ago," he said. "There is nothing you can do about it. It's a legal document, carrying with it the full force of the law." Morty watched Leo snap his Bijan shirt cuffs forward, first one, then the other, as if making exclamation points at the end of his statement. Morty enjoyed that gesture. It looked like Gilman was earning his money, he thought. Maybe we've got this one nailed shut.

But Diana continued without missing a beat. "Hardly. Mr. Gilman," she continued in her deep, soft voice, "it's our contention that Mrs. Cushman's legal representation might be in conflict of interest. As I understand it, you represented Mr. Cushman in the divorce, and my client, at *your* suggestion, was represented by a young man just out of law school, who *you* had engaged for her, a Mr. Barry Marlowe. Now we find that he also became an associate of *your* firm only a few months after the divorce decree. We think these facts may change the perspective of the settlement."

Leo Gilman licked his lips.

"Balls!" Morty shouted. "A deal's a deal." Diana smiled at him.

Leo Gilman straightened up in his chair. "Let me handle this, Morty.

"Ms. La Gravenesse, I don't like your innuendo. This firm has a spotless reputation, and you should know better than to make baseless accusations. Anyway, the burden of proof is on you. One thing has nothing to do with the other. Mrs. Cushman acted on her own free will as an informed adult. *She* retained him, and then came to an agreement with benefit of counsel. We subsequently hired Mr. Marlowe because we were impressed with his work. It's too late to change her mind. It's unjust to try to take advantage of Mr. Cushman's success since the time of their divorce. It had nothing to do with her marriage. And we're prepared to enter a long, expensive court case in the interest of justice. As Mr. Cushman so aptly says, a deal is a deal."

"We are quite prepared to dispute that," Diana said. "We have information and proof that the business was established by Mrs. Cushman and her parents. That Mr. Cushman actually played a minor role."

Leo smiled. "Ms. La Gravenesse, the world knows Morty the Madman. He *is* the firm. I'd hate to see you spend your time and Mrs. Cushman's resources trying to prove otherwise."

Brenda's stomach lurched. She could feel a film of sweat developing on her upper lip and forehead. It was so unfair! She knew that Diana was bluffing on this shit—she and her father had kept no records, and she could prove nothing. If she sued, what would happen? How would Angela and Tony feel to see their grandfather's name in the papers again? Who didn't like and believe in Morty the Madman? The guy with the deal for you?

Diana took off her glasses and cocked her head. Then she sighed. Is she giving up? Brenda thought, panicking. Maybe it's too late now to do anything. God, why was I so stupid, so scared then? Why did I settle for so little, why did I sign that damn thing anyway? Her disappointment was so intense that she actually felt dizzy for a moment. I should have known not to get my hopes up, she told herself bitterly. And there was all that paperwork I did, rooting through our old receipts and the time I wasted with Diana. And now there would be her bill. Oh, Christ.

Diana remained silent, however. Then she reached her long arm across her flat chest and into the attaché case on the floor next to her chair, snapping the latches open and taking out a thick file, which she noisily smacked on the table. Morty recognized it immediately. His stomach lurched. The bold letters across the front read, "PHOTOCOPIES. Tax returns for Mr. and Mrs. Morton Cushman, tax years 1980, 1981, and 1982."

Morty blinked.

The implication was clear to everyone in the room. Leo and Morty locked eyes. "What the fuck is this?" Leo telegraphed to Morty, who looked for the moment like a wounded bull elephant, unsure whether to charge or die. This was clearly a mortal blow.

Before Morty recovered, Leo spoke directly to Diana. "Ms. La Gravenesse, I'd like to consult privately with my client. I may have been mistaken. Perhaps we do have the basis for a more up-to-date agreement."

"I can't believe it!" Brenda laughed again, her deep voice trembling as the Asian masseuse hit her flesh. Brenda heard Diana's deep-throated moan. She opened her eyes and smiled.

On the massage table next to her, Diana turned her head, looked at Brenda, and grinned back. Their eyes locked, and then together they shrieked with glee, like two kids who just found out they had a snow day. As the giggles died down, Brenda continued to look at Diana. With her glasses off and her hair mussed, she was surprised at how attractive Diana was. Not pretty exactly; more like handsome.

Brenda had found out more about Diana from Duarto. She was a crusader, a fighter. She'd worked for seven years as assistant DA in charge of sex crimes prosecution. After that burnout, she'd moved into her private practice and now only handled cases involving women's and children's rights. She had sued the city on behalf of a foster child placed in a home where the child was being molested and had won a settlement for her. She'd just defended a woman who'd murdered her abusive father and had gotten her off. Now she was working on another divorce where the husband had stolen his wife's idea and patented it under his own name. Brenda admired Diana's mixture of coolness, caring, and activism. But most of all, she admired how Diana handled Leo and Morty.

"We rattled their cage," Diana agreed.

"Rattled? Jesus! Leo Gilman nearly took a dump in his pants. His seven-hundred dollar pants. I couldn't believe that look he shot Morty. God, it was delicious. Hey, Diana, some suit!"

"Well, let's not eat out on it until the agreement is signed and the checks clear. You know what they say—'It ain't over till it's over.' Or isn't it, 'It ain't over till the fat lady sings'?" Diana continued. "Well, Brenda, we'll have you singing before too long."

Brenda, somewhat taken aback, paused to see if she was offended by the "fat lady" remark. But Diana was looking at her with such warmth that she knew in an instant Diana would never hurt her. After all, I *am* fat, she thought. She threw back her head and laughed.

It was a good idea to come here, to the Salon de Tokyo. It was an Asian massage house, a no-nonsense, no-frills place on West Fifty-seventh Street, where Brenda would sometimes stop on her way back from a visit with Angela, who had a tiny summer-sublet apartment on Fifty-third and Ninth Avenue.

The little Japanese woman who was working on Brenda grunted and climbed onto the massage table. Overhead was a pole suspended from the ceiling, which she clung to, monkeylike, as she began to walk on Brenda's back. Now it was Brenda who grunted.

Diana laughed. She had a nice laugh, Brenda thought, throaty and warm. "Well, if anyone was going to walk all over you today, thank God it was a woman," Diana said.

"No, thank *you*, Diana," Brenda parried. "Are you sure he'll sign the agreement? Two checks, a million each? One now, one before Thanksgiving?"

"There are no guarantees, but I think he will. We got them on the run. It was a dirty trick, but an effective one. Let the IRS be your enforcer if he doesn't come through. I'll draw up the papers and get them over to him tomorrow, before he changes his mind." She paused. "You know, Brenda, we could have gotten more. A lot more. I'm certain of it."

"Maybe. But a bird in the hand, you know. And I've never been a vulture. Two million bucks, tax free, and some stock is all that I'll ever need. And my kids don't need more, either. I might be a cow, but I'm not a pig." She laughed. "Two million dollars! I can't believe it. It's like winning Lotto. I feel good!"

Diana smiled across at her. "I'd feel better if this woman would get off my back," she said, wincing. "To show your true appreciation, how about telling her to stop?"

"Only if I can take you out for dinner."

"It's a deal."

Brenda motioned for the masseuses to finish, which they did. Then, bowing, they quietly left the room. Diana sat up, and the towel fell from her. Before she picked it up, Brenda saw that Diana's chest was almost as flat as a boy's, her shoulders as broad. Goodness, she's as handsome as a man, Brenda thought. Then she blushed and turned away. How odd, she thought. How very odd.

5

The Frog Pond

Elise was showing a hell of a lot of character. "It's outrageous!" she said as she stared at the column Brenda had torn from the *Post*. "How can a man announce his engagement when he is still legally married?" she asked, more exasperated than upset. Two decades of respectability and discretion, of living well but unostentatiously, of practicing noblesse oblige and trying to be appropriate, were now being blown away by her future former husband, who was making a fool of them both. She wouldn't just *stop* him personally from handling her business, she was going to pull it out of Cromwell Reed altogether, even though they'd been handling her family since her grandfather's time. That ought to put Bill in bad odor with his partners. And maybe that would hurry the divorce as well.

"It must be male menopause," she said. "Otherwise, how could he say it?"

"Well, *he* didn't exactly," Brenda pointed out. "It says there that *Phoebe* announced that it would be announced, which is different, I think, isn't it, Annie?"

Annie would have smiled, but her concern for Elise prevented her. "Well," she admitted, "it's not the form they taught at Miss Porter's."

"She was probably stoned—Duarto says she's usually flying."

Elise seemed not to hear. "Bill knows I have a horror of the tabloids. Next the *Enquirer* will headline how Phoebe is having my baby by Elvis." Then she smiled in spite of herself. "Well, as a lawyer, he has to realize that this is not the smartest move toward a financial settlement. Not to mention that it is in the worst possible taste." Elise thought of her mother. Those words were her mother's harshest criticism. Small blessing, Elise thought, but at least Mother, wrapped in her cocoon of Alzheimer's, won't know about this.

"By the way, I saw your picture in *People*, Elise," Brenda said. "You looked pretty good, considering." Brenda pulled out another clipping.

Elise stared at the photo, then shuddered to herself. She was rarely in the news, her press agent saw to that. This picture wasn't authorized. She read the credit. Larry Cochran. My God. She remembered Room 705. What other pictures had he taken?

"You look good, considering," Brenda repeated.

"Considering what?" Elise said, a bit defensively.

"Considering you just came from a funeral, Elise," Brenda snapped back.

Elise caught herself and smiled back. "Of course. I guess publicity just upsets me."

"So, speaking of taste, let's have lunch," Brenda suggested brightly. If Elise feared the papers, Brenda was at least as frightened of the courts. And Diana La Gravenesse still hadn't gotten the signed agreements or the first of the checks from Morty. She hoped nothing would go wrong. She was counting on that money now. She'd be independent at last. The whole thing made her ravenous.

Today they had met at La Grenouille, the only place
Brenda knew of where the food was as good as the flowers.
And for a $36.50 prix fixe lunch she could have almost any-
thing she wanted. She'd been worried about that. Until things
were straightened out with Morty, she couldn't afford to blow
a hundred bucks for lunch. The big menu cheered her up.
Here they were, the three of them, set in the middle of the
choicest frog pond in the city.

Brenda enjoyed baiting Elise, and she always enjoyed
Annie. Even if nothing came of this, if they got no justice for
Cynthia, it was pleasant to have a reason to get dressed up and
eat out. Of course, Brenda was happy just staying involved
with her children. In fact, she'd called Anthony only this
morning, offering to come up to his school and pick up his
laundry. It was no trouble. But Tony said no. He was at that
age now when parents embarrassed him. Brenda still longed to
spend time with him. She liked to clean, and it kept her mind
off food for a while. She didn't know how Annie was coping,
being separated from Sylvie, and with both her boys so busy
with their own lives.

She was worried about Annie. Since Sylvie had left, Annie
was down, real down. It was that bastard Aaron.

For Brenda, her children were everything. Unlike Annie,
Brenda wasn't busy with the Special Olympics Committee or
volunteering at Beckstein Burn Center. She had never been a
real part of the social world, never wanted to be, but she was
enjoying the look she was getting at it now. Secretly, Brenda
devoured the columns, and she loved society gossip. She'd die,
however, before admitting it. And when Morty had tried to
push into this world, Brenda had dug in her heels. She knew
the picture they would paint. Unattractive parvenus trying for
the big time. *Feh!* Well, at least she knew her limitations.

Annie was real class, and Elise, she had to admit, was real class *and* big-time bucks. She wondered whether Elise followed the columns.

"I think what we should do," Elise was saying, "is prepare a brief, a sort of report on Gil and each of the others. Include their work life, and their social life. And the trophies, of course. And then, after we know them better, we'll be able to spot their vulnerabilities.

"What we need is a dossier. Anything and everything. The stuff from *Advertising Age,* or the *American Bar Association Journal,* their high school yearbook or whatever. Their horoscope sign. Their favorite color. Their stockbroker, banker, tailor. How they take their coffee."

"Sure, you know," Brenda continued, "dental records, scars, tattoos, favorite sex positions, worst nightmare." She paused. "My ambition is to be Mort's worst nightmare."

"That's what I want to hear," Elise said, nodding her approval.

"Except I can't. I still haven't gotten my money from him, so I'm skating on thin ice," Brenda said.

She saw Elise's face tighten. Brenda knew that like other Greenwich WASPs, Elise got icy when she was angry, and she was angry now. She stared coldly down at her. "Don't be a pussy, Brenda," Elise said, echoing Brenda's own taunt at Annie.

Brenda felt stung by the barb. I'm fighting to stay alive and this rich bitch calls me a *pussy?*

Brenda felt her skin grow hot as she leaned forward, her face very close to Elise's. "What the fuck do you know about being a woman at the mercy of a man, fighting for her survival? Everything you have has been handed to you. You've never had to kiss a man's ass to make sure you got the maintenance paid so you can look the president of the co-op in the eye in the elevator, or try to figure out if you can afford a thirty-six-dollar lunch because your alimony check might be late again. Do you know how I have to degrade myself with Morty—month after month—because I have no control over *anything*? You don't, Elise, and you never will."

Brenda's anger came quickly. She realized that even though she was trying to control her voice, she was beginning to attract the attention of some nearby diners. But Brenda didn't give a shit.

Annie leaned forward and said, "It hasn't been easy for Elise, either, Brenda."

Brenda looked over at her and said, "Not now, Annie. Don't do 'good girl' now."

"I can take care of myself, Annie. Besides, Brenda has a point," Elise said, and turned her attention back to Brenda.

Brenda continued, her voice now more subdued, "Do you know what I think, Elise? I think this is just a game to you. Something to do until you get over losing your man. Something to do instead of going to the south of fucking France, or taking a three-month tour around the world on your fucking yacht. It's like another toy. Well, I'm fighting for my life here, little Miss Rich Spoiled Brat. This isn't a game." Brenda took a quick gulp of water from the stemmed goblet. She put it down and looked at Elise, squinting her eyes just the way her father used to. "So don't 'pussy' me. When *you're* willing to lay everything *you* own on the line, *then* you can criticize me. But until then, keep your righteousness to yourself."

Elise continued to look directly at Brenda. Brenda saw something in Elise's eyes, something she hadn't really noticed before. "I'm sorry, Brenda," Elise finally said, speaking slowly. "I was thoughtless and insensitive. You *are* right, you know. I don't know what it's like to be at the mercy of a man for my financial security." Elise blinked her eyes quickly, lifted her head, and said, "Please forgive me, Brenda. I should have thought."

Brenda, surprised, leaned back in her chair, her breath coming slower. "Sure. Yeah, it's okay, Elise." Brenda instantly regretted her outburst. "I shouldn't have been so hard on you."

"But I *do* know what it's like to depend on a man for *emotional* security. To depend on a man for anything is degrading, it appears." Elise smiled. "So that's that. We don't do anything about Morty until after he settles with Brenda. Agreed, ladies?"

Annie smiled back at the two women and nodded. Somehow, when they had decided to get together, she hadn't quite foreseen this. In fact, she realized uncomfortably, the whole thing seemed to be getting beyond her control. And her years with Dr. Rosen had taught Annie she was nothing if not a control freak.

Annie shook her head, as if to dislodge something in it. Thinking of Aaron and Dr. Rosen was a dangerous business. She kept herself busy, but at night, alone in the apartment, he was there in her thoughts. He had been so funny, so witty. He had made her laugh. And he had understood her, gotten her own mild jokes, admired her wit. At least at one time he had. No one had really known her since.

"Well, what are we looking for?" she asked now.

"I don't think we'll know yet. I mean, in general, we're looking for the chinks in their armor, aren't we?" Elise asked.

"The soft white underbelly," Brenda added, patting her own.

Elise pursed her lips. "For Gil, it's obvious. I say we move on two fronts: we find out who his next takeover target is and screw that up, and also see how he's been a bad boy on past offerings or takeovers. Involve the SEC, and if we can mole into his personal finances, maybe the IRS. I don't think that we can do much with the police—I mean, that note from Cynthia proves it *was* a suicide. But socially we may have something. The new wife, what's her name?" She consulted her notes.

"Birmingham. Mary Birmingham," Brenda prompted.

"Yes. Well, she wants a new apartment on Fifth. Lally is on that board. Maybe we can keep them out of the building. And I think we can blackball her from any social function that matters."

"I can get all the old stuff I have on Morty's company. I used to save it all. Maybe there will be something there," Brenda offered.

"Great. And Annie, didn't you say you were dining with Stuart Swann?"

"Well, he invited me out," she answered, blushing slightly.

Brenda noticed the blush and wondered. Is Annie feeling guilty because she has a date and we don't?

"Good," Elise said. "Pump him. Let's find out who Gil is about to gobble up next." Annie nodded reluctantly. "Maybe I'll talk to my uncle Bob about Gil, too," Elise said. "He might help." She looked at her notebook again.

"Now, Bill is more difficult. Of course, I've cut him off without a sou, and I'm pulling my business out of Cromwell Reed. But I think we might be able to do something with the Van Gelders."

"Break up their love nest?" Brenda asked.

"Break up the trust fund, more likely."

"Do you know she's a drug addict?" Brenda asked.

"So you say. That might be useful. How do you know?" Elise asked.

"We are not without resources." Brenda smiled imperiously.

"Maybe I could mention the problem to Dr. Girton on my

next visit. He's the Van Gelder family physician, too. I think it's my duty to help them help the girl, don't you? Could there be a Ford in her future—as in Betty's detox place? That ought to hold Bill and his 'fiancée' for the present. He's clean on taxes, and he has no friends to alienate, so that's him for now." She paused, flipping pages.

"Brenda," Elise continued, "your husband isn't un-impregnable. After your settlement goes through, let's have my boys go over those business papers and the entire offering. We might take down two birds with that stone. And you could sue him for more."

"No, Elise. Let me just get what he's promised. I don't want to screw up the deal." Brenda was getting nervous again.

Elise looked at her with understanding. "Well, of course not. No sense in cutting off your nose to spite your spouse. So we can't use the IRS either?"

"No." For once, even Brenda didn't make a joke.

"Well," Elise said cheerfully, crossing that off her list, "we can at least have him kept out of the Union League Club, and the Maidstone."

"Has he applied there?" Brenda asked incredulously.

"Apparently. The wife wants in."

"How do you know?"

"I'm not without resources." Elise smiled back at her airily. "They wouldn't have been accepted, anyway." She shrugged. "You know the attitudes there—NOKD . . . 'not our kind, dear.' We can also try to get his wife's new art gallery panned. We can make sure when they give a party nobody comes. And I understand she's applied to the Junior League." She looked over at Annie. Brenda knew that was the most exclusive women's club in New York. "She is not going to be accepted," Elise said. "Not a husband stealer." She paused and looked at

Annie. "Speaking of husband stealers, there's the good doctor's new husband. Shall we try to close down Aaron's agency?"

"No, Elise. That isn't fair," Annie said. "It would make his partner suffer. Jerry's a good guy." Annie couldn't add that she still didn't want to think of Aaron hurt.

"We're not playing fair," Elise reminded her. "They didn't."

"No. Nothing like that," Annie protested. "He's the father of my children, after all."

"A penis is no longer a passport to safety."

"Was it ever?"

"Well, perhaps we'll save Aaron for last," Elise said, snapping her book shut.

"Now, Miss Elliot," Brenda said, dimpling. "Did anyone ever tell you you're beautiful when you're angry?"

Elise smiled at Brenda. "No. Mostly they liked me passive. But those days are over, my friend. I'm changing." She looked around her at the elegant, tasteful room. "I don't want to roll over anymore. I want blood."

"Anger mutation," Brenda said, nodding. "Very common during nuclear holocaust or divorce."

"So, are we now Middle-Aged Mutant Ninja First Wives?" Annie asked.

"Cowabunga," Elise answered.

6

Dinner at Eight

The sun was setting on the glittering city, putting on a spectacular sky show, as Annie turned from John Finley Walk onto East Eighty-fourth Street and headed for her apartment building on Gracie Square. As she got into the elevator, she looked at her watch, realizing she'd lost track of time again. With Sylvie gone it was easy to do.

It was six. Only an hour till she was to meet Chris for drinks, then dinner with Stuart Swann at eight. She had cut it too close, but she always found it hard to leave the hospital. Hard to go to, hard to leave, she thought ruefully. Now she'd have to rush to get ready. But better to be rushed than nervous, she thought. I don't want to think about this date too much.

Annie hadn't dated since the separation. In fact, she'd rarely dated before her marriage. Serial monogamy was more her style. She'd met a nice Amherst boy when she was at Miss Porter's, and they had necked and written to one another. They'd managed to make love once, right in the living room of his parent's New York pied-à-terre, but it had still been a furtive affair. Then she had met Stuart on a weekend visit to Cynthia's home, and they had dated until she met Aaron. But they had never slept together. It had embarrassed her to tell Dr. Rosen how inexperienced she really was. And here she was, even more pathetic now, divorced and obviously incompetent at mating.

Well, she wouldn't consider this a date; it was simply a dinner between old friends. And if something came of it, well . . .

Men. There was something wrong with men Aaron's age. Something that she didn't think—something that she hoped—wouldn't eventually prove to be wrong with her sons.

Well, of course, the men of Aaron's generation had grown up with a set of different expectations: they expected both to dominate women and to be cared for by them. At least that was the example Aaron's father had set for him. Then the rules changed, but the men didn't. Annie could see that both Chris and Alex had less need to prove themselves, more willingness to share with their girlfriends.

Still, Aaron and Morty and Gil and Bill all went on, needing to be looked up to yet resenting the burden. Annie supposed that the new wives were light to carry but still kept that glow of idol worship going. Was Stuart just another angry, resentful member of that club, or was he different? God, she thought, is my view skewed with bitterness, or is that exactly what's been happening to men and women in the last decade?

Maybe tonight she would uncover something useful: what Gil was up to, where he might be vulnerable. Corporate Espionage 'R' Us, she thought. But she would also do her best to enjoy the evening. Heaven knows, there hadn't been many opportunities to enjoy men, but that was what happened to middle-aged women who lost their husbands. Of course, a few of her friends had made "suggestions." But Annie shrank from the idea of men like Felix Boraine, an unattractive, wealthy seventy-year-old widower, or Georges Matin, an amusing but obviously gay social escort. Such men were beneath her after Aaron. She'd rather be alone.

Once inside her apartment, Annie longed to remain there. She had things to do, the mail to go through, her letter to Sylvie to write. She longed for her daughter. She tried to write each day. Well, she'd have no time for that or the mail now. She'd make it an early night and do it when she came home. The order and beauty she had created here made spending a comfortable evening at home a sure thing. With Stuart she couldn't be so sure.

But God, she knew she should go out. She spent so many evenings, had so many dinners, alone. Lunches were no problem, and the days were slowly getting filled by her work at the hospital, her plants, her writing, and the First Wives Club, but the evenings! She had to start doing something. Aaron gets remarried and I don't even date, she chided herself.

Although she had less than an hour, she poured herself a tall glass of Evian and sat down in her favorite chair. She wanted to think: about Sylvie and her life at Sylvan Glades, about herself and her own life without Sylvie, even without Pangor. She not only missed her daughter, she missed her sweet Siamese cat as well. Yet she hadn't the heart to get a new kitten. That's me all over, she thought. The tom is gone but I can't replace him. She drank the water down. Chris would be at the Russian Tea Room at seven, then Stuart at Petrossian at eight. Damn, and I have to get there, she moaned, getting up. She hadn't engaged Hudson for the evening, so she'd have to take a cab. She hoped she could get one, that it wouldn't smell, that the driver would speak English, that he'd have change for a twenty. She'd better hurry.

It never took her long to dress. At 6:35, Annie slipped into a pair of slim ivory silk trousers and pulled a matching silk knit top over her still-damp curls. She sat at her dressing table and opened the velvet box that contained the jewelry she'd been left when her mother ran off. The gold ear clips and necklace set that she'd seen so often on her mother were now her favorite pieces. She looked at her reflection in the mirror as she put them on and almost saw her mother there. But I'm not as tan, she noted. Or as beautiful. No, the nose is too long, the face too round, the chin too short. Best I can do is pretty, if that. Maybe only attractive. But tonight is a night of intrigue. Perhaps I'll look more the part if I put on more eye makeup, she thought. But her round eyes refused to look mysterious, no matter how much eyeliner she applied.

She glanced at her Waterford clock and quickened her pace. Scent, keys, bag. Over her silks, she put on a modified Japanese kimono by Hanae Mori, beige with subtly colored, widely spaced markings in pale rust and ocher. She saw herself in the hall mirror and was pleased. I can still pull this off. She smiled at herself trying to build her own confidence. I look great. Aaron was a fool to leave me. As if to match her positive mood, a cab pulled up as she stepped out of the lobby. Perhaps this would be fun.

The Russian Tea Room was decorated for Christmas. This wasn't jumping the season, as so many New York retailers did. The Tea Room was *always* decorated for Christmas because the owner, Faith Stewart Gordon, liked it that way.

The desirable tables, always surprising to Annie, were not the ones at the center of the long, narrow restaurant, but the red semicircle banquettes at the entrance corridor. Well, as at Le Cirque, see and be scene, she supposed, but the draft was terrific on your legs there, despite the beautifully polished brass revolving door. No, Annie didn't mind that she was always seated in the back. Tonight, though, she'd just take a seat at the bar, she thought.

Yet Chris was already there waiting, and in a banquette! She supposed she'd have to suffer the draft. Annie returned his welcoming smile and was pleased when he stood to receive her. "Chris, how nice! But we're only having a drink; how did you get a table?"

"Well, maybe I'll force some blini on you, you anorectic." Chris smiled. "Anyway, Faith knows me now because of Dad."

Of course. Aaron knew all the first-class restaurateurs in the city. Nice of him to initiate Chris, she thought. Part of the Paradise legacy, she supposed, always to be given a good table.

"What would you like?" Chris asked her.

"Just some white wine, I guess."

He waved toward a waiter, placed her order, and asked for another Perrier.

"Well, so how are things?" Chris asked. His tone seemed overly hearty to Annie, unlike him.

"Fine," she said. "Sylvie seems fine, and Alex called Saturday."

"Uh-huh. Anyone else call?"

She looked at him. "Brenda Cushman," she told him. For a minute he looked confused.

"Who?" he asked blankly.

"My friend Brenda. Chris, what is it that you're trying to find out?"

"Dad didn't call?"

Her stomach tightened, but she was sure she kept her face blank.

"Mom, Dad's asked me to his wedding."

She tried hard not to let her face change, not to show her feelings. "Well, I'd expect him to. You *are* his son."

"His *second* son," Chris said, almost bitterly, Annie thought. "Anyway, did he call you and tell you about it?"

She had always hated the thought of this moment. She'd decided long ago that she wouldn't drag either of her sons into her private life with Aaron nor would she attempt to tarnish him. It was a reprehensible thing to do. She smiled at Chris.

"No, but he doesn't have to. He's divorced. He's free to do what he wants—"

"Oh, come on, Mom! Stop protecting him," Chris broke in. "Stop being so goddamn fair." He looked away, collected himself, and turned back to her. "You know, I'm not a kid anymore. I deserve to know what the hell is going on!"

"Well, apparently, you do. Your father is getting married."

"Yes, to your psychiatrist."

Annie blinked. "I terminated with Dr. Rosen some time ago."

"Jesus, Mom." Chris shook his head. He sighed. "Mom, I'm trying to find out how I feel about this and you're not helping."

"It seems to me that you're trying to find out how *I* feel about it."

"Well, that's part of it, Mom. I haven't really been comfortable with some of Dad's behavior at work. He's . . ." Chris paused, and Annie saw the hesitation, the pain in his eyes. Chris was loyal, she thought. He was loyal to his sister, to her, to his father. Would it be possible to be loyal to all of them at once, or would he be torn apart? Lucky Alex, removed from it all, she thought. Alex was like Aaron; Chris, she recognized with a start, was more like herself.

"Dad's tougher than I thought," Chris finally said.

"You have to be tough to run a business, Chris."

"He embarrasses Uncle Jerry. He does it in front of the other staff members. He blames him when it's not his fault."

"Partners often have problems," Annie said.

"I don't think Dad wants to be partners with Jerry anymore. Wouldn't it be better if he just said so?"

He paused and reached out and took her hand. "Mom,

I was there at Alex's graduation. I *saw* the two of you, Dad and you, holding hands. And then I left when we got back to the hotel." He sighed. "Mom, I'm involved with someone. A woman that I think I could really love, and it's made me, well, sensitive to things. So I know what was in the air between you and Dad up in Boston. I wasn't just being a child when I thought that maybe the two of you were getting back together."

Annie felt her lips tremble. There was no way to protect anyone in this bitch of a world, she thought bitterly. "No," she told him, "you weren't just being a child."

"But it didn't work out?"

"No. It didn't."

"But has Dad been a complete bastard?"

Oh, God. How could she answer that question? How could she be fair to Chris, to Aaron, and to herself?

"No one is a complete anything, Chris." It was, at the moment, the best she could do, and perhaps it was good enough. "Chris, go to your father's wedding, if you can. He isn't a monster." She was suddenly exhausted. The thought of dinner with Stuart Swann was almost more than she could bear. She took a deep breath.

"And now," she said, "I have to go. I actually have a date."

"Well, actually, Mom, so have I. And I wanted you to meet her." He raised his head to a woman at the bar, a real woman, not a college student or a girl, Annie saw with surprise. Why, she had to be ten years older than he! But she was, Annie saw immediately, a nice-looking woman. She wore a white jacket, long, and a short beige skirt with matching hose and pumps. She was far more finished, more sophisticated, than anyone whom Annie expected Chris to be with.

The woman, dark haired, dark eyed, approached the table.

—

She smiled, and it was a nice smile, a bit tentative, and it showed the fine wrinkles around her eyes.

"Mrs. Paradise?"

"Annie."

"Annie. We met last Christmas. I'm Karen Palinsky." She slid beside Chris in the booth and he took her hand.

Of course. Annie recognized her. She was one of the staff at Aaron's shop. "Yes, I remember you. Nice to see you again." Karen looked better, softer, than the last time Annie had seen her.

"Mrs. Paradise, Annie, I just wanted to thank you for raising such a wonderful man," Karen said as she turned to smile at Chris.

"Pshaw," Chris said.

"No, I mean it. It's so rare to meet a man who isn't closed off or defensive or who doesn't hate women."

"Is it?" Annie asked.

"Well, you haven't been single for long," Karen said, and laughed. "That or you've been lucky."

"I have? Perhaps," Annie said, feeling dazed. "And now, I've got to go." She rose and turned to Chris. "I see I leave you in good hands." She kissed him before she left.

Ten minutes later, Annie stepped into the magnificently ornate building on West Fifty-eight Street that housed Petrossian's. A baroque, cast-concrete extravaganza, it had been reclaimed from the pigeons only a few years ago and was now the elegant site of the best caviarteria in the city.

She hoped Stuart would not be late, although if he could be late for Cynthia's funeral service . . . Annie had never felt comfortable sitting alone at a bar. Not enough self-confidence, she supposed. She always thought of poor Alice Adams, sitting at the sidelines of the dance, forcing herself to make bright little smiles as if she were remembering something amusing.

Dr. Rosen had been right about one thing: Annie identified with victims. Well, she just wouldn't, not now, anyway. This evening she was nervous enough. She was a cross between an adolescent wallflower and a middle-aged Mata Hari. And she was still reeling from her meeting with Chris. Aaron's getting married, she thought, and then tried to push it from her mind. If Stuart wasn't there, she'd just order a Campari and stare at her manicure until he arrived.

But Stuart was already seated, having a drink. He stood up and smiled at Annie. They hugged briefly.

"You look wonderful, darling," he said, looking at her intently. "I'm so happy to see you."

"It's good to see you, Stuart," Annie responded, returning his direct gaze. And it was. Stuart was still good-looking, in his scrubbed way. Of course, he had gained some weight, but most people did. Light, as Cynthia had been, his hair and lashes and brows were all a beige color that blended with his skin tone. He had those fine tiny freckles, the kind that seemed more like careful little dots than splotchy freckles. His eyes were brown, but a brown with a lot of yellow in it. The iris was multicolored. Annie remembered with a start that she used to call him Speckle Eye. She smiled at him. Yes, perhaps this *would* be fun.

"I'm so grateful that you came. I don't see you often enough." He paused. "And it was so awful last time, at the cemetery. God, I was so wretched. I rushed like hell from Tokyo—almost got angina in the process—only to find the service over. Damn Gil. But seeing you there did me good." He picked up his drink, something colorless on the rocks, and sipped it. "I know I behaved badly that day. Of course, it was a shock. And I was jet-lagged. But beyond that it all seemed so damn false and wrong—like not one person there cared about my sister—except you, that is. I just felt somehow, when I looked at you, that you were real and that you actually did care about her." Stuart stopped abruptly.

"Stuart, you don't have to apologize . . . ," Annie began. Inopportunely, the waiter arrived.

"Good evening, madame, would you like something to drink?" he asked.

"Yes, please, a Campari and soda."

"Yes, and I'll have another. Make it a double." Stuart turned to Annie. "And if it's all right with you, let's start with their special salad!"

Annie nodded. "Fine." How much had he had to drink? she wondered. Was it gin or vodka? It must be gin. She felt her eyebrows begin to furrow. Stop it, she told herself.

"So, what's it been? Maybe ten years since I saw you last? I mean, aside from the cemetery."

"Yes. Well, no. I saw you at Carla's funeral, and then we saw you in Vail, remember?" He had been with his second wife, very drunk, standing outside Cookie's, the *après ski* rendezvous that everyone went to when they were in Vail. Yes, she realized. He had been very, very drunk.

"No. Did you? Well," he said, smiling, "perhaps you did." They were silent for a moment. Covertly she looked at his face. Puffiness under the eyes. She sighed, feeling like a tire with a slow leak. It was her hope deflating, she thought ruefully. Well, at least she could still drive somewhere before she was flat out of air.

"So, what's going on at work?" Anne asked as casually as possible.

"Oh, the usual. Nothing new to talk about."

"It must be exciting, being involved in all those takeovers and big deals." Oh, for heaven's sake, she thought, I sound like Lorelei Lee. Next I'll be calling him a big, strong man.

Stuart didn't seem to notice. "Not very inspiring, actually."

"What's the next target for takeover, or aren't you allowed to tell?" she asked, feeling guilty at her probing.

Stuart started to look at her more closely. "Annie, are you looking for a tip? Do you need money?"

She blushed. How dreadful. "No. Not at all. I'm quite comfortable."

"You're not thinking of gambling in the market. It's no place for a small investor. Believe me. I know."

"Is it as crooked as they say?" She hoped he wouldn't ask who said.

"Let's just say that an outsider doesn't have a chance. And when he does move in big, he's destroyed. Look at Milken. He was handed over. Pissed off too many of the *real* powers." Stuart took another drink.

"So I shouldn't invest? Not at all?"

Stuart paused. "Look, I shouldn't say anything, but I do know that Gil Griffin is about to go for Mitsui Shipping. If he gets it, the stock will rise. Buy some of that, if you have to, but only spend what you can afford to lose."

"Is it great working with Gil?" She blushed. Oh, she had to drop this ingenue bit.

But Stuart didn't notice, he only snorted. "Yeah, if your last job was as Prometheus' stand-in. Gil only picks out my liver once a week or so."

"He's that bad?"

"Let's talk about something else."

"Does he still drive that XKE of his?"

"Are you kidding? It's his life."

"Where does he park it?"

"It has its own office."

Annie laughed. "No, really?" she pushed.

"Annie, what's with all these Gil Griffin questions? Are you in love?"

Annie was startled. "Of course not. *Au contraire* . . . well . . ." She paused, confused.

Stuart nodded. "So what about Gil?" He looked at her closely. "Annie, you're not thinking of trying to antagonize him?"

"Well . . ."

"Annie, don't be crazy. He's not human. Leave him alone. You know, when Cynthia died, Gil didn't tell me. If my secretary hadn't wired me condolences, I wouldn't have known."

"That's incredible."

"Don't even *think* about crossing him. He's worse than a cobra. He's invincible. And the bitch that he's married is almost as bad. They deserve each other." He took another swig of his drink. "The thing about Gil that you have to try to understand is that he doesn't like to crush people." Annie nodded while Stuart finished his drink. "He doesn't *like* to—he *needs* to."

Despite herself, Annie felt a shiver run up her back and make gooseflesh along her arms. Once again, she was cold. But she wasn't frightened. This was drunken exaggeration. This was melodrama.

"Come on, Stuart. Isn't the destruction just a side effect of his steamroller will? I used to know the man. He's immature, selfish, but he isn't the devil."

"Oh, no. No. That's where you've got it wrong." He motioned for the waiter and got another refill. "I'm no psychiatrist, but there's something really wrong with the man. I've never been spooked by anyone the way he spooks, me. You look into his eyes, and there's nothing there, Annie. Nothing."

"Do you mean he has no soul? Come on, Stuart."

"Listen, I don't know about God. Let's face it, who does? But there's the Light. You know, the Organizing Principle."

"I was always in trouble with the assistant principal," Annie joked, trying to lighten things up.

"Annie, there's no light in Gil Griffin's eyes. Only darkness."

Annie tried to look calm. What were she and Brenda and Elise getting into? Was Stuart right, or was he just a bitter, frightened drunk, excusing his weakness by exaggerating his foe's strength?

The waiter came to take the rest of their order. Annie ordered caviar, hard-boiled egg yolk, and toast points, all the little bits she loved to mix into minute open sandwiches. She never ordered blinis or, worse yet, potatoes with her caviar. And she was a strict vegetarian, but for caviar she made her one guilty exception.

"And I'll have the steak *au poivre*," Stuart said. "And another double."

They were silent for what seemed like several minutes, both aware of the awkwardness, the strain.

"How is your daughter?" Stuart asked suddenly. "You said she was away at a new school."

"She's adjusting. Sylvie's fine." Annie felt herself start to choke up. She hoped Sylvie was fine. She herself wasn't. Aaron was remarrying. Gil was an invincible monster. Stuart was a drunk and certainly not right for her. She felt herself sigh again, and to her embarrassment, her eyes filled with tears.

Stuart reached over and patted her hand. "And Aaron? Are you over him yet?"

Annie withdrew her hand abruptly. "Please, let's not talk about him *or* Gil Griffin. Oh, look, our dinners are coming."

It actually hadn't been such a bad evening, Annie thought as she let herself into her apartment. Chris was a delight to be with, although his news and meeting a woman in his life had given her a start. And once she'd given up on Stuart as a possibility, he had charmed her with gossip and triviality. He could be amusing, even if he was under the influence. And maybe *I can use that information about Mitsui Shipping. Maybe Brenda and Elise will be interested.* Despite her disappointment she felt all right, she realized. It would be a coup to tell them about her discovery. But she wouldn't tell them about Aaron's marriage. She couldn't. Not just yet.

In her foyer, she opened the hall closet and hung up the kimono. There, on the console in the hall, still waiting in a neat pile, was the mail. She picked it up and made her way to the bedroom.

Throwing off her shoes, she lay on the bed, for once oblivious to wrinkling the bedspread and duvet. Quickly she sorted through the mail. A few bills, a note from her aunt, some catalogues. And the Federated Funds Douglas Witter trust fund statement. Annie opened it with a sigh. She glanced at it quickly, ready to put it on her bedside table to file. Then she stopped and looked again. It was a trade notice. A trade. A huge trade. Virtually all the balance, and the margin, too. What the hell was this? There had to be some mistake. She checked the name, then the account number. What the hell was going on?

Jerking upright on the bed, she reached for the phone. It may be eleven-thirty and it may be awkward, but she was going to find out who the hell had put in an order for all those shares of Morty the Madman stock. Neatly filed in her Rolodex was her broker's home number. Her heart pounded. She had never authorized this. There had to be some mistake.

7

Larry Cochran

Larry stepped out of the cramped bathtub onto the worn linoleum of his kitchen floor. "Only the poorest of the poor in New York have a bathtub in their kitchen," he said out loud as he always did after using the ancient tub and the hand-held shower. He had a front room, twelve by twelve, a kitchen with a tub and old cabinets infested with five hundred generations of roaches, a tiny back room on an air shaft, and a toilet in a closet. He washed and shaved in the kitchen sink. And all this for only $742 a month.

Self-pity and panic were twisting in his insides. This month he didn't have the $742. Since his encounter with Elise Elliot, his writing had taken a dramatic turn. He had become obsessed. Time had passed in a fever of creation. Now, at last, he finally had a plot for a screenplay clearly in mind, and he saw Elise playing the starring role. He was writing night and day, not stopping to think of anything. Not about his press pass, soon to expire again, or even where his rent was going to come from.

Usually, he was able to support his simple needs by taking pictures of empty-eyed celebrities and selling them to the newsmagazines and tabloids. But he had been so obsessed with Elise and the screenplay he was writing for her, he hadn't thought of money until the rent notice arrived. And Mr. Paley, the landlord, eager to turn over tenants to increase the stabilized rent, was never patient.

This work was good. It really was. He knew it. He'd already completed three screenplays since getting out of graduate school, but they had been commercial crap. Or as close as he could get.

But not close enough, Larry-boy, he told himself. No one had bit. He didn't even have an agent. What do you do after you sell out and nobody buys? he asked himself as he picked up the thin, torn towel. You go back to art. Drying off his long, lean body, he shook his head, dripping water onto the torn linoleum. *La Bohême*. The haven for failures.

He padded into the tiny space where he slept on a single bed, reached into the mess of clothes hanging from a suspended broomstick that he laughingly called his closet, and took down his old, very old, standard dress-up outfit. Just as he viewed the apartment lately through the eyes of poverty, he now saw his blazer and gray slacks as they really were: worn, shiny, and frayed. This is no way to live, he thought for the hundredth time in the days since his encounter with Elise.

He took down a blue oxford shirt from the wire hanger, smelled the armpits to see if it could make it through one more wearing, and clipped some frayed threads off the collar. The loafers were scuffed and run-down at the heels. He threaded his pants with his black snakeskin belt—a present from an ex-girlfriend who bought it on employee's discount when she had worked at Bloomingdale's one Christmas. Now it was peeling away from its backing. Let's see, he thought, how long ago was that? Three years? Four years. I haven't bought a belt in four years, for chrissake!

He picked up his watch from the sink, fumbled, and dropped it. Perfect. Just what I need. But when he snatched it up off the floor, it was fine, if a Timex could ever be called fine. Takes a licking and keeps on ticking, he thought, snapping it onto his wrist. It was already five past five, and he had told Asa he'd be there at six. Jesus, if he had to hit up his best friend for a loan, at least he could be on time to do it.

He rushed out of the apartment, locking the double locks as he went. What a laugh, he thought. What am I protecting? A broken TV I can't afford to have fixed and an ancient KLH turntable. Who the fuck uses a turntable anymore? Only CDs. I'm so out of it, I haven't even gotten around to a cassette machine that's already obsolete. Take that, Madison Avenue. I missed a whole generation of obsolescence.

He passed down the dimly lit hall, the creaking floorboards muffled by the arguing from the super's apartment. Rosie was drunk again. Well, she wouldn't be up to see him about the rent tonight or tomorrow morning. Let's hope for a bender, Larry thought. I might get three days' grace out of it.

Reaching the sidewalk, he immediately felt better, felt freed from the oppression of his poverty prison. Autumn in New York. The ginkgo trees lining York Avenue were shedding yellow fans onto the gray sidewalk. He walked briskly toward the Seventy-ninth Street crosstown bus and remembered to ask for a free transfer as he boarded. Every little bit helped. He had $216 available in his checking account, and $31 in his pocket. And no other resources. His mom, back home in Missouri, lived on her teacher's pension. She saved some of it, he knew, but he'd never take a dime from her, he had sworn to himself after he graduated. His dad had abandoned them when Larry was still a baby. Someday, he'd give *her* money, not take it. But what will I do now? Larry knew his charge cards were up to their limit—he had even used up the cash advances on them both. Asa was his last shot until the money from *People* magazine came in. He winced, remembering how painful it had been to sell the picture of Elise.

He had thought he wouldn't stoop to selling her picture. No, he had thought, he could never do that. But out of desperation, he had. It had felt like an act of betrayal, now that he had crossed over the line from being in love with her image, her picture on the screen, to loving her, actually loving her. And he did. He loved her. He'd developed the photos he'd taken of her and hung them all over the apartment. He obsessively went over every moment they had spent together in Room 705. He took breaks from his writing only to go to her films when they played at the Thalia or Biograph. He loved her, and his work was showing it.

He began to go over how he was going to ask Asa for a loan. After all, they used to do this back and forth all the time when they were in college, and even after that whenever one of them was short. But neither had borrowed from the other for a long while. Asa got by on his modest salary at the *Wall Street Journal,* and Larry managed to keep his bills up to date through occasional picture sales. Until now, the situation had been okay. Not great, but okay.

But not anymore. Larry was sick of it. Five years out of school, and still feeling like a broke student. No resources, no assets. Nothing to sell. Except, of course, the picture of Elise.

God knows, he should have been out there this week, hustling. But he hated it, snatching pictures of the greats, the near-greats, and the ingrates. It made him sick. He just hadn't been able to make himself do it. Plus his writing had become an obsession. And it was going so well, so smoothly.

Larry understood women, worthy women, lonely women. Jesus, he'd been raised by one. And this screenplay, this story of a lonely, mysterious woman, was coming along so beautifully. He'd hate to have to stop it all now and risk losing his vision, breaking the spell. He'd just *have* to get some money from Asa to tide him over until *People* sent him his check.

At Fifth Avenue he transferred to a downtown bus and his meeting with Asa at the opening of some stupid exhibit. Asa had insisted, had gotten them both invitations. Well, who knows, he might luck into a few pictures there *and* get a loan. He stepped off the bus at West Fifty-seventh Street and walked to the address he was given.

Getting into the elevator, he thought, please, Asa, please loan me just enough to pay the rent this month, just until the end of October. I know I'll have the screenplay done by then, and the photo money will be in. I'm so close, Asa. And it's great, Asa, really, really great. You never heard me say that about my writing before.

And once I get the loan, I'll get on the stick and shoot every fucking asshole celebrity in New York! I promise.

8

West Fifty-seventh Street

W hen Annie arrived at Elise's corporate office at 30 Rockefeller Plaza, she found Brenda waiting for her at the information desk in the lobby. "Elise's office is on the thirty-ninth floor," Brenda said.

The building was the focal point of Rockefeller Center, and a perfect exemplar of art deco design and architecture in New York. As they walked toward the elevator bank, Brenda looked around and said, "It will always be the RCA Building to me," and sighed.

"I know what you mean," Annie said. "Somehow I can't bring myself to call it the GE Building." She, too, sighed. "I guess everything is changing."

"You got *that* right," Brenda said. "And so are we."

Elise had been cheerful when she called. In fact, for a woman in the midst of divorce negotiations she seemed almost too cheerful. Annie hoped she hadn't been drunk. It wasn't polite to mention it, of course, but Elise's drinking was apparent to everyone, though over their last lunch she seemed to have slowed down. Well, sometimes a shock, such as a divorce, actually helps people to reassess themselves, Annie thought. And of course, this support group of theirs could be helpful, too. Anyway, Annie hoped it would work that way for

Elise. And she hoped—no prayed—that something, *anything*, would work for her.

Now Annie was distracted by the trouble with the trust account. John Reamer knew nothing about the trade. Then she had tried Aaron, but he hadn't returned her calls. She figured her broker would straighten it out, yet it was making her jumpy. Then Brenda shook her out of her thoughts. "Annie. It's our floor."

The elevator doors slid back to reveal Elise standing at the receptionist's desk, waiting for them. She turned when she heard the elevator open. "Well, girls, you're right on time. Come on into my office."

"Wow," said Brenda without a wisecrack for once. The window behind Elise's desk overlooked Central Park and as far north as the eye could see.

"It's beautiful," breathed Annie. "What a view, Elise. It's like sitting on a cloud."

"Well, let's call the meeting to order," Elise suggested.

"Now *you're* taking over," Brenda told her. "*I'll* call the meeting to order this time. And I've got some news to report: Angela told me Shelby was rejected by the Junior League and that she's furious at Morty."

"Why at Morty?" Annie asked.

"She says she was turned down because of his Hebrew heritage." Brenda hooted with laughter. "He's had to promise to take her to Aruba for Thanksgiving to make up for it."

Elise smiled. She took out her notebook and checked that off. "Now, I found out something, too. Unfortunately, Gil has already been accepted at the co-op on Fifth. Lally wasn't very cooperative. However, the good news is that the Securities and Exchange Commission has been investigating Gil Griffin for years. A man named De Los Santos is in charge."

"Why hasn't he ever been indicted?" Brenda asked.

"Who knows? Maybe no evidence, maybe Gil bought his way out. Annie, I think you should go see Mr. De Los Santos at the SEC."

"Why me?" Annie asked, fearfully thinking of Sylvie's portfolio.

"Well, you were Cynthia's best friend. Maybe you should share Cynthia's letter with him. After all, it was you who received it. See if he is serious. Has he been paid off by Gil? And if not, see if he can help us or if we can help him. Poke around. Is he friend or foe?"

"All right," Annie agreed. "Now, what about Bill?"

Annie could see Elise's mind working. "Brenda, could you get copies of Bill's client billing sheets through Angela? Didn't she work at Cromwell Reed during the summer?"

"Yes, she interned there. She's friends with some of the secretaries. But I don't know. Maybe. Why?"

"Well, I don't want your daughter to take any risks, but I have an idea. Let's not talk about it until we see if we can get the billing sheets."

"Okay."

Now Annie saw both of the women looking at her. "So what about Aaron?" Brenda asked. "Any ideas?"

Hearing Aaron's name, Annie reminded herself to try him at the office again before she left. "Not yet," Annie admitted. She didn't want to admit that she was having dreams about him almost every night. She was too ashamed of it.

She noticed that Elise and Brenda looked at one another and raised their eyebrows. "Get your dossier started," Elise told Annie. "Remember, Aaron is last, but he's not left out."

"Well, how was dinner with Stuart?" Brenda wanted to know.

Annie made her report, stressing Stuart's warnings. Instead of alarming her, however, it seemed to Annie that Elise became even more animated. "But dear, this is wonderful! Mitsui Shipping. I shall look right into it."

Annie hesitated. "But remember about Stuart's warning," she cautioned.

"Oh, come on, Annie," Brenda chided. "Stuart's a wuss."

"And Annie; Aaron is last, *not* forgotten," Elise reminded her as they all rose to follow Elise down to her waiting limo. Today the club would lunch at a charming French bistro on East Fifty-seventh Street.

On West Fifty-seventh Street, Shelby Symington was nervous. Of course, she'd never admit it, but having a show at the opening of your own gallery was a heady experience. And this gallery wasn't in some grubby basement space off Wooster Street, but here, uptown, where the big boys played.

She couldn't wait to see who came. They had better *all* come. She had spent enough time kissing heinies to wear her lips right off. And Shelby Symington didn't like kissing heinies. Down in Atlanta, where she was from, people used to line up to kiss *hers*. The Symington family had been running the town for the last five generations at least, and there was no one of any importance in the South whom Shelby wasn't kin to by blood or marriage.

Things were different, though, in New York, and she knew it was a great big world out there. Besides, Atlanta had started to feel too small. Shelby had big ambitions, if only a small trust fund. And she had already learned that the larger world was just filled with people who had money but no taste. Well, she would be just too happy to relieve them of some of the former, and they might even end up with some of the latter.

She was a little upset, though, about the Junior League. How could they reject a Symington? Her mother would be shocked, and then she'd begin harping again about "that

Jew," as she called Morton. Still, she knew her mother would get some of her pals to come through, and that would almost ensure a mention of the gallery in the society columns.

She had covered the art scene with millions of little favors since her marriage to Morton: introducing society people to the promising young artists before they got well-known; arranging for loans of art; actually loaning money to talent and small gallery owners. Well, now it was payback time, and they'd better be here. If only she could be sure that Jon Rosen would come.

Rosen was, without doubt, the most influential art critic in New York, maybe in the country. He wrote for *ArtWorld* and was on every damn grant committee in the state. Shelby tried hard not to be anti-Semitic, despite what her family said and especially since she had married Morton, but this guy was the worst. At least Morton was pathetically grateful to have her on his arm. Jon Rosen was a whiner, a supercilious misanthrope who loved to feel superior to everyone, to point out the flaws, never the triumphs. And he was a tomcat, always on the prowl.

Shelby knew that her husband had his flaws, but promiscuity was definitely not one of them. If he was unimaginative and somewhat selfish in bed, at least she didn't have to worry about finding him there with someone else. Shelby could imagine a discreet affair of her own—where was the harm?—but was damned if she'd have a man cheat on *her*. It had been damned difficult to get Morton into bed, and she had only done it to clinch the deal. He wasn't going to bed with anyone else, not if she kept her eyes open. It wasn't easy to land a rich man in New York, especially one who would be as grateful as Morton, so grateful in fact that he would give her anything she wanted, including her own business. And she could control him, something Brenda hadn't been able to do. Since the day Duarto had brought Morton and Brenda to the gallery, Shelby knew he had everything she wanted. New money, no taste, and the drive to be even richer.

But Jon Rosen couldn't keep his long, soft, white hands off *shiksas*. It seemed to Shelby it was the Yiddish form of alcoholism. That and therapy. Wasn't his sister a psychiatrist or psychologist or something even more disgusting? Well, she'd just have to hope that Jon Rosen would get lucky tonight and be in a good mood when he wrote up her show.

Now she looked around the gallery with pride. The show was profound: deeply felt, but with that twist of irony or neurosis that was necessary to capture attention in this city. The four main rooms of the gallery were hung with Phoebe Van Gelder's mammoth collages; the two smaller rooms contained the work that even Shelby felt might be objectionable. After all, it was art, not dirty pictures, but some people didn't know the difference. Look at the flap that Jesse Helms had started. Of course Shelby wanted, needed, to shock the audience: otherwise this would be just another opening, another show. But she didn't want to shock them so badly that they wouldn't buy.

Well, there was the insurance of Phoebe's family. The Van Gelders were to New York what the Symingtons were to Atlanta, but perhaps more so. Power and money. The Van Gelders had been in international banking and shipping in New York since the place was Dutch. And when that family showed up, all of New York would follow. After all, Phoebe's uncle had once been vice president, and another uncle had been the city's mayor for three terms. But mostly the Van Gelders were known for being what the Symingtons had never been: wildly rich.

Well, this show would start to change that. No more sweet little jobs as gallery slave to Leo Castelli while he and the other established art crowd made fortunes. Shelby would start to do it herself now. And she wouldn't be the first woman to connect commerce and art. It was just too bad she had had to marry to do it. Shelby sighed.

Well, I'm doing the best I can. Maybe I could enroll Morton in the SoHo School for the Terminally Unhip. She smiled and comforted herself by surveying the gallery—*her* gallery. Once again Shelby walked through the rooms, admiring the gleaming floors, the virgin white walls and the utter havoc displayed on the vast canvases.

Over and over Phoebe had depicted lips—lips more luscious than life could produce, lips pulsating, pushing off the canvas. Some were three dimensional, built up by layers of gesso; others were plaster mounds glued on the painted surface. All looked wet, gleaming, dripping open, with promise. If de Kooning's frightening women were the last word in *vagina dentata*, Shelby was certain that these massive works by Phoebe would become the dernier cri in female acceptance. They were disturbing, certainly, but they were alive. They were this generation's Georgia O'Keeffes. And if she was lucky, several dozen would be hanging in libraries and salons all over the city in just a few months' time. And she'd be off and running. Wait until Ross Bleckner and Richard Prince saw this.

Speaking of which, she'd better be off and running now. She had to check the sound system, since Phoebe insisted on playing her own recording of new age music as part of the environment. And she'd need to freshen up, and see to the refreshments.

The elevator doors pulled open to reveal the caterers.

Usually, these things were white-wine, green-grapes, and cheese affairs, but Morty had suggested more, and for once Shelby agreed. But it all had to be done immaculately, or not at all. She showed the white-jacketed crew where to set up and left them to be handled by her very own gallery slave, Antonia.

9

Art for Art's Sake

Morty stood awkwardly at the elevator, watching Shelby's gallery as it began to fill up. *Exhibition* was certainly the word for this show. If these huge pictures weren't enlargements from *Hustler*, Morty didn't know what was. But what did he know about fucking modern art? He figured you could pick this stuff up on Forty-second Street, but Shelby used to be a curator at the Museum of Modern Art, so she ought to know. Still, he had never paid for snatch in his life, and he couldn't imagine that these people would either. They didn't look shocked, though.

Even though there was not much of a turnout yet, there were men in dinner jackets and women dressed for parties later wandering around, munching pâté. At least the food was good, as good a chopped liver as his mother, may she rest in peace, used to make. It was only the panpipes, or whatever the hell it was playing over the sound system, that would make him *meshugge*.

Bill Atchison kept one arm around Phoebe. As usual, she was wearing something outrageous, and as usual, Bill couldn't take his eyes off her. She was really something, and everyone knew it. She had it all, he thought: money, breeding, creativity, and sex appeal. Bill felt himself stand taller. Everyone was looking at her, and he could feel their covetousness, their envy. Not bad for a man pushing sixty. Not bad at all.

As he always did, he became anxious when he thought of his age. He didn't look fifty-seven. Christ, he didn't look *fifty*, and he felt twenty years younger than that. He thought like a young person, therefore he was young. Phoebe said so, even though, in their most intimate moments, she called him Daddy.

He looked around the gallery. People were beginning to arrive. Now they'd all see the fabulous talent that he had recognized and nurtured. Now she would belong to the world.

But just for a moment, he pulled back from the idea. Two young men had joined them. One looked a pansy, but the other . . . was Phoebe looking at him? Bill wished his divorce was over, so he could marry Phoebe and be sure that she was his. Oh, but what was he getting nervous about? She loved him. He knew that. She was staring because of all the coke she had done. Just opening-night jitters. Only he could understand her. Such an old soul. Once more, he looked at her paintings. Such an old soul, and so very hot.

Aaron Paradise and Leslie Rosen were on their way to the opera, but had to stop in for the opening. It wasn't just that Aaron had to show up to please Morty, his valued if somewhat crass client. "I want to see what this girl produces, Aaron," Leslie had admitted. "From what I've seen of Phoebe, I think she needs help, and I'd like to be the one to help her." Leslie was sure Phoebe's art would be very revealing to her and would help her understand Phoebe better. Besides, both she and Aaron could scout around for clients. Not a bad idea. And Gil Griffin would be there. It never hurt to press the flesh of the CEO of a major account.

Aaron was, he had to admit, a little uncomfortable about the possibility of seeing Annie. But, he told himself, it had to happen sometime. He was prepared. And as Leslie had said many times, they simply had to refrain from allowing Annie to play the martyr.

Leslie looked beautiful tonight, Aaron thought as they stepped off the elevator and into the new gallery. She dressed not merely simply, but almost starkly. Tonight her hair was pulled back, revealing her creamy neck. Her strapless black dress hugged her ample cleavage, then dropped severely to the floor. It was a McFadden, he thought, in that crimped fabric that made women look like classical statues. And she did look classical. She was so much more female than Annie. "I love you," he whispered into her hair.

"Good," she said as she looked around the room, raising her eyebrows as she did. Aaron followed her look.

"Oh, my Holy Redeemer," he breathed, staring at the enormous genitalia on the wall.

"Wait until Jon sees this!"

Aaron wasn't sure if Leslie meant the display on the walls or the one Phoebe Van Gelder made. She was standing in front of them, beside Bill Atchison, wearing a kind of transparent, black body stocking and limp tutu-like skirt. "What do you call that?" Aaron asked Leslie.

"Exhibitionism."

Aaron laughed. "Shall we?" he offered, and they moved together toward the couple. It was time to hustle.

Larry Cochran stepped off the elevator and saw Asa standing just inside the door of the gallery. He went up to him, smiling. "Asa, so sorry I'm late." Larry patted his friend on the back. Asa awkwardly gave Larry half a hug, somewhere between a handshake and an embrace. Asa was gay, or maybe bisexual; it seemed to Larry that Asa never quite got it straight in his own mind. He was not a physical person. Larry sometimes wondered if Asa had ever had a crush on him, but it was something he didn't like to dwell on.

"Larry, good to see you. Just got here myself. Just in time for champagne," Asa said as he hailed a passing waiter.

Larry slowly scanned the room, then guided Asa over to a quiet corner. "So, what's new, Asa? What's been happening?" Asa shrugged slightly. "Same old, same old, pal. And you?"

Larry had hoped that Asa would get the conversation going until he found an opening to casually ask for the loan. He'd like to get it over with. But he could see something was bothering Asa. He's as down as I am, Larry thought. Not unusual for either of them, of course, since their common lack of money and success seemed to be the thing that kept them friends for all these years. It wouldn't be easy to stay pals with a guy who skyrocketed to fame and fortune.

Larry asked Asa his usual question whenever they met. "Got any good stock tips for me?" As if he could invest in them even if Asa gave him a tip.

Asa smiled, as usual and said, "Nothing we can make use of." Larry shook his head. He was aware of Asa's ethics when it came to his career. No insider info, just keep it clean. But then, surprisingly, Asa added, "Everyone's gotten rich but me, and I know more than most of them. Wish I had some cash; the way the market's going, it looks like no one can lose."

Larry's stomach flipped. "Do you mean you have none?"

"Broke as a two-dollar watch," Asa admitted grimly. "Living on my privileged checking. Hardly a privilege to my way of thinking."

"I was going to hit you for a loan today," Larry moaned. "Holy shit, Asa. I owe seven hundred and forty-two dollars rent now or I'm out on my ass." Larry took a long gulp of champagne.

"Yeah, well, I've only got plastic money." Asa paused for a moment, then added, "But if you can hold off until the end of October, I'll be able to help you out big time."

"At the end of the month, I have some money coming in, too. No, I need it now," Larry said swallowing his disappointment.

Turning to look up at Asa again, Larry asked, "What's going to happen at the end of the month? Going to win the lottery?"

"I've got a deal working," Asa said, trying to deflect Larry's curiosity. "But you've been writing and not taking pictures. I figured *you* were in the chips."

"No," Larry said, "just hot water."

Gil and Mary Griffin were pounced on by Morty and Shelby as they stepped into the gallery. "Oh, am I evah happy to see you," yellow-haired Shelby drawled. "I can't wait to see your reactions."

Gil looked around. A bit much. Personally, he was repelled by this sort of thing publicly displayed, but he knew enough not to show his feelings. He was a follower, not a leader, in the world of art and was wise enough to know it. It was Mary who looked somewhat taken aback. He'd have to talk to her about that.

"I wanted to take you into the private viewing rooms," Shelby gushed. "I have some of Phoebe's select works there."

Gil wasn't interested. Mary had all these social aspirations, such as the Fifth Avenue apartment and those ridiculous charity committees. Gil could care less. Cynthia had done the society nonsense, which had helped him once upon a time.

But no more. He was beyond it now; besides, it bored him. But if Mary wanted it, he was willing. To a point. Still, she wasn't hanging *this* on their walls, no matter how fashionable it might be. It was nice to be taken into the private rooms, though, far away from the hoi polloi. Taking Mary's arm, he followed Shelby and the detestable Morty Cushman, crass and so nouveau. Morty was getting a little too pushy lately. Gil had made him a millionaire, but the little weasel kept sniffing around for more. Gil would unload him soon enough.

At that moment Shelby also wanted to unload Morty. She was worried. Why was the turnout so bad? She let her eyes scan the room, but couldn't bring herself to count heads. She knew it had to be low, since it was possible to get to the bar without pushing and shoving. Where were the socialites? People like Gunilla Goldberg and Khymer Mallison? Was it Morty that was keeping people away? Maybe my mother was right. He is, after all, only a New York Jew, rich or not. And art was a sensitive thing; these works particularly so. She was charging a lot for a relatively unknown artist. She sighed. She just hoped Morty would keep his mouth shut.

It was Gil's mouth that opened when Shelby led them before the smaller pictures. Sexual positions, with women as receptacles, filled each canvas. The images were disturbing, sadistic, and deeply erotic to Gil. He involuntarily squeezed Mary's arm.

"Interesting," was all he said, recovering quickly.

"Yes. Very," Mary agreed, and Gil heard the breathlessness in her voice. One of these, perhaps. Yes. One of these in their bedroom. Silently, they toured the two small private rooms, viewing each of the canvases of writhing forms.

Shelby had heard Mary's breathlessness as well. She turned to Morty and raised her brows. He shrugged and said nothing, thank the Lord. Shelby watched the other, mesmerized couple. She could smell her first sale. And if she sold to Gil and Mary Griffin, others would fall over each other to follow suit.

Back in the public viewing rooms, Duarto had just arrived. And he couldn't believe his eyes. It wasn't the show that shocked him, however. There, in the middle of all these useless pussy pictures, was the man he'd like to spend the rest of his life with. He'd never felt such a strong tug in his loins, and he'd felt plenty of tugs in his time. He'd come here, as always, to scare up a little business, and his special target was Mary Birmingham Griffin. He'd just heard from a mole in Linda Stein's office that Linda, the nouveau society-apartment broker, had sold the Griffins the penthouse in Jackie Onassis's building at 1040 Fifth Avenue, and Duarto badly wanted the job. But he also wanted this man who was standing beside one of these awful, offensive Phoebe paintings.

It was clear he was gay, but was he available? He was standing before a dark, tall, gangly, good-looking student type, but Duarto had never gone for the Jimmy Stewarts. He always yearned toward the sandy-colored, freckled little *maricones*. Who could figure these things? He even liked the guy's receding hairline.

These days, of course, a date with a stranger was taking your life in your hands. So many of Duarto's friends were dead, it was too painful to count anymore. After the seventeenth memorial-quilt square, Duarto gave up. He himself had always been careful, and lucky. He'd lived with Richard for eleven years, never cheated, and after Richard had been diagnosed, Duarto had tested negative. He should consider himself lucky, and he did. Duarto remembered how supportive of his work Richard had been. But even with Brenda helping out, he felt overworked without Richard's help. And since Richard's death, he was lonely. Now he stared at Asa Ewell, and visions of vine-covered cottages and beagle puppies flashed before his eyes.

"So instead of the old click-click, it's been scribble-scribble?" Asa was asking Larry.

"Yeah, I've been writing. I've been inspired." Yes, Larry thought. And Elise Elliot is my inspiration.

Dear Elise. I sold the picture I took of her to *People*. Now I'll have to give up the hope of ever seeing her again. I sold her out. She'd never understand, he thought. She'd believe that he was just using her when she saw the published picture.

He tried to shake off the dark cloud. Asa, he noticed, also seemed grim; the two of them were a pathetic pair. "Inspired? That's great, Larry. But why so down? You got more than just money problems?"

Larry was grateful for the offer of an ear and a shoulder, but afraid to talk about how he was really feeling. Christ, what would Asa think of him if he knew what he had done? Well, he'd have to chance it or go crazy holding it all in. Slowly, he began to unravel the story of Elise to his old friend.

"I couldn't believe it, Asa. Elise Elliot, right there on Madison Avenue. I kept snapping pictures of her as she walked down the street. When she went into the bar at the Carlyle, I was beside myself. There was no decision. I just followed her in. It was dark and cool, almost empty. She was sitting by herself." Taking another sip from the fluted glass in his hand, he said, "So I sent her over a drink."

"And then?" Asa asked.

"And then she accepted. I joined her at her table and we talked. Then we spent the afternoon making love." Larry lowered his head.

Asa laughed. "So what's the problem? Seems to me you have no problem."

"There's a problem. I just told you how broke I've been?"
Asa shifted uncomfortably. He nodded.

"Well, I had to sell one of the pictures I took of her. Shit,
Asa, I betrayed her. After having spent the most wonderful
afternoon of my life with a woman, I betrayed her to survive."

Larry thought his guilt must be contagious. He noticed
Asa flinch when he said the word *betrayed*.

Asa looked up slowly. "I know something about big mistakes. Some can be forgiven just by saying 'I'm sorry.' Some
need to be atoned for. But Larry, I think this one's easy. Just
write her a note and tell her you're sorry you did it, and ask her
to forgive you. No explanations, no buts, just 'I'm sorry.'"

"But she'd never see me again."

Asa nodded in agreement. "So then, what have you got to
lose?" he said, biting his lip.

Even in the midst of his own problem, Larry noted his
friend's discomfort. "Are you okay?"

"Who's okay?" Asa asked. "Anyway, we were talking about
you. Ask her forgiveness."

"But suppose she won't?"

"Then you haven't lost anything trying. Larry, just do it."

Larry chewed on Asa's very sound advice. He's right, as
usual. I'll write to her. Confession is good for the soul, he
thought, feeling lighter already. He began to pay closer attention to Asa. Good idea. Good friend. But why was *Asa* so
down? And was that a new suit? Why was frugal Asa living on
plastic? What's going on here?

"Asa, what's with you? You got something on *your* mind?"
Larry was sure Asa wasn't only picking up his own guilty mood.
Asa did have something on his mind, or on his conscience.

Larry, leaning toward him, said gently when Asa didn't
respond, "You know you can tell me, buddy. Out with it."

Asa half-turned away from Larry, avoiding his eyes. "I sold out, too, Larry. Big time. And like I said, some things take more than an apology to fix."

"What are you talking about? What have you done?" Larry asked, almost in a whisper.

Asa turned back to the bar, dismissing Larry's question. "I don't want to talk about it right now, Larry. Wait until Halloween." They stood in silence for a moment, looking over the sparse crowd. "Sorry I couldn't help you out right now, Larry. What are you going to do?"

Larry paused, then said as if to himself, "I'm going to do what every other failure in New York does. I'm going to call my mother." Then he noticed the rather exotic-looking man staring at them, or rather, at Asa. Grateful for the chance to change the subject, he said to his friend, "I think you're being paged."

Asa, following Larry's glance, stared into the melting brown eyes of a tall, thinly mustached Hispanic man. Asa looked away. He never did know how to do this stuff.

Looking in the other direction, however, he was confronted by Gil Griffin. Jesus, he didn't want to be seen talking to him! Gil had gotten a message to him to put off the column until Halloween. He'd agreed. It was going to be tough to make it look natural. Asa wished he could back out of the deal. But it was too late. He'd already spent most of the money that was coming to him.

"Let's go over and take a look at some of these paintings," he suggested to Larry, taking his friend by the arm.

"Do we have to?" Larry asked.

Jon Rosen didn't share Larry's aversion to looking at the art. It was simple, really. Arriving late, as he always did, he had taken in the show at a glance. Derivative, purposely provocative. But ultimately unimportant and uninspiring. Phoebe Van Gelder, on the other hand, was extremely inspiring. Jon waited until Shelby Symington, the Atlanta Barracuda, gently grabbed him, as he knew she would, and led him to Phoebe and the small crowd congregated around her. They were an interesting study—Shelby all tanned and blond and lush, Phoebe pale and raven haired and bony. Two extremes of the female of the species.

"Phoebe," Shelby drawled, "I want you to meet Jon Rosen. *The* Jon Rosen."

"Hello, *the* Jon. Are you related to *the* Donald?" Phoebe looked right into his eyes, her own dilated with excitement, or something more. Her tiny, almost boyish body was barely concealed by the chiffon draped around. She extended her hand to him. It was very small, and very hot.

Jon wasn't sure how he wanted to play this one. He knew immediately that she was available, and he liked to divide and conquer old money. I'm just like my sister Leslie, he thought. No sense of guilt. He only wondered whether he'd prefer to take her and write a scathing review, or whether it would amuse him more to do her *and* the public by praising her in print. The choice was interesting, and he felt a pleasant quickening. Shelby was watching the two of them intently, as was an older man. Before Shelby could bother with other introductions, Jon took the first step.

"Why don't you show me what you have to show?" he asked her.

Phoebe smiled. Wordlessly they left the group.

Larry Cochran was shocked by this stuff. It wasn't the subject, it was the stupid, tawdry, lifeless execution of it. "What was it?" he wondered aloud to Asa. "Self-hate, do you think? Or a political statement of some kind?" He stared over at Phoebe

Van Gelder. She looked utterly stoned, incapable of any kind of statement. A rich little princess of entitlement. Though he had his camera with him, he'd never be able to sell a photo that had one of Phoebe's pictures as a backdrop. Larry tried not to think of the beauty he could create if he had her resources. Too much resentment there.

His mother would send him a check, and he'd finish the screenplay and take pictures of these morons so he could keep eating. He sized up Phoebe for a shot. She stood beside a tall, silver-haired man. He was wearing a really ridiculous black leather blazer with gold buttons. Chanel gone butch. Maybe worth a shot of the two of them. It was tricky, getting a photo without a labial lip intruding into the viewfinder. But she was this month's media darling, so he could probably eat on this shot for a week. Larry had wandered the four main rooms. He'd gotten a few shots, but not many. Not much hope. Sylvia Miles, but she was the one who Warhol said showed up at the opening of an envelope. Castelli, Harris, some other big-time art boys. A few minor Broadway types, desperate for some PR. Not worth wasting the film on. He would have to ask his mother for a loan. And he'd have to get a straight job. And he'd write an apology to Elise. Not that it would do any good. Well, at least the food was good.

"Is that her father?" he asked Asa.

"Hell, no. That's Bill Atchison, her fiancé."

"*That's* Bill Atchison?" Larry couldn't believe it. This man was leaving Elise Elliot for a kinky piece of ass like that? Larry shook his head. He looked over at Phoebe, who was now draped over Morty Cushman, the guy from the TV ads. She was arching her back, the little buds of her breasts clearly visible through the filmy blouse that covered her body stocking.

"She's demented," he told Asa. "I wouldn't fuck her with your dick."

"Well, that's a relief."

The gay guy finally made his move, and Asa went off to talk with him. So now Larry stood at the buffet alone, nibbling on cold shrimp.

Staring moodily at one of the canvases, Larry was thinking it might be time to go home when he noticed the gallery hostess, or whatever she was called, coming out of one of the private rooms. Larry wondered what was in there. People had been in and out with the woman all night. Maybe it was the VIP lounge. Larry decided to give it a try.

Looking as blank as possible, he wandered over to the door. He tried it, and it wasn't locked. He turned the knob and slipped in.

The room was relatively dark, with smaller pictures illuminated by recessed lights. In a moment his eyes adjusted, and he saw the incredible obscenity of the stuff. And then, in another moment, he saw them.

Jon Rosen stood with his back toward the door, his arms braced against the far wall, facing it. For a moment, from the way he was hunched over, Larry thought perhaps the guy was sick. But then he saw Phoebe Van Gelder, almost hidden by him, sandwiched between his body and the wall. She was there, on her knees, her own red mouth open, taking Jon Rosen's dick deep into her throat. I wonder if *ArtNews* would be interested in a shot of this, Larry joked to himself as he backed silently out of the room.

10

The Debacle

Aaron reached out to answer the phone that was ringing beside his ear, interrupting his dream. It was a good dream, too. Big, with lots of colors. And a girl. Too bad, he thought, and had to let it go.

"Yeah?" His voice was hoarse. He turned to see if Leslie was beside him in bed, but she was gone—up already and probably at the gym by now. She was amazing. He glanced at the clock. It was seven-thirty. Who'd be calling him now?

"Look, we got a situation." It was Morty Cushman's voice, loud and upset.

Christ, was there a problem with the new series of Morty the Madman commercials? Aaron wondered. What did the guy want? He'd taken Jerry off the account, for chrissake. Had Drew and Julie fucked up?

"What is it?" Aaron sat up, reached for a cigarette. Leslie didn't like him to smoke in the bedroom, but she wasn't here now.

"The shares," Morty said.

Aaron sat up straighter. "Yes. What about them?"

"Oh, Christ," Morty groaned. "Have you seen the *Journal*?"

"No." Jesus, it was 7:32 in the fucking morning! Aaron was never a morning person. His hours, now that he was the boss, were usually ten to ten. He'd supervised a presentation rehearsal last night until sometime past eleven. He'd had to scream at Karen and his son Chris because of a stupid mistake. If he didn't check on every goddamn thing, it would all go wrong. So now, how the fuck could he have seen the *Journal?* And what did it say? Was this some kind of a fucking guessing game?

"Well, this schmuck Asa Ewell ran a column this morning and took a crap all over me. All over *us*, I should say. Listen to this," Morty said. " '*As the dust settles from the public sale of Morty the Madman stock, chinks in the corporate armor are now becoming visible. Once a pioneer in automated inventory control at point-of-sale, Morty the Madman now appears to be stuck in an over-automated system too complicated for POS control. That coupled with a bad cash-flow problem makes the stock at its current rate per share overvalued.*' Jesus Christ, he fuckin' nailed us."

Was that all? Some two-bit columnist giving old Morty some bad press? Morty was all worked up over nothing. "Don't worry, Mort, we'll make it up in the new ads. Everyone will love you."

"Aaron, will you listen, for Christ's sake? You don't understand. I'm not talking about my fuckin' public image. I'm talking business, not PR. It's all true. And it's going to affect the stock prices. Christ, it probably *already* has."

Aaron felt his heart lurch in his chest. "How did the guy get hold of this stuff?"

"I don't know, but I have a good guess. I think it was that prick Griffin. He's the only one outside my firm who knew this."

"But he took you public."

"Yeah, and he must have sold me short." Morty explained about overhearing the phone call, and about his idea to buy more stock because of it.

"I figured Ewell would be giving it a glowing recommenda-
tion and that we'd cash in on Griffin's shirttails. That cock-
sucker! He *must* have sold short. He knew in advance; he set
it up. Then he bailed out, and he's made another fortune, and
he's movin' on. Meanwhile, I'm bleeding."

"Shit, Morty. You mean we *lost* the money?" Aaron felt his
heart pounding. He hadn't even told Annie about the trade
yet. He'd been ducking her calls for more than a week.

"Not yet, but we will. Place a sell order as fast as you can.
Get out. Meanwhile, my net worth is going to go into the toilet.
Fuck that bastard. He used me like a twenty-dollar whore."

"But the loss, Morty. How much will we lose? I can't afford
to lose that money, Morty. It isn't all mine." Christ, Aaron
thought, panicking. None of it was his. Only the profits would
have been. Shit, he should have known. There was no free
lunch.

How could he have been so fucking stupid? Had he started
to believe his own fucking PR? Years ago, he had given up on
the market. He'd never wanted something for nothing. How
could he have trusted a *putz* like Morty? And gambled his
daughter's money? And Annie's?

It was the pressure. His support payments to Sylvie, carrying the weight of the business on his shoulders alone, and
his new life. It was always something. Leslie expected to live
a full cultural life. *And* a sexual one. He hadn't even been up
to see Sylvie yet.

Christ, how could he have let Morty talk him into it?
What could he do now? He'd like to grab Morty by the neck,
if he could find it under his chins, and snap it like a match.
He listened to Morty's breathing and wished he could make it
stop. The asshole was still talking.

"Okay, so call your broker. Tell him to sell. And I'll make
it up to you, I promise. Just get that call in."

"Sure. Sure." Aaron heard Morty hang up. He sat up, nervously running his hand across his brow; he was covered with sweat. Christ, that bastard Gil Griffin was unbelievable. Playing both sides of the fence. And paying off that Ewell jerk, too. Wasn't it typical that Morty would get stuck with his dick in the wringer? But my dick, too, he thought, wincing. Well, he'd call John Reamer at Federated Funds right away.

He sprang out of bed. But it was still only twenty to eight. There was nothing he could do until Reamer's office opened. He went into the bathroom, showered, and brushed his teeth.

It was still only five to eight when he was through. He dressed, made himself a pot of coffee. As he lifted the cup, he noticed his hand shaking and put it down abruptly. He checked his watch. Still, it was only a quarter after eight.

Already wired, he drank cup after cup. Visions of murder danced in his head. But who should he kill? Morty. Gil, Sylvie, himself? Jesus, it wasn't that bad, he told himself. Get a grip. Get a sense of perspective. At last, at five to nine he got through the switchboard to Reamer's office.

"John, it's Aaron Paradise."

"Yes, Aaron?" The broker's voice was cool. Probably pissed off that I went over his head on the trade. Well, he'd fix it now. He knew how to ingratiate himself when he had to.

"John, I've miscalculated a bit. Could you sell off the Madman stock I bought and repurchase CDs?"

"Well, I'd be relieved to. But I can't. I got a call from Annie and I must say she was adamant. Apparently she didn't know about the transaction. Neither did I." He sounded frosty. "Frankly, I was taken off guard. Anyway, we can't make a trade without her approval. Does she approve of this, Aaron?"

Aaron tried to think. How had Annie found out? Oh, Christ, the trade notification! He should have gotten to her before it did. He had been ducking her calls for three days now. He had meant to call her to explain. Well, what now? He could try to bluff John, but he had the feeling that a bluff wouldn't work at this point. Christ, didn't Morty say the stock would go into the toilet? How long did he have?

"No, no. But she will approve. I'd like to have all the shares sold, as soon as possible. She'll call you right back with a confirmation." Snotty little fuck, he thought. Aaron wondered if he had the nerve to call Gil again, decided he didn't, and picked up the phone.

It was five after nine. He dialed their old number. One ring. Two. Then three, four, five. Aaron imagined the four extensions ringing in all the empty rooms. Jesus Christ, where was Annie? Was she sleeping out? A man in her life? Couldn't be. But where *was* she? How long would it take to track her down? And what would happen to the portfolio in the meantime?

II

A Bill of Divorcement

Elise sat at the desk in her office, the letter from Larry Cochran crumpled on the desk before her. She smoothed it out and read it again carefully.

Dear Miss Elliot,
I met you on Memorial Day weekend at the Carlyle, and
I felt that I had to write you to let you know how much I
valued our brief time together. I did, however, do something
I am very sorry for: necessity forced me to sell your picture.
I was working on the enclosed, which you inspired. It is a
piece of me. I hope both that you'll like it and forgive me,
though both are unlikely.

Larry Cochran

Elise crumpled the note again, for the tenth time. She didn't know what to do. Was he blackmailing her? He certainly must know about her pending divorce. Was he threatening her? Did he want money? Were there more pictures? Were there pictures of the two of them at the Carlyle? If only she could remember. How much had she had to drink?

She was getting a headache, one of those awful ones with needles that mercilessly drilled her behind her left eye. If only

Chessie, her maid, were here, she'd bring a cool cloth and close the curtains, and after some Valium and a rest, Elise would feel better.

But here there was no one to look after her and no one to talk to. Although she loved Annie, and was even coming to like Brenda, she could never talk about this sordid liaison with a stranger. She was from a generation where nice girls did it, but never admitted it, and her own sexual appetite, once loosened, had frightened her. She had stopped herself back in Hollywood; she had seen what those promiscuous marriages had done to other women. Elise had sworn it would never happen to her. Yet this indiscretion, this single awful event, could ruin her. What if Bill found out? Could it stop the divorce proceedings? What if this Cochran person sold pictures to the *Enquirer*? And a story? Was she still hot enough news to matter?

Now, this letter, the photo, and some kind of a screenplay he had sent lay before her on the desk. She couldn't even bear to touch them. Was he trying to force her to put up production money? She shivered and felt her headache intensifying. She remembered her mother's stricture: "Never back a production, never support a husband." Well, so far she hadn't stooped to either, but her mother hadn't said, "Never pay off a blackmailer," and she didn't know what to do. Unfortunately, her mother, in her addled state, couldn't help her now. But maybe Annie and Brenda could, she thought, as she reached for the phone.

Brenda had spent hours each day at Elise's office, rooting around in Elise's files and her own, looking for anything that would help them in getting even with the four pricks. Surprisingly, she found that she liked it. Her bookkeeping skills—taught by Mrs. Goldman back at Julia Richman High—were coming back to her. Plus it was interesting. Slowly, slowly, from papers and memos and tax returns and financial statements, she was disinterring the bones of the skeleton in Morty's closet.

Today, as she walked as briskly as she could to the Algonquin Hotel to meet Annie and Elise for drinks, she mentally went through some of the findings. It should be a good meeting. Elise said she had news, and Brenda couldn't wait to spring all the dirt she'd unearthed.

And if she did it with Morty's stuff, why not with Bill's or Gil's or Aaron's? She wondered whose financial files she could get her hands on and how. Columns of numbers, receipts, tax claims, all those bits and pieces of paper were under her control. They couldn't yell or pout or hit you the way men could.

Those men, those big, powerful, scary men—they weren't so tough or invincible, not when you really looked at the facts. Sure, they ran the courts, the crime, the corporations, but you could, Brenda was starting to believe, you could, perhaps, use their own institutions to bring them down. Because Brenda, staring at Morty's confused and confusing paper trail, could clearly see malfeasance.

Maybe these guys weren't perfect, invincible. Maybe they were just schmucks with good haircuts. And maybe she, Brenda, was good at something. Maybe she could be more than just a fat ex-wife. But what?

That was where she got stuck. Because going back to school, getting her CPA or some other stupid series of initials behind her name, wasn't for her. The idea of doing other people's tax returns revolted her. Nah, she'd like to manage a little business, handle the accounts payable, deal with the tax boys, manage cash flow. But what business would hire a fat, middle-aged housewife without a degree or a résumé? Brenda sighed as she stepped into the Algonquin's dowdy lobby. In a quiet corner, she saw Annie and a pale and agitated Elise.

"What's up?" Brenda asked brightly, shocked at how upset the usually unflappable Elise appeared. Annie silently handed Brenda a crumpled piece of paper.

"What nerve!" Brenda said after reading Larry Cochran's note. "He takes your picture, sells it to *People,* then sends you a screenplay to read? I don't know, Elise, but it doesn't sound kosher to me."

"It's not, Brenda," Elise agreed. She took a sip of her martini. "What do I do about it, is the question. I couldn't bear to go to the police."

Elise noticed Annie lean into the upholstered arm of her chair. "First things first, Elise," she said. "Maybe you should give him a call. I'm sure if you talked to him, he would be reasonable." She picked up her San Pellegrino and held it in her hand. "After all," she continued, "what harm could be done by just talking to him?"

Elise tried not to let her irritation show. Before she could speak, Brenda jumped in.

"Plenty!" she told Annie. "It would just encourage him." Brenda signaled a passing waiter for a diet Coke, thinking to herself how silly it was, since she was already so fat. "We have a way of dealing with blackmailers and rats where I come from. I could call my Uncle Nunzio. Send someone around to break his legs." Brenda smiled at Elise's discomfort. "He'll get the message."

This isn't helping me at all, Elise realized, feeling suddenly very alone, and very upset. The martini wasn't helping her, either. As she always did in times of severe stress, she thought of Uncle Bob. I'll go to see him, Elise thought with relief. He'll know what to do. And maybe *he'll* take care of it.

"Leesie, my dear, how good to see you." The tiny man stood up, almost stiffly erect; even so, he wasn't five feet high. He walked toward her, his step brisk as ever. Elise was frightened that someday Uncle Bob Bloogee would begin to decline like her mother had, that she'd see the beginnings of that long slide to death, and once he was gone, she'd be completely on her own. All alone, forever. But reassuringly, he looked much as he always did: thin, bald, tiny, and wrinkled. He must be well into his seventies now, Elise knew, but as long as she had known him, it seemed to her he had looked much the same.

Robert Staire Bloogee was, arguably, the wealthiest man in the United States, perhaps even the world. His mother had been a Pittsburgh Staire and the heiress to both a steel and a coal empire. His father was the notorious Black Jack Bloogee, son of an Oklahoma wildcatter smart enough to tie up the mineral rights to more than eight hundred thousand acres of oil-rich Southwest land. As a result, his vast holdings dwarfed even the immense ones of Elise.

In addition to their individual fortunes, he had inherited his father's shrewdness and lust for life, and his mother's love of beauty. If he regretted that his physical stature never echoed his fiscal one, he didn't seem to show it. After all, Andrew Carnegie, that other rich Pittsburgh boy, had only stood five foot three. It hadn't hurt his career. Bob Bloogee had long ago gotten the point: life happens once—enjoy it and try to do some good.

Uncle Bob did both in a big way. He made huge contributions to charities—anonymously—and he entertained lavishly and often. He was only Elise's courtesy uncle, really a distant cousin. Since they'd met, when Elise was seven or eight, "Uncle" Bob had taken her on as one of his interests. He was always there for practical advice, a shoulder to cry on, a friend with whom to celebrate.

And he took care of things for her. He had gotten her first, disastrous marriage annulled and had himself given her away at her marriage to Bill. Now he was helping with her divorce. He was good at divorces, having had so many himself. He never judged Elise and always seemed thrilled by her achievements. He cultivated a wide, diverse circle of friends and was on excellent terms with his previous three wives. Currently he was at work on his memoirs, which he was calling *The Autobiography of a Nobody*. Altogether, he was a darling little man.

As always, it was so good to see him, Elise thought as he crossed the big room to meet her. She had to stoop to receive the kiss—a real kiss, no social air-smack—that he planted on her cheek.

"How is your mother?" he asked. "I haven't seen Helena since last month."

Elise sighed. "She's as good as she can be. It's me I'm worried about."

"Leesie, you didn't sound well on the telephone, and now, if you'll excuse me for saying so, you don't look well. Sit down, dear."

No one called her Leesie anymore, not even her mother. It was her baby name, the name her father had given her, that only he and her mother *ever* used. It felt good, comforting, to hear it again. Elise gratefully sank onto a down-cushioned fauteuil. The room, Uncle Bob's library and office, was lined with his magnificent collection of books, volumes that he actually read. The walls, where not covered by books, were hung with paintings, several of which were important. A Van Gogh self-portrait was over the enormous Gothic fireplace. Opposite his desk was a Vermeer, exquisitely depicting a woman reading a letter, an expression of deep concern on her face. How appropriate, Elise thought as she wordlessly handed Larry's crumpled note to her uncle.

He scanned it quickly and then looked back at her questioningly. "What is it, dear? What is this 'piece of himself' that he sent you? Something distasteful?"

Elise nodded. She thought of the screenplay and blanched. She knew how pale her face must be. His own paled.

"Not a body part?" he asked.

"Of course not." The surprise almost brought Elise back to herself. "No!" She shivered with repugnance.

"These things happen," Uncle Bob said. He inclined his head toward the Van Gogh. He paused a moment, delicately. Then he cleared his throat. "So what *did* he send?"

"A screenplay." It was worse, in its way, than an ear or a tooth. It was an insult, a demand. Elise knew that.

But Uncle Bob didn't seem to see it that way. "Was it any good?"

"I don't know!" she almost snapped. "Uncle Bob, that isn't the point. I'm worried about the implied threat."

"What threat?"

"Well, the tone."

"What tone?"

This wasn't going well at all. Usually Uncle Bob picked up on everything. He was usually so very intuitive. Elise sighed. She had hoped she wouldn't have to explain it, all the sordid details. But she supposed she would.

The whole story tumbled out. Cynthia's suicide, the funeral, Bemelman's, and her indiscretion. She laid herself bare. When she was done, she could hardly bear to look at him. "Are you very disappointed in me?"

But he was smiling, beaming at her. "I could never be disappointed in you, Elise. You are wonderful and so talented. I regretted it when you gave up your career—but not if it was what you wanted." He smiled at her and patted her hand. "I'm glad you got what you needed when you needed it."

Elise sighed. She had been so concerned Uncle Bob would

judge her harshly. She hadn't realized until this moment how much like a father he was to her.

"But now, are you afraid that this young photographer-cum-screenwriter has indecent photos?"

"I'm not sure."

"Do you think you were set up?"

"I don't know."

"Unlikely, my dear. Your behavior in the past would make you a long-shot candidate. Do you think your drink was spiked?"

"No! No, Uncle Bob, it's nothing like that." She couldn't tell him about her drinking—about how often she lost control. She couldn't tell him that she had simply blacked out, that she didn't remember getting home. Anyway, what difference would that make? She tried again. "It could affect the divorce."

"Well, I suppose anything could, but I've got Bill in a reasonable position. He wants to remarry ASAP, so it seems to be 'in one heir and out the other,' if you'll excuse the pun." He chuckled. "I'm delighted you're unloading that stiff at last. Frankly, Leesie, he bored me to death. Always did, the pompous ass. Well, at any rate, I expect we'll have papers ready to sign by next week. So what difference does this note make, even assuming it *is* a threat?"

"Oh, I don't know." Elise took a deep breath. Perhaps Uncle Bob was right. She wished she could feel more comfortable. She wished her head would stop hurting.

"Listen, dear, if it's bothering you so much, why don't I invite the young man up for a little chat? I'll have my man in McLean, Virginia, check him out a bit, too. And if he's clean, and I suspect he is, it looks like you have a fervent admirer, that's all." Uncle Bob smiled. "Was he any good?"

She was shocked. Uncle Bob was outspoken, but this . . . She thought of Larry's arms around her, his flat, broad chest against hers. In truth, it was something she thought of often. And the things he had said. She blushed. "Yes. Yes, he was."

"Then maybe you want to send the screenplay over to my man on the coast."

"Oh, the *screenplay* . . . ," Elise breathed. "No. It's not . . . I mean, I haven't even looked at it. I thought . . ."

"Elise!" Uncle Bob said, and now he sounded shocked. "What did you think I was asking about? Really!" But his eyes twinkled. He laughed, and she joined him.

"Uncle Bob, there's one other thing." She described the First Wives Club to him briefly and talked about their project.

"A worthwhile undertaking, my dear. Sounds like a lot of fun. You know, I've always despised men who got stingy with old spouses or women they'd made promises to. And Gil Griffin has been on my personal shit list for a long time. I was friends with Jack Swann, Cynthia's father. Good friends."

Uncle Bob came through again. She should have known she could always count on him.

He sighed. "Well, I don't suppose you'd let me be a member of the club, but you can count on my support."

"What an idea," Elise said. "Of course, I'll have to check with the other women, but you know you have my vote."

"Well, then. What's up?"

She told him about their plan. "We've already gotten a tip on Gil—he's planning a takeover of Mitsui Shipping. We couldn't pursuade Lally Snow to keep Gil and Mary out of her co-op, but Annie has blocked Shelby from the Junior League, And Brenda thinks she's found a way to put the screws to Morty. Things are moving along nicely, I'd say."

"Mitsui Shipping, huh? That's what Stuart told Annie? An odd target, though." The old man stood up briskly. "Very interesting."

She nodded. "What do you say to buying shares in volume while the price is still low? When word gets out that Gil Griffin is interested in Mitsui, the price will go up." Elise allowed herself a small smile. "Then we will make money, too."

"A dangerous ride, but interesting. Like riding a luge," Bob said. "But if you're going to ride a luge, you should first know three important things: what the highest point is, what the lowest point is, and when to bail out." Bob paused for a moment, letting this sink in. "People break their necks on luge rides, Elise."

"I'm aware of that, Uncle Bob. But I'm hardly a novice."

"That you're not," he said, laughing. "You've always used common sense in your portfolio." Then he added, "I'll get my man on Wall Street to do a little checking and then I'll throw my weight in, too, if it looks viable. How's that?"

"Great. Really great, Uncle Bob." He was so good, so reliable. And he threw around a lot of weight.

"By the way, I've heard a piece of news about Bill's new lady-friend, Phoebe Van Gelder. Are you up to hearing it? It might be information for your club."

"Uncle Bob, I'm years past being sensitive about Bill and his women. What's the scoop?" She sat back to listen. I hope it's something good, she thought.

"I ran into Wade Van Gelder at the University Club the other day. You know him, Elise. He's Phoebe's uncle. Anyhow, he tells me Phoebe's family is in an uproar over her drug use."

Elise smiled. "Well, news travels fast." She had dropped a word with her doctor. "In fact, she's doing so much cocaine that they ought to have her hospitalized for detoxification."

"That's what they're planning to do." He studied Elise for reaction.

"This *is* good news. Wait until I tell the girls. Brenda always says, 'What goes around, comes around.'"

He looked up at her. "Now, I'd like to ask a favor from you. Not a quid pro quo, of course, but something I'd appreciate. Something for my wife."

"Anything I can do. You know that."

"Well, Bette is having a hard time with a few of the society babes. You know, Lally Snow and that set. I don't know *why* they continue with the cold shoulder. Lally Snow has sucked more cock than Bette, and to less effect, I'll bet. Personally, if she'd stop speaking to me, I'd be grateful. But it upsets Bette, and that upsets me. She's such a sweet girl. And if she wants to chair charity balls, I say she shall. But those cunts keep getting in her way."

Elise blinked at the C-word, but she had to admit that it fit Lally Snow. "How can I help?"

"Get Bette her chairmanship and make the thing work. You know all the girls. Could you do it?"

Bette wasn't unpleasant, but she was dumb as a plank. Still, Elise would do anything for Uncle Bob. She knew how entrenched these old-guard New York women could be. Well, she would just have to be tough. I'm owed a lot of favors by this crowd. I'll just call some in, she thought. Bette is special to Uncle Bob. And he's special to me. "Of course. I'll do my best."

"Thank you, dear. I'd appreciate it and so would Bette." He bent forward. "You know, dear, getting it up at seventy-seven isn't easy, but Bette does help me manage it almost every night. She's a gift, and I'd like to see her get anything she wants."

"Absolutely." Elise nodded. It was always good to see Uncle Bob. He had such a real set of values.

Bill Atchison got into the Lincoln Town Car that waited for him outside Bob Bloogee's attorneys and gave his driver

Phoebe's downtown studio as his destination. He was, of course, being a gentleman about the financial settlement. He'd asked for nothing from Elise. And if all he had was his salary, his clothes, his very valuable collections, and Phoebe, that was enough. More than enough.

He was living with her at her loft in Tribeca now, but tonight they were meeting at her studio in SoHo. Now that he no longer had Elise's Rolls-Royce at his disposal—and couldn't afford his own car and driver—he had taken to using his firm's car service, billing it to various clients. Nothing new; he'd been charging things off for years. He thought of it simply as extending his income, one of the perks of the profession. And with the huge fees the firm charged, a few extra dinners or nights on the town never registered with clients. It helped make ends meet.

As he settled into the upholstered seat and thought of Phoebe, Carly Simon's "Anticipation" came through the car's speakers. How appropriate, he thought, for he was filled to the brim with it. He reached for the car phone and punched in Phoebe's number. He'd called her four times during the day, but he couldn't wait another minute.

"It's me," he said when she answered.

"Oh, Bill," she said anxiously, "where are you? When will you get here?"

"I'm calling from a car phone, honey. I should be there in about twenty minutes. What's the matter?"

"Bill"—she began to cry—"it's my uncle Wade and the others. They want me to see a psychiatrist." Her voice became smaller at these last words, and she continued to sob.

"Psychiatrist? What for?" he asked, trying not to show he was upset.

"They're saying I have a drug problem. Can you believe that? For Christ's sake. Just because I do a little cocaine socially, those tight asses think I'm a fucking junkie. Jesus, Uncle Wade thinks *two* glasses of sherry before dinner makes you an alcoholic. Anyway, they say I either have to see a psychiatrist or they will put me in a detoxification place."

Bill began to calm down. He knew how to control the situation. "Is that all? Don't worry about a thing. I've got just the psychiatrist for you."

"But I don't *want* to see a psychiatrist. There's nothing wrong with me. I'm the first artist in the family, and they just don't understand the artistic temperament."

"Slow down, honey," he said soothingly. "Why antagonize the family if you don't have to? You'll go see Dr. Leslie Rosen, Aaron Paradise's fiancée; she'll tell your uncle Wade that all you need is a few sessions with her, and then it will all blow over. Don't panic. I'll call her first thing tomorrow. Just relax, okay?"

"Okay, I'll relax. Just hurry and get here. I need you."

Bill hung up the phone. He congratulated himself. He had handled the situation just right. Now he was going to have a good time, just as he'd planned.

The irony of the moment caused Bill to smile to himself. While at the offices of Elise's attorneys, signing the divorce settlement not fifteen minutes ago, he knew he appeared to the distinguished partners as somber, grave, in the face of what, for most, would have been a sad time. And, since he was coming away from the marriage with nothing, in accordance with the prenuptial agreement he had signed, he also appeared to be taking it all like a gentleman.

But with Phoebe on his mind, he could afford to be gracious. There was no real loss here, he assured himself. For him, it was all gain. Money, beauty, youth. Phoebe, young Phoebe, was so like Elise in the early years of their marriage.

He had loved the unconventional bohemian life Elise had

exposed him to in Europe. They had been the only married couple in that circle in those days, and they had played at being poor to fit in. Long after she quit the film business, she was welcomed by prominent intellectuals and film greats all over the world. He had been proud to be seen with her as she escorted him through the demimonde. It gave him the feeling of being on the cutting edge. If it were possible for a rich man to be avant-garde then he had been, or at least felt as if he had been. And now he was again. It felt right: it was where he belonged. He shrugged out of the suit jacket he had been wearing and put on the baby-skin soft black leather blazer that he loved. Slick, hip, but tastefully so. Just like Phoebe.

Phoebe had seemed so beautiful and unreachable when he first met her. Like Elise, Phoebe came from an obscenely wealthy family who provided for her while she developed her art. He had recognized her talents, all of them, and she had exposed him to the greats and soon to-be-greats of the very fashionable downtown art scene.

It was so exciting. Phoebe gave him back his youth, reminding him of the happy times with Elise. It's like a second chance, he thought. Again, he had a young, rich creative woman who wanted him. And I want her, he thought. The art crowd, the openings, the gossip. And the constant round of parties and events. The similarities of today's downtown scene and the film world of Europe in the sixties excited him.

Of course, living with the rich has its own set of problems, he reflected as his car inched along Park Avenue South. Even though he didn't have a monthly mortgage or rent to pay as other men did, a certain standard had to be maintained when married to a wealthy woman. And $250,000 a year from Cromwell Reed wouldn't quite do it.

When his car stopped for a red light, he noticed the clusters of business executives making their way home to Long

Island and New Jersey. What do those guys make, $50,000 a year tops? he thought. They go out once a month, it costs maybe a hundred bucks for the night, dinner and a movie with friends. What a life.

If I hadn't figured out how to lay off some of my expenses to the firm, I could never have afforded to escort Elise around. As the car gathered speed after the light changed, he thought about the article in the *New York Post* his secretary had shown him: *"$15,000 for a night out for Ivana and Donald."* He remembered how the secretary had laughed derisively at the amount. Bill knew it was true; he could even count it up. Ten units for a dress she could only wear once. (He had trained himself to think of $1,000 as a "unit." It was less nerve-racking than thinking in thousands.) Hairdresser, manicurist, masseuse, makeup artist, jewels, car, ball or theater tickets, dinner out for ten. "See what I mean?" he had told his secretary. "It all adds up. Fifteen units easy." His secretary had nodded in stunned silence. "It's difficult to live with the rich," he had added.

And he meant it. I never took a dime from Elise, he thought. I never wanted to give up the control, be dependent. It's not good for a man, he thought.

Of course, he *had* had to develop his little system of creative billing of some of his expenses to both his clients and his firm, but didn't he bring in Elise's business? And now that he'd lost that, look what Gil Griffin was earning the partnership. *I* brought in Gil Griffin. No matter that the firm would be losing all Elise's financial management, estate planning, and legal counsel, now that they were divorced. Gil's business will give me back more muscle. My *own* muscle. He smiled. You win some, you lose some.

Client billing had covered the cost of nights at the Waldorf with girlfriends. As well as his new two-unit tuxedos bespoke by Savile Row's best. And the bespoke shoes! Oh, yes, he acknowledged confidently. I'm covered and won't have to change my lifestyle one bit. Good-bye, Elise.

As the car pulled up at Phoebe's studio on Spring Street, Bill jumped out and hurried up the steps to the entrance. Phoebe responded to the buzz in her tiny, almost childlike voice. "I'm on my way," he yelled into the speaker, and pushed his way through the now-unlocked door.

As he waited for the lumbering freight elevator to respond, he felt the excitement of being close to Phoebe. So young, so sexy. So *young*.

In a moment of truth, he would have to admit that he felt a certain sexual excitement when he looked at the young. The younger the better. As he got older, his women seemed to get younger. It had troubled him for a while, but Phoebe had been the one who had recognized the unseemly side to his sexuality, and by articulating his fantasy for him, she had removed most of the guilt he felt after fantasizing about adolescents. He had never discussed it—this need—with anyone. Not until Phoebe.

Walking onto the elevator, he felt his erection strain against the fly of his trousers. He wanted to touch himself badly, but held off the moment of contact, only increasing his excitement.

Without being told, Phoebe had known each part of his very private fantasies, and slowly, over time, with gentle and tender understanding, she was helping him express his need, experience it, and find release in it. "Because it is good," she had said. So long as they acted it out together.

And so they had. They had come to call these sexual encounters their own "performance art." Bill had little use for actual performance art, but to Phoebe and her sophisticated circle, it was de rigueur, even old-fashioned. They accepted it. They accepted him.

He got off the elevator and walked down the hall to her studio door. He rang impatiently and heard her bustling activity on the other side. A moment more, and he rang the doorbell again, longer. The door finally flew open, and Phoebe jumped excitedly into his arms, slightly out of breath.

"Baby, what took you so long?" he said into her soft neck.

She pushed into his nuzzling and said, "I just wanted to make sure all my work is covered. You mustn't see it yet. Not till it's perfect."

She pulled back and tugged him into the massive work space. He looked around at the sheet-covered work that took up much of the vast floor space.

"What's all this? What are you working on?" he asked with feigned interest as he walked to the messy table that held both sculpting tools and vodka and tequila bottles.

"My best work so far, Bill. At least I think so." She hesitated. "Fix me a drink, too."

He quickly complied, handing her an iced vodka as he fell onto the king-size futon on the raised platform in one corner of the loft.

"Come here," he said, reaching for her and pulling her down to him. "Whose girl are you?" he asked from deep in his throat.

But Phoebe jumped up and said, "Wait, not yet. First, take your drink and come with me."

And the ritual began. The long, slow, hot shower together, more chilled vodka, some lines of snow that amplified the excitement, and then, the tableau.

They had acted this out many times after Phoebe uncovered his particular need, always embellishing it slightly, and always ending in the same way.

At last he had her, trapped in the corner the way he liked

it, the way she liked it. He asked her again, "Whose little girl are you?"

And she answered as she always did, answered as she did now, straddling him like a little girl on her daddy's lap. She alone controlled him. She rode him slowly, her flat chest glistening with sweat, her almost hairless body swallowing his organ deep, deep within her. "I'm Daddy's little girl. Daddy, Daddy." This simple phrase had become the key to their perfectly timed release. She had him and he knew it.

12

Crying All the Way to the Bank

T he day after Halloween when Brenda received the first million-dollar check from Morty, she felt as if she had won the lottery. And there was another one yet to come! She could hardly believe it. She remembered the "Millionaire" series on television when she was a kid and wished she had a John Beresford Tipton she could kiss.

She kissed the check instead, then held it over her head as she danced around the room—until she caught a glimpse of herself in the mirror over the sofa. She came to a stop, the image of herself as one of the dancing hippos in *Fantasia* too vivid to ignore. Still, the exercise classes with Bernie and his twin were having some impact. Maybe now she looked more like the little elephant that danced around the Delacorte clock at the zoo. Even her weight couldn't dampen her spirits for more than a moment today.

She imagined a week in the Hotel Sacher in Vienna surrounded by mounds of spicy, warm potato salad and veal cutlets, Sacher torte and apple strudel with fresh whipped cream. She hugged herself at the imagined tastes and smells. "Fuck it, make that two weeks."

Oh, but her weight. Sobering for a moment, she thought, maybe one week Sacher, one week fat farm. No, that didn't sound like fun. She sat down glumly. But why be glum? Money and time were unlimited. "Okay, two weeks Sacher, one week fat farm. And that's my final offer," she said out loud.

Then she went to the phone and called Annie, knowing how happy Annie would be for her. She had become very fond of Annie. They had always been friendly, but lately it seemed warmer, deeper, like having a best friend.

Annie answered on the second ring, "Kiddo, I'm rich," Brenda announced. "Guess what the postman did, and don't get dirty." She laughed. "I got Morty's check. With all those zeros. Now I know what they mean by round numbers."

Annie listened as Brenda continued to crow. "I don't know about you, kid, but the only other time I've seen that number written out was in Trump's first book."

She paused for a response, got none, and went on, not skipping a beat. "You know the nicest part? It's thinking of the pain it must have caused Morty to write the check. I woulda *loved* to have seen that bastid's face when he signed it." The image of Morty chomping mercilessly on a cigar, his face burning red, eyes bulging in rage, popped into her mind. She patted her hairdo in satisfaction. "Whattya think, Annie? Help me spend it?"

Annie's voice sounded strained in spite of the obvious effort she made to pick up Brenda's enthusiasm. "Congratulations, Brenda. What wonderful news."

"Is there something wrong, Annie? Did I call at a bad time?" Brenda asked, beginning to feel her enthusiasm wane. "Here I've been running off at the mouth and haven't asked you how you are."

"No, no, Brenda. I'm fine. I just have something on my mind. But what great news, Brenda. You did it. You won."

"Yeah, I guess I did." Brenda was amazed.

"Now what are you going to do with all that money?"

"Feed the hungry," Brenda said, and burst out laughing.

Then Annie laughed, too, in spite of herself. "Oh, Brenda, I shouldn't encourage your eating problem, but you always can make me laugh." She paused. "It's just that I've had some really bad financial news."

"I knew it, I *knew* something was wrong. Here I was thinking you were envious or something. Hey, don't do that to me. I'm half-Catholic, too, you know. I'll imagine the worst. What's up?"

Then Annie told her the whole story about Aaron's stock deal, about Sylvie's trust fund, and about how it was mostly gone now. Brenda could hardly believe it.

"Wait. So he finally got in touch with you and says it was a miscalculation? A mistake? He's a piece of shit, Annie. A piece of shit!"

"No. He says he'll pay it all back. By the end of the month. He promised."

"Yeah, he also promised till death do him part, but he parted. He's a piece of shit, Annie."

"He's only a piece of shit if he doesn't make up the money," Annie said. "Anyway, I'll deal with it. In the meanwhile, *you* must celebrate. Dance naked on Madison Avenue. Take a vacation." She paused, then continued, sounding more serious, "I'm so happy for you, Brenda. You deserve only the best. Now, there is one thing you absolutely *must* do before you do anything else." Jesus, Brenda thought. She's gonna tell me to get an IRA or a CD or one of those damn things. "You have got to go out and get yourself a very expensive, very self-indulgent present. Not for Angela. Not for Tony. For *you*. Will you do that?" Annie asked in her very best good-mommy tone.

"Yeah." Brenda paused, suddenly shy. "Annie, where do you get your shoes? Those really nice ones?"

"Helene Arpels. They'd look great on you."

Brenda was touched. "Annie, thank you." Then she added, "Will you come shopping for them with me?"

"Would I? We'll make a day of it, Just the two of us."

Brenda felt her eyes begin to fill. Before she lost it, she hurriedly said, "Thanks, Annie. You're the first person I thought to tell." Gaining back her bravado, she added, "Now, gotta go. Gotta call Elise. See you round the clubhouse."

Next she called Elise, who took Brenda by surprise with her excitement. "You don't mean it, Brenda? You really have it? That's wonderful," she said, drawing out the first syllable of *wonderful.* "And you have another check coming, don't you? Well, good for you. Good for us. It was brave of you to go up against him. I know you didn't want to go to court, to drag out dirty linen. And I know how threatening bad press can be. You never cease to amaze me, Brenda," she had added with genuine warmth.

Brenda was moved, but managed to give credit where credit was due. "And Diana amazes *me*. I don't know what I would have done without her." She realized, as she said it, how very much she meant it.

"What are your plans, Brenda?" Elise asked. "You know, if you invest that money properly, you can get yourself both a tidy little income for the rest of your life *and* a very small tax bite." She paused, not wishing to offend, to find the right words. "If you like, I could get you investment and tax advice. I've organized my portfolio now. I could help. I mean, if you wanted me to."

Brenda was having a good day. Money and friends. "Elise, I would be very grateful if you would do that. Thank you."

After she hung up, Brenda left her hand resting on the receiver while she took it all in. I have girlfriends, she thought, tentatively adding Diana's name to the short but distinguished list. Growing up in the Bronx, with her dad busted so often, she had never gotten close to anyone outside the family. "I have girlfriends." It sounded good out loud.

So good that Brenda shouted, "And another million bucks on the way!"

Two weeks later, just a week before Thanksgiving, Brenda was having a very different conversation on the same telephone.

"Welshed? Are you trying to tell me that prick welshed on our agreement? Morty's not going to give me the second payment?" Brenda screamed into the phone to Diana.

"So it would appear, Brenda. I'm sorry. His lawyer said that he doesn't consider the agreement binding. It's outrageous."

"Tell me straight, Diana, so I can understand this. When Leo Gilman tells you, 'Mr. Cushman no longer considers our agreement binding,' he's really saying the prick welshed? Right?"

"Right."

Brenda felt the dampness of her hands, her heart pounding. But through her rage, she began to sense Diana's discomfort on the other end of the line and realized how difficult it must be for Diana to make this call.

"You have every right to be furious," Diana said. "It isn't a rational decision on Morty's part. Even Leo Gilman seems surprised."

"He just couldn't take it. Seeing his net worth diminish."

"I'm so sorry."

"I'm sorry too. Diana, but I'm not mad at you," Brenda added, lowering her voice. She didn't want to hurt Diana. "It's just that I like to call a spade a fucking spade, in the loudest voice I know, just so I get it. So I don't forget it. I should have known the cheap fuck wouldn't pay up. I blame myself."

"Well, I blame *myself*. I should have pushed for more, and a heftier payment up front. Of course, we'll sue."

"Sue, shmoo. It will be a long time before I see another

check. Tell you what," Brenda added, trying to sound cheerful. "How about I take you to lunch today. I'm always more under control when I'm eating."

"I'd love it. But honestly, Brenda. You don't have to control yourself around me. I love the way you just let go. What a gift."

Brenda, pleased, said, "You think so? You ain't seen nothin' yet." Diana made her feel so good, despite the bad news. "Carnegie Deli at one o'clock? And you'll recognize me immediately. I'll be the 'full-figured gal' with a corned beef sandwich between my teeth. And steam coming out of both ears."

At the Deli, Brenda had time to take a table before she saw Diana stride confidently into the restaurant. Something about Diana made her excited, like a girl on her first date or something. She paused and hung her head, not liking the simile; she looked up to find Diana towering over the table.

"I'm not late, am I?" Diana asked, glancing both at her watch and the plate of potato salad in front of Brenda.

"Nah, this isn't lunch. This is just like, you know, pickles on the table. Something to nosh on while you're waiting for the real food."

Diana smiled and nodded, slipping into her seat. As the waitress approached the table, Diana asked Brenda if the fruit salad was fresh here.

Brenda almost choked on the last forkful of potato salad. "What, are you crazy?" she asked incredulously. "You're in a Jewish deli, for chrissakes, with a Jewish food maven."

"I don't know much about deli food. What do you suggest?"

Brenda turned to the waitress and without pausing for a breath, reeled off a list of dishes. "Give this *shiksa* white-meat turkey on rye with Russian dressing, lots of Russian dressing. Even some on the side. And give her an order of nice fried potatoes, well done, not those white things. *And* an order of coleslaw."

To Diana she added in explanation, "We'll share the slaw."

Turning back to the waitress, who was expertly getting it all down, she continued, "I'll have corned beef on rye, not too lean. I hate it dry. And an order of *kasha varnishkas*—put some brown gravy on that."

Turning to Diana, who was mesmerized by this litany, Brenda asked, "You ever had a knish?" Diana hardly got the word *no* out before Brenda, rolling her eyes, continued to the waitress, "And to start, let's have a potato knish each."

"Where've you been? China?" Brenda asked Diana. "And don't worry, you'll love it," she assured her. "And two cream sodas. I'd order you a celray, but I don't want to shock your system. We'll start gently. And yeah, do you have any sour pickles? Really sour. I hate the half-sours. Too much like a fresh vegetable. And those will kill you."

Diana laughed as the waitress strode away. "I'll never eat all that food. I'm used to very light lunches, Brenda."

"Yeah, and look at you. Skin and bone. Anyway," Brenda continued, "you need your strength to help me deal with Morty, the cheap fuck. I'm helpless without you. And now we have some money in the war chest."

And despite her bravado, Brenda knew that she did feel helpless. She paused. "What am I going to do, Diana?" It wasn't the money. With a million bucks Brenda didn't have to worry. But Morty was cheating her. He had another 30 or 40 million. It made her furious. All at once tears sprang to her eyes. Brenda was embarrassed.

Diana reached across the table and placed a comforting hand on Brenda's. "Don't cry, Brenda. We'll figure out a way. We'll get him."

Brenda couldn't understand why Diana's gentle hand felt

so good on hers. And why she was so moved, and so comforted, by Diana's saying "we." Why do I feel so good while I feel so bad, she thought, and once again, pushed the confusion from her mind.

"So what do we do now?" she asked, wiping her eyes on the paper napkin and then taking a bite of the knish the waitress had placed before her. "Do I sue him for it, or do I just give up? And if I accept the fact that it will take years to fight him in court, and maybe lose in the end—who knows?—what do I do then, go for revenge and turn to Uncle Sam? If we really turn him in to the IRS, I still won't see my money."

Diana thought for a minute. "You could take him to court, and it could take years. But if you're worried about the legal fees, I could work on contingency. I feel partly responsible. Let me do it this way: you would only have to pay me if we won. After all, I'm beginning to feel like we're in this together."

"Diana, you're one of the most decent people I have ever met. And just about the *only* decent lawyer. Thank you."

Diana smiled and continued, "Of course, you can go for revenge. That's an emotional payoff you can get sooner, but in my opinion, it doesn't beat money."

Brenda wasn't paying too much attention to the sandwiches that had been placed on the table. She was thoughtful, as if she were about to make one of those important life decisions. Slowly she said, "Diana, what would happen to me if I really turned Morty in to the IRS, with all the documentation they needed? What would they do to me? I mean, most years they were joint returns."

Diana shrugged. "I think we need an expert tax attorney on this, Brenda. We never meant to actually do it. It was a bargaining chip. We thought it was worth two million, and stock, but it turned out to be worth only a million. At least for now. Let's give this some thought."

Brenda nodded and began eating. "Remember my men-tioning Elise Elliot to you? *The* Elise Elliot? Well, she offered to help me with investment and tax advice. If anyone has a pipeline to the workings of the IRS, it would be Elise." Brenda looked up at Diana. "That is, if you don't mind."

"We can use all the help we can get," Diana said. "And by the way, the knish was great. I don't even remember eating the whole thing."

"Yeah, I know what you mean, kid. I have the same prob-lem myself. How's the turkey?"

Diana took a bite and moaned with delight.

"Speaking of food, what are you doing for dinner next Sunday?" Brenda asked.

"Nothing," Diana admitted.

"So, how about comin' over to my house. Tony and Angela are going to be home and I'm cooking up a storm. How 'bout it?"

"I'd love to."

By the time Brenda got to Duarto's office, she was confused. How could I go from total depression this morning to feel-ing so happy this afternoon? she thought. Nothing's changed. I'm still not going to get what Morty owes me, that's a fact I accept. So what's different?

Diana was so kind this afternoon at lunch, she remem-bered as she began opening that morning's mail, bills and important correspondence to one side, dropping third-class advertising unopened into the waste basket. What was it that Diana had said? she thought. "Don't cry, Brenda *we'll* figure out a way." *We.*

Brenda sat back for a moment, staring into space. "We," she said aloud. That feels so good, she thought. Maybe even too good. What exactly is going on? She went to the small refrigerator under Duarto's worktable and took out the box of cream-filled cupcakes she had put there yesterday.

I'm happy when I'm with Diana, that's what's going on, she thought. I'm happy because I feel she cares about me, wants to help me, and doesn't judge me. So what's wrong with that? she asked herself. What's wrong with being drawn to a woman who offers me kindness and friendship and very real help?

So then what's the problem? she continued to probe. She took another cupcake from the box and walked to the window that afforded a view of Fifty-eighth Street at Park Avenue. The problem is that I don't know what I feel, nor what I want, and there is no one I can talk to honestly right now. Not about this, anyway.

Brenda thought of Annie, and their date this evening to meet at the Metropolitan Museum. It wasn't that she felt Annie couldn't handle it—she was sure Annie could. That wasn't it. It was saying the words out loud to someone else. It seemed that once they were said, they were permanent, irrevocable.

No, she thought, I have to go slowly with this. Small steps.

Later that evening, Brenda fell into a cane-backed chair in the restaurant at the museum and let out a loud sigh.

Annie, sitting opposite, started to laugh. "Honestly, Brenda. You've only walked around for a little over an hour. You're not *that* out of shape anymore."

"It's not the shape *I'm* in, it's the shape *my feet* are in." She took off a shoe to massage a foot. "Tony told me about a friend of his that went to France one summer. The kid came back with one of those laser disks he got at the Louvre. It had a picture of every one of the works of art in the museum. All you had to do is lie on the couch and click a little button on the TV's remote control to move to the next picture." Brenda now massaged the other foot. "Those French are sure civilized. Why can't the Met do that?"

"You're missing the point, Brenda."

Before Annie could continue, Brenda raised one hand and said, "Wait, don't tell me. It's 'no pain, no gain.' Right? That's the point, right? Must have been one of those New England WASPs that coined that one."

At that moment, the waiter came to the table. "Bring me a pan of hot water and some Epsom salts, and a cup of tea for my friend," Brenda directed.

"Would that be a large pan of hot water or a small one?" the good-looking young man said, not missing a beat.

Brenda laughed out loud, and so did Annie.

After their tea arrived, Annie leaned forward on her elbows as she spoke to Brenda. "I'm so sorry about Morty backing out of his agreement, Brenda. It's a rotten thing to do." She placed her hand gently on Brenda's. "How are you doing?"

"Oh, I've been worse. But I've been thinking, Annie. You know, life is funny." She took a sip of tea and placed the cup gently on its saucer. "I never loved Morty, never even thought I loved him. In fact, I never thought it was possible for me to love anyone, anyone else, I mean. I felt love one summer at camp, when I was sixteen." Brenda paused, not sure if she was going to be more specific, and deciding she had to tell someone something about how she felt.

"Her name was Ivy and she was a counselor. We used to sneak into the craft room after lights-out and cuddle on the floor on a blanket." Brenda didn't look at Annie. "We talked about everything those nights. During the day we ignored one another, but those nights, snuggling into her in the damp darkness, not able to see her face, I knew something special was happening to me. The night before I left for home, we made love. I should say she made love to me, I just accepted it. The next morning I went home, and I never saw her again."

Tears glistened in Brenda's eyes. "Don't get me wrong, Annie. I wanted to, but she said it would be best not to, to just hang on to what we got, because it might have to last a long time. So, it lasted me while I was married to Morty. Now it's run out, and I feel so empty and alone." Brenda allowed the tears to fall. "I want to feel loved again, Annie. I know you can understand that, can't you?"

"Of course I can. Honestly, Brenda, you have so much love to give. Don't hold back."

Brenda blotted her eyes with a crumpled Kleenex. "Thank you, Annie."

Elise stepped into the dark interior of Shea's Lounge on Second Avenue and stood nervously, her eyes straining to adjust to the subdued lighting of the bar-restaurant that so contrasted with the sparkling sunlight at her back. Although she lived on Park Avenue only three long blocks away, they were in the wrong direction. Park Avenue matrons did not shop or dine on Second. But she had been here, once or twice, long ago. The barkeeper approached and asked, "Ms. Elliot?" She nodded, surprised, having gotten used to being unrecognized. But he had been sent by Larry. The barkeeper led her to a corner table in the back room, replete with red-checkered tablecloth and regulation candle in a Perrier bottle. Two decades ago, when she had last dated, she thought wryly, they had been Chianti bottles. Larry stood up as she approached and, reaching for the chair opposite before the maître d' pulled it out, settled it under Elise as she dropped her bag on the table.

Giving herself time to also settle her nerves, Elise pulled off her gloves and looked around the room with obvious pleasure. "You picked the perfect place, Larry," she said, turning her attention to him and smiling. "It's a nice old-fashioned bistro, despite the cutesy name."

Larry beamed with pleasure. He had obsessed for days about where he could take her to lunch. He wanted it to be perfect. Someplace inexpensive, but good. Not too new. Definitely not flashy. "When I was at Columbia, I had a friend from school who worked here as a waiter on weekends. So this was always our jumping-off spot on Friday nights. I had some great times here."

Elise noticed how much like a college boy he still looked, dressed in his tweed jacket and blue oxford shirt. "Me, too," was all she said. "A long time ago, I used to come here also. It was after the summer I had spent in Rome. That was the year every publication in America had that picture of me 'cavorting' in the Trevi Fountain, with two *carabinieri* wading in to arrest me." She smiled at the memory.

"I remember that picture!" Larry said. "I've seen it. It was a great shot. The reporters said you jumped in, but you insisted you were pushed. Which one was it, Elise?"

Her eyes narrowed for a moment, over the memory. "Neither," she said with a self-satisfied grin. "I was carried in. Publicity for a movie. Even the *carabinieri* were actors." She looked down at the martini Larry had ordered for her and longed to take a drink. No, she thought, the double I had before I left the house will have to be enough. She'd stick with the Pellegrino in the water glass. "And when I came back to New York, I came here with friends. There was an Australian soccer team celebrating a victory, and they recognized me from that picture. They made me the team mascot that night and taught me naughty words to 'Waltzin' Matilda.' I had such a wonderful time. It was 1961."

"That was the year I was born," Larry said.

An embarrassed silence fell between them. Elise was

relieved to see the waiter appear at their table, pad in hand. "Would you like to order?" he asked. Elise didn't need the menu. "I'll have a small salad," she said. "And your famous ranch dressing, if you still make it."

Larry ordered a chopped steak and fries, then turned his attention toward her once again, picking up the thread of their conversation. "Elise, I'm so happy you agreed to see me. I wanted so badly to see you again. I did everything I could to reassure Mr. Bloogee I mean you no harm." He paused, then stammered, "In fact, I hold you in the highest regard. I would never hurt you." He felt himself flush.

Elise was moved. He was, in a way, wonderfully old-fashioned, she thought. He seemed mature beyond his years. Uncle Bob was right. He had said Larry was a unique individual. Elise was beginning to see what he meant. His manner was almost courtly, she realized. When was the last time Bill, or any man, had been tender to her?

Not wanting Larry to misunderstand the reason she was meeting with him, she quickly said, "Larry, I've read the draft of your screenplay." She could see Larry take in his breath and hold it for what seemed like minutes. "And I think it's wonderful." He exhaled. "You have a very visual eye. It's as if it were written with a camera. Do you know what I mean?"

He blushed. The boy actually blushed. Elise sighed. He was nice, maybe *too* nice. And young. Too young. "There are some things, though, that I think won't work."

"Really, what?"

"When she goes into the church. All of that seems so, well, self-conscious."

"Too arty, you think?"

"Yes. And the ending. Why the happy ending? It seems so unlike the rest of the piece. So tacked on."

"I know. I didn't see it that way originally. I think I just couldn't bear to see you unhappy."

"Well, it's the wrong ending. Wrong for the *character*."

"Elise, I wrote it with *you* in mind. This film is for you."

Elise had already known that. Every page of the script was written as if through her character. Nonetheless, she hadn't been prepared for Larry's statement. The screenplay seemed so personal, which was what made it so powerful. There was something about him that made emotions safe. But she wanted to defuse the heightened atmosphere.

This is only a business meeting, she reminded herself. Don't make a fool of yourself again, she told herself sternly as she pushed her untouched drink away and picked up her fork. She wished for—longed for—a real drink, not the useless Pellegrino water. But she didn't touch the martini. She was determined not to lose control today. "To be honest, I haven't considered acting for many years, Larry. But my life is chang-ing now; perhaps the timing is right. I think I could play this role better than someone else."

Their food arrived and looked uninspired. Well, the place was a dive, really. Larry didn't touch his plate, his excitement at seeing Elise again and the possibility of her taking the star-ring role—*her* role—tying his stomach into knots. "There is no one else, Elise," he said almost in a whisper.

Elise, purposely misunderstanding, said, "Of course there is. Dina Merrill could play it."

"That's not what I mean, Elise. I mean, I have never felt this way before in my life. I'm in love with you."

Elise lowered her head to hide the blush of pleasure his declaration brought to her cheeks. This was ridiculous! He was talented, and the screenplay was a good one, but the rest was nonsense, she warned herself. "You don't know me," she said as quietly as he. "It was just one afternoon."

"I've known you all my life. I've always loved you." He touched her hand holding the fork, then seeing her face, let go quickly.

Oh, this has to be a scam, she thought. Or he's deluded. Thank God I'm not drinking or I'd fall into bed with him and be in real trouble. Her lips trembled.

Before she recovered, he asked, "Can I see you again, Elise? I *must* see you again. We could just talk. About the screenplay. Or your career. Or mine, if I had one. I want to make you happier than you've ever been."

Then she remembered. That was what he had said that afternoon at the Carlyle. "Oh, God, Larry, I don't know. I don't know." I can't give in to this, she thought. He's less than half my age. He's a child. He's a manipulator. Or else he doesn't know what he wants. I'm just an experience. "Larry, let me first make a decision about acting again. Let me start there." His face tightened. Oh, God, I've hurt him, she thought. "I'm so confused. Please, Larry, leave me alone. My life is upside down right now."

She reached for her pocketbook and the check at the same time. Larry reached over quickly and took the check. "This is on me, remember? I asked *you* to lunch. And I appreciate your advice on the script."

She stood up and offered him her hand. He held it for a long moment while they both looked at each other. "Fine," she said. "And I would like to see the screenplay when it's revised." She impulsively leaned forward, kissed him on one cheek while holding the other in her warm palm, then turned and walked quickly to the door.

"I'll wait for your call," she heard him say as she stepped out into the glaring sunlight. She put her sunglasses on, grateful to them for hiding the tears welling up in her eyes.

．　．　．

But that night Elise slept well, for the first time in weeks. The next morning, going up to her office in the elevator, she replaced her sunglasses in her bag and gave another quick look at herself in her mirror. She was surprised to see a glowing, happy face reflected back, instead of the sad, bloated one she had expected. She took this as a good sign.

As she walked into her office, she was again surprised, finding Annie and Brenda sprawled on her couch in excited, happy conversation. They both looked up at her with pleasure. Brenda, of course, was the first to speak.

"Where have you been, kid? Hot date?" Brenda had the uncanny ability to pick up the truth from the air like a radio. This time, thank goodness, she didn't know it.

Annie said, "What a beautiful outfit," eyeing Elise's Ungaro. "It makes you look twenty years younger, I swear. Or is it your hair? What have you done?"

"Oh, I've been making a new life for myself," Elise said airily as she sat down on the chair angled next to the sofa, crossed her long, slim legs, and turned her attention to her friends. "I think I might act in a film again. And who knows, maybe even produce it."

"Wonderful," Annie said. "It's just what you need, Elise. Do something for yourself."

"Good girl," Brenda said. "Do you have a movie in mind, or are you doing a remake of *Sunset Boulevard?*"

Elise laughed. "Yes, I have a script in mind. But before I do that, I have other unfinished business to handle. Which leads me to my question: What are you two cooking up? Brenda, you look like the cat that ate the canary."

"Make that a rat," Brenda said. "Here's the thing: Morty's welshed on our agreement. He's not going to give me the second check. So, I figure, what's the next best thing to money?

Revenge. Let's give him to the IRS. I'm ready. I got a shitload of goods on him."

She threw a handful of jelly beans into her mouth from the bowl Elise now kept filled on the coffee table. "Whattya think?"

Elise didn't hesitate. "I say stick it to him. If you really believe you're not going to get the money, throw him to the lions. This may be the crack in the wall." She sat back and shook her head. "What a bastard!"

"Diana suggests I get a tax expert to go over the returns to determine how this would affect me. Diana says maybe I could get immunity when I turn him in."

Before Brenda could continue, Elise joined in. "Why don't I call my tax attorney and get him over here? He's the best, Brenda."

Brenda was happy that Elise offered before she had asked. "Yes, please, Elise. And the sooner, the better."

Annie watched. Brenda had lost a million dollars and could laugh. Why couldn't she? That morning Aaron had called to say he'd hit "a little glitch." He wouldn't be able to make up the losses until after the end of the year. But meanwhile Annie had to pay for this quarter of Sylvie's school, and the next would be due before the end of the year. Aaron had been sharp with her. He called her a nag. She'd threatened to go to court or go see Gil Griffin. He'd warned her not to.

"Annie, are we all together here?" Brenda asked, sensing that Annie's thoughts were focused elsewhere.

"Sure." She nodded and spoke for everyone when she said in a mock Brooklyn accent, "Are we good, or what?"

They laughed together, like sisters.

As Bill got off the elevator on the fortieth floor of Wade Van Gelder's office building, he felt his courage wane. Walking toward the gleaming reception desk at the end of the large, carpeted room, he reminded himself why he was here.

Last night, lying next to Phoebe, listening to her breathing, he realized that unless he took steps, his future with Phoebe was seriously threatened. The one person standing in his way was Phoebe's uncle Wade, the spokesperson for the Van Gelder family and the trustee of the family's huge trust. Bill had called for an appointment first thing this morning and had been surprised to be given one so soon.

"Thank you for seeing me so quickly, Wade," Bill said as he settled into the leather chair in front of the mahogany and leather desk. He looked past Wade's head, noticing the collection of antique flintlock rifles hanging on the wall.

"I assumed I would be hearing from you one of these days," Wade answered.

"I think we have some mutual concerns," Bill said a little too hurriedly, "so I thought it best to get them on the table. I have a feeling our concerns are similar."

Wade looked down at his hands clasped on his round abdomen, then back at Bill. "I don't believe they are. My concerns have to do with Phoebe's well-being. Quite frankly, it seems that the escalation of Phoebe's drug use and the decline, shall we say, of her artistic expression seem to coincide with the beginning of your relationship with her." Wade's hands moved to align the already perfectly positioned blotter on his desk. "You can see how this coincidence could lead to the very unfortunate conclusion that you are not good for Phoebe." He tilted back in his swivel chair.

Bill had expected this and was prepared. "As a matter of fact, Phoebe's drug use is a growing concern of mine. So much so, Wade, that I finally got her to agree to see a very well-known psychiatrist. I've no doubt that with Dr. Rosen's help,

Phoebe can begin to stop taking drugs." Bill lowered his eyes. He secretly feared that the drugs had more to do with their sexuality than he cared to admit. "It's very painful to watch." Then he looked up, smiling. "But I'm much more optimistic now that Phoebe has agreed to treatment. It's the first step."

Wade flicked the thumbs of his clasped hands. Bill could see that he was beginning to make an impression.

"And did you see Jon Rosen's review in the *Times* of Phoebe's show?" Bill continued while he felt he had the edge. "Rosen said that Phoebe's art 'sucks one dry of emotion.' Wade," Bill chortled, "it may not be what *we* would call art, but Rosen does have clout, and an eye."

Wade was quiet for a long moment. Bill's anxiety didn't show, but he felt it in the moistness in his armpits. Everything I want is hanging on this meeting, he thought. Phoebe most of all. I can't let them take her away from me.

"Bill," Wade said with a frown on his forehead, "there is another consideration. As you know, the Van Gelders have been friends with the Elliots for generations, have done business with them, socialized, intermarried, and we are more than a little upset at how Elise will fare in the divorce."

Bill felt Wade's eyes boring into him now and knew Wade's real concern.

"I admire and respect Elise, and in my way, love her. I assure you, in no way would I injure her. I am not taking a dime in settlement from her. The only assets I have are my collections—the Imari, the coins." Looking up at Wade's antique rifles, he continued, "Also my musket collection, and of course, the medieval Italian armor. I've asked Elise to sell them for me at her discretion and send me the net proceeds after expenses, and she's agreed. It's my intention not to profit financially from our marriage." His brow wrinkled with his seriousness. "After all, I *am* a gentleman."

Wade smiled broadly.

"And I'm sure I don't have to tell you, Wade, that I have a rather substantial income of my own. After all"—Bill crossed his legs—"I'm a partner in Cromwell Reed."

"Bill, it seems to me that you're doing the proper thing." Wade reached over as he spoke and opened the humidor on his desk. Offering a cigar to Bill, he continued, "If you can assure me that Elise will not be humiliated by having to pay you a settlement as a condition for your divorce, and that you are willing to sign a prenuptial, I can't see any further reservations the family would have to your relationship with Phoebe."

Wade clipped off the end of his cigar, passed the clip to Bill, and lit up. After several slow puffs he said, "Welcome to the family, Bill."

Bill exhaled a long thread of smoke. He thought this was the best cigar he had ever had.

13

The Visit

The destruction of Sylvie's trust fund by Aaron had at least one positive effect: Annie was angry, and she knew this anger was energy—energy that could help her do what she had to do today. Today, she was going to see Gil Griffin, and then she would have lunch with Jerry Loest, to find out how things were financially with the agency. She had to know where she stood.

She knew she was obsessing, but Annie found it impossible to think of anything but her visit to Gil Griffin. Staring off into space, chewing her breakfast slowly, she realized she had no idea what she was eating. She had to look down at the bowl before her to remember what it was. Strawberries? Ah yes. And yogurt. God, she was out of touch.

Maybe she should have told Elise about what Aaron did with Sylvie's fund, but she simply couldn't. Brenda already despised him; she couldn't face telling Elise as well, because in their crowd this simply wasn't done. This was such dirty laundry. It showed all of them in the worst light: she as a victim, Aaron as an incompetent, Gil as a crook. She'd try, simply, to fix it.

Annie felt an unusual fatigue as she readied herself for the trip downtown. She was grateful for Hudson and the limousine, cushioning her against unpleasantness until she would have to face the personification of it in the form of Gil Griffin. But I can't afford Hudson now, she realized with a start. What will this day cost me?

At the Federated Funds building, Annie was on the list of expected visitors but had to wait nearly half an hour to see Gil. She was nervous, and the air-conditioning chilled her to the bone. Why air-condition in November? But of course, it was because the windows could not be opened. What a waste of energy. She leafed through a current *BusinessWeek* but paid little attention. What did she care about breakthroughs in microprocessor technology?

Finally the receptionist flashed a tight smile at Annie. "Mr. Griffin will see you now. Mrs. Rodgers will take you to him." An older woman appeared and led the way down the silent, blue-carpeted hall.

Annie had never been in Gil's office before, and the size of it astonished her. Walls of glass faced south and east, commanding a view of the Manhattan harbor that was breathtaking. She had to tear her eyes away from it to look at the figure who had risen to greet her.

She expected some social pandering, some "how are you's" to break the ice, but Gil didn't bother. "I understand you have some kind of problem, Anne," he said even before she was seated. He looked her over. She wished she'd worn something more formal, more businesslike, than her simple black Calvin Klein. He looked at her as if she were in a bathing suit. His smile was narrow, as were his eyes.

"Yes, Gil, and I'm very upset," Annie began. She spoke slowly and deliberately. "You know that Aaron and I set up a trust fund for Sylvie here. It was almost twelve years ago. And the fund is essential for Sylvie. Without it she cannot live a decent life."

"Yes, I remember." He was cool. His eyes, a pale, frosty blue, looked at her mechanically. Then they flicked away, wandering the room.

"This is the fund which Aaron has, with your cooperation, thrown away."

Gil listened impassively to this accusation. Annie waited for a reaction, but there was none. None at all. They sat together in the big room, in silence. I won't speak again, she thought. I'll wait until he says something. She was embarrassed, though she knew she shouldn't be. But he simply sat, not even fidgeting, staring at her. Her anger rose, catching in her throat. She could hardly believe how cold, how impassive, he could be. But then she remembered Cynthia's letter. Her rage drove her on.

"It was illegal for you to allow Aaron to have access to that account. My permission was required, which I did not give and which I never would have given."

Annie's voice had started to climb and Gil held up his hand in a stop gesture. Now he wanted to talk. Well, too bad. "Don't interrupt me or tell me to calm down, Gil. I'm furious and I'm not stopping till I've finished. I hold you legally responsible for the loss of this money, and it must be replaced somehow. If it isn't, I'm going to press charges."

Gil flashed her a contemptuous smile. "Against whom, Anne? Aaron? Aaron's the one who broke into the fund and lost the money. Am I wrong to assume he's a responsible adult?"

She felt her stomach flip. "I will sue *you*."

"Sue away. I'll simply say that he lied. That he told me he had your permission, and I believed him. After all, we're old friends. I trusted him. I'm not the first one he's fooled. He fooled you, too."

Was it her imagination or was he leering at her? He was

despicable. And if he lied in court, he'd probably be believed. She'd try, one last time. She clasped her hands tightly together, hoping the pressure would keep her calm, then said, "Gil, what you did was illegal. What on earth do you think . . . ?" Annie turned her face away from him. She couldn't go on, looking at that impassive hawklike face. Stuart was right—she was dealing with someone who was not human.

"I facilitated a business transaction for an associate." Gil affected a voice of exaggerated politeness, mocking her. "It's not an uncommon practice in business. Aaron is president of his own firm. He is neither underage nor incompetent."

"Aaron's age or competence is irrelevant! Two signatures were required to withdraw or sell assets from that fund, Gil. God, doesn't that mean anything? What the hell is the point of establishing that kind of rule if the rules don't mean anything? What kind of business do you run?"

Gil closed his eyes and sighed. "So what do you want me to do, Mrs. Paradise? Give you the money your husband blew? Should I take it out of my own pocket?"

For a moment Annie was at a loss. She remembered what Stuart had told her about Gil: he needs to make people suffer. Then she forced herself to speak quietly. "Yes, Gil. That is what you should do. Replace the money, not out of charity or because Sylvie needs it, but because you fucked up. Make restitution, Gil."

Gil looked at her as if she were mad. "Good joke, Anne. Cute. Now can we get realistic, and quickly please"—he glanced at his watch—"because I have a squash game in less than ten minutes."

Annie wouldn't let Gil see how offensive she found him. And she wasn't going to be rushed. I came here to say something, and I'm going to say it, she thought. Annie took a deep breath. "Gil, I've gotten Sylvie into a place now where she's happy. It costs money. A lot of money. That is what her trust fund was for. If you think I'm going to just let this go, you really are crazy."

She stood up and found that her legs were shaking.

Gil looked at her coldly. "Do what you have to do . . . and see how far you get." He rose and, clutching some kind of remote control, made the doors swing open.

Annie turned to go. If she had wished to say anything more, it was too late now. Nancy Rodgers entered. Reinforcements. Annie felt as if the bully's mother had come to stand up for her son. Either one of these two was bad enough, but together they formed a wall of resistance that was too much for her. She had an urge to reach across his desk, pick up a paperweight, and hit Gil over the head. Instead, she left without another word.

In the car, with Hudson taking her uptown, the rage that had maintained her subsided, and she cried. They were too big, too powerful for her to tackle. If she tried to sue Aaron, to sue Gil, they'd have their lawyers all over her. And how could she drag Aaron's name in the mud like that? It would cost both of them money, money she didn't have. Money Aaron swore he'd replace. But *when* would he restore the money? And *how*? What could she do? The tuition for Sylvie's school was due soon. Dr. Gancher had told her she would give her some time, but how much time would she need?

Mrs. Rodgers, her dictation book raised, accompanied Gil down the hall as he strode off to his squash match. She could see how angry he was by the clipped way he was speaking.

"Cancel lunch with Gilhooley," he said. "Don't reschedule. We'll call sometime next week on that. Be sure the Mitsui partners' memo is on my desk, ready to be signed by the time I get back."

"Yes, Mr. Griffin."

"Oh, and call Gibson in marketing. I want a review of our advertising program. I saw one of our ads last night and they've got to be changed."

"Yes, sir," she said, feeling a moment of sympathy for Gibson.

"Perhaps it's time for a new ad agency to get a shot with Federated. No more Paradise/Loest. Tell him I mentioned that."

Annie slipped into the booth across from Jerry Loest. Pete's Sweet Shop, on Lexington Avenue and Eighty-third, hadn't changed since her nana used to bring her here thirty years ago. It looked as if Archie and Veronica would soon slide onto metal stools at the soda fountain and order cherry Cokes. It was a safe place, a calming place to sit after a meeting such as the one she'd just had with Gil.

She looked across at Jerry. He was safe and calming too, though right now he looked less than well. So do I probably, she thought as she smiled at him.

"Thanks for going out of your way to meet me, Jerry." Jerry and his wife, Eunice lived in Jersey, and the Paradise/Loest offices were on Twenty-third Street.

"It's good to see you again, Annie. I don't see nearly enough of you."

"How's Eunice? I don't get much news from Aaron. We . . . we haven't talked in a while."

"We don't talk much either," he said, smiling ruefully.

"It must be affecting your work."

"No worse than usual, according to Aaron."

Annie sat back against the booth. When the waitress came, she ordered a lettuce-and-tomato on whole wheat and a glass of lemonade. Jerry waved the woman away.

"Chris is doing very well, by the way. You know, he's a great kid. He's the son I never had." Jerry smiled.

Annie nodded. Jerry and Eunice had twin daughters. She always felt Jerry had wanted a son.

"I wanted to know how the business was going, Jerry. I hate to ask you, but I don't like to involve Chris in my problems with Aaron, and I can't really get a straight story from him."

"Business is up, but expenses are up higher. Aaron's brought in some big accounts, but lately we've lost a couple." Jerry paused, looked down at the table, then turned his eyes back to Annie. "I feel like I'm left on by sufferance. My relationship with Aaron has disintegrated. We hardly pass a civil word to each other anymore." Annie could see how upset Jerry was. "I believe he's trying to push me out of Paradise/Loest. And if he comes up with the money, he can do it."

"Maybe it's just all the pressure, Jerry. I can't believe that Aaron would betray you. No, Jerry. Aaron needs you."

He shook his head. "Not anymore. He's changed. You know, you're not the only one betrayed by Aaron Paradise."

14

Step by Step

Annie awoke early the next morning, feeling full of energy. Things never seemed as bleak after a good night's sleep. In her cotton pajamas she hopped onto her Exer-cycle and did her twenty minutes of aerobics. Is this what they meant about being in touch with your anger? she thought, feeling powerful. Today she was going to visit Mr. De Los Santos at the SEC. She walked to her closet and opened the door. The light inside went on, revealing a marvelously ordered selection of simple, elegant clothes, mostly in shades of black, ivory, and beige, but with a splash of color, mostly pink, the color of most of her summer cottons and silks.

Now, what do you wear to the SEC? Annie asked herself. She thought of how uncomfortable Gil had made her feel in her simple little black jersey, and the leering once-over he had given her. I've got to be more formal, she thought. It's an old, establishment, bureaucratic kind of place. Probably stuffy. They're into money and law and order, and I need them to take me seriously. I need to be adult and conservative.

She decided on an old classic Chanel suit, the only Chanel she had, a beige and black, nubby tweed. With it she could wear a beige silk blouse and beige and black Chanel pumps. And maybe a hat, she thought, reaching for the black one with the net veil that she had worn to Cynthia's funeral.

In the limousine on the way down to Federal Plaza, Annie reviewed what she would say. She hoped she would not feel overwhelmed as she had in Gil's office. *I hope he's not just a dumb bureaucrat or a corrupt bastard. I hope we've got a case.*

At Federal Plaza, she found it was no easy matter finding her man. From reasonably spacious hallways and modern-looking offices she proceeded to the basement and a maze of smaller corridors and tiny, old-fashioned offices with doors holding panes of frosted glass. In one of these, she finally found Miguel De Los Santos.

Her heart sank a bit at the sight of the left-wing posters and slogans, kept, she couldn't imagine why, from the seventies. But the lawyer himself seemed to be an alert and up-to-date-enough fellow, so she withheld judgment. He was tall, with olive skin and hair as dark as Aaron's. His face was long and lean, with deep-set, large eyes. As she entered, Miguel De Los Santos whisked off a pair of glasses and stood up, looking her over from top to bottom. For a moment, she was a sure she saw a flicker of something in his eyes. She was overdressed! she thought immediately. It must be the hat. She wished she hadn't worn it.

"I'm Miguel De Los Santos."

"Annie Paradise. Miguel De Los Santos. That means Michael of the Saints, doesn't it?"

"Very roughly translated," he said. "So you want to talk about Gil Griffin?"

"Yes, do you know him?"

"Who doesn't?" Miguel shrugged. "But of course, I don't know him personally, if that's what you mean. I assume you do?"

"Yes. He's a horrible man." Annie looked down and bit

her lip. The conversation had just started and she was already showing her hand, being too emotional.

"Yes, well, you don't get where he is, as fast as he has, if you're not fairly ruthless."

Mr. De Los Santos' tone sounded condescending. Another big man explaining things to a stupid woman, Annie thought. If he was so smart, why was his office here, lower than hell?

"His wife was my friend, Mr. De Los Santos. She committed suicide a few months ago, as you may know. She wrote me a letter in which she told of the dreadful things her husband had done—how he had taken over her family's company and pushed out her father and her brother."

Annie unfolded the letter and handed it to De Los Santos.

As he studied it, Annie tried to read what she could in the physical appearance of this stranger in whom she was confiding. Cheap, rumpled suit, frayed cuff. Missing button on his shirt collar. But good bone structure, attractive, short, curly black hair, a little gray here and there, furrows between well-shaped, dark eyebrows. His lips were full but compressed now in an attitude of concentration. The intensity of his eyes and the set of his jaw further reinforced the impression of disciplined energy. She wondered, for a moment, how old he was. Younger than she, but not by much. And much more attractive than she would expect. She cut short her analysis when he looked up from the letter with an expression of puzzlement.

"It's certainly a harrowing document, Mrs. Paradise, but I'm afraid there's nothing here that could be considered 'evidence.'" He refolded the letter.

"I understand that, but doesn't this indicate that Gil must have done something wrong to achieve these results? Cynthia says he managed all the family portfolios and he never went wrong once. I mean, don't you think that if someone really investigated him *thoroughly*, they would find some 'evidence'?" Annie had leaned forward on her chair.

Miguel raised his eyebrows at her emphasis on the word *thoroughly*. Then he sighed loudly. "Why, exactly, do you want to see Gil Griffin indicted, Mrs. Paradise?"

"Mr. De Los Santos, I knew Cynthia very well and for many years. I knew her deep down, and she didn't have a mean bone in her body. If I hadn't received that letter from her, after she was dead, maybe I could have let it go, but it's just too unfair." Annie paused. "He's a horrible, heartless man, and it's wrong for him to get away with such atrocities."

"Well, I agree with you on that, but actual proof of criminal activity is what is needed. You have to 'get the goods on someone,' as they say." He handed the folded letter back to her.

Annie took it and closed her eyes. It was her turn to sigh. She couldn't tell this man about Aaron's stock trade. Bad as it had been, she couldn't risk Aaron in prison. "I might be able to get more information. More 'goods' as they say."

Miguel looked more closely at her. He liked her face. It was thoughtful and intelligent and she had good features and healthy skin. Her clothes and jewelry put her way out of his realm, however. He looked at her suit. It's actually pretty, he thought. But the hat—ridiculous. Is she playing the merry widow? Is she married? Hey, forget it, Miguel. The whole outfit just shouts *money*. Miguel resented the chasm money could create between a man and a woman, but he was a realist. He made a scornful face, which Annie looked up just in time to see. He saw her face redden.

"I'm sorry," he said quickly, "I was thinking of something else."

Annie blushed anew at this frank admission of disinterest, but this time Miguel misinterpreted. He thought she was touched by his apology. Must be something she's not used to, in her crowd, he thought sympathetically. And how very appealing.

"I could leave the letter," Annie said hesitantly. "Maybe you could look at it again later. If you're interested."

Miguel couldn't imagine what he could do with poor Cynthia Griffin's suicide letter, but he wasn't about to offend this lady again. Maybe there was more that she could offer. He felt his reluctance at ending this meeting.

"Of course, please do leave it. There might be something." He smiled at her, but she couldn't tell if it was a dismissive smile.

She rose to leave and he rose to accompany her. "I'll show you a quicker way out," he said.

He can't wait to get rid of me, Annie thought. She tried not to let her disappointment show on her face when he brought her to the elevator. Walking behind him, she couldn't help but notice his build—he was thin, almost skinny, with long legs. Even in a cheap suit, he looked good from the back. Was he Spanish? Puerto Rican? Annie wasn't quite sure. They arrived at the elevator. Well, she thought to herself, I tried.

"Call me next week to talk over what other information you may get," he said. Annie nodded. "And call me before then if you think of anything else," he added as he was about to turn from her.

"I was going to say the same thing to you." Annie smiled. "Good-bye."

"Good-bye, Mrs. Paradise."

Miguel shook his head on the way back to his office. This is the vaguest complaint I've ever received, he thought. He sat down at his desk, took off his glasses, and rubbed his eyes. "Call me next week." It had come out before he even realized it. And she agreed, he remembered.

When he reopened his eyes, he saw Cynthia's letter. All right, he thought, putting his glasses back on, I'll read it once more. The woman did come all the way down here, all dressed up, to this dingy place.

So Miguel read it again. As he did, he envisioned the despondent woman, articulate and tidy to the end, needing to unburden her heart and tell the truth about a husband who had destroyed her life. What a bastard, he thought angrily. Why do people let him get away with it? God, I'd like to nail him on something.

Not for the first time, Miguel turned his total concentration to the matter of Gil Griffin. As he read the letter a third time, a thought occurred to him. He went to his file cabinet and pulled out back issues of the *Wall Street Journal*. Maybe there was something here, after all.

15

And Now, Miguel

Miguel De Los Santos sat at his scarred desk in the basement office at the Securities and Exchange Commission in Federal Plaza. He scanned the *Wall Street Journal*, as he did every morning, not to find the biggest gamble of the day, but to unearth the biggest gamblers. Because they frequently turned out to be the biggest crooks.

And there were plenty, he thought. Printouts sat on the clanking radiator, printouts that contained all trading "irregularities"—thousands of trades that broke patterns, were linked to other trades, made an abnormal amount or lost big—waiting to be reviewed. On his desk, on the top of the old green file cabinets and stacked on the floor, were folders filled with what he called Alleged Perps. Some he'd been following so long, he called them Old Faithfuls. So many crooks, so little time. Actually, Miguel sighed, there was plenty of time. He had been at it for years. He had apprehended several, made the indictments stick, even got them a few months of jail time. But there was so little hard proof. And so much power to cover things up. And so little motivation from his bureaucracy. That was the problem.

Mrs. Paradise's visit had excited him. He wasn't sure if it was the prospect of landing Gil Griffin or if Mrs. Paradise had touched him in a sensitive spot, but either way, he was going to see her again.

Miguel Carlos De Los Santos, Esquire, leaned back in his broken-down swivel chair until his head almost touched the back wall of his office. He put his feet up on his desk and stared at the wall opposite, just six feet away. Yesterday he had been to the eye doctor because of the headaches he'd been getting. He'd been shocked when the doctor had prescribed reading glasses. Poring over these files would do that to you, Miguel realized, but it offended him. He hadn't expected to age. It was a sign of the times, a reminder. He was getting older, but making little progress.

When the phone rang, he jumped, then reached for it.

"Mike?" It was his wife. Or his ex-wife, he supposed he should say. Milagros was Cuban, not Puerto Rican, and unlike Miguel, she was eager to assimilate into the melting pot. But only if that meant that, like cream, she could rise to the top.

"Mike?" she asked again. Christ, he wished she'd call him Miguel and stop the Anglo shit, but it was too late for that. About ten years too late, he reminded himself.

"Yes?" he finally responded.

"Listen, can you come out tonight and watch the boys? We've got a late closing and I've got to be there."

"What about Carmen?" She was the au pair.

"She's baby-sat two nights this week already."

"Well, don't you think two nights out is enough? Do the boys actually get to see the mother who has custody of them?" It hurt him that the courts had automatically given her temporary custody. Still, he reminded himself, it isn't as if she's a drunk or a child abuser. She's just a loan officer.

"Mike, I have to work, okay?"

"Hackensack Federal is more important than my boys?"

"*Our* boys. And give it up, huh? Will you sit or not? Spare me the sermon. I've got calls to make."

"Yes, I'll come out. But I can't get there until six-thirty."

"Fine." She hung up.

Stupid to expect a "thank you" he told himself. Stupid to expect a "how are you." Almost a dozen years of marriage and they were like strangers. Milly wanted things, not people: the house in Teaneck, the Chinese rugs, the Mazda. She was going for the American dream, minus the husband with the low-paying government job and the inconvenient idealism.

But Miguel had never been able to let go of his idealism. Or his pride. It had cost him monetary success, recognition, and recently, a wife and two children. At thirty-eight, he no longer thought of himself as a *niño*, but there, were times when he thought he might be *loco*. Today was one of those times.

For Miguel had done just what he said he would do: he had become an honest lawyer fighting dishonesty and corruption. As a Hispanic he had, at first, been pathetically grateful to the establishment for taking him in, giving him a place at their table. He admired the *gringos* and their ordered world. In time, however, he had come to see that there were those, born to wealth and stature, who used their advantages unfairly, who spoke of laws and justice but broke the former and escaped the latter, who made fools of the rest of the people who had to play by the rules. In Puerto Rico there was a tree with deep green leaves. But when the wind blew, and the leaves were turned, the underside showed white. *Yagrumo*, it was called. Puerto Ricans in New York still called hypocrites *yagrumos*. And Miguel still hated hypocrites and thieves.

In this miserable office at the SEC he had done the tedious work of carefully tracking the financial bullies of Wall Street. Hired during the Carter administration, he had several victories: Maple Oil, the Thomas Harding thing. But in the last decade he had followed up scores of leads and investigated hundreds of irregularities, discovering new hotbeds of corruption and wrongdoing, only to see his cases fall apart. Each time the well-heeled, well-connected wrongdoers had managed to pay off the right people, cover their tracks, and appear as innocent as lambs in the face of actual accusations. The eight years of Reagan's administration had not been a good time for muckraking or corporate law enforcement. And the Boesky thing, and Milken—they were essentially outsiders, easy to pick off. It was the insiders, the *jefes*, who got away.

Today had brought news of another failure, another "misplaced accusation." Miguel had had it. He looked at the photo of his wife and his two kids. They lived in New Jersey now, far from El Barrio; Miguel only saw them every other weekend. He was a family kind of man, and he missed them.

They had been separated now for almost five months. Miguel had found a cheap studio sublet near Columbia and was back to eating out of cans, sleeping on a mattress on the floor. He hated living this way, but he would not concede, would not do his wife's bidding like a dog. She called him crazy, and bitter. Well, perhaps he was, but he was also right. It amazed him that if he'd chosen to be a run-of-the-mill accident-claims lawyer, he might still have a home and family and a wife who didn't think he was *loco en la cabeza*.

Miguel thought again of Mrs. Paradise. She certainly didn't look like any other woman he knew. But her appeal wasn't just the way she looked. She had seemed so vulnerable, yet so determined. Miguel reached for the phone at the same time he flipped through his Rolodex.

"Mrs. Paradise?" he said when she answered. "This is Miguel De Los Santos at the SEC. I wanted to talk to you some more about Gil Griffin. Could we meet for lunch?"

After the date was arranged, he found that he had actually

been nervous asking her, and when she accepted. He couldn't promise her an open-and-shut case, but he could promise her—and himself—some action.

His eyes focused once again and took in the photo of the U.S. Senate he had mounted on the wall. Under it he had put his own caption: *White, male millionaires working for you.* He *was* bitter, no doubt about it. You guys are not going to win, he thought.

Four more months. That was it. I'll nail one of these guys in four months. Sweeping his feet off the desk and changing from a man of thought to one of action, he walked to the Year at a Glance calendar on his wall. He picked up a thick red marker and circled a date.

He walked back to his desk and with a sigh, reached down for one of the Old Faithfuls. He picked it up and laid it on the marred surface of his desk. Maybe this time, he thought. Maybe this time I can bring down one of the corrupt *jefes*. Putting on his new reading glasses, he opened the file titled *Gilbert Griffin—Federated Funds Douglas Witter.*

16

Out to Lunch

Bill watched Gil enter Bankers and Brokers restaurant and, like a politician, maneuver between the crowded tables, handshaking and backslapping. He made his way to Bill, who sat in the much sought-after corner booth reserved under Gil's name. "What a mob scene," Gil said, pretending he didn't like the attention his entrance brought.

After ordering drinks from the hovering captain, Bill got right to the point. "Have you heard about Morty Cushman and the IRS?" Gil nodded. Christ, the guy knew everything. "He called me. Asked if we could represent him. Imagine." He spoke with disdain. The firm didn't like dirty clients.

Gil shrugged and said, "You ever hear of an overnight millionaire who didn't have tax problems? It'll blow over. Anyhow"—he took a sip of his San Pellegrino—"it's not our problem."

Bill twirled his martini around in the stemmed glass. "I know it's not our problem. It's just that when I hear the IRS is sniffing around one of the principals of a company we took public, it's just a little too close to home. It makes my partners nervous." He took a big gulp of his drink. He was uncomfortable with it as well, but wasn't going to let Gil see him sweat. "And I heard something about a meeting you had with the

SEC—nothing serious, I hope, Gil. No relation to the Cushman deal."

"Just the usual compliance garbage. Routine." Gil seemed impervious, very upbeat. "Look," Gil continued, "from what I hear, this IRS flap has nothing to do with the stock issue. It has something to do with his divorce. It's his personal taxes, his personal problem." Placing his hand on Bill's shoulder, Gil smiled. "I hear she's going for his balls."

Bill smiled grimly, reassured but insulted; Gil, knowing about Bill's own divorce, wasn't very tactful. And Gil knew about Phoebe, too, although Bill knew that Gil could never understand what he had with Phoebe. He could never appreciate a woman like her.

"And speaking of balls, I had to take Federated's business away from Aaron Paradise's ad agency. Aaron is having his own financial problems and tried to get me involved. He pulled a number on Anne, and I was supposed to take the weight. Can't have that, now, can I?"

Bill nodded, but his thoughts were still on Phoebe. Gil brought him back to the present when he nudged him and asked, "What's worse than getting married to a broad like that Brenda?"

Bill shook his head.

"Getting divorced from her," Gil said, and laughed out loud. Bill joined in. Gil called over his shoulder to the waiter. Turning again to Bill, he said, "Speaking of Brenda, I'm so hungry, I could eat a cow."

"So everything is fine?" Bill asked.

"Hey." Gil looked him in the eye. "It would take more than a greedy Jew to bring me down."

Elise sat across from Larry on the banquette in the dining room of the Algonquin Hotel, nervously twirling her drink in damp circles on the white tablecloth. He looked so nice, his long, kind of hound dog face smiling. He looked so handsome, and so damn young. How old *was* he? She couldn't remember what year he'd said he'd been born. Please, she prayed, let him be at least thirty. He couldn't be *less* than that. She took a sip of the vodka and orange juice while waiting for their omelets. Although she'd prefer her vodka neat, she didn't want to shock Larry.

Elise was, she admitted, embarrassed that she had used the excuse of the screenplay to invite Larry to lunch. Not that the revised screenplay wasn't extraordinary. It was. But she was as interested in him as she was in the screenplay. She'd thought of him every day, every night for weeks. Arriving at the decision to call him had been agonizing. She'd hoped that *he* would call *her*, that *he* would seduce *her* into a relationship with him, even though she had been so clear at their last meeting that that was not what she wanted. And it seemed he had respected her decision. A gentleman, she thought, miserable, a perfect gentleman.

Was she obsessed? She fluctuated between gratitude for his gentlemanliness, and longing for his pursuit. The struggle between the old Elise and the new, she thought grimly. But there had been no ambivalence about how she felt remembering the time they had had together in the Carlyle. That, she now knew, had been nothing but good. And now, so was his screenplay.

Elise cleared her throat and smiled. "This ending is much more real." She tapped the blue-bound manuscript between them on the table.

Larry smiled proudly. "It is, isn't it? Well, let's be honest. The ending on the earlier draft was sentimental trash, but I didn't have the courage to do it honestly. You gave me permission."

"It's painful this way, but it's right." Elise took another sip of her drink, though she wanted to gulp it and order a double. "There are no happy endings in life."

"Do you believe that? I don't."

"When I was your age, I didn't either. But enlightenment comes later. Life wears you down."

"Yes, but it also builds you up. I mean, at any time, things could change. Look what happened to me. At Campbell's, seeing you, and then the idea for the screenplay, and these lunches. God, you never know what could happen. Tomorrow, your whole world could change."

She envied him his enthusiasm and felt saddened that she couldn't share it. "Yes, and probably for the worse."

He frowned at her. "I don't believe that you're really that cynical. Cynicism is just a cover-up for despair."

Elise hated how the conversation was going, hated hearing the world-weary tone in her voice. Then the waiter arrived with their omelets, and Elise changed the subject. "Larry, I've come to a decision." She picked up a stem of parsley and twirled it between her fingers before placing it back on her plate. "It's about something that affects both of us." She took courage from the bright smile on his face. "I want to do that role, and if it means producing, then I'll have to do that, too."

She wasn't prepared for the sudden look of sadness on Larry's face. "What's the matter?"

"Nothing," he said, but his eyes began to dart around the room, avoiding her eyes.

"Don't lie."

Larry looked down at his plate, his hands in his lap. Without looking at her, he said, "I thought you were talking about a personal decision. About me."

"This *is* a personal decision and it *is* about you. Don't you want to see this film produced?"

"Of course. But it's not the most important thing to me. Maybe I'm wrong, and I might be naive, but I think I could get this script produced without you." Now he looked directly into her eyes. "I think about you all the time. What I can't do is go on living without you."

Elise shook her head. "You don't have to keep up the sales pitch, Larry. You've already closed. So cut the idle flattery."

Larry drew back as if slapped, the suddenness of his movement upsetting Elise's water glass, spilling it across the table and onto her lap. Elise sucked in her breath at the shock of the ice water. Well, she thought, I deserve that. She quickly regained her composure. But Larry looked stricken, his anger fighting with his embarrassment and concern.

"God, I'm sorry . . . ," he began. "It's just . . ."

While Elise mopped her skirt with the napkins the waiter handed her, she said, "I owe *you* the apology, Larry. What I said was insulting and provocative. I'm not usually so insensitive. I'm just frightened."

"Of *me?*" he asked incredulously.

"No, not of you. Of my own feelings. You have to understand. I've always had a horror of bad publicity, and to imagine myself a laughingstock, well, it's too painful."

"Why would anyone laugh at you? Am I so disreputable? I know I haven't had a movie produced, but I *am* a fairly decent photographer."

"Yes, an excellent thirty-year-old photographer."

"Well, twenty-eight, actually."

Elise dropped her head, then spoke to the top of the table. "Oh, Jesus." She looked up and saw awareness grow on Larry's face.

"Is that what all this is about, Elise? My *age?* For God's sake, are you going to pass up something as good as *this* over something as irrelevant as *that?*"

"Easy for you to say," she said, but with a little less conviction.

"It's easy for you to say, too, Elise. Just say it. Are you going to let morons—fifty-year-old men who would date eleven-year-olds if they could get away with it—be the ones to set the social standards?"

"The standards have already been set. And not only by fifty-year-old men. By women, also. By women like my mother."

"Yes, and probably my mother, too. But those rules aren't carved in stone. Things change. *You're* changing." He leaned across the table and took her ice-cold hands in his. "I'd be so very proud to be with you. Elise. We could have fun. We could make this work." He paused. "God, your hands are ice-cold."

"You should feel inside my underpants."

"That's just what I've been trying to tell you."

Despite herself, Elise laughed. This was it then. She prayed that the Algonquin Hotel had a room available. "Waiter!" she called. "The check, please."

Aaron strutted into the dining room of the Advertising Club, the former Phipps mansion on Gramercy Park. With him was his star, his centerpiece, his advertising triumph, Morty the Madman, and his son Chris, his rising star. Aaron liked to think of Morty as his creation, and he expected others to do so as well. As he followed the headwaiter and Morty and Chris to their table, he felt people pause and stare. As they sat down and ordered drinks, Aaron said, "Morty, you're an adman's dream come true. Everyone's looking at you."

"Bullshit," said Morty, squinting at the menu. "They're looking at *you*. They're envious. Look what you pulled off." Putting aside his menu, he looked directly at Aaron. "You're a genius. You made us both rich. You made my name a household word. I paid you a bundle, but it was worth every penny. And it didn't hurt when I went public." Aaron noticed Chris's eyes on him and felt a surge of pride.

Chris leaned back in his chair and patted Aaron's back. "That's my dad."

Aaron looked around the former ballroom of the mansion. Always in good taste, he thought. Turning back to Morty, he felt the wolves at the surrounding tables nipping at his heels. Yeah, he'd made them both rich, and as a payback Morty had made him poor. Today he needed two things: assurance that Morty would expand his advertising budget in a big way, and confirmation that Morty would cover his losses.

He needed both badly. Aaron was still reeling from the loss of the Federated account. Their advertising manager wouldn't give him any reason for their decision to pull out. And Gil Griffin wasn't returning his calls. It was as if an ice curtain had dropped between Federated and the agency. He desperately needed Morty's budget to double in order to cover the loss of the Federated account. Christ, I need Morty to cover *all* my losses, he thought.

Pulling this one off would be a trick. Well, love the bastard up and then see what you can pull out of him. After all, it is Thanksgiving, a time when even Morty should be in a good mood. And, Aaron told himself, I'm the phoenix, ready to soar again from the ruins of a disaster. But instead of the surge of adrenaline he usually managed, there was merely a trickle. Maybe I'm a bit of a bedraggled phoenix, he thought.

Leslie hadn't taken the news of the loss on the Morty the Madman stock very well. In fact, she'd been a bit of a bitch. Aaron was ready to admit to himself that he'd been a schmuck, but he wasn't ready to admit it to Leslie. And he certainly wasn't ready to be called one.

Annie had been furious. Well, of course, she would be.

She'd threatened to go to Gil Griffin, to raise a stink, to hire a lawyer. He'd promised her he'd have the money all back in six months. The problem was, he didn't know how.

He looked across the table at Morty. Fat bastard. He wondered how long it took him to shave all those chins. But Morty was his only hope. Now, if he'd double their budget and cover the loss, Aaron could straighten things out with Annie, buy out Jerry, *and* make things okay with Leslie as well. He felt his stomach knot. He hated being so much in the power of another. Well, he was the phoenix, he reminded himself again. He'd get this buffoon to do what he wanted, and in the process maybe teach Chris a little bit about how it's done.

"So I took a bath because of that bastid Ewell's column. But business is booming. It'll be all right. And Shelby's excited about her new show. What's with you?"

"Nothing much," Aaron said, smiling. "Except, Morty," he added as he cut into the very rare roast beef they all three had ordered, "we have to talk about a bigger advertising budget for next year. You know, the only way you can stay rich is by getting richer." He looked over at Chris and winked. Chris looked properly impressed.

Morty put a forkful of Yorkshire pudding into his mouth, ignoring the gravy that dripped down his chin. "Hey, I like you, kid. Always have. Have I ever let you down? I'm with you." He pointed his fork at Aaron. Turning to Chris, Morty said, "We're a good team, your father and me. And we'll get even richer together." Morty returned his attention to his food, while Chris excused himself and went to the men's room.

Aaron saw his opportunity and took it. "Which brings us to another matter," he said, a lot more offhandedly than he felt. "We need to talk about the margin I covered for you. And my losses. We haven't really talked about that yet, Morty."

Putting down his fork, he added, "I took a bath with that one. On your say-so, Morty."

Morty snapped, "Hey, I can't help it if you couldn't get out of it when I told you to. Whose fault is that?" Morty shrugged and took a sip of seltzer.

Aaron's resentment at Morty's shrug welled up, ready to burst out. Stuffing down his anger, he said in a monotone, "You told me to cover you and I did, Morty. And then you told me you would cover me, but so far, nothing." He'd better keep his temper. Keep control. New tack.

Now Aaron stared directly at Morty. "This isn't like you, Morty. You've always been straight with me." Leaning slightly forward, he asked kindly, "What is it, Morty? This IRS thing bigger than you're letting on?"

"No, no, that's not it," Morty answered, maybe a little too quickly. "I mean, sure, it's on my mind, but it's no big thing." He forced a big smile. "My lawyers are handling it." Yeah, and Leo was having a shit fit. He'd found out about Morty's accounts in Europe and was screaming like a stuck pig.

He continued, "Listen, kid, I said I'll take care of you and I will. Okay, you got the account budget expanded. Trust me, I'll make up some of the losses to you soon. Just give me a little time. After all, you can't afford to let go now." He smiled at Aaron.

Aaron forced himself to return Morty's smile. He's right, of course, thought Aaron. But still I wish Morty didn't have IRS problems, too. I don't want this guy to get distracted.

"You're right, Morty," Aaron said as Chris returned to the table, "I can't afford to let go now."

Brenda was happy to see Diana, but not happy with Diana's choice of lunch spots. "Hey, Diana, I'm no Hindu, remember? I'm a not-so-nice Jewish-Italian girl from the Bronx." She pushed her chair into the table. "What the fuck kinda name is 'Nirvana,' anyhow?" Brenda looked around at the incongruous setting. "Now. Diana, let me get this straight, just so as I don't get confused. I'm a Jew about to eat a meal prepared by Hindus in a restaurant decorated for Pilgrims, is that right?"

Diana laughed out loud and said, "Yes, that's absolutely right, Brenda. So, should I order for both of us?"

"Sure. Anything, so long as it's not green or brown."

Diana ordered an array of Indian vegetarian dishes that Brenda thought sounded pretty unappetizing. Oh, well, I should be dieting anyway, she thought. As the waiter walked away, Diana turned her attention to Brenda. "You haven't talked very much about your job with Duarto, Brenda. How do you like it?"

"Just being with Duarto is great. We laugh all the time. *Nothing* is sacred to him." Brenda noticed Diana's nod to continue.

"You remember I told you Duarto landed Gil and Mary Griffin's decorating contract for their new Fifth Avenue apartment? Well, I got inside it with Duarto yesterday. I am his assistant, after all. There was no one there except some workmen, so I did some snooping."

Brenda saw Diana's eyebrows rise slightly. "Oh?" Brenda said, feigning surprise. "Do I detect some disapproval here? You mean you *don't* want to know what I read in her diary?"

Diana couldn't resist. "Her *diary?*" Diana was incredulous. "You read her diary, Brenda? What was *in* it?"

Brenda looked off into space, as if she hadn't heard Diana.

"Okay, okay, I don't disapprove. I'm dying to know. Now come on, tell me."

Brenda giggled. "I didn't really read her diary—I couldn't find it—but you know those yuppie organizer-appointment books that are about twelve inches thick? Well, I found last year's copy in a box." Brenda now spoke emphatically. "She has 'Mrs. Gil Griffin; Mary Birmingham Griffin; Gil loves Mary' scrawled on practically every page. Like in high school. What a hoot!" Brenda said, hitting the table with her hand.

Diana threw back her head and joined Brenda in the laughter. "Brenda, you're one in a million. Don't ever change." Diana looked up as the waiter approached. "And here comes our lunch."

"I can't believe it," Brenda said to Diana after she had tasted each of the dishes. "This stuff's great."

Diana, watching Brenda dig into the feast she had ordered for her, couldn't help adding, "See, I told you food can taste good and be good for you, too."

"Now you sound like my fourth-grade teacher, Mrs. Wasserstein. 'Children, what are the four important food groups?'" Brenda asked, mimicking her teacher. "I used to say to Ginny Skelton, who sat next to me, 'Chocolate malted, cheeseburgers, french fries, and coleslaw.' I could make Ginny wet her pants at the drop of a hat."

Diana smiled, then became serious. They looked at one another in silence for a moment. Then Brenda lowered her eyes and began to fuss with the silverware.

"You know, Brenda, you've become very important to me." Diana paused. "I know the last time I tried to tell you how I feel about you, you cut me off. But you're very special."

Brenda reached across the table and took Diana's hands in hers. "You don't have to say anything more, Diana. I know. Ever since that conversation, I've been thinking myself. No one has ever been so good to me, so accepting. You're on my mind all the time. You've really helped me and I love you for it."

"That's what I've been trying to say. I love you."

Brenda felt her heart leap in her chest. She wanted to say, "Me, too," but the words got stuck. She coughed and finally, after a pause, heard her own voice. "Me, too, Diana." It felt so good.

Diana smiled and they sat in silence for a moment, looking at each other. Then Brenda, remembering there was food on the table, broke the spell. "Whatever. Now that that's settled, let's eat. What do Indians have for dessert?"

Shelby Cushman was lunching with Jon Rosen. It was, of course, a business lunch, and she, of course, would pay. She was taking him to the Boxtree, partly because it was very expensive, but also because it was very *in-time*. Jon Rosen wasn't only the most powerful art critic in America, he was also a very attractive man.

If Morton saw the bill, he'd scream, but he wouldn't see the bill. Shelby was using her own money. Well, it *was* her own money now. For the last few months, many of the paintings that Shelby bought for the gallery she bought with her own money. Shelby bought them from artists, raised the price, then sold them to Morty's gallery. And at a hefty profit for her.

Well, Shelby thought as she put mascara on her long, long lashes in preparation for her lunch, a girl has to do what a girl has to do. No one was married forever, and Morton was not a generous man. Fact is, he screamed when he had to write checks. I've simply got to look out for myself, she thought.

The money was tucked away in a safety deposit box in Zurich. She had an arrangement with a courier, who delivered it there. And the key was safely hidden in the gallery. In some ways, she was an old-fashioned girl. No bank accounts with messy paper trails and taxable interest for her. She felt that the gallery was enough of a marital asset. And if it lost money, well, it wasn't *her* money.

In fact, it wasn't doing as well as she had hoped. Despite her mother's prodding from down in Atlanta, and all the New York prodding she could do, she had not been getting enough of the monied crowd at her gallery. She couldn't think why. Was it because of Morton? Other people had overcome a Hebrew background. It wasn't as if he were Negro or anything.

Shelby finished with her eye makeup. She fluffed out her long, yellow-blond hair. She looked good, really good. She ran her tongue over her red, red lips. She couldn't wait to see Jon Rosen.

Mary Birmingham Griffin wore sunglasses and had her pale hair pulled back into a tight ponytail. A bulky car coat and a pair of old jeans added to her unusually casual look and to her—she hoped—disguise. As she stepped from the cab, she threw the driver a crumpled pile of singles. The fare was eight dollars and change, and she only had eleven dollars, aside from the ten thousand in crisp, new hundred-dollar bills stuffed in her coat. Rich people never seemed to carry much cash, she'd learned. Well, she could take the crosstown bus home, if she had to. She'd taken it before, God knows.

Mary stepped across the littered sidewalk at Amsterdam Avenue. The majestic spire of St. John the Divine rose up on her left, but a filthy vagrant, standing by the fence, and another human form crouched in the doorway, were more immediate scenery. She strode by them with her habitually purposeful walk. Ten thousand in cash was a lot of money to lose to a crack freak or a wino who decided to get aggressive.

In just a few strides she was at the door of V & T's. She paused for a moment, her hand on the doorknob. She hoped ten thousand would be enough. She would give him ten times that if she had to, but she couldn't let him know that.

Mary pulled the glass door open and walked in. The place hadn't changed much: the same worn linoleum, plastic table-cloths, gloomy, cheap wood paneling on the walls. The front room, reserved for smokers, was separated from the back one by a hip-high divider that housed planters of plastic orange and yellow flowers, none of which even made a pretense of resembling anything that had ever actually grown. How many years of grease coated them? she wondered. They were the same ones from her years up here at Columbia, getting her MBA. Nothing else here had changed either. The same mural of Vesuvius on the wall, the same fake-wood captain's chairs, the same Bobby.

She walked into the room, and as she did, her ex-husband smiled. His teeth still looked beautifully white in his dark face. His hair was different. Instead of the Afro he had worn, it was in one of those new hairdos, a high-top.

"Hello," Mary said coolly.

"Hi, babe. Good to see ya." He looked up at her, turning on the charm. Voice like warm molasses. Eyes full of puppy pleading. Same old Bobby. He reached out, took her hand, its whiteness stark against his ebony skin. His hand felt undeniably good around hers. Well, sex had never been their problem. Only everything else.

"What do you want?"

"Hey, baby. Nuthin'. Just to see you, just to talk. For the holidays, you know."

"Oh, come on. Cut to the chase, homeboy."

He smiled. "Same ole Mary. Won't you sit down, at least? Have a bite with me?"

Mary sat. She'd picked this place because it was the most unlikely she could imagine to risk running into any of her new group of friends and acquaintances. The last thing she needed was for anyone to find out about her first marriage:

short-lived, emotional, and to a black man. Christ, Gil wished she had been a virgin, and the women in his circle acted as if they were. They would never understand what Bobby had done for her.

Bobby handed her the menu. It felt sticky. She looked at it. In her Bobby years, V & T's had been the treat of the week, something they could afford only occasionally. Now, well, she looked at the heavy Neapolitan selections and repressed a shiver. She only ate Northern Italian now.

"I don't want anything," she told Bobby. "What do *you* want?"

The smile finally left his handsome face. Mary watched as he made the expected transition from Fun Bobby to Earnest Bobby.

"Babe, I been thinkin'. I got to make a new start." Bobby smiled again. "You know, like you did. Take a step out and a step up."

"Yes?" Don't act too interested; Bobby, she knew, got to believing his own bullshit and could go on all day. But today he seemed a little intense. Too intense, she thought, trying not to show her anxiety.

"I thought I might try Las Vegas. I got a friend thinks it's the place for a guy like me . . . a guy with ambition and some workin' capital."

"What's her name?"

Bobby gave her that slow smile again. "Never could fool you for long, Mary. Name's Tamayra. Workin' at the Sands."

"That's fine, Bobby. But what has this to do with me? We're annulled. That's like saying we were never married. I want you to remember that. So why did you call?" she asked, even though she knew. It was like the other shoe had dropped, hearing from him. A part of her had been waiting all this time.

"Saw your picture in the paper. Said where you worked. Made me think of old times. Thought maybe I'd come see you." He smiled wolfishly. Mary stifled a shudder. "Then I figured, maybe not."

Bobby shifted slightly in his seat. Mary kept looking at him. Coming here in the cab, she was sure she could outlast him. Now, well, Bobby seemed different, harder. He had been a local boy, raised in Harlem, attending Columbia on an athletic scholarship. All he wanted was to play ball and to party. When she hit New York and saw him at a Columbia game, she'd been knocked breathless by his skill on the court. And as a lover, he was even better. She hoped to see him make it in the NBA, a star, a dark horse she could ride to success with. But he couldn't stick to his training or his books and had eventually flunked out. He was a failure, but *she* wouldn't be, and she wouldn't be brought down by him. But now he was dangerous. Now he *knew* he was a failure. Her dark horse had become her dark secret.

"Okay, Bobby. I can help you out, but just this once. I swear to God, if you call me again for any reason, I'll put the cops on you. And you know I can do it."

"Hey, baby, I don't like to be threatened. Nobody does, know what I mean?"

Mary did, but wouldn't acknowledge it. "Here Bobby. This is it. It's all my savings. Take it and go, and don't call me again."

She pushed the envelope across to him. He looked in side it, and his eyes opened. She saw his jaw muscles pop as he gritted his teeth.

"Oh, now. Hey."

"Hey yourself, Bobby."

"You married to one of the richest men on Wall Street, baby. And you got a Fifth Avenue apartment, the newspapers say." His voice became almost a whisper. "So don't shovel none of your bullshit about your 'life savings.'"

He stuffed the envelope in his pocket. "Tell me it's all the cash you got on hand. Even, 'This is all you're going to get, Bobby.' But don't cry poor to me."

He sat back and smiled. "I think we understand each other."

He looked her over. "You was good, Mary. Hey, *we* was good, wasn't we, baby?"

She nodded.

"You interested?"

She felt a tightening at her crotch. Just what she needed, now. She shook her head.

"Too bad, baby, 'cause you the best white pussy I ever had."

She stood up, pushing her chair out from behind her.

"Happy Thanksgiving, Bobby," she said, and walked out of V & T's, hoping never to see him again, but certain that Bobby wasn't out of her life yet.

Miguel De Los Santos took a certain pleasure in baiting Annie. He knew it wasn't his best trait, but he couldn't help it sometimes. Despite that silly hat, the Paradise woman had really gotten to him. She was undeniably attractive, even on that first meeting, mincing around the subject. Jesus. Now they'd met twice more for lunch and once for dinner. But it had all been on her turf. So when he called to firm up his invitation to her for lunch today, he had picked Asia de Cuba to see her reaction. A Cuban-Chinese place, it was affordable *and* on the West Side of town, closer to his neighborhood, not hers. Not that they'd go back to his place. Certainly not. He chose it just to see her reaction. Well, what the hell, he thought. He did it to make her squirm.

"I've never been here before," Annie said as she took her seat opposite Miguel in the vinyl-covered booth.

"I'm sure you haven't, so let me explain. This is a Cuban-Chinese restaurant—"

"Oh, I know that. I just haven't been to *this* one before. I've been to Estrella de Asia on Seventy-eighth and Broadway near the Beacon Theatre. But I think Mi Chinita in Chelsea is more authentic." She leaned back and smiled.

Miguel laughed. "So, I guess I'm guilty of stereotyping. I'm sorry."

"All's forgiven," Annie said, smiling, and began to sift through the contents of her oversized bag.

"Well, what have you got to show me?" he asked, smiling at her. "Ready to work?" They were still using the fiction of the investigation to justify their meetings. At least, Miguel hoped so.

"Perhaps. Why don't you start by calling me Annie."

"All right. And I'm Miguel."

"I've got a lot of files here—some records of the Morty the Madman offering, and some information from Cynthia's bank. It seems she was close to penniless when she died." Annie paused. "Also, I was thinking, Gil invested for her family. She mentioned that in her note. Well, she had an Aunt Esme. Esme Stapleton. Could you see what trades were made in her name? Maybe Gil used her portfolio."

"A long shot," Miguel said, but he was impressed with her persistence. "You really mean this, don't you?"

"Oh, yes." Annie paused for a moment, then seemed to make a decision. "Miguel. Can I tell you something else that might help in the investigation? But something I'd prefer you not use unless you have to?"

"Well. I suppose."

Miguel listened as Annie told him about Aaron and Sylvie's

trust fund, and about her visit to Gil Griffin. "It doesn't sound like an SEC matter to me, but I'll check into it. There might be a chance Gil violated some SEC regulation," Miguel said. "It's a pity about your daughter's trust fund. Maybe she could apply for some scholarships." If the kid was anything like her mother, she'd sail into a good school.

"The fund wasn't meant to pay for her education. It was meant to provide for her care." Annie paused. "Sylvie has Down's syndrome."

Miguel felt his face redden. "Annie, I'm so sorry. That's twice this afternoon I put my foot in my mouth."

"Don't be too hard on yourself, Miguel. Why shouldn't you presume a child is born into this world normal?" Miguel noticed Annie's voice get very soft. "It's the birthright of every child. Anything else seems to be such a gross injustice; at least, I used to think so."

Miguel recovered from his embarrassment. "Injustice, of course," he said adamantly. "But what do you mean you *used* to think so? What changed you?"

Miguel waited for a moment. Annie first looked off into the distance, then back to Miguel. "Sylvie changed me." Miguel nodded, gently urging her on. "She changed Aaron, too. But in the opposite way."

"You must have been very lonely."

"I was." Annie lowered her head and added, "I am lonely."

Miguel was touched by Annie's honesty. He refrained from reaching out and putting his hand to her face. A moment of silence passed between them. Then Miguel asked, "Was Sylvie the cause of the breakup of your marriage?" Miguel didn't want to pry into Annie's life, but she seemed so ready to talk.

"I'd say Sylvie's birth was the catalyst rather than the cause. If there had been no Sylvie, perhaps Aaron's shortcomings would never have become apparent to me. Perhaps I would never have been given the insight I gained." Annie paused while the waiter placed the covered dishes on the table.

Miguel ignored the interruption. "And that was . . . ?"

Annie's hand fell slowly to the top of a covered dish, then stopped. "Sylvie taught me to live in awe." She spooned some fried rice onto Miguel's plate, then her own. "Do you have any children?"

"I have. Two. Two boys who live with my ex-wife in New Jersey." Miguel shifted slightly in the booth. The woman was brave, braver than he'd thought, he realized guiltily. *Madre de Dios,* how would he cope if one of his boys . . . ? He couldn't bear to think about it.

"Then you know what I'm talking about. Do you know the way young children, when they make a discovery on their own, seem so in awe of what they've discovered?"

"Of course," Miguel said. "I remember when my first boy discovered the mobile that had been hanging over his crib since he was born. One day he noticed it and gurgled and kicked frantically at the moving colors." Miguel lifted his fork. "But then he got used to it and moved on to his next discovery."

"Exactly. Except with Sylvie, it was always the first time. She sees the colors in bath bubbles, and it's like the first time all over again. And stars, and ice cream."

"I call it the 'wow' experience," Miguel said. "It's a shame, but it seems that as they get older, it gets harder and harder for them to have that experience." Miguel chewed a piece of sweet and sour chicken. "Well"—he shrugged—"what can we expect? I read somewhere that before a child reaches his teens, he has seen twenty thousand violent deaths on television. That's enough to take the 'wow' out of anyone."

"Do you see your boys much?"

"Every other weekend, or when Milly asks me to baby-sit."

"What happened?"

Miguel understood what Annie meant. "We had different dreams, I guess. She's chasing the American dream . . . you know, car, suburban house, vacations."

"And what is your dream?"

"That's easy. Family and work, in that order." Miguel dabbed his mouth with the corner of a napkin. "Milly thinks it should be the other way around. She couldn't stand to be married to a government employee. She used to call me a crusader."

"I take it you have different ideas on child-rearing."

Miguel snorted. "That's an understatement. Milly talks about 'quality time' and all that other yuppie crap. Then she takes them to McDonald's and out to play video games." Miguel paused. "I tell her she's a long way from her roots. Not *everything* the *gringos* do is better."

"And how do you spend time with your children?"

Miguel leaned forward on his elbows. "I had heard about a veterinarian in Pennsylvania who raises llamas. Breeds and raises them! Now you can go to the Bronx Zoo and look at llamas twelve feet away and read the little card with three lines of information about llamas. But when do you get the chance to visit a llama farm and touch them and hear how they're cared for? I mean, *I* was excited."

"And your boys weren't?"

"The woman was nice enough to invite us down to see the animals. Then we went to a Pennsylvania Dutch restaurant for a family-style meal." Miguel lifted the napkin off his lap and tossed it on the table. "Guess what? The boys wanted to go to McDonald's and then play video games instead." Miguel couldn't hide his disappointment as he remembered. "But I keep on trying. Next month I'm taking them to a town on Cape Cod where there is a large population of deaf people, so the entire town uses sign language."

"Honestly?" asked Annie. "That's incredible. That would be a wonderful experience."

Miguel really liked this woman. He considered, for a moment, asking her to spend Thanksgiving with him. But that was too much. "Would you like to go to dinner with me Saturday night?" Saturday night meant a real date, no more pretend business meetings.

"I'm sorry. I already have plans. But thanks anyway." She paused. "I wonder if I could ask a favor, though."

She blew me off and she's asking favors? Miguel wondered.

"I'm going to visit my daughter on Saturday. Want to come? It's a long drive. I can't afford a chauffeur anymore, and I don't want to go alone."

"I'd be delighted."

Stuart Swann sat back in the limo parked outside V & T's, his camera resting on his lap. He saw Mary Griffin hurry out the door of the restaurant and approach the corner for the crosstown bus, getting one immediately. Stuart watched as the bus pulled out into traffic, then noticed the black man he had seen Mary sitting with leave a minute later.

Stuart had decided to follow Mary whenever she left the office unexpectedly without Gil during the day. He wasn't sure why he was doing this; he just knew there was something not right about her, and since he was feeling the pressure of her dislike for him at work, he figured he had better have some ammunition. At least I've learned *something* from working for Gil Griffin, he thought. Now, after only two outings, bingo!

Except he didn't know what "bingo" was exactly. Not

yet, at any rate. He'd barely been able to glimpse her and her companion through the dirty glare of the restaurant window. But the combination of this out-of-the-way restaurant, a black man, and an envelope he'd seen her pass over were enough ingredients to cook up a Mary stew, he was sure. Drug addiction? Sex? Something worse? He ordered his driver to follow the black man as he walked quickly toward Broadway. At Ninety-sixth Street the man walked into the lobby of a newly constructed luxury apartment building, incongruously set amongst tenements and *bodegas*. This, Stuart decided, was a good day for him. A bad day for Mary, he believed. It was becoming more apparent every day that Mary Griffin was not a woman of integrity.

Stuart looked at the sign on the side of the building and copied down the name of the management company, recognizing it as one of his pension-fund accounts. One step closer to bingo! he thought. Directing his driver back to Wall Street, Stuart smiled to himself as he began making calls on the car phone.

17

Queen for a Day

Annie smiled to herself as she turned off Montauk Highway and crossed the railroad tracks. This would probably be the first time Elise visited the wrong side of the tracks out here in the Hamptons.

Annie's little house, which she had inherited from her grandmother, was truly a cottage, not one of those enormous beach-side mansions that the wealthy persisted in calling "cottages." The place was in Devon, a small corner of Amagansett, on the north and unfashionable side of the main road. Seventy years ago, her grandmother had seen this old farmhouse on a small peninsula called Promised Land and had fallen in love.

It was easy, now, in the dying autumn light, to see why. The misty blue trim on the windows perfectly set off the brown cedar shingles of the little house, set on a gently sloping lawn. One side of the cottage was a single lofty room—the living room—with a peaked roof and big French windows on three sides that opened onto an old brick terrace.

The other part of the house was two storied, with a kitchen, bath, and study below, and two bedrooms and a bath above. A glassed-in porch on the west side of the house served as a dining room and conservatory. From the west windows, one could see the little orchard, and behind it the beach and the bay, now silvery gray in the late-autumn afternoon.

As Annie pulled up the drive, the crunching gravel seemed to welcome her. She'd have just enough daylight to check on the woodpile, to air out the house, and perhaps make a mulled-cider punch for the holiday tomorrow. It was unseasonably cold, really almost winter cold, and she'd have to bring in lots of wood.

First, though, she'd unpack the car. She had bought whole-wheat croissants at Dumas and raspberries and cream at Frazier Morris, along with some fabulous-smelling fresh Jamaican coffee beans and, finally, indulged in a big bunch of peonies from her florist. She looked guiltily at the huge, fluffy blossoms. They were four dollars a stem. She had bought a dozen, then was shocked by the price. *I can't even pay my daughter's tuition and I blow forty-eight dollars on a bunch of flowers.* Annie sighed. Well, what was forty-eight dollars in the face of the million and a half that her husband had squandered?

Now she was certain she wouldn't see the money anytime soon. Perhaps never, Aaron had called and stiffly said there were some problems with the business right now. Annie wondered if it was true. Armed with her knowledge of the agency from both Jerry and Chris, she had been silent for a moment. Then her anger had gotten the best of her. "Can't you sell the business?" she asked.

"Sell it?" he'd exploded. "I want to *buy* it."

"But if you sell it, you could replace Sylvie's money."

"Oh? And then how will I make a living?" he asked bitterly. She hadn't pushed, and now she shook her head as if to clear the memory. She wouldn't think of it now.

For the next hour she unpacked and stowed away the provisions, dusted the house, and brought in wood for a fire. Then she went up to the guest bedroom and down to the study and prepared them, the first for Elise and the other for Brenda.

Annie put out clean towels, flowers in pottery jugs, fresh soap, and a few magazines beside each bed, then went onto the porch that served as a dining room and set the table for the next morning's breakfast.

Elise and Brenda didn't arrive until half past eleven. She heard the car pull up—it was Elise's Lincoln limousine. The driver carried in the women's bags and a big turkey, then left to spend the night at Elise's East Hampton mansion.

Both Brenda and Elise complained about the holiday traffic and said they were tired, wanting nothing more than to go to sleep. Annie showed them to their rooms and went to bed herself. They had both seemed especially grumpy and irritable. They had probably offended one another half a dozen times on the long drive out.

The next morning Annie awoke early and showered and dressed as quickly and quietly as she could. Then she padded across the hallway balcony that overlooked the living room and took a moment to survey it.

Below her, the living room was already bathed in the early light of the sunrise, which poured in through the two sets of east-facing French windows. In the west wall, opposite the windows, a large fireplace with a simple white-painted pine mantel had pride of place. Facing the fireplace was a long, deep sofa, covered in her grandmother's favorite blue, rose, and white floral print, and flanked by a couple of cretonne-covered armchairs, each with its own hassock. I must remember to be thankful for all this. For everything, Annie reminded herself.

On the wall between the French windows, Annie had placed her desk—an English Regency *secrétaire*, the only really fine antique in the house. This would be a good place to write, she thought suddenly. I could write a book here, without the distraction of New York. Now that Sylvie is gone . . . but I'd be lonely. The room was lovely, the house was lovely, and she was lucky to have it. But it was so isolated here. Oh, I'm so foolish, she thought. I can't work with distractions and I'm afraid I can't live without them.

She had to smile. The peonies looked spectacular on the table behind the sofa. Their fat white heads drooped with just the right amount of heaviness. In the warmth of the room they had opened wider, and now, even from up above, Annie could see the few magenta petals that flecked the heart of every bloom. Lovely, she thought again as she went down the stairs as silently as possible.

Before her, the white-painted dining room table and the white Windsor chairs surrounding it looked fresh and inviting. The blue-and-white-checked cloth and the three places she had set all charmed her. But she needed something for a centerpiece. She decided to go outside and see what she could scout up. She shrugged into an old duffle coat and boots.

It was cold, with a breeze blowing from the south, filled with the fresh scent of the sea.

At the far end of the garden, Annie spied some fire thorn. Perfect for the table, a Thanksgiving color, a little gift to enjoy over breakfast. Annie cut some branches, feeling the stab that she always did when she sacrificed something from the garden for the house.

She walked back, admiring the place as she did. She loved coming here. It had been her grandmother's and it still remained so in Annie's mind. Annie's taste was more toward the simplicity of design of the Japanese, but here Nana's hand still prevailed. It comforted Annie.

She even used her nana's now-ancient percolator on those rare occasions when she made coffee. Its strange internal sounds and its pleasant perk had so often kept the two of them company.

Oh, God, she thought. Perhaps I'll have to sell the place. How much could I get for it? she wondered. How many tuition payments would it cover? The thought of giving up Nana's house brought tears to her eyes.

Now, the percolator was making its strange grunts and burps. Soon the delicious smell of the vanilla-almond coffee would waft up to the bedrooms.

"What the hell is making that noise?"

Annie spun around. Brenda, disheveled and in a fantastically colored muumuu stood in the kitchen doorway, sleepily scratching her head.

"It's the percolator."

"Jesus, it sounds like it's taking a dump on the counter."

Annie laughed. "Well, it's old. It struggles."

"So do I." Brenda moved to the refrigerator and opened the door. "Have you got anything to eat?" Before Annie could answer, Brenda had picked up a banana from the blue and white china bowl on the top of the refrigerator.

"Yes, there's plenty. But let's wait for Elise."

"Your waiting has ended," Elise said. She was impeccable as always, dressed in simple cream-colored slacks, a crisp cotton blouse, with a deep green sweater elegantly tossed over her wide shoulders. "Annie, what an absolutely charming little house."

"It is, isn't it?" Annie agreed. If there was a tiny note of unconscious condescension in Elise's compliment, Annie chose not to hear it. "Breakfast in the dining room?" she asked. They moved to the porch.

"Annie, what an absolutely charming little breakfast," Brenda said in a perfect imitation of Elise, and then grinned wickedly at her. "And I do mean little." Brenda looked down at the single croissant on each plate, the berries, the pretty but inadequate swirl of butter. These goyim don't know how to eat, she thought. Luckily she had brought a little something to keep in her room, just in case.

Elise, too, had brought "a little something," hidden at the bottom of her bag. The idea of visiting someone who might have no liquor available was terrifying, so Elise had stooped to packing a bottle of vodka. She'd been trying hard to control herself, drinking much less lately. But Christ, holidays were too depressing to get through sober. She would attempt it with these two friends, but she might as well face it, this was pathetic.

After breakfast they took a walk to the farmer's market, where they bought a lot of side vegetables to go with the turkey (not that Annie would eat turkey) and planned a strategy session and drinks to follow. "Now, let's spend the afternoon without men or food or children on our hands," Annie said, trying hard not to miss Chris, away at his girlfriend's, or Alex at school, or Sylvie.

Brenda napped while Annie stuffed the turkey and put it in the oven, and Elise lay beside the fireplace leafing through annual reports and taking notes. By one it was overcast, looking like snow, and Annie went up for a hot bath while the others started to set the table for the holiday dinner.

Trying to think of something positive, Annie smiled at how well Elise and Brenda were getting along. It was fun to be with them together. Brenda's earthiness offset Elise's tendency to be cool, and Elise's class contrasted vividly with Brenda's admitted vulgarity. Annie had to smile again. She really was having fun.

The dinner was delicious. Chris called from Pennsylvania where he had gone to meet Karen's family, and Alex from California at school, and then Brenda called her kids, who were spending the holiday with their father. Annie looked over at Elise, staring at a magazine she wasn't reading, Elise who had only her senile mother. But she'd had more than a bottle of wine.

As they finished dinner, it began to snow, and the sight of the big flakes was a pleasant end to the pleasant meal. Elise and Brenda cleared the table and washed up despite Annie's protest, so she filled her nana's percolator and added decaf this time.

"Well, who wants to tell what they are thankful for?" Annie asked.

"Not without another drink," Elise said.

"Not even *with* one," Brenda corrected. "Annie, stop being such a damn goody-goody. The nuns aren't here taking notes."

They had drunk almost all of the white wine, but when Elise asked for another glass, Annie opened the red. She had trouble with the cork. "I really miss having a man around when it's time to open the wine."

"Get screw caps," Brenda suggested. Annie began to giggle. It wasn't that funny, but Elise joined in. Then Brenda. The three of them stood in the warm kitchen, laughing. We may be getting drunk, Annie thought. Just then the percolator began its gruntings. This set them off again.

"It's disgusting," gasped Elise.

"It's obscene," agreed Brenda.

"Oh, stop picking on the poor thing. He can't help it. Anyway, who wants cream on their pie?"

"How decadent!" Elise shook her head.

"How delicious," Brenda approved. "The pie is what *I'm* grateful for."

Annie carried the coffee into the cozy living room and added another log to the fire. They settled in, each of them finding a comfortable seat before the fireplace. There was a silence. Annie took a deep breath. It was now or never, she thought. Confession is good for the soul, so why is this so difficult for me? She looked at the other two women. I don't think they'll judge me or pity me. I hope not. "I'm grateful for friends like you two," she began. "Friends I can confide in." She paused. "I'd like to tell you about my divorce."

Slowly, calmly, she told them about the unpleasantness at the Carlyle: her eagerness, her desperation, Aaron's betrayal, and worst of all, the final horror of Dr. Leslie Rosen lurking in the other room, hearing her beg Aaron for a reconciliation. She was thankful she could get it off her chest.

"Did you used to tell Dr. Rosen *everything?*" Brenda asked. Silently, Annie nodded. "Well, I hope you told her Aaron had bad breath in the morning, or was getting soft in the gut. Something she'd tell him and he'll eat his heart out over," Brenda cried. "I can't believe you're still wearing his wedding ring!"

Annie looked down at her hand, self-conscious. "You're wearing *yours!*" Elise said to Brenda.

"Yeah, well, my finger's too fat to get it off. What's *your* excuse?"

"I paid for it. It's a perfectly good Winston. Anyway, we were talking about Annie at the Carlyle," Elise said coldly. "What did you do?" she asked Annie, her voice warm with sympathy.

"I ran."

The two women nodded. "But now I'm tired of running. And I'm tired of blaming myself. And I'm tired of excusing either of them. And I'm tired of loving a man who doesn't love me." Annie paused. "There's something else. Something worse. Aaron's lost the money from Sylvie's trust fund and I don't know when he'll pay it back."

The two women looked at her. Brenda knew about the loss, but not about Aaron's refusal or inability to repay it. And Annie hadn't ever told Elise about it at all. Now she expected to feel the shame over what he'd done. But for the first time, instead of feeling Aaron's feelings, too, she felt the tear, the true separation from him. He had left her, he wasn't part of her, and what he did didn't reflect on her. She wasn't ashamed.

Her chest hurt, as if something physical had been pulled apart, as if a rib had been torn away. Involuntarily, unconsciously, she put her hand to her heart. Telling them, her friends, had made this possible. She wasn't ashamed anymore. Hurt, yes. And angry. But no longer ashamed.

"Something's different," she said, and she knew how stupid it sounded. "Something's changed." She sat quietly for a moment while they waited. She bowed her head for a moment, bit her lips. What was it? What was it? "I don't love him anymore," she said simply.

Brenda raised her hands in triumph. "Hallelujah," she yelled. "A wonderful Thanksgiving. The worm has turned." Then she calmed down. "But how much money are we actually talking about?"

Leave it to Brenda, Annie thought. If sex was secret and dirty and shaming, money was more so. "Almost a million and a half dollars. The money for Sylvie is gone."

"Yeah, but you said he's paying it back," Brenda said. "He's not a lying cheapskate like Morty. It'll be made up, right, Annie?" For once, Brenda sounded like a child, a hopeful little girl.

"Well, now Aaron isn't so certain. He doesn't know when he'll be able to replace it. He said business isn't great right now."

"You didn't tell us that!" Elise accused her. "Anyway, how did he do this? You can't simply break into a trust fund."

Annie shook her head. "He did it without my knowledge. It probably was illegal, and perhaps he could be sued, or even worse, but what's the point?" Then she told them about her visit to Gil Griffin's office, of his threat. Tears filled her eyes. "I can't sue. Aaron can't pay Sylvie's tuition from jail."

"I'll lend you the money," Brenda offered.

Elise shot her a look. Why was it people with so little could be so generous? she wondered. She thought of her mother's rules. She was already breaking one, trusting these women, so different from her. Should she break another? She loved Annie too much to risk losing her friendship. But Annie had given them a gift tonight. A gift of trust. All at once, Elise, too, wanted to share.

"Well, now I have something to confess." Elise paused. "I slept with a man who is half my age. I was drunk. I was lonely. And now, I think that I'm falling in love with him. I'm ashamed. And I'm afraid of what people will say."

"They'd probably say, 'Lucky her!'" Annie smiled, but thought for a moment of her reservations over Miguel, just a few years younger than she, and a minority. Wasn't she uncomfortable about that? It was so hard to break away from conditioning.

"Hey, never mind what they say," Brenda told Elise. "Fuck 'em if they can't take a joke. But neither of you has won 'Queen for a Day' yet," she added, tissue box in hand. "Jack Bailey hasn't heard from the last contestant yet. I'll see you and raise you," she said with more bravado than she felt. "This ought to win me the washer-dryer *and* a big hand from the crowd. I've got something to be grateful for, but I warn you, it's pretty weird." She paused.

"Morty told my father something . . . a secret I had once told him about this counselor at summer camp I'd had an affair with." Elise and Annie were gazing at her. "The coun-

selor was a woman. A girl, really. The swimming instructor."
There, it was out.

"When Morty told him that, spitefully, my father looked
at me, and I looked away. I couldn't lie to him about anything.
I never had."

Brenda looked at the two of them. "My father never mentioned it again, but it changed him. Deeply. Daddy loved me,
I knew that, but from then on, he never looked me in the eyes
again. And when my father died four months later, Jesus, I felt
terrible. And I blamed Morty. Christ, I still do. Of course, I
never should have told him."

"Well, many girls have crushes on women when they're
in their teens. It's normal," Elise said soothingly. "Your father
just didn't know that."

The three women sat silently, the fire making the only
sound in the room. "I think it's more than that, Elise." Brenda
looked at her two friends directly. "I've been trying to sort it out
since I met Diana. You know, the only real physical affection I
ever felt for anyone in my whole life was for that counselor at
camp. Nothing else physical was ever good . . . certainly nothing with Morty. I figured it was just our bad marriage. At least
I wanted to believe that. But it was deeper." She spoke softly,
even gently, but with conviction.

"Diana makes me very happy. I love her. And I'm thankful." Brenda leaned back and folded her hands in her lap. For
the first time in her life, she realized, she didn't feel the need
to explain herself, to make any more excuses. She had stated
a fact. Now the rest was up to them. I accept myself, Brenda
thought, and felt the warmth in her chest.

Elise looked at Brenda and said, "From what I hear, Brenda,
Diana is a very impressive woman. Bright, committed, and
sensitive." Elise broke out laughing. "I'm sorry, but I just had a
thought. She's all the things Morty's *not*."

Annie said, "Well, I hope you get what you want. You deserve someone in your life who will love you. I'm very happy for you both, Brenda."

Brenda cleared her throat. "So, did I win the washer-dryer?" The others both smiled. "This is a helluva weird Thanksgiving. I thought I'd mope around and miss Anthony and Angela. I didn't know we would be playing 'truth.' I thought we were *supposed* to be moping."

"Let's *do* something, not just talk about things," Annie said. "God knows, I'm sick of moping. Let's *really* do something about Aaron, and Morty, and Bill."

"We should have taken more action before, but we'll do it now," Elise said. "You're already started, Brenda. So far, you're leading us all. Sending in the tax information to the IRS was the first step. Remember our goals: Morty broke, Gil powerless, Bill castrated, and Aaron abandoned. I've already started to work on Gil. We know from Stuart and Uncle Bob's contacts that he's going to go into Mitsui. And I've told my uncle to throw all of his weight and mine against Gil now."

"How?" Annie asked.

"Get behind Mitsui. Buy it up in a big way. And do it strategically. Once we've bought in at a low price, talk it up. Make it a hot ticket. No takeover possible. Get the word out. We'll make enough to buy Sylvie her own school."

"Say that again?" Brenda asked.

Elise explained the whole process. Annie listened, too. Elise was so wonderful, she thought, almost ready to cry again. She bit her lip.

"You want my settlement from Morty?" Brenda asked. "To invest? Maybe I could help fuck Gil over and wind up with what Morty promised me!"

"Certainly," Elise agreed. "But be practical. You need something to live on, but we could invest the rest for you.

Then we've got a little more working capital and it's Gil who gives it to us."

"So, that starts Operation Gil. Then there's the SEC investigation. Any word, Annie?"

"De Los Santos hasn't made much progress yet. I'm seeing him again right after Thanksgiving. I'm not sure we're going to get anywhere with this, but I trust the man." Annie didn't have the courage to tell them how much she liked Miguel. She was just beginning to admit it to herself. But soon. Soon she'd tell them, but not yet. She wanted to be more sure of how she felt. And of how *he* felt.

"What do you mean we're not going to get anywhere?" Elise demanded.

"Oh, I don't know. Gil seem so, so . . . impervious."

"Don't be ridiculous. Everyone is pervious."

"Pervious? Can you say *pervious?*" Annie wondered.

"I just did," Elise snapped. "It means accessible, vulnerable."

"Oh, you know what Annie means," Brenda said. "Aaron and the pervert headshrinker, they have their careers, their reputations, and each other. They look fine; we're the losers. And Morty, the fat slob, gets millions of bucks and a blonde from Savannah, or wherever the hell she was spawned, and now he's hanging out with the beautiful people, and he's in the prime of his life, while I'm fat, over forty, and finished."

"And whose fault is that?" Elise asked, exasperated. "Your only exercise appears to be lifting the fork."

"Don't throw rocks at me; keep them floating in your drink," Brenda said sweetly. "I eat too much, you drink too much, Annie worries too much. What's the diff?"

Annie stared at the two of them. In a moment they'd gone from friends to adversaries. They looked like two cats with their backhairs up. But very different cats: Elise was an elongated, elegant Siamese purebred, Brenda a roly-poly tabby with claws. Would they tear into each other? Would the holiday be spoiled?

And then, Elise smiled grimly. "I guess you're right."

Brenda smiled back. "I've got a stash up in my room. Do you?"

The smile left Elise's face, but Brenda continued, "I tell you what. I'll trade you my six Milky Ways for your bottle of Stoli."

Elise hesitated, for a moment looking like a cornered cat. Then, taking the challenge, she raised her eyebrows. "What else have you got?"

Now it was Brenda's turn to stop smiling. "Gummi Bears," she admitted. She paused, as if fighting some internal battle. "And some peanuts. But that's all. I swear it."

"Oh, certainly. Next you'll tell me you've got a bridge you want sell to me. Well, I'll go get yours if you'll get mine. Is it a deal?"

"From now on, no drinks for you before dinner," Brenda warned. "And no wines."

"You're the one who whines," Elise batted back. "And no dessert for you after meals."

Annie had to hide her smile. Maybe Brenda had bitten off more than even she could chew. And for once Annie wasn't being the nag.

"You're on," Brenda sighed, and trudged up the stairs to the guest bedroom, while Elise went into the study and pawed through Brenda's bags. Annie sat, astonished and delighted as each triumphantly returned, Brenda waving the bottle of vodka over her head, while Elise dumped sweets on the coffee table. In addition to the candy bars, nuts, and Gummi Bears, she had found a big bag of Raisinets. She added it to the pile of contraband with a flourish.

"You neglected, somehow, to mention these." She smiled.

Brenda glared at her. "Silly me. So forgetful. So we're off the stuff for the duration? Cold-turkey time? We clean up our acts?"

"*I* will if *you* will. No more booze until these husbands pay the price."

"It's a deal."

"Okay, so back to business," Elise said, pulling out her Hermès notepad and a gold Montblanc pen. "We start on Mitsui and the SEC with Gil, and we've sicced the IRS on Mort." She looked up at Annie. "Now, what about Aaron?"

Annie shrugged. "What about him? I don't know."

"We have to get him for this trust busting. We *have* to, Annie."

"So long as it doesn't hurt the children."

"Well, where's his soft white underbelly?"

"Not the shrink, that's for sure," Brenda said. "I saw her picture in *Vanity Fair* and she's scary looking. Harder than diamonds."

Annie smiled. "I can't think of what he would miss. He's not involved much with Sylvie, and I would never involve the boys. He's never been promiscuous, he has no bad habits—"

"Except for betraying his wife."

"And squandering his daughter's fortune."

"Yes, well, except for that."

"What were his goals?" Elise asked. "What was really important to him?"

"The boys, of course, especially Alex, but they're off-limits. That and his work, I suppose."

"What about his work?" Elise asked, beginning to take notes.

"Well, I think the agency is the most important thing to Aaron. And I know he's been planning to buy out his partner,

Jerry, for a long time. But now, he doesn't have the money. First, the divorce cost him, and then . . ." She stopped. "We can't hurt Aaron's livelihood. Sylvie will need the money. But I'm so angry, I'd like to kill him."

Elise thought for a moment. "Well, it couldn't hurt if Aaron's *partner* got some new accounts, would it? Make it harder for Aaron to buy him out. Why don't you call Jerry and see? Meanwhile, I could ask Uncle Bob to find out if any of the companies *he's* involved in want a new agency. We move them in through the partner. At the least, Aaron makes some money for Sylvie. And if it gives his partner some leverage over Aaron, so much the better."

Annie wiped her eyes and nodded. "Jerry could use a break right now. Elise, you're brilliant. Thank you."

Elise smiled. Perhaps, just this once, for a retarded girl's tuition, she could make an exception to Mother's rule. She could do that for Annie. She'd figure out a way to make Annie take the money. She turned to Brenda. "So? Anything else?"

"For Morty, it's money. It's always been money. Of course, since he's welshed on his deal with me, Diana is dying to sue him. She says she'll do it on contingency. She's furious."

"Suing him isn't enough," sniffed Elise. "How strong was the package we sent to the IRS? What did Klendenning say?"

"It looked good to me." Brenda shrugged. "Your attorney promised that I'd have immunity, and that I won't he responsible for the fines, if there are any."

"Not if you'll testify and help them make the case."

"Brenda Cushman, girl stoolie."

"Better than Brenda Cushman, girl patsy."

"I never would have turned him in if he hadn't welshed. His lawyer, Leo, told Diana that he'd had some reverses. The stock had gone down." She stopped, thinking hard.

"Annie, do you think that Aaron's tip might have come from Morty?" she asked slowly.

Annie stared at her. "I don't know. It's possible." She reflected for a moment. "Aaron's never done anything like it before. He's very conservative. He isn't interested in the market."

"That might be something to look into," Elise said, briefly taking more notes. "What stock did he buy?"

Annie's mouth opened, her face reddened. Of course! "It was Morty the Madman," Annie admitted, feeling as dumb as she ever had in her life.

"Eureka!" Elise shrieked. She and Brenda began to hoot.

"Why didn't you tell us that?" Brenda screamed.

"Because I'm stupid," Annie said. "Should I tell Miguel De Los Santos about this?"

"Only if you want to see how Aaron looks in stripes."

"Insider trading!" Elise chortled.

"But I don't want to see him in prison!" Annie cried.

"Look, I think we could get them all on that stuff," Brenda said earnestly. "I mean, the stock was completely inflated. I used to know that operation, and it was totally fly-by-night. Couldn't we bring them all down with it? Griffin underwrote it. Bill did the contracts, Aaron bought stock—"

"Please! I have to think of Sylvie. I can't get Aaron into that kind of trouble," Annie cried.

"And Bill would never do anything he could get caught at," Elise said. "He's the original Philadelphia lawyer." She pursed her mouth. "No, each man gets the punishment reserved for him. What did they say in *The Mikado*? 'The punishment fits the crime.'"

"Come on, Elise. Each one of us says our husband is the hardest to get. Don't hold out. I'll go for it if you will. There's got to be a way," Annie said.

"Well, I do hear from my uncle that there's trouble on the Phoebe front."

"Maybe that could be exploited," Brenda suggested cheerfully. "Though I think she's a time bomb that will self-destruct anyway."

"Well, where else is Bill *pervious?*" Annie asked.

"I'm not sure. Of course he's most vulnerable around the woman thing. Show him he's a bad lay and ruin him for life."

"Well, is he?" Brenda asked, hopeful.

Elise looked back at her, as if considering whether or not to respond. Then she sighed. "Unfortunately, no." She giggled. "Although it's been a long time."

"Well, maybe we can break up his marriage plans completely. Then he'd be broke," Annie suggested.

"Not exactly. He's collected some antiques over the years that are now worth quite a bit. And he does make something at his job."

"Oh, he'd just charm some other rich woman," Brenda said. Then she stopped. She didn't want to hurt Elise.

"That's all right, Brenda." Elise shrugged. "You're right. But I'm sure there must be *something.*"

Then Brenda stood up. "That reminds me. Guess what gift I have for you?" From under a seat cushion she pulled out a file folder. "What would you give me for all of Billy-boy's client billing records and expense reports? Angie got one of the girls from the typing pool at his law firm to get copies of them last week. I don't know what's in 'em, but maybe something."

"Brenda, you're a genius," Elise said. "I think this could be a wedge."

"And what about Gil? We haven't done anything about his car, yet." Brenda reminded them. "But, you know, I'd like to see him punished physically." In response to the looks of disgust she saw on her friends' faces, she continued, "I know, I know, you white people don't get violent. But in the Morrelli family, it was an eye for an eye. Hey, remember, Gil hit Cynthia. He should be beaten. And we should take an oath on it. A pact signed in blood."

Annie shook her head. "No violence. None. Absolutely none," she said firmly. Then she smiled. She filled a champagne flute with bubbly and set it on the table. Then she took off her wedding band—the ring she couldn't bear to remove. "There!" she said, and dropped it in the glass.

"Okay!" Elise said, looking at her two friends. She laughed and nodded. Then she pulled off her ring and flung it into the golden glass. Brenda, grinning, struggled to get hers off her fat finger, finally did, and threw it into the flute, which toppled over, smashing on the floor.

Brenda laughed and nodded. "I'm proud of us."

"Me, too," Annie agreed.

"Then we're agreed." Elise turned to Brenda. "And no eating sweets for the duration."

"And no drinking," Brenda reminded her. "Not till it's over."

"And it ain't over till it's over," Annie reminded them both. "Happy Thanksgiving."

That night, Annie lay in bed awake, grateful for her friends and wondering if they would succeed. She thought about Aaron with Dr. Rosen. She thought about her daughter, and De Los Santos.

Brenda was also awake, alternately wondering if Tony and Angela were enjoying Aruba with their father, if she could sneak into the kitchen unheard, and if she was now, officially, a lesbian. She thought of Diana and wondered some more, and wished for, longed for, *craved*, just one candy bar.

In *her* room, Elise, desperate for a drink, considered slugging down her perfume, but wound up eating four of Brenda's Milky Ways and finally fell asleep near dawn.

18

Sylvan Glades

Miguel drove Annie's gray Jaguar smoothly along the Taconic headed north. Getting out of the city was always confusing, but from this point on the trip was direct. Annie could relax. Well, at least she could try. She hadn't been to see Sylvie since Memorial Day, but now the six-month resettling period was over and it was time to see how she had adjusted, if the special community was right for her.

Annie took a deep breath and turned to stare out the window. It was nice to be with Miguel; he respected silence, seemed comfortable with it.

"It's beautiful here," she said aloud. They were about seventy miles north of the city, in New York's Dutchess County. The trees were coated with an icy shell that sparkled in the sunlight, and clean snow was still on the ground. The Jag moved easily over each rolling hill, effortlessly eating the miles, gliding her toward Dr. Gancher and her daughter. She smoothed the skirt of her Donna Karan cashmere sweater dress. What would her nana say was appropriate dress for visiting your retarded daughter at her new group home? Annie shrugged. Peering at the barren trees that lined the highway, she could see the waves of drifts that the snow had made across each enormous meadow. "I'm always surprised there are farms so close to the city. This is real country."

"Yes, and it's always here," Miguel answered quietly. "When I see all this, I think of myself hemmed in down there at Federal Plaza and wonder what the hell I'm doing with my life."

Annie nodded. Lately she'd found the city even more crowded and oppressive than usual. More crowded and more lonely. Of course, the holidays make things worse. Maybe if Sylvie isn't happy here, she suddenly thought, I'll sell the co-op and the cottage and live in the country with her, somewhere cheap, where Sylvie could find some kind of help.

But where would that be? she wondered. And what about me? Could I get along without my friends? Brenda made her laugh, no matter how bad her jokes. And Elise always had a plan, plus she was loyal, and solid. And there was her work at the hospital. Maybe it didn't add up to a lot, not much to build a life on, but it was something. Oh, but she missed Sylvie. It had been so long since she'd seen her.

She checked herself again. Visit Sylvie with an open mind, free of tension, anger, or projection. First Sylvie, then Dr. Gancher. One thing at a time. She was going to do each thing until everything was done. Too bad she already felt exhausted.

Annie relaxed, letting her eyes rest on the white landscape until Miguel turned off the Taconic and stopped at a red light. Then the tension returned. It was this money thing. Annie had never thought of her family as rich, not really rich, like Elise, but of course wealth was relative. And her family was wealthy. They had the house on Main Line, and the camp in the Thousand Islands. And they'd gone up to Palm Beach. Annie smiled. Never *down* to Florida, always *up* to Palm Beach. It was part of the code of the wealthy.

Of course when she was growing up she knew there were poor people. But poverty had had no reality for her; Annie had thought everyone lived as she did. Her trust fund wasn't large, but it paid for Smith College, and for her clothes after she dropped out and married Aaron. It wasn't until then, when she was first married and they had almost nothing that she saw firsthand how impoverished families lived. Then she finally realized how money, or the lack of it, affected her own kind.

Well, it had affected Aaron, but not her. She had found living frugally rather charming. She was ashamed of herself. A Marie Antoinette in a milkmaid's costume. Playing at being poor, while Aaron wrote. And then she had gotten pregnant with Alex, and Aaron had gone to work to earn more money. Eventually they'd had enough, and then more than enough. And her father had given them the down payment on the Greenwich house.

But now there wasn't enough. Only this time it wasn't cute, or charming, or unimportant. It was frightening. And I don't have any experience in dealing with these things, she thought. How do you beg them not to throw your child out of school? How do you tell them you don't have enough money? Think of the welfare mothers who have to fight for their children daily. Annie was washed with a wave of shame.

In ten minutes they were turning into the driveway of Sylvan Glades. The English Tudor mansion never failed to impress her and since her very first visit she had expected Laurence Olivier to emerge from the doorway to greet her. The house with its huge, snow-covered lawn was like a movie set, or a dream. Last night I dreamt I went to Manderley. She sighed. The sight of the other buildings brought her back to reality, however: cracker boxes, ugly modern cracker boxes. Couldn't they have . . . ? Well, she stopped herself. Apparently they couldn't. And if they had, the tuition would be even more astronomical.

Annie and Miguel walked to the reception office and were greeted by Dr. Gancher.

"You've had a beautiful day for a drive," she said, smiling at them. "I'll take you to Sylvie, and then you can come back here and we can talk."

Sylvie was working at the canteen. Annie saw her at once. She was clearing dishes off the tables and scraping the plates before carefully stacking them on a tray. Annie felt a stab at her heart when she saw Sylvie's face. Never before had Sylvie looked so absorbed, so satisfied. She glowed. In fact, in the six months since she'd seen her, Sylvie seemed completely changed. Annie had a moment of panic. Now I *am* completely alone, she thought. Miguel fetched two cups of coffee from the machine, and when he returned and pulled out a chair for her, she sank into it. They watched Sylvie silently, until she looked up and noticed them.

"Mom-Pom!" she cried. "You're here! You're here!" She ran to Annie and hugged her. "Come here! Look!" Annie bit her lip and breathed deeply, but Sylvie didn't notice. She was too excited.

"Here's what I do, Mom! Look! When somebody eats something, they leave their plate and I can take it away. It's my job." She was very excited, and saliva had accumulated at the corners of her mouth, as it always did when she was excited. Other residents and staff were sitting at tables, but no one turned to look. Annie stifled her need to wipe her daughter's mouth. "I have to do it every day. No misses. And Jim says that I'm the best bus-girl he ever had here!"

Annie felt a twinge of guilt. This was what Sylvie had needed, and this was what Annie had selfishly kept from her.

"I'm so proud of you, Sylvie!" Annie said, hugging the beaming girl. "And you look wonderful!" She was wearing a jumper, too tight across her chest, and the blouse under it was missing a collar button. But these things don't matter, Annie told herself, and smiled. "How's Pangor?"

"Great. He caught a mouse! And do you know what he did with it?"

Annie winced. Did the residences have mice? she wondered. "What, honey?"

"He put it on my pillow!"

"Like a present to you? I once had a cat that did that. She even caught rats," Miguel said.

Annie wondered where it had been that Miguel lived with rats. Then she remembered herself and forced a smile. She turned to Miguel, who was also smiling. "Oh, I'm sorry! Miguel, this is my daughter, Sylvie. Sylvie, this is my friend Miguel. He drove me up."

"Hello, Mr. Me Kell," Sylvie said. "I'll clear your cup for you."

"May I finish my coffee first?" Miguel asked.

"Yes." Sylvie giggled.

"Then that's a deal," Miguel said.

"I have to go back to work now," Sylvie told them, her flat face serious. "Work during work time."

"I understand. And I'll come back after work is over," Annie told her.

Annie left Sylvie at the canteen, but once outside she turned to watch her through the window. Her daughter, scraping plates. Her life's work. Miguel stood silently beside her. Once Jim, the supervisor, came over and spoke to Sylvie, who nodded earnestly.

Annie sighed. What was her own life's work, to make

scraping plates look so unappealing? Holding the hands of burn victims? Writing useless, unfinished short stories? Sylvie was happy. Who was she to judge?

"It's very hard," she said aloud. Miguel nodded and said nothing.

Annie left Miguel outside and walked across the snowy campus to Dr. Gancher's office. All right. Sylvie first, now Dr. Gancher. For it was clear to Annie that this place was right for Sylvie. She walked along the avenues of massive plane trees, their limbs coated with snow and ice. The beauty, the restfulness, reinforced her feelings of the rightness of the place for Sylvie. It gave Annie courage.

Dr. Gancher's door was ajar and she called to Annie to come in and sit down. "So, what do you think of Sylvie?" the doctor began.

"She looks good. And she's trying so hard. People always think that—"

"There are none of those people here, Mrs. Paradise," Dr. Gancher interrupted. "That's what makes Sylvan Glades a haven. But it's more than that. We have great hopes for Sylvie. In a month or two we'd like to try a job for her in a restaurant in town."

"Really? So soon?" Annie felt a lurch in her stomach. People could be so cruel, so impatient. "Is she ready?"

"She has been very well raised." Dr. Gancher looked straight at her. "I think she has plenty of resources."

Annie didn't thank the woman, but felt herself tremble from the approval. She took a deep breath. "I understand. It's just that . . . it's almost more than I hoped for. I'm very grateful."

"Now it's my turn to understand, Mrs. Paradise." Dr. Gancher smiled. "When parents come here for their first visit, it's often a disturbing experience for them. The six-month separation is hard. They may have struggled for years and made many sacrifices and changes in their lives, to give their children happiness. They feel that their children can't survive without them. Then they come here and see their children living on their own and happy in the bargain. The parent can feel unnecessary and even intrusive, and perhaps foolish for having kept them home so long." The doctor smiled at her. "Sylvie needed the time alone. And she needed her years with you, too. All of them. I'd say your timing has been amazingly good."

Annie did not respond immediately. She looked at Dr. Gancher with a keener gaze. In this pause she took in the largeness of this person's character and involuntarily contrasted it with the smallness of such people as Gil Griffin, and yes, of her husband, Aaron.

"Thank you," she said finally. And if only she could just leave now, secure in her happiness for her daughter. But she'd have to start the other business now. She'd have to. "Unfortunately, though, I do have a problem." Annie sat up taller in her chair.

"Yes?"

"I'm not able to make the quarterly payment in full and I need to . . . I hope to pay . . . to get completely caught up by spring."

Dr. Gancher looked puzzled. This obviously wasn't the objection she was prepared for. "I'm surprised, Mrs. Paradise. We are aware of Sylvie's trust fund. There isn't a child with Down's who doesn't deserve a Sylvan Glades. It's my heartbreak that so few can afford one. Since there are so many candidates, ability to pay is one of our first considerations. Your ability to pay was never in question." She paused. "What happened?"

How could she explain? You see, Dr. Gancher, Sylvie's

father is a liar and a thief. Oh, God, she couldn't. Why the hell didn't Aaron come here himself and beg, she thought bitterly.

"My husband, my ex-husband, made a bad investment," she finally blurted out.

Dr. Gancher's puzzlement gave way to a look of concern. "But what about the future? You know we feel that long-term residency is the only really beneficial treatment. An aborted stay does more harm than good, not only for Sylvie, but for the community."

"Dr. Gancher, I promise that I'll get the money to restore Sylvie's trust fund. I do have some resources. I'm just not very liquid right now. I see how happy Sylvie is and I won't allow this life to be taken from her. Please just give me some time."

"Yes, Mrs. Paradise, I can do that." Dr. Gancher's face relaxed. "I'll explain to the bursar. But we will need a letter from you with a payment schedule. And some idea of Sylvie's financial future."

"Of course." Just let me out of here, dear Lord. It was worse than I imagined. Let me out without crying like a little victim. "Thank you," she said, standing.

Annie headed out the front door so she wouldn't run into Miguel or Sylvie until she had time to collect herself. Just a few deep breaths, she thought. She walked along the drive, breathing in the crisp, cold air, staring at the wide, empty white lawn. All right. That was done. But she would never forgive Aaron. Never. And she would do whatever it took to keep Sylvie here.

She would spend the afternoon with Sylvie. She would play with Pangor, see Sylvie's room, take her out to lunch, watch Sylvie open the gifts she had brought. She would enjoy her new, grown-up daughter.

And then there would only be Miguel to contend with.

She wondered how much he liked her, and if that might help him indict Gil. Because now the gloves were off. She'd give Miguel De Los Santos everything she had. And if Aaron was implicated, so be it.

She turned and began walking back to the parking lot. In the distance, outside the canteen, she could see Miguel and her daughter sitting, throwing snowballs at a plane tree and talking. Sylvie seemed to be laughing. Annie smiled. She would keep her laughing, whatever the cost.

As they drove home in the winter twilight, the silence between Miguel and Annie deepened.

"She's a nice girl, Annie," Miguel said. "Funny, too."

"Yes," Annie agreed. Sylvie had a host of faces that she used to express herself. When she had seen Miguel's poached perch at lunch, served with its head, she had wrinkled up her nose and made a fish face.

"The school seems a good one."

"Yes. Too bad I can't afford it." She took a deep breath. "Miguel, I have some more information for you. I don't know if it will help in the Gil Griffin investigation, but . . ." She took another deep breath. "We think Aaron invested in Morty the Madman because of a tip from Morty Cushman, the owner. But we have no proof. Then the stock took a nosedive. Something happened, Miguel, but we don't know what. And we also know that Morty Cushman may be in trouble with the IRS. We think there might have been collusion between Gil and Morty and Aaron."

"Good. Maybe I can use that. I'll see Mr. Cushman. Meanwhile, what are *you* going to do?"

"About what?"

"About Sylvie's school. It can't be cheap."

"I don't know." Tears began to fill Annie's eyes. "I don't

know," she repeated, and then, despite herself, her sobbing began. Miguel pulled the car to the side of the highway. It was almost dark. He took out a folded white handkerchief, handed it to her, and she wiped her eyes, but the tears kept coming. He leaned toward her, putting his arm awkwardly around the back of her seat. At his touch, Annie put her head on his shoulder and sobbed. He held her for a long, long time.

19

Morty Suffers a Setback

Morty settled back into the plush seat of the limousine and lit a cigar. "Christ, what a day," he said, then took a long pull of smoke. His cigars were his one real luxury. They were Havana, of course, same brand as Castro smoked and purportedly hand-rolled by teenage girls, on the inside of their virgin thighs. Guys swore it gave them a special sweetness.

"What a night." He leaned forward to get a can of seltzer from the compact refrigerator and felt the ache in his back muscles brought on by the twisting and turning of the sleepless night before. Just age, he thought, but his mind leaped back to the parade of money grabbers on his tail who had nipped at his heels every time he closed his eyes.

Jesus, Thanksgiving with Tony and Angela in Aruba had cost him a bundle. And they both hated Shelby. His gaze fell on the driver's copy of the *New York Post* with the headline, "Leona Helmsley Denies Tax Evasion Charges" and a picture of Leona being escorted in tears out of court by her gaggle of lawyers.

Morty snorted. Poor bitch, he thought. He was probably the only person in the city who pitied her. Why don't they leave her alone? Evade taxes! Didn't she pay more than

$3 million? How the fuck much more does she have to pay? When is enough going to be enough?

He tossed the paper aside, took a gulp of seltzer, and continued to work on the cigar while scanning the crowded streets through the smoked glass. "Enough is fuckin' enough!" he said out loud.

"Excuse me, Mr. Cushman?" the driver said.

"Forget about it," Morty told him roughly.

He leaned his head back and closed his eyes, trying to calm down. He didn't want to spoil Shelby's cocktail party and the play—no, what was it?—performance art. Right. Whatever. She had maneuvered the grants committee of the Museum of Modern Art into attending this party, to be followed by a "living sculpture" piece of performance art. If the committee takes the hook on this one, Shelby will have made a real splash in the art world. That's what she says, anyway. But, Morty had to admit, all this stuff bored the shit out of him. He and Shelby were donating a painting to the museum, and it would have his name on it. "Donated from the Morton B. Cushman Collection." Somehow, it didn't thrill him as much as he had expected. And the gallery wasn't doing any business. Shelby couldn't get the social crowd in, but she could sure as shit pull in bills.

"Enough," escaped his lips involuntarily. Enough for Leona *and* me. When are they going to leave us alone? They think I'm a bottomless pit of money. Well, they're wrong! There's not enough to go round, he thought resentfully. Someone's going to come up holding the short end of the stick and it ain't going to be me.

Why not Brenda? Two million dollars to "reevaluate" their divorce settlement? Thanks, Leo, you asshole. Why should she get one more dime? Two checks, a million each. His stock was depressed right now, and so was he. Well she can fuckin' die waiting for the second check. Fuck her, and fuck Leo.

"She got a signed contract, Morty. Signed, sealed, and delivered," Leo had sputtered in anger. "Okay, Leo," Morty had said, "let her sue me. You're a good lawyer, right? Just tell her and the dyke that I want to 're-reevaluate' the agreement."

They're all over me, he thought, as he fanned himself with Leona's picture. And now Aaron. I'm going to have to increase my advertising and cover my losses with Aaron. Plus bail him out? All right, so Aaron's not so bad. But more money going out. Shit!

Everywhere he turned, he felt the grabbing hands. Except, of course, Shelby's. He didn't like to think about whether Shelby would have married him if he hadn't bought her the gallery, but if he was honest with himself, he would have to say no. Fat Jew bastid. "*I wouldn't fuck a poor one, either,*" he said, and laughed.

The limousine turned onto Fifty-seventh Street from Madison Avenue and slowed to a halt in front of Shelby's gallery near Fifth Avenue, half a block past Tiffany's. The crossroads of the world, Morty thought, and it's costing me a fucking bundle.

But this was one of those rich men's moments that he loved. Limos could double-park anywhere in this city, he knew. So, as his came to a halt, he savored the moment. The chauffeur went around the car and opened Morty's door.

Over his shoulder, he called to his driver, "I'll be a while, so stick around." The security guard greeted him by name as he ushered Morty into the cool, rich, marble-faced interior. Then Morty stepped into the elevator and pressed the button.

When the doors opened, Morty stepped out, then stood

still for a minute and took it all in: the expensive paintings on the walls, the deep-piled carpet underfoot, knots of sedately but expensively dressed people holding drinks and talking in suitably hushed tones, waiters noiselessly passing drinks and hors d'oeuvres among the crowd. Morty grabbed a drink from the tray of a passing waiter and continued to eye the room for Shelby.

Not seeing her, he made his way reluctantly toward Josiah Phelps and the rest of the museum committee. Forcing a smile, he surprised himself by remembering to greet each one of them by name.

I'm getting good at this shit, he thought. His father, Sy, would never believe it. Me, Morty Cushman, grandson of Russian Jew pogrom survivors, standing in one of the most expensive cocktail circles in America. Morty figured there was over $3 billion net worth in that small group. At least that much. He wondered if they felt the money grabbers as bad as he did.

Nah, he thought, they don't feel nothin'. After three generations with money, "go fuck yourself" comes very easy. These bastids don't bend. Well, neither will I, he thought.

Just then, from the door to her office in the middle of the near wall, he saw Shelby beckon to him. He began to excuse himself from the group when two men in nondescript suits pushed past her coming out of her office and began to walk purposefully toward Morty. Shelby nervously followed them, until all three of them came to a stop in front of Morty.

Shelby hurriedly said, "Morton, these gentlemen would like a word with you. Why not come back into my office?" She looked imploringly at the two strangers. "So you can discuss this in private."

Her voice had risen, and the entire room, guests and waiters, turned to face her.

Morty was confused and pissed. These guys better not rain on my parade, he thought. Clenching his teeth, he said, "What can I do for you gentlemen?"

The first suit said, "Are you Morton Cushman?"

Morty barely got out, "I am," when the second guy took a laminated card from his jacket pocket and began to read. "You are under arrest. You have the right to remain silent."

"What the fuck is going on?" Morty gasped. "What do you mean 'under arrest'?"

"You have the right to have an attorney present when questioned." The second G-man had pulled Morty's arms back and was putting cuffs on his wrists. Oh, Jesus, not this, he thought. This couldn't be happening. Sweat started to roll down his sides from his armpits.

And handcuffed behind my back? Morty thought. What the fuck's happening here. Like I'm some *schvartzer* pocket-book thief.

"Wait, there's some mistake."

"You have the right to court-appointed counsel if you can't afford your own."

"Morton, what should I do? Morty?" Shelby, now shrill, said, "Morty, what's this about?" forgetting the roomful of people all watching this event as if it were performance art.

"Anything you say can and will be held against you."

Shelby's high-pitched voice caused Morty to begin to regain his composure. "It's okay, Shelby, just call Leo Gilman. He'll take care of everything. Just a misunderstanding, honey."

Turning to the arresting officers, he said, "It's just a misunderstanding, right, guys?"

"No, Mr. Cushman, you're under arrest for tax evasion." Leaning toward Morty's ear, the fed whispered. "This is big time, Morty," and stood back and grinned complacently. Then he gave him a little poke and took him by the elbow, steering him from the room.

Shelby ran up to Morty, tears streaming down her face. "Morty, how could you do this to me? After how hard I've worked. We're ruined, Morty." She took a deep breath. "Tell me everything's going to be okay."

"Honey"—Morty was straining now, forcing out the last wisp of bravado left in him—"just remember this: once indicted, always invited. We're going to be able to dine out on this story for years."

Shelby began to collect herself and tried to smile.

The two officers tugged on Morty's cuffed arms and kept him walking to the door, while the crowd of guests parted for them as if they were afraid arrest were contagious.

Morty caught a glimpse of Josiah Phelps and made a huge effort to smile nonchalantly. Josiah dropped his eyes and turned away.

Morty was hustled into the elevator, then past the astonished security guard, and Morty could see his chauffeur run to open the door to his limousine, while trying to make sense of the scene of two men and Morty walking toward a plain brown Chevy sedan.

The two men pushed Morty into the backseat, then they got in the front. The Chevy pulled out around the limousine and headed toward Fifth Avenue.

Morty turned painfully on the seat and saw Shelby, composed and in control once again, emerge from the building and walk briskly toward his limousine and get in. Then the car turned downtown and he lost her. Well, Morty thought, I guess the party is over.

20

Chopped Mitsui

Gil stepped on the gas of the Jaguar XKE and thrilled to its great thrust of speed as it accelerated past the snow-dusted delivery van. He felt the familiar quickening in his groin in response to the car's acceleration. The 1962 XKE had been his first "rich-man's toy." He had seen one for the first time parked in front of Doney's on the Via Veneto in Rome that year. His parents had given him the family's traditional college graduation present when he got his bachelor's degree from the University of Virginia—the grand tour of Europe for three months. Not too grand, actually, with a Eurailpass for travel and an International Youth Hostel membership for shelter, but it had been the best the family could do. Since the crash of '29, his father's reaction to adversity had been a glass of bourbon. Gil had been grateful for any trip at all.

And he'd had his eyes opened in Europe. By the women, the luxury, the cars. There the XKE had sat, shiny fire-engine red, seemingly in motion even as it sat parked at the curb.

He had taken a table at Doney's, ordered a Negroni, and sat staring at her. The car had become "her" the moment he had seen it. I want that baby, he had thought, knowing with all the certainty that was the most outstanding characteristic of his youthful but defined personality that he'd have one someday. Smiling to himself, he promised that as soon as he got his first million, a car like it would be his reward.

And he had gotten the car with his first million, only it wasn't technically his. It had been his wife's money. But what the hell, he thought now with a grim smile to himself. I didn't say I was going to *make* it, just *get* it, and he chuckled again as he usually did at this thought. He lost his wife, but kept his car. He'd rather lose five wives than his XKE. He drove in every morning alone. Mary took the limo.

He slowed slightly, held back by a knot of lesser cars. All the jerks slowed down on the Merritt at the first sign of ice. Well, they didn't hold him back for long. Seeing a brief opportunity, he swung out into the left lane, shifting for speed, and insinuated himself into the almost-too-small space two car lengths up. Horns of protest blared behind him. Fuck 'em.

I did it, he thought. Two car lengths. Those pussies wouldn't even try, but I did.

He reached across the seat to the inside pocket of his suit jacket, fumbled out a pack of Dunhills, and tapped one of the cigarettes between his thin lips. As he lit it from the dashboard lighter, the words came into his mind again.

Held back, he thought, as he exhaled a steady stream of white smoke. Nothing, no one, can hold me back, he told himself, his eyes on the curving road ahead.

The Swanns had tried but failed. He had known they didn't want Cynthia to marry him just as he had known that she would, no matter what they thought. From the first moment he heard her last name, his future brightened. He had wanted her and he had gotten her. She was necessary to him. She had helped him with that first giant step.

But she had ultimately failed him. The more compliant she had become, the more contempt he had for her. She was weak, he thought, and he hated her for it. He liked to believe it was his strength that made him succeed, but he sometimes knew that that was not the way it had been at all. It wasn't his strength, it was the weakness of others that had helped him. That and his own ruthlessness in the face of trust and honesty. It had all been necessary, he told himself. Whatever he had done had been necessary.

Mary isn't weak, he thought. She's a killer, worthy of my talent. A fit partner. We're going to climb higher together. We'll be world class.

Gil sped down the FDR Drive and screeched to a halt in his assigned space in the underground garage of his office building. Next week he and Mary would permanently move to the new apartment on Fifth, although it still seemed a shambles. He wouldn't get to drive as often, and he'd miss that. He patted the dashboard. Then he got out and in three strides reached the elevator to the lobby. As he stepped off the elevator, Gus, the guard on duty, tipped his hand to the visor of his cap in a respectful salute and immediately buzzed the receptionist on the forty-fifth floor to alert her to the arrival of the company's president.

A second guard stepped quickly in front of Gil and, taking a ring of keys from his hip, unlocked the door to his private elevator. Gil stepped in and the guard pressed forty-five and said, "Good morning, Mr. Griffin."

Gil ignored both the guards and snapped open *Barron's*. If he said hello to every one of the little people who greeted him, he'd have no time for work.

In the reception area at the executive floor, he found Mrs. Rodgers, his secretary, waiting for him, as he knew she would be.

"Good morning, Mr. Griffin."

Walking past her without breaking his stride, he said, "What's my calendar for the day?"

Mrs. Rodgers scanned her notebook while she tried to keep up with his brisk walk. Overweight and near retirement, she found the pace of Gil Griffin's business life more and more difficult to keep up with, but after sixteen years with him, she was determined to maintain his speed until she reached sixty-five. She was up at five-thirty every morning so as to be in the office by seven-thirty. It seemed as if the commute from Queens got longer all the time, and sometimes, especially on cold winter mornings such as this one, as she mounted the long flight of steps to the F train in the predawn darkness, she felt ready to give up. "But I'm going to make it to the finish line," she would say to herself at these moments.

As they continued down the silent, carpeted hall toward Gil's corner suite, Mrs. Rodgers breathlessly ran through Gil's schedule for the day. Poor, luckless Stuart Swann picked this moment to come out of his office. Typical of his timing, Gil thought as he saw him out of the corner of his eye. Without turning his head, he said, "My office, fifteen minutes, Stuart."

Just as he reached the entrance to his office suite, Mrs. Rodgers jumped ahead of him with a great effort and opened the door for Gil without causing him to stop. He rewarded her with a nod, but didn't break his pace.

Gil proceeded to his desk and stood behind it, while Mrs. Rodgers, now out of breath, seated herself on one of the burgundy leather chairs across from him.

"The executive committee wanted to know if the two P.M. meeting is a luncheon meeting in the private dining room, or is it a meeting in the boardroom?"

Gil's mouth turned up at the corners very slightly at the thought of having to eat an extra meal with those sycophants, and he said, "One P.M., boardroom." He was going to pitch the Japanese deal. The real one, not the plant he had thrown them.

"Anything else, Mr. Griffin?"

"Yes. Have someone wash the salt off my car. And when Stuart Swann shows up, don't buzz me. Just tell him I said wait."

He noticed her drop her eyes at his comment. In sixteen years of dedicated service, she had never once commented negatively about him or anything that he did. If he thought about it, he would have guessed she didn't particularly like him, which was all right with Gil, just so long as she did her job, and did it well. She had two assistants to help her do it, too. Highest-paying secretarial job in New York City, he thought. And there's the profit sharing. *And* her portfolio. She couldn't afford to leave. He knew it and she knew it.

Gil walked to the window and stared out. He had never gotten over his fear of heights, but always took great pains to keep the fear hidden from others. He kept his back to the view and only looked out the bubbled, old panes. "Never let them see you sweat" was his motto, and he lived by it. So, when planning his space in the new building he had had the company buy, he insisted on not only the highest floor, but also the largest picture windows. However, the antique windows with their tiny, wavy panes had been installed on one side. Those were for him.

Had he looked down, he would have seen the one street in America that was important enough to dominate all the others—Wall Street. And Gil was the current "king of the mountain." From his perch, looking straight ahead, the view of Manhattan's financial district with New York Harbor as its backdrop gave him the tight feeling in his groin that he lived for.

This is it, he thought, this is the ultimate thrill. Not car racing, not speedboating. Not even sex. This, the feeling of having control over billions of dollars of other people's money. This is what I need.

The connecting door between his office and his wife's swung open, and Mary came in with a rush.

"Gil, I'm so glad you're in. Look at these," she said as she dropped paint chips and upholstery samples before him on his desk. "What do you think?"

He took a moment to compose himself, staring at the fabric and color chips without seeing them. Then very quietly with all the restraint he could muster, he asked, "What's this, Mary?"

"Gil," she reminded him, as if he were stupid, "these are the samples for the apartment." He could see she mistook his annoyance for lack of understanding. "I have to get them to Duarto this afternoon if we're ever going to get the new apartment finished."

Gil, still cool, said, "If you have a decorator, why are you bothering with this stuff? Why am I? We're paying him to decorate. Let him decorate."

He brushed aside the samples and his own misgivings and asked, "Have you prepared the final figures for my meeting with the executive committee today?"

His irritation was clear to her now. Quickly gathering up the samples from his desk, she recovered and matched his tone, saying, "I just have to run through the analysis one more time. I'll have it on your desk by one P.M." She turned toward the door to her office.

"By twelve, Mary. I had asked you to have them for me by twelve noon so I would have time to review them before I take them to my meeting with the executive committee. By noon, Mary."

Mary, becoming vice president of Federated once again, had the good sense to say, "Twelve noon, Gil," before closing the door behind her.

Gil sat back and tapped his index finger against his lip

as he tried to come to terms with his disquietude. I thought she was different, he mused. Hard-nosed, ambitious, greedy. Like a man. I thought she was the one worthy to be my other half in business, my partner. Now give her four walls and she becomes like every other Greenwich housewife—decorators, color schemes, wallpaper.

Cynthia came to mind. He had been forced to almost accept this nesting trait in Cynthia. It was so mindless and she had been able to do nothing else. But not Mary.

Still, the worst women were those combinations of fuzzy thinking and aggressiveness, such as that useless bitch Anne Paradise. He fumed each time he thought of her. Who did she think she was, coming into my office and telling me what to do? He hated women who talked back, who disobeyed. At least Cynthia never did that. He thought of Mary. They really had something together. Was she going to ruin it? he wondered. Softly, out loud, he said to the empty room, "Don't fuck this up, Mary."

He reached over to the intercom and slapped Mrs. Rodgers's line open. "Send him in," he growled.

He had looked at his watch and realized that if Stuart Swann had been on time, and he wouldn't dare not be, he'd been cooling his heels in Mrs. Rodgers's office for twenty-eight minutes.

He heard Stuart's one light tap at the door. Knock like a man, he thought; and he decided to make Stuart do exactly that. He did not respond.

After a too-long wait, two more taps, only a little harder this time, but Gil knew this was the best this wimp could do. Magnanimously, he called out for Stuart to come in. Stuart stepped into the room with a scared smile on his face. "You wanted to see me, Gil?" He didn't close the door until Gil answered with an abrupt motion of his hand.

He kept Stuart standing in front of his desk, not asking him to sit down. Without preamble he said, "Stuart, I've been reviewing the figures for the last quarter on the corporate pension funds, and what I see is that your funds are the three lowest in the firm. Why is that, Stuart?"

Stuart was never prepared to handle these sessions, Gil knew, and he listened to Stuart stutter and stumble through an explanation. He cut him off midsentence. "Stuart," he said as if talking to a retarded child, which is exactly how he thought of Stuart Swann. "if these figures aren't turned around by the end of next quarter, you're going to have to answer to an executive committee review. I won't be able to protect you if that happens.

"And Stuart. There's been word on the street about my interest in Mitsui Shipping. That leak wouldn't be from you, would it? Only the executive committee members were aware of it."

"No, not from me, Gil."

"Good. If I hear different, your seat on the committee is jeopardized. You know that?"

Stuart looked at him for a moment, opened his mouth, then closed it. He nodded. Gil gave him a curt, dismissive nod and turned back to his desk.

Stuart's silent departure left Gil both pleased and angered. What a wimp, Gil thought. There wasn't a Swann who could stand up to him. Not the old man, not Stuart, and certainly not Cynthia.

They go soft after generations of wealth, he thought. Those families need an injection of new blood every other generation. The gene pool needs stirring up. Even though he saved their precious family business by merging it with Federated, they still had not accepted him as one of their own. And all the rejections he had felt at the hands of the rich families, all the contempt they had shown him for being aggressive and single-minded, was now focused on the one remaining Swann in his life.

Stuart Swann, he knew, had to pay for the offenses of the past. Gil hated to admit it, but in some ways, he needed Stuart. Like all great kings he needed a whipping boy, a focus for the hatred he felt for the weak, a place to contain the overwhelming hatred he felt for all those who were not on his level.

Stuart Swann, my whipping boy, he thought with a chuckle. Well, not quite a whipping boy, but almost. Not quite a king, either, but almost, he thought, now laughing to himself.

His reverie was broken by Mrs. Rodgers's buzz on his intercom announcing Dwight McMurdo to see him. He greeted the partner casually, but his stomach still fluttered at having a member of one of the oldest New England families beholden to him. He had made McMurdo, as well as the other partners, millions of dollars.

Dwight was smiling nervously. He asked, after the basic pleasantries, "What's with Mitsui Shipping, Gil? What's our position on the stock? I just heard from the specialist handling Mitsui; the guy's sweating bullets. He tells me there's a run on the stock. I swear, it's up five points over yesterday."

"Dwight, don't worry. We're positioned perfectly." Gil could see that Dwight had let the tension of the game get to him.

Dwight continued as if not hearing Gil. "I mean, Gil, with the price of the shares going up, we're going to be pushed off the playing board. This will blow the whole deal, Gil. What's going on?" His voice had gone shrill as he came to the end of his harangue.

Gil leaned back in his chair, his fingertips touching in an arch, savoring the moment. This asshole, he thought. All his years on Wall Street and he still didn't understand the game.

Slowly, relishing the power he had, he said, "We don't have any position on Mitsui, Dwight." He watched Dwight try to absorb that, then continued, "We're as safe as a babe in its mother's arms, Dwight. I was never interested in Mitsui— that's not my target." He watched Dwight's shoulders relax at the same time a quizzical look came over his face.

"But I don't understand. You told the executive committee . . ."

"Two things are important, Dwight," Gil continued, as if he were instructing a young trainee in the business instead of talking to a seasoned veteran. "How you play the game, as well as whether you win or lose. And you can't win if you don't know how to play."

Gil's contempt for these tail-riders put a sour taste in the back of his throat. He continued, "Because I *told* the executive committee that we were going after Mitsui for a takeover, there was a leak and every asshole on the street jumped on the bandwagon. So, no one noticed when I started to quietly go after my real target."

"Wait a minute," Dwight said. "You lied to the executive committee when you said Mitsui?" He was near panic in his disbelief.

Gil smiled his best little-boy smile. "Yeah, well, I lied. Just goes to show you, Dwight—can't trust anyone. I knew there was a leak, so I made it work for me instead of *against* me," he said proudly. If he had been alone, he would have exhaled onto his fingernails and buffed them briskly on his lapels. "Now, this afternoon's special meeting will announce that. Oh, and you *are* invited to attend."

Dwight got it, the corners of his mouth flickering up. Gil continued to smile and finished, "Stick with me, kid. We're about to pull off the biggest takeover in the history of Wall Street."

Gil mentally slapped himself on his back for having had the foresight of getting the go-ahead from the very special executive committee—the four largest shareholders in the partnership corporation plus himself. The Gang of Four as he thought of them, the Central Committee. You want something done, you go to the doers. He got *their* permission to go after Maibeibi after telling them about the "disinformation" on Mitsui. And these guys don't talk, he knew. They understood their bottom line.

That's one of the reasons he had been so hard on Mary today. He knew he had the executive committee in his pocket. But he could only keep them there by having accurate numbers and a plus sign on the bottom line.

Leaning forward and speaking in a conspiratorial voice, he said, "More money than even you could imagine in your wildest dreams of avarice," and winked.

Dwight clapped his hands, then grabbed for Gil's hand and shook it vigorously. "Gil, you're brilliant. A genius. I knew the minute I first set eyes on you."

Gil watched him dance out the door, where he pirouetted and said, "Great work, Gil."

As the door closed behind Dwight, the intercom buzzed again.

"Mr. Griffin, you have the SEC compliance meeting at three P.M. after the executive committee. Where do you want it set up?"

He had forgotten about the regulatory review. It was routine to the securities industry but not to be taken too lightly. And if there's a problem, Stuart is the company's compliance officer.

"Right in here, Mrs. Rodgers. Make sure they have something and keep them occupied—coffee, drinks, whatever. I might be late. Keep them happy. And let Mr. Swann handle it."

"But Mr. De Los Santos asked specifically to meet with you."

"Don't worry about it."

As he rang off, he swiveled his chair to face the great expanse of the Manhattan harbor visible through his picture window.

Today, more than usual, he tingled with the sensation of anticipated victory. McCracken and Steinberg had jumped on the Mitsui bandwagon, he had learned, and now they were going to take a fall while making him the richest, most powerful takeover king in the world. Cover of *Time*. Man of the Year, for chrissakes.

It was only fitting. Look what I've accomplished in a few years. I brought the oldest family private bank in the country public and merged it with an international financial conglomerate. Me! I did it. If the Swanns had manipulated their holdings the way I did, they, too, could have made millions.

But they fucked up, he thought. They didn't know how to play, so they should have gotten off the court. But Mary knows how to play. She'd better not lose *her* focus. He remembered Annie's attack on him the other day. Who was she to come in here and accuse me of underhanded tactics? If Aaron Paradise had made a bundle instead of losing a bundle, she'd be kissing my ass. She doesn't understand the game. Another housewife-bitch with too much time on her hands. Well, he had too many other things to think about. Two big reviews today: the executive committee and the SEC. Piece of cake, he thought.

The executive committee meeting would be short. They always were. First, start out by giving them the bottom line— how much profit we could make if we go for Maibeibi. After that, there was little else to say. They'd buy it.

And the SEC? Today's meeting was just the opener. They'll

be here about a week, usual crap. I can stroke them for about an hour, get them off on the right foot. Fifty-thousand-dollar-a-year bureaucrats, he thought. Fifty thousand and a pension. My guys at a million plus a year can run circles around them. Even Swann. Get a couple of broads to wine and dine them at night. No problem.

And of course—he smiled to himself—I had the foresight to have Stuart Swann sign off on all the compliance crap to the SEC, so if worse comes to worse, I'll toss them Stuart to keep them off my back.

I got it all covered, he thought. Got a wife who knows how to do business, got my partners in my hip pocket, and a virgin to sacrifice if the SEC digs too deep. And the biggest takeover coup just around the corner.

He got up and stretched, then continued to stand with his arms outstretched, as if embracing the scene beyond the window. There were times, bad times, when he believed he won not because of his own greatness but because of the weakness of others.

But this was not one of those times. He ran through the succession of names in his mind once again: Swanns, Milken, Mary Birmingham, yeah, even the SEC. He thought of his afternoon squash game: one of the Young Turks had challenged him in a meeting yesterday and would be crushed on the court this afternoon. Then he and Mary were going to a party. It was a good day.

He spoke out loud through clenched teeth. "Nothing can stop me now."

BOOK THREE

—⁂—

The Wives
Getting Even

I

Gil Goes to Japan

The apartment was a shambles. Gil strode through the marble-floored gallery, flinging open the immense mahogany doors. Library, study, some other goddamned room, all in various states of chaos: furniture covered in wrapping, sealed cartons, rolled-up rugs, fabric tacked to walls, paint cans littering the floor. The only room finished was their bedroom, which functioned also as a home office. And nowhere a suitcase. They were leaving for Japan tomorrow and not a suitcase to be found, much less the packing done.

Gil had been more satisfied living in Greenwich. Despite her flaws, Cynthia had given him a perfectly run house. And Gil was entitled to that. Then he had the commute, his quiet time every day, to drive his beloved E and think. And there he had a proper garage, not a cramped space in a basement. Here there was nowhere to tinker comfortably with his car, nowhere to commune with it. Missing that, and deploring this half-finished apartment, he felt worse than irritated.

He felt murderous. What in Christ's name was Mary thinking of? He'd let her move him out of Greenwich and then out of their perfectly comfortable pied-à-terre on Park so that they could wallow in this sty? Where did she come off assuring him that it would be comfortable in no time? It had been weeks, and things still were in tumult. Couldn't he trust her? Couldn't she manage one damn thing?

He continued down the gallery to their bedroom wing. Here, at least, there was some order, but not nearly enough. He had suggested that they stay at the Waldorf for a few more weeks, but no, Mary had all but guaranteed him the spic queer she had hired was nearly finished with this faggot decorating shit. Well, by the time they returned from Japan, he had better be.

Gil crossed the huge bedroom and approached the walnut butler's tray that held several crystal decanters and a half dozen cut-glass tumblers. He poured himself two fingers of Scotch and opened the ice bucket. He couldn't believe his eyes. No ice, only some lukewarm water. A household staff of four, not counting their butler, and they couldn't even manage to keep ice in the ice bucket! He rang for Prince.

As he turned from the bellpull, he couldn't help but survey the view. Dizzy for a moment, he automatically stepped back from the bay window, then hated himself for the weakness. Christ, you'd think he could conquer that foolishness by now. And the upcoming eighteen hours enclosed in an aluminum tube hurtling through space at six hundred miles an hour, thirty thousand feet up in the air—that was another weakness he worked very hard at concealing. He couldn't let himself think about that one now. Anyway, on the plane Mary would distract him. Sex on the plane—silent, always in danger of discovery—both excited him and calmed his fear of flying. He took a long breath and looked out the window.

He had to admit that the view was spectacular just now. As the sun set behind the Central Park West skyline, he could see the entire park spread out before him. It was a marvelous skyline with the distinctive silhouettes of the San Remo, the Beresford, the Majestic, all backlit by the setting sun.

Well, attractive yes, but there was no one over on that side of the city but Democrats, parvenus, and Jews. He would never live there. Gil paused for a moment. It had been strange that this building's board had seemed reluctant to approve him. Their reluctance had made him all the more determined. Ironic, since he had actually preferred the Park Avenue pied-à-terre, and its lack of views. Yes, that place had suited him just fine.

He heard a noise at his back and turned to see Mary enter the room, with Prince close behind her carrying a Bergdorf bag. More new fripperies. His anger came back, and he looked coldly at both of them.

"Ice."

"Sorry, sir," Prince apologized.

"Hello." Mary smiled.

It was clear that she was cheerful, and this only irritated him further. "Where is the luggage?" he asked. His voice was calm, as always, though she should be able to hear the edge in it.

"Who knows?" she said, shrugging. "I'm not Cynthia, Gil. Ask Prince."

He let that pass. Now was not the time, although he could feel the hairs rise on the back of his neck. Mary paused. He could see she was bursting with something.

"I've got some good news," she said. Gil sighed.

Prince returned with the ice and a tray of the Norwegian flatbread that Gil favored, as well as a small wheel of Explorateur cheese. He placed them on the low table in front of the sofa, a sort of peace offering. Gil sat down, his drink still uniced, his anger undiminished.

"Gil, I'm going to co-chair the Fantasie FunFaire."

Gil shook his head but restrained a groan. More of this completely useless social nonsense. He felt himself losing his patience. Somehow, she'd gotten onto this kick of committee work, charities, and volunteering. Didn't Mary realize that she'd never be the real article, that she'd be suffered by those women only because of the contributions she'd bring in? Gil had a horror of looking foolish, of letting her look foolish. He got up to put ice into his glass.

"Well, that's what you wanted, I suppose."

"It's going to be *the* new event of the season. And Bette Bloogee, Lally Snow, Gunilla Goldberg, and Elise Atchison are all on the committee with me. It will be such fun and great for business, too."

That was a lot of bullshit as far as Gil was concerned. He had yet to do a deal as the result of one of those affairs. *Business* was what was great for business, and he wished Mary would get her head back into it.

"Well, good," he managed.

"Is that all you can say? Gil, this is *the* board to be on. All of the women who count are on this committee. I'll get to work with them all."

His back turned, he winced. For God's sake, she didn't even begin to see the distinctions between the others and that Bloogee woman, prostitute or call girl or whatever she'd been. Mary just didn't know the ropes, and it was embarrassing. Well, they could talk about it on the flight to Tokyo.

"Have you started packing?" He added another finger of Scotch and, at her silence, turned to look at her. She was standing beside their bed, her dress off, her pink silk slip shimmering against her creamy skin. Despite his irritation with her, he felt a stirring.

"Well?" he asked.

"Gil, I'll have your bags packed in an hour. But I'm not going to pack mine."

He stood silent, absolutely still, staring at her. What the hell was she talking about?

She dropped her eyes. "The committee meets next week and I need to be here. It took so long, Gil, to break into this. I can't not appear." She looked directly at him for the first time. "I'm not going to go to Japan, Gil."

He felt the anger rising in him, but he made himself continue to stand utterly still.

"You have everything under control on Maibeibi. All the research is complete. And over there women in business are more of a liability than an asset. I've asked Kingston to go instead. You don't need me, and we do need this."

She was talking faster and faster, he noticed. Almost bubbling. But for him everything seemed to go in slow motion. The anger, the absolute rage at her insolence flooded. Was she mad or completely stupid? How had she dared to decide all on her own to replace herself with Kingston? That jabbering smart-ass, what good was he to Gil? He couldn't fuck Kingston. Mary stood there, looking at him, blinking, like a deer caught in the headlights of an oncoming truck.

"I'm not going," she said.

And then he was on her, his left hand gripping her slender throat, his right pulling on her hair, propelling her across the bed, forcing her down, his hand tightening on her neck. Straddling her, his legs pinning her across her chest, he watched as her expression changed from one of surprise to disbelief to horror. It was almost comic, and he couldn't help but smile. Then, raising his left hand and clenching it into a fist, he hit her.

2

Is You Is Maibeibi?

Brenda was still breathless as she hurriedly paid the cabbie and rushed across the broad sidewalk and into the Rockefeller Center building that housed Elise's office. Elise's call this morning had brought the worst possible news. As she hustled past the security desk, the elevator doors were just closing. She clutched her bag tightly under her arm and ran for it.

All those fucking aerobics classes were paying off because she made it easily through the doors, which, though narrowing, were still wide enough to let her pass. Of course, she was narrowing, too—she hadn't cheated once on her bet with Elise, and she could tell she was a lot slimmer. Elise hadn't been drunk, as far as she knew, so it seemed she wasn't cheating either.

But as Brenda stepped farther into the elevator, she saw someone who was. She knew her instantly, though they had never met face-to-face. Shelby Cushman, Morty's society wife, was embracing a good-looking man, her hands cupping the crotch of what looked like an expensive pair of slacks. Brenda had seen Shelby's picture too many times to forget it, though now the Southern mouth was open and this hunk had his tongue deep into it.

"Oops," Brenda muttered to herself, and turned to the front of the car. No question of what she'd seen, but the suddenness of it and the intensity of the atmosphere in the elevator car shook her. For a moment, upset as she was about Elise's phone call, she smiled. Why should she be surprised that Morty's little *shiksa* was cheating on him while he was in jail? It looked like lunch at the Rainbow Room, with an appetizer on the elevator. Brenda knew what dessert would be. But I got problems of my own, she thought, and this ain't one of them. In fact, it was a reason to rejoice. There was a God.

In case she had any doubt about what she'd seen, when the elevator stopped at Elise's floor, Brenda turned and looked at the little tart and her hunk as she got out. Neither Shelby nor the guy looked at her. Brenda wondered who he was, and how she could find out.

But then she was on Elise's floor, and remembering why Elise had called her here. "Elise! Elise!" she called. "What happened? How much have we lost?"

Annie stuck her head out of the cubicle that she had started to use as a writing room. "Oh, Brenda. Elise told me about the Mitsui stock. I'm so sorry. Are you okay?"

"Okay? Hell, no," Brenda spat. "That schmuck Stuart Swann gave us the wrong dope. Gil wasn't interested in Mitsui. That must have been a blind. We lost money big time." She thought of her million dollars, her freedom money, now drained away. Christ, how could this have happened?

"Elise is very upset," Annie told her. "She's been working over the computer all morning."

Hearing her name, Elise stepped out of her office. "Don't panic, Brenda," she snapped. She looked pale, though she wasn't perspiring. She didn't like losing money, either.

"I'm not panicking," Brenda snapped back. "I'm beyond panic. I'm somewhere around frenzy right now." Brenda felt like crying. "Everything I had I put into Mitsui, and now you're telling me it's gone south?" Sure. Easy for Elise to say don't panic. What was a million dollars to the snow queen? "I mean it, Elise. This means I lost *everything*."

"I know," Elise said, and Brenda could see her concern now. "It was a stupid move on my part."

Great, an apology. As if that would pay the maintenance or the phone bill. "Listen, Elise. Please. What can we do?" Brenda pleaded, trying to sound reasonable.

"Yes, what does this mean, Elise? I feel responsible. After all, I supplied the tip from Stuart," Annie added. Brenda knew Annie had no money to invest, in fact she'd been agonizing over her own financial plight. Still, Brenda was happy to see Annie upset for her.

"We invested in Mitsui believing that this was Gil's take-over target," Elise explained. "Uncle Bob checked it out with someone at the Exchange and felt it was worth the gamble. Now we find out that Gil obviously has no interest in Mitsui, because the stock went to the basement this morning. There's no demand for it out there." Elise paused. "So Brenda and I and Uncle Bob have lost much of what we put into it. I was incautious, and I'm very sorry. It's my fault."

Brenda sighed. "Oh, well, it's not your fault. It's mine. I shouldn't have gambled with the grocery money."

"Well, I'd like to make it up to you." Elise, taking a deep breath, continued, "I'd like to pay you back." She looked at Brenda.

"What?"

"I'd like to make up your losses."

Unbelievable. The ice queen was offering her money. Boy, for Elise that was a big deal. Brenda couldn't get over it, but she also couldn't accept. "Forget about it. I'm no welsher. I'm a big girl, Elise."

Elise nodded. "I've been giving this some thought this morning, Brenda, and I think there might be something you'll agree to. It would actually help me out and move me closer to club goals."

"Then that would make you a miracle worker," Brenda said.

"Yes," Elise said slowly. "I don't mean we haven't lost the money we put on Mitsui. We have. But there is a way *you* can recoup your losses, Brenda, and *I* can help."

"Elise, just tell me how," Brenda begged. She had calmed down considerably since seeing Elise's genuine concern for her predicament.

"I feel somewhat responsible for your investment, Brenda. I mean, despite my anger at Gil I should have discouraged you from putting up your whole nest egg. What I and Uncle Bob lost we could afford to lose. We probably needed the tax break anyhow."

Brenda interrupted. "Wait a minute, Elise. Thanks for your concern, but I told you I'm a big girl. You *did* try to dissuade me from investing, remember? But *I'm* the one who insisted. So, you're not responsible." Brenda wanted to be fair to Elise. After all, she was becoming a good friend.

"Well, at any rate, Brenda, I've got a proposition. How would you like to buy Bill's collections from me?"

Brenda thought Elise was losing it. She hadn't been drinking, had she? No, her eyes were clear.

"You mean his china and antiques and stuff? Bill's collections must be worth a couple of million at least, Elise. How could I buy them? I'm broke."

Elise smiled. "When Bill left, he signed an agreement that instructed me to sell off his collections—you know, his Imari, his antiques, the muskets, stamps, coins—everything. He was being a gentleman about it all. The stuff is spread all over my houses. Well, I told him I didn't know the exact value of the stuff, so he told me he respected my judgment and would accept whatever I chose to pay or got for it. I could buy what I wanted and I was going to put the rest up for auction at Sotheby's. I'm just to deduct my expenses and send him the balance. He was being very magnanimous."

"So?" Brenda asked, still not getting the point.

"So, Brenda, why don't you and I agree on a price, then it's all yours. And if you were able to resell them at a huge profit through Duarto, well, that's just free-market enterprise, isn't it?"

"Elise, what do you have up your very expensive sleeve?" Brenda asked cautiously. She was beginning to enjoy this, even if she didn't quite understand what it was.

"If you were to offer me a fair price, say one dollar, Brenda, I would consider it. In fact I'd accept it."

"One dollar! Holy shit, you got it, Elise." Brenda laughed out loud. "But is that legal?"

"Absolutely. He even put it in writing, and I checked with my lawyers. 'I'll accept whatever you can get for it, less expenses.' So, the way I figure it, he'll wind up owing *me* a couple of thousand dollars since I will have to calculate the expense of packing and shipping to the new owner." Elise smiled for the first time that morning. "I'll just send him a bill."

"Elise!" Annie gasped. "You wouldn't!"

"Just watch me!" Elise said. "That's it, then. Done deal. And you're a witness, Annie. Brenda can't back out now." Turning to Brenda, Elise said, "There's just one stipulation. You must invest the proceeds in a business of your own."

"What? Another fat lady boutique?" Brenda sneered.

"Find a small company that needs capital, buy in, and help run it," Elise said.

Brenda's eyes lit up. "Like Paradise/Loest?"

Elise leaned back and laughed. "Brenda, you are a very astute businesswoman. Yes, Paradise/Loest would be the perfect company for you."

Brenda laughed and said, "It's a deal." She hugged Elise, then the two women shook hands. "I'll have Duarto call you and arrange to pick up the stuff. He'll know just what to do with all that crap. Some very newly rich people are going to pay a bundle for those things."

Brenda felt the tension suddenly lift. "Whew!" she breathed, and collapsed into a chair. "I nearly had a stroke over this. But that still leaves us with a problem. We got Bill nicely on this, and you saved my ass, but Gil remains unscathed. If Mitsui isn't his target, what is?"

The three women looked at each other. Annie remembered her meeting with Gil, and the way he had dismissed her. "He can't go unpunished."

"Brenda," Elise asked, "aren't you working with Duarto on the Griffins' apartment renovation? Maybe it would be a good idea if you got in there with Duarto and nosed around again. You might come up with something."

"Hey, I'm strictly back-office stuff. I'm organizing his records and accounts—it's the Augean stables—but Duarto goes there every day or so. Mary is constantly on the phone to him about one thing or another." She paused. "He's such a good pal, I can't risk getting him in trouble. But I'll ask." Turning to Annie, Brenda added, "Boy, fuck that Stu Swann. He can take his 'insider info' and blow it out his ass. Don't date him, Annie. The guy's a loser."

"No fear. Now tell me how to get rid of him."

"Oh, is he becoming a pest?" Elise asked.

"Well, he keeps calling."

"Annie has a boyfriend, Annie has a boyfriend," Brenda sang. She was almost giddy with relief. Everything suddenly looked bright again, thanks to Elise. And Annie. What good friends. Then she remembered and stopped. "Speaking of boy-friends, guess who else does?" she asked, and told them what she'd seen on the elevator.

"When the cat's away . . . ," Elise began.

"The mouse fucks like a bunny," Brenda finished for her. "Isn't nature beautiful?"

"Now, remember, Duarto. You're going to keep chickie for me while I take a look through their desks," Brenda told Duarto as they rode in the wood-paneled elevator to Mary and Gil's penthouse. Today Brenda was a woman with a mission.

"What ees 'cheeckie,' *cara?* I thought I was going to be chour lookout."

"Same thing, Duarto. But you had to have grown up in New York in the fifties to know that." Brenda sighed and con-tinued her lesson. She knew even if Duarto raised his eyes to the heavens, he always enjoyed stories of her childhood.

"When I was a kid," she said, "whenever the teacher left the room, one of the kids always stood 'chickie' at the door to warn us when the old bat was coming back so we wouldn't get caught making noise, tearing the place apart. So that's what you're doing today. You're standing chickie for me while I see what I can find in Gil's or Mary's desk. Got it?"

"Eet's like what Ethel Mertz do for Lucy Ricardo, no? I love that chow. I love Desi Arnaz."

Brenda turned her head to him in disbelief. "*Desi?* You loved *Desi?*"

"Chure. He was my idol."

"You're the only one I know, Duarto, who loved the 'Lucy' show for Desi Arnaz. Nothing personal, but that's weird. I mean, how many times can you listen to 'Babalu'?"

"Eet was not only hees singing, *cara.* I owe everytheeng to heem. Hees style. Hees humor. I learn to speak my Engleesh from watching Desi."

"That explains *everything*, Duarto."

The elevator came to a stop on the penthouse floor and opened onto the Griffins' private foyer. Duarto pressed the buzzer as the elevator door closed behind them; then he turned and said to Brenda, "There ees no one here today, except Preence, the butler."

"Preence? Oh, you mean Prince."

"Yes, tha's what I say, Preence, but really, he's just another queen." Just then the door opened and revealed a gaunt man in his forties.

"Preence," Duarto cooed, "we've come to take some measurements for wallpaper."

"It's about time," the man snapped. "Mr. Griffin wants the job finished. He's adamant about it."

Stepping into the apartment and looking around the gallery, Brenda said, "We're really speeding it up. We're working overtime. But you can go back to polishing the silver or whatever you were doing. We'll be quiet as mice and out of here in just a few minutes." She looked Prince up and down. "Nice apron," she said, and walked down the corridor toward the Griffins' shared office.

When Duarto caught up to her, she said in a whisper, "An English butler, for chrissakes. I never even *saw* an English butler before, except in movies."

"Thees one eesn't really Engleesh. He's Irish, but ees passing. He say, who would hire an *Irish* butler?"

When they walked into the office, Brenda paused and looked around. She hadn't seen it since the furniture had arrived and the storage boxes were unpacked.

"Oh, Duarto, it's lovely. It really is." Brenda turned to face him. "I'm so proud of you."

She took in the rice-papered walls, the needlepoint rug, the raw silk curtains. Walking around the room, she said, "They don't deserve such beauty." Brenda walked over to the exquisite antique partner's desk that stood elegantly between the French doors to the terrace. "And this desk is gorgeous, Duarto. What a find."

"Mrs. Greeffeen said to make thees a very personal work space. That they spend almost as much time een thees room as een the bedroom." Looking over at the desk, he continued, "So I figured they needed a king-sized desk." Duarto looked down at his watch. "What exactly are chou looking for, *cara*?"

Brenda had her index finger on her chin. "I'm not sure, Duarto. But something that will tell us what Gil is up to with a Japanese company. There was a reason he allowed that leak of Mitsui. I don't know what I'm looking for, but I'll know it when I find it. Now you go outside in the hall and pretend you're measuring for wallpaper. If Prince comes snooping around, let me know. Give me a signal."

"Chure, but what kind of signal?"

"I don't know, Duarto. Just start singing or something. Anything," and she pushed him out, leaving the door slightly ajar behind him. She walked over to the desk once again and began opening drawers. What *am* I looking for? she thought. She wasn't so optimistic now.

The first couple of drawers she tried were obviously on Gil's side of the desk. File folders, nothing interesting in them. Proposals in acetate covers, word-processed financial reports. She knelt, removed an armful, and started to thumb through them. Nothing here. Nothing at all. She began to replace them. Brenda froze, holding a bunch of documents in her hand. Duarto was singing.

"Someday my preence weel come." Jesus, she half-laughed

in her panic. Leave it to Duarto to go camp even as he warned her, she thought, and she ducked down into the leg well of the desk. She crouched as low as she could, realizing that for the first time since she was a little girl, she could touch her knees to her chin. As she heard the door swing open on its hinges, she pressed deeper into the well, but her hips wedged tightly against the sides.

"Duarto," she heard Prince call in his clipped accent. "Are you in here? Mrs. Griffin is on the phone for you."

From a distance outside the room, Brenda heard Duarto answer, "I'm out here, Preence, een the hall." Duarto's voice was in the room now. "Shall I take the call een here?"

"Yes," Prince said, adding, "the line on the desk phone that's lit up." With a sigh of relief Brenda heard Prince close the door behind him as he left.

"Brenda, where are chou?" Duarto called out in a hoarse whisper.

"I'm stuck under the desk, Duarto. Get me out." She saw his legs and feet approach, but he didn't bend down to help her.

"Chust one meenute, *cara*. Good morning, Mrs. Greeffeen. Yes, but chust for the hall for now." Brenda heard Duarto's best client-voice and realized she would just have to sit it out. Suddenly she thought, I never knew I had a scar on my knee! I wonder when I got that? Then she remembered the roller-skating accident when she was nine. And I haven't been able to get my knees this close to my eyes since. Thank you, Bernie and Roy.

"Of course, Mrs. Greeffeen. We weel rush. We weel be ready very soon. We are working day and night." He paused. "Yes, I'm here weeth my girl. She has a very good eye."

My girl, my ass, Brenda thought. He's going to pay for that.

Duarto finally hung up the phone and peered under the desk.

"Oh! *Cara.* There chou are." He extended his hand to her. Brenda pulled on him but couldn't move. Duarto started to laugh, although he tried his best not to.

Brenda began to laugh also. "Don't, Duarto. I'm afraid I'm going to wet my pants. Just get me the fuck out of here!"

Duarto reached down, braced himself, and pulled Brenda's legs straight out in front of her. Then he tugged. Three heaves and he moved her enough so that she could wriggle until she freed herself.

"I didn't realize that space was so small, *cara.*" He had stopped laughing, but the glint of a smile was still in his eyes.

Brenda got to her knees, then pulled herself to her feet. "Duarto, you're both a pig and one of the sweetest men I know. Now just let me put back these files, finish this side of the desk, and we're out of here."

Brenda turned her attention to Mary's side and began opening and closing drawers. Nothing of interest. Nothing, until she tried to pull out the bottom drawer. Locked, she realized. Goddamnit. She looked at Duarto and saw him smiling as he reached into his trouser pocket and came up with a small brass key on a ring.

"I must have forgotten to geeve the extra key to the Greeffeens when the desk was delivered. Tomorrow weel be soon enough." He shrugged.

Brenda kissed him hard on his mouth, then turned and unlocked the drawer. All of it was Japanese, she saw that right away. Sony, Nissan, Mitsui, Awai, Maibeibi. Pay dirt! But how could she know which to take? She couldn't take them all. What to do? She saw a file marked *Memos—Japanese Acquisition.* She took it out first. Maybe there'd be something to clarify it all in there. And there it was! She picked up the document and waved it in front of Duarto, her eyes glistening.

"'Confidential: Memo to Mary Birmingham from Gil Griffin. Re: Maibeibi Research Acquisition versus Mitsui Disinformation.'"

"Lucy, Lucy, you found it," Duarto mimicked.

"Come on, Ethel, let's get out of here," Brenda said, stuffing the memo and the Maibeibi file under her sweater.

Twenty-five stories above Elise's office at 30 Rockefeller Plaza, the three friends sat in the Rainbow Room, New York's oldest drinks-with-a-view bar. The view of the sunset from their table was spectacular, and the setting sun cast a red-orange glow over the file laid out in front of them on the white linen tablecloth.

After a moment of silence spent gazing out the window, Brenda finally said, "There you have it. I've gone over the figures with a fine-tooth comb, and the net of it is"—she indicated the Maibeibi file—"this isn't just a good company, it's a great company. The only reason I can see why it isn't making a fortune is the shipyards. If Mr. Tanaki closed them down and sold the land to real estate developers, he'd be in the black again with a large cash reserve for more profitable acquisitions."

"Easier said than done," Elise said. "Remember, he's a traditional Japanese businessman. Even though land in Japan is at a premium, the shipyards division was the base for the entire company. His father started with it. And despite the fact that the electronics end is their most profitable, he's not going to put tradition aside and put all those people out of work."

Brenda, crestfallen, said, "I thought it was too easy." After a moment, she continued, "Then why not sell it as a shipyard? Isn't there anyone who needs a shipyard in Japan?"

Now Annie chimed in. "Maybe there is, but they haven't asked because it's known Tanaki doesn't sell."

"Then what about a trade instead?" Brenda said brightly. "Who has something Tanaki would trade for?"

The three women looked at each other, then Annie and Brenda turned to Elise. "I don't!" Elise said, the surprise showing in her voice.

"Aren't you two going to see Bob Bloogee? I bet *he* has something in his toy chest he'd like to swap with another overgrown little boy."

Brenda, once again, had cut two business giants down to a more manageable size.

"You know that I'm doing this only for you," Annie reminded Elise as they got out of the limo in front of River House, probably the most exclusive co-op in the city. "I've been extricating myself from these charity committees since Sylvie was born. And spending time with Gunilla and Lally is not my idea of fun."

"Yes, it's an ordeal, and I'm forever grateful, et cetera, et cetera, et cetera," said Elise, rolling her eyes. "But what could I do? You were the only one I could count on not to let Bette get into too much trouble, and not broadcast her phenomenal stupidity. Not that the world hasn't already noticed." Elise sighed. "Lally has been an utter bitch to the poor girl. At least she and Gunilla won't be here today. And you also have something riding on Uncle Bob's reaction to Brenda's 'swapping' suggestion. And," Elise continued, "you know Uncle Bob is the key to Gil Griffin. If we're serious about evening the score with Gil, we need Bob's support, and to get it you'll sit on this subcommittee with Bette, and I'll present the Maibeibi scenario to Uncle Bob."

"A high price to pay," Annie grumbled, but she smiled.

The planning for these parties meant a great deal of work for a small reward. The affairs often cost hundreds of thousands and brought in only a small percentage of that for the charities. They were really an excuse for the women to flex their muscles and to dress up. That meant that the organizers fought small wars over the decor, the theme, the menus, and the seating arrangements. Especially the seating arrangements.

It was a sign of social prestige to be asked to serve on a committee, assuming you hadn't simply bought your way on as Mary Griffin had. But to Annie it was all tiresome. Now the committee had broken into small groups, and Bette, she, and Elise were in charge of tickets and seating. But though she complained, Annie had actually found herself enjoying Bette. She was, to put it mildly, refreshingly unpretentious.

"I'll need to spend some time with Uncle Bob on this Mai-beibi deal. I'm not sure that after the Mitsui fiasco I have much credibility, so I'll need time to convince him. Time alone, so keep her talking."

"It isn't keeping her talking, it's getting her to stop that I worry about."

They entered the building, passed the concierge desk, and took the elevator up to the penthouse floor. There are penthouses and there are penthouses, Annie thought, surveying the huge marble-tiled entrance gallery that was roughly the size of her entire apartment. A uniformed butler led them in. Before them, an enormous Sargent, a painting of three women in dressing gowns, dominated the twenty-foot-high wall. On either side, arches flanked by marble columns led into the salon, where Bette lay stretched on a récalmier, dressed in exactly the same satin robe as the central woman in the Sargent portrait.

"She's putting us on," Annie murmured to Elise.

" 'Fraid not," Elise told her, and swept into the ornate chamber, her hand out to her "aunt." "Bette, dear. How wonderful to see you!"

Bette Bloogee rose from the divan. "Hoy, Elise," she said in the unmistakable accent of Bayonne. "Hoy, Annie. Good ta see ya. I was dyin' ta tell ya the news. We sold out every seat in da house. There ain't a table left."

"That's great!" Annie said.

"No kiddin'!" Bette agreed. "Those poor peopul with the ca-ca talk disease will get a lot of help now. Right?"

"Tourette syndrome, Bette," Elise corrected gently.

"Yeah, yeah, I know but I keep forgettin'. Jeez, you want to hear bad language, you shoulda heard me. Before Bob cracked down on me, I used to talk like that, too. No offense meant, right?"

It was mesmerizing to watch her, Annie thought. She was one of the most breathtakingly beautiful young women that Annie had ever seen. Her hair was auburn, lustrous and thick. Now it was tied up loosely with a black velvet ribbon, but when undone, it must cascade to the girl's small waist. Her skin was pale and clear, unblemished by the tiniest freckle. Her turquoise blue eyes were enormous, fringed with thick black lashes. She was a ravishing creature, physically perfect, yet, when she spoke, perceptual dissonance set in: how could such unappealing sounds pass from those perfect pink lips? But they did. Over and over again. Annie felt an almost overwhelming need to giggle.

"So, like, ya wanna beer or somethin'? Anythin' ya like."

Elise said she'd like some coffee, and Annie managed a nod.

"Regular or black?"

But just then the butler returned and hearing her question, cleared his throat. He carried a sterling coffee service on an immense silver tray. He walked slowly and carefully with the heavy burden. "Don't rupture yourself," Bette warned him, and jumped to help.

The three women moved to the seats around a Louis Quinze fruitwood table. Annie couldn't help but admire it. Tiny cherubs danced around the table edge, all shaped in various shades of satinwood, the garlands that stretched between them perfect in each tiny detail. It was a masterpiece of the *ébéniste's* art.

"What a wonderful piece!" she exclaimed.

"You like it, it's yours," Bette offered.

The butler cleared his throat. Bette looked at him. He raised his eyebrows. "Oh, come on, Smitty. Let me do it. Bob says I can if I want." She turned to Elise and Annie. "Smith here gets pissed when I give shit away. But we have so much, what's the diff?" She turned back to the butler. "Hey, one less thing to dust, right?"

Annie smiled at the girl. She was irresistible, and Smith seemed to think so, too. "I don't want the table. I just wanted to compliment your taste. But thanks for the offer. It's thoughtful of you to want to share."

"Sure. Anytime." Bette looked at Annie. "You're very nice, you know that?" she asked. Annie smiled.

When Annie asked to use a lavatory, Bette jumped up. "Sure. Come use mine."

She led her through several suites of rooms to a bou doir that seemed transported from Versailles. Behind a tapestry door, a stunning onyx bathroom was hidden. "It's got everything you need. Even a pie washer," Bette said, indicating the bidet. Annie laughed out loud, and Bette joined her.

When Annie was done in the bathroom, Bette was still waiting for her. She was holding her hands together behind her back, and she looked down at her shoes like a shy six-year-old.

"Listen, do you think after this party some of those babes will like me?" she asked. "I know Lally Snow hates my guts, but you think maybe Mary Griffin or Gunilla Goldberg might come over sometime?"

Annie looked at the girl. "I don't know, Bette, but *I* certainly would like to."

Bette smiled, her pleasure making her face almost luminous. "Okay!" she grunted, making one of those victory jerks with her forearm. She led Annie back to Elise, waiting in the drawing room. "So, what are ya goin' as?"

Bette had insisted that the event be a costume ball, and though the idea was always unpopular with the men, the women seemed delighted at the chance to don even fancier dress than usual.

"I haven't had a chance to think about it," Annie admitted. She actually had no interest in going at all. But the First Wives Club had held a meeting on it. They'd each admitted that they were hesitant to be seen publicly with their new partners. And then they'd decided to take a stand. They'd worked out a costume scheme and had taken a whole table. It might actually be fun.

"How about you, Elise?" Bette asked. "Who're you goin' as to the party?"

"Maybe I'll go as an aging movie actress," Elise said dryly.

"Hey, then I'd go as a retired porn star," Bette said, laughing. "But it's a costume party, not come as you are."

Elise blinked, then began to laugh. Annie joined in. The three of them were at it when Bob Bloogee entered the room.

"Well, that's what I like to be greeted by when I come home. The sight of three beautiful women laughing."

Elise sat beside her uncle Bob on the south-facing terrace. From her chaise, she could see the East River, Roosevelt Island, and all of Manhattan spread out before her. He was also lying on

412

a chaise longue, all four foot eleven inches of him, carefully reading the Maibeibi file that Elise had given him.

He looked up. "Thank you for being so nice to Bette. She really likes Anne Paradise. And she told me how you protected her from Lally. Thank you."

"She's a nice girl, Uncle Bob."

"I know." He smiled, then returned to the file laid out before him.

"How have things worked out with Jerry Loest?" he asked.

"Wonderfully well. We've brought two other new accounts his way. Thanks for your help."

"No problem. We could use some new blood on our marketing. My man on Madison Avenue says Loest's a very talented guy. He's worth an investment."

"Really? That was my reading, too. Good. I'm glad you told me that." She paused. Taking care of Aaron Paradise was small change compared to their main target, Gil Griffin. "Uncle Bob, I feel terrible about the loss of the Mitsui stock. I feel so responsible."

Bob looked up quickly. "No need to, my dear. Remember, I put some very good people on it. They came up with the same thing. Gil Griffin was very smart in how he handled it. He lied to his partners, so they confirmed the lie to my man at the Exchange." Bob patted Elise's hand. "These things sometimes happen when you play the market, my dear. You're not used to losing, you're such a good player. It's too bad, because Griffin is such a bastard. This isn't the first time he's cost me money."

Elise pointed to the file. "So, is it all over?"

Tapping the file on his lap, he said, "It's not all over yet, thanks to Brenda. This is very doable. As it happens, I owe Tanaki at Maibeibi a favor, and telling him about Gil Griffin having his eye on Tanaki's company might pay off my debt. Of course, it would take some delicate handling. Tanaki's ship-building subsidiary has been losing money for years. If he sells it off to real estate developers, he'd make a bundle, but he's against development and would never lay off the employees at the works. But if we found something he wants of ours . . . well, we might not recoup our Mitsui losses immediately from it, but we could, just possibly, do Gil in on this one. I'd like to see that happen. I don't like him. Never did. And the goodwill we might reap with Tanaki is always worth something."

"Then let's do it," Elise said.

"Done! I think we ought to visit him in person. Yes. That would be best. I'll get my man in Kyoto on it tomorrow." He closed the file, and then he, too, looked out over the city. They lay there, quiet for a moment.

"So much wealth, so much poverty," Bob said, staring. "Elise, do you know the rent for an apartment in those build-ings there, across the street?"

Elise looked at the old low-rise he was pointing at. She knew his penthouse was worth a lot more than the fourteen million he had paid for it ten years ago. "No," she said.

"Two hundred and sixteen dollars and nineteen cents a month. It's rent-controlled, and an old woman, Mrs. Willie Schmidt, has lived there since 1939. Same view of the East River I've got. She's close to ninety now, and it's a fifth-floor walk-up. I offered her a hundred thousand dollars to give me the apartment, but she wouldn't. Said she was happy there. So I offered her a quarter of a million. She turned me down. 'No use tryin', young fella,' she said. 'There's nothing I need that money can buy.' I know just how she feels."

They sat for a little while longer. "Know why I wanted the apartment?" he asked at last. Elise shook her head. "For security reasons. My man in McLean thought it was a good

— 414 —

idea." Uncle Bob sighed. "What a world! I've got more ex-Secret Service and CIA staff members on my payroll than Gorbachev does."

Elise laughed.

Uncle Bob looked over at her. "Are you happy, Elise?" When she didn't answer, he paused. "What did you do about that Larry Cochran?"

"I'm seeing him, Uncle Bob."

"Well, good for you. He seemed like such a nice person."

Elise thought of Larry, and then she thought of her mother. Helena would not approve. And while Helena was hardly in a position to judge, Elise felt both judged and grateful, too. Grateful that her mother couldn't meet him. How dreadful, she thought: I'm glad my mother is incapacitated. Her lip trembled.

"Oh, he *is* nice. Very nice, Uncle Bob. And funny, and considerate and talented. But he's out of work. He's a nobody. And he's half my age!"

"So help him get a job. Help him be a somebody. About the age, however, you can do nothing, except learn to live with it gracefully. When waiters ask me what my daughter wants for dinner, I tell them Bette's my granddaughter. So what? She's a good girl, and we're contented."

"But Uncle Bob . . ." What could she say? How Bette would never be with him if it weren't for his money? How his old body must repulse her in bed? How humiliating Elise would find it to be used? How her mother might be right? To her horror, she felt a tear roll out from her right eye. And she was about to sob, she realized, if she didn't do something. Because the truth was, she wanted Larry Cochran desperately. More, it felt, than she had ever wanted anything in her whole long life.

She stood up abruptly and strode halfway to the balustrade. But before she could get farther, Uncle Bob was beside her and had taken her hand.

He turned her to him. "You married a fool, Elise. A pompous, boring fool. Why? To be safe. But you weren't. No one ever is. Follow your heart, Elise. Don't waste the second half of your life."

3

Strangers in Paradise

Aaron shifted uncomfortably in his chair. The pants Leslie had bought for him were too damn tight. He was not a thirty-four anymore, thank you very much. He'd asked her to pick up a pair of his standard khaki chinos, and when she had asked him his size, he had said thirty-four. What in the world had possessed him? And who would have thought an inch made such a difference? Size thirty-five is hardly disgraceful for a man in his late forties, he thought to himself. I'm over six foot one. I haven't been a thirty-four since I was at Choate. I'm in excellent shape.

And really, he was. He ran three miles four or five times a week, and he still played the occasional game of tennis. Maybe he didn't play as much as he used to when he was married to Annie, but it was harder now to find a partner. Leslie wouldn't play. She worked out alone at her damned machines—she said they were more efficient, and he supposed she was right. Still, he missed having an in-house tennis partner.

He patted his sides. Maybe he was thickening a bit around the waist, but he still didn't have love handles. He would never let that happen. Aaron had a horror of fat. It said weak, it said lack of discipline, it said old and unattractive. He was none of those things, he told himself. Only vain enough to tell a white lie to his fiancée.

Things had not been good between them lately. That was why he'd lied. After he'd confessed to the Morty the Madman stock loss, Leslie had gone berserk. He wouldn't even have told her but he'd passed the tip on to her brother, Jon, who'd also lost a bundle. Leslie had called him irresponsible and immature. She'd told him that she wouldn't use her money to pay his expenses. Not that he'd asked. She'd cooled to him and not only socially. She'd turned her back on him in bed for more than a month now. And she'd looked more alluring than ever. It was torture. No wonder he'd told the stupid lie. She made him feel bad about himself. A man with an erection and nowhere to put it was a pathetic sight.

Aaron looked at his watch. Forty minutes to De Los Santos's visit. Why had he asked to see me? Aaron thought again. He shook off his nervousness, stood up, opened the closet that was concealed by a wall panel, and surveyed himself in the full-length mirror. He felt the need for some reassurance, and ever since he was a little boy, his appearance had given him that. Now he critically surveyed himself: his long frame, piercing blue eyes, dark hair. Some gray just starting to show at the temples, but hey, that just made him Butch Cassidy instead of the Sundance Kid. No problem.

Nothing wrong with aging, as long as you did it like Paul Newman. And that's how Aaron intended to do it. He was still damn handsome, and his casual clothes showed off his looks without giving him a peacock air. He changed his style a bit depending on his audience, but he always looked good, though he tried to be subtle about it. He might admit to being vain when he was alone, but he never wanted anyone else to suspect it. This, he decided, was a good, casual, but solid look.

Damnit, too bad the pants didn't fit. He really was uncomfortable. And it isn't just the pants, he finally admitted. It's everything. It's Leslie's coldness since the debacle with the stock. It's the problem with Sylvie's trust, the visit from the lawyer from the SEC this afternoon, and losing the Federated account and the meeting with Jerry this afternoon, and the waiting on Morty to get out of jail so he can sign off on the new campaign and float me the loan he promised. No wonder he was uncomfortable.

Well, he had at last convinced Leslie to lend him the money to buy out Jerry. He'd pay her back out of the profits, or out of the money that Morty would lend him. Leslie did, after all, still believe in him despite his poor judgment on the stock deal. And as soon as Morty paid him off he'd be fine.

Christ, he cursed inwardly, it's not enough to have suffered that enormous fucking loss. Now he had to sit waiting for Morty to get out of jail to make up for it. Why was he in jail, anyway? Christ, couldn't he make bail? Aaron secretly feared that maybe it wasn't only Morty's tax problems that got him in jail. He prayed it didn't have anything to do with that stock purchase. He'd bought nothing in his own name, had only passed on that tip to Jon Rosen and, of course, used Sylvie's trust. But it was legal to have bought as much as he wanted: the stuff was already public and being traded over the counter. No one could know about Morty's tip, unless Morty told them, and he'd never tell. Especially now that he had the tax problem. There was absolutely nothing to worry about, damnit! Then why was De Los Santos's impending visit making him so edgy?

He walked to the door of his office and opened it. Then he turned and surveyed the space he'd created and worked in for the last nine years. The hallway was bustling. The agency now had three floors in a cast-iron building on West Twenty-third Street right near the old Flatiron Building. He'd been right to move them down here, though Jerry and everyone else had said no at the time. He'd been a pioneer, and it had paid off. Now every boutique in the ad game wanted space in this neighborhood. He'd come a long way, baby. And he loved it.

He went over some comps from the Larimer account while he waited for De Los Santos to arrive. These were good. They were very good—clever. Aaron had assembled a talented staff. Jerry hadn't done that.

He's really dead weight, Aaron thought to himself for what must have been the hundredth time. There was nothing personal here. And no room for wimping out with guilt and all that bullshit. He thought of Leslie and her therapeutic disgust with guilt. It was unproductive. This firm will be a lot better off without Jerry.

He rubbed his hands through his hair and tried to relax. He looked at his watch. In a few minutes he would have to see this guy, then go into the meeting with Jerry and make perhaps the best business move of his life. It would mean more money, and God knows he needed it. He had to try to replace Sylvie's trust fund and . . . it was expensive living with Leslie. She didn't really have much tolerance for anything less than abundance, and Aaron was feeling pressured.

His secretary announced Mr. De Los Santos. Aaron snugged up his knit tie, tucked in his shirt more neatly, and walked to the door. Miguel De Los Santos was surprisingly good-looking. Aaron always noticed that in a man. Here he was expecting a bureaucratic drone and this guy looked built for action. Cheap suit, of course, but sharply angled planes in his face, wide shoulders, and a walk more like an athlete's than a desk jockey's. Not what he'd pictured at all. It was disconcerting. He thought again of Butch Cassidy and the Sundance

Kid, but this time he remembered how they'd been pursued by the Pinkertons. Who was this guy?

"How do you do, Mr. De Los Santos." He said it as a statement, leaving off the questioning inflection. It seemed a powerful opening, polite but lacking interest.

"Hello, Mr. Paradise. How are you."

His response lacked the questioning tone as well. The man looked him up and down, taking his time about it. Aaron wished his pants weren't so tight. Well, he'd make the guy his friend.

"Fine, fine. Come in and have a seat."

"Thank you." But he didn't move toward the Barcelona chairs that surrounded the low table, even though Aaron sat there. Instead the guy walked over to the windowsill and perched on it. "Great office," De Los Santos said, looking around the spacious room.

"Thank you. I like it a lot." Aaron smiled. Definitely time for a new role, here. Casual, equal to equal.

Aaron crossed his legs and looked at the guy. He looked smart. Shit. Well, he really had done nothing wrong. It wasn't illegal to lose money, for chrissakes.

"So what can I do for you, Mr. De Los Santos?"

"Well, as I told you on the phone, I'm investigating the Morty the Madman offering. I'm in a fact-finding phase right now, sniffing around." He paused. "There have been some complaints."

"Is this related to the tax thing? I understand there is a tax problem that Mr. Cushman has on his hands now."

"Well, all things are interrelated in the end, aren't they?"

"Uh-huh."

What was this guy, a fucking philosopher? Aaron felt his hand close into a fist. Keep it open. Seem interested. But casual. Get the bastard to like you. Aaron crossed his arms, leaned back in the chair, and smiled at De Los Santos.

—

De Los Santos seemed not to notice. "I understand you're the advertising agency that handled the Madman account?"

"Of course. You don't need me to tell you that. It's a matter of record." Whoa, partner. That sounded a bit defensive. Smile again.

"Right. . . . And are you also personally acquainted with Morton Cushman?"

"How could I not be? We've had the account for seven years." Christ, the guy got on his nerves. It was almost impossible not to be nasty to him.

"And do you see Mr. Cushman socially?"

"Not really."

"What does that mean?"

"Oh, occasionally we may be at the same party, but we don't go out together."

"But did you in the past?"

"God, maybe years ago. He's a major client. I don't avoid the guy."

"Uh-huh. So, did Mr. Cushman tell you he was going public?"

"No, he did not." Aaron was surprised to feel a light sweat break out on his forehead. Once again he asked himself, who *was* this guy? "That would be illegal, wouldn't it, Mr. De Los Santos?" Shit, he didn't like the man.

"People make mistakes," De Los Santos said.

Was it his imagination or was the guy glaring at him?

"So it wasn't until September that you liquidated your daughter's assets and purchased the Madman stock?"

Aaron felt the blood rush to his face. He could hardly believe what he'd heard. How the fuck did this guy know about the trust fund? No one knew about it except Annie and Leslie. Surely Leslie hadn't said anything to anyone. She was angry, but that would be insane. Did Annie sic this trouble on him?

"Mr. Paradise?"

Christ, he had to say something. Get a grip, Aaron warned himself. "Yes."

"You purchased seventy-six thousand five hundred and sixty shares on September the third?"

Aaron nodded. He was sweating all over.

"So you never bought *any* shares, though anyone who had before that date had made a major killing. You just happened to buy the stock right before the Madman plunge began. How is it you did this?"

"How is it? How is it that I lost my shirt? Since when is losing money on the market an indication of being privy to inside information?"

"I said nothing about insider trading."

"It's what you're implying, isn't it? Well, my losses should prove that there was none of that. Insiders don't lose."

"Oh, not necessarily. It may only mean that something didn't go as it was planned. When much money is lost, just as when much money is gained, it can mean that there has been insider activity." De Los Santos looked at him blankly, expressionless.

"Well, I've told you as much as I know." Aaron tried to calm himself and attempted an innocent smile.

"Thank you, Mr. Paradise," De Los Santos finally answered.

His expression was blank, his face unreadable. To Aaron's enormous relief, he stood up.

"I may have to call you again."

"Feel free," Aaron replied, rising. Anything to get rid of the guy. Get it over. Put it behind him.

"Thank you," De Los Santos repeated, and turned to leave. Then he stopped and faced Aaron again. "Oh, you're not planning to leave the country in the near future are you?"

Aaron gave him a look of disbelief. The man must be joking. "No . . ." he said hesitantly.

"Well, let us know if you're planning any trips. Okay?"

They shook hands and Aaron made an effort to keep his grip firm, though he couldn't prevent his palm from being damp. Then he walked the guy to the door. He watched him until he was completely out of sight and then walked back to his desk. He fell into his chair and covered his eyes with his hands. He felt exhausted and frightened, more frightened than he could remember being in years, since he'd moved out of his father's house. He wondered if there was any way they would find out that Morty was paying him back some of the money lost. If Morty was. Aaron had heard from Morty's lawyer that all was well, but for some reason Morty was still being held in jail. Christ, he felt cornered.

He went to the closet mirror again. The face that looked back at him looked as bad as he felt. He looked old, and his clothes were all wrong for his next meeting—too conservative, too predictable. He looked like a loser.

Aaron made a quick decision. He got up, put his jacket on, and told his secretary that he'd be right back. Out on Twenty-third Street, he turned right at Fifth Avenue and walked downtown a few blocks. There he entered Paul Smith's, the trendiest of the downtown stores.

"I need a shirt, a tie, and a pair of pants that I can wear out of here." he told the salesman. "Waist size thirty-five."

He took a deep breath. He'd go back and present the plan. He'd convince the staff. They should all back him. Christ, *he* was the talent, and he'd hired them. They all owed him. And they better come through for him. Still, he had a nagging fear in his gut. Who knew with this generation? Who knew what had become of loyalty and commitment?

4

A Cot and Three Hots

Downtown in the Federal House of Detention near the Hudson River, Morty Cushman was lying on his cot, wondering the same thing.

He had been wondering for almost two weeks now. When he'd first arrived, the processing of prisoners moving down the receiving hall was painfully slow. Morty Cushman had been on one line after another for hours, none of which seemed to produce any results other than to test the limits of patience of the prisoners. He had stared at the institutional gray that coated everything: walls, desks, counters, guards' shirts. He had been instructed to follow one of the various colored stripes painted on the floor: the stripe he was following was brown. The new prisoners were wearing jumpsuits they had been issued earlier in the day and had been given their choice of color: gray, brown, or blue. Why he picked blue he couldn't say.

Now, in his blue uniform, he lay on his cot waiting. He cursed Leo Gilman again for not getting him out on bail. "I will, Morty, it's just that these things take time," he had said. "I got to convince them that you're not going to leave the country. But Christ, it was stupid to put so much of your assets abroad. They're afraid you'll abscond. It looks bad when you do that, Morty." Morty couldn't believe the bastards wouldn't let him out on bail, but he had to admit that after two weeks of prison, leaving the country felt very attractive. Being any-where but here right now was attractive.

When he'd first gotten in, he looked around for a buddy. The guy in front of him in line seemed not to have a care in the world. Morty had liked the guy until he found out that he had kidnapped his ex-girlfriend and her new boyfriend in the Bronx, killed them in New Jersey, and thrown their bodies out of his van in Maryland. The guy behind him had tried to hijack a plane out of Kennedy Airport, with a bomb tied around his ankle. Morty shook his head and wondered where the country-club prison for white-collar criminals was. He'd been glad when the guard stopped them from holding any more conversations. He didn't want these kinds of guys to hear he was in for *tax evasion*, for chrissake. He was sure that was not the kind of thing these guys would respect.

When his turn came for a physical exam, the trustee fill-ing out the questionnaire asked him if he had dentures. When Morty said he didn't, the trustee shrugged in feigned pity. Morty's stomach tightened. What the fuck did that mean? Was it some kind of code, some kind of jail lingo?

Finally he was ushered down long hallways, each with a guard station that closed the gates behind him with a clang. After several of these passages, he and the other new admis-sions came to the cellblock that would be his temporary home. As they progressed down the catwalk, prisoners from other cells began calling out their choices for future mates. Everyone on the cellblock was hanging on to the bars, watch-ing the passing parade.

"Looky, looky, looky. Hey, sweetcakes, you with the peach ass. You're mine, honey. Don't forget, you're Al's, anyone asks. Al'll take care of you. You take care of me, I take care of you. Remember me, sweetcakes, 'cause *I* ain't goin' forget *you*."

"Hey, whitey, fatboy, you take your teeth out? I got plans for you, baby. You got dentures, I can get you work day or night. My name Rocket, baby. Rocket got you in his pocket." Oh, Christ, that's what the trustee had meant.

Morty kept reminding himself that he'd been raised in the Bronx, so he could do the rolling gait that the homeboys seemed to have developed to an art. He felt foolish walking that way, but he was a man intent on saving his life. He always used to get beat up by the Irish kids in Kingsbridge when he was growing up, but he didn't know then that you have to walk tough to be thought tough. And he was tough, for a Jew. Christ, let me get through this, he thought.

Morty was the last prisoner to be dropped off at a cell. His forced bravado immediately left him when he saw his cell-mate. The ebony figure stretched out on the lower cot looked like his worst nightmare. About six feet four inches, 275 pounds, and muscles that bulged at every seam of his clothing; his black skin was tight and shiny, and his shaven head made him look even more menacing. Morty paused for a moment at the cell door. Christ, he wouldn't even step into an elevator with a character like this.

The guard pushed him in and closed the cell door behind him. "Hey, Mo, look who I got for you. He can't take his teeth out, Mo, but you'll work it out. You got a genuine celebrity here. Ever hear of Morty the Madman? Well, here he is. Only now he's Morty the Badman." The guard laughed and strode away. Morty was sure that the heavy hitters weren't treated like this. Boesky was probably given his own cell. And each of Gotti's boys would get a red carpet, he was sure. Tax evasion, he thought again. Too wimpy. Too Jewish.

Big Mo continued to flip through the pages of *Playboy* before finally raising his dark eyes in Morty's direction. But when he did look up, his tense face relaxed, his eyebrows raised. "You the guy what's on TV selling portable telephones and shit?" Morty, relieved at the lack of outright hostility, immediately jumped into his madman persona.

"That's me, Morty the Madman," he cried in the hyper voice he used in the ads, and extended his right hand. Mo took it, gave it the uptown double shake with the five-finger slide. Morty pretended he shook hands this way all his life, but Mo was no fool: major heroin dealer and sometime pimp, arsonist even, but no fool. Still, he was impressed by this face that he'd seen so often on TV. This Jewboy was really Mad Mort. He grinned.

"Since you a celebrity, let me tell you how it is here." Mo put his magazine aside. "I'm Big Mo D.C., and I'm the guy that gets things done. If Big Mo your friend, nobody messes with you. So if I can do something for you, just let me know. The way I sees it, one hand washes the other. Right, Little Morty?"

Mo moved over slightly on the cot to make room for Morty to sit. The timing was perfect because Morty's trembling legs couldn't hold him upright much longer. Morty continued his bravado, however, and set out to make Big Mo D.C. his best friend. "Mo, for you I can do things."

"You know, Morty, I was thinkin' the same thing myself. Like I got my woman back in my crib all alone and lonely for her man. So maybe you could like get her something nice. Something that will remind her of me."

"I got the perfect thing, my man. I can get her a thirteen-inch combination TV and built-in VCR. It's a beauty, and no bigger than a toaster. How's that sound?"

Big Mo considered, then shook his head, as if Morty didn't understand. "No, man, I want her to get something that will keep her thinking of *me*. I'm a *big* man. No thirteen inches. A little toaster-size TV just ain't gonna do it."

By way of impressing Morty with his pull in the joint, Mo reached under his cot and pulled out a bottle of Scotch, some brand Morty had never even heard of. "Want a taste? Or would you prefer a hand-rolled?" He extended an open gold cigarette case and offered a perfectly rolled joint.

Morty again thought of Leo Gilman, how gladly he would kill him. Somehow, to Morty, Leo was more responsible for his being here than Morty himself was.

"Well, how 'bout a fifty-four-inch giant screen? And a job for you, when you're out." Morty blessed all the powers that be for his good luck in a cellmate. "Mo, leave this to me. Just tell me where you want the TV delivered, and I'll have it there in two days. I'll even put a gift card on it."

"Now we talking business, my man."

After they each had a couple of pulls on the Scotch, Big Mo was Morty's long-lost friend. "Ain't never met no real-life celebrity before, man. You my first."

Morty didn't miss an opportunity. "You want to meet more celebrities? When we get out, I'll take you places you never even dreamed existed." Mimicking Mo's dialect he said, "We friends, man."

"Okay, Little Morty. Okay." The big man stretched out on his bunk.

Morty climbed up into the upper bunk and stared at the ceiling just inches over his head. He was terrified, he had to admit that. And very angry, although he wasn't exactly sure why or at whom. Leo, yes. And Bill Atchison. And Gil Griffin. And somehow at Brenda and Shelby. All their fault. Bloodsuckers. All of them.

Morty fell into a troubled sleep, wishing he had a friend.

Morty sat behind the bulletproof glass wall that separated him from his visitors and watched the group of women walk through the door at the far end of the room.

There she was, dressed in his favorite color. He didn't know that it was a buttercup yellow Azzedine Alaia; he didn't know it had cost him almost four thousand dollars; all he knew was how glad he was to see her.

He watched Shelby move along the row of cubicles until she spotted him sitting at one of them. She smiled. Shelby always looked good to Morty, but today she looked like a sun-goddess. He took a deep breath, feeling a surge of comfort. She was bought and paid for, he knew, but now, seeing her here in the midst of this sleaze, he felt hope, he felt remembered. He felt cared about. And he needed care. Christ, he felt like he needed his mother.

But Shelby sat down and immediately began to cry. Well, it showed she loved him. Morty motioned her to pick up the phone and tried to calm her. "It's going to be all right, Shelby. I'm going to be home real soon. Please, don't cry."

But Shelby didn't stop, even when she had picked up the phone. Then, at last, when she began to speak, she turned on him. "Morton, do you know what they put me through to get in to see you?" she snapped, her drawl turned treacherous. "Ah waited for hours, then Ah was body-searched by a woman who looked like Arnold Schwarzenegger. And the other women! They treated me like dirt. Me! And they all smelled so bad, and the children had filthy diapers and . . ." Shelby started to cry in earnest again. "Ah can't be put through this, Morton. Ah may just die."

She gulped air, trying for some control. He watched her coldly. "And they've gone through the apartment. Those people from the Treasury were there for hours. And they searched the gallery, too. They went through *everything*."

Jesus, Morty thought, those fucking feds are like cockroaches in New York; they're all over. What would happen next? He felt his scalp tingle with sweat. What could they uncover? Morty knew he was in a vulnerable position. How far back will they go? He swallowed the panic that was beginning to tingle the back of his throat. How had this happened to him?

"Shelby," he said gently, "I told you. Everything's going to be okay."

"That's easy for you to say. I'm the one that has to deal with the authorities; I'm the one that has to face our friends." Starting to cry again, Shelby dabbed at her eyes. "You're in here not seeing anyone you know." She continued to whimper. "But what about me?"

Morty had never deluded himself into thinking that Shelby was loyal, certainly not like Brenda. That wasn't why he wanted Shelby. But hearing her now whine about herself, while it was *him* in jail, hit him in a way that made him swallow hard. But Morty was a realist, and the moment passed. You get what you pay for, he reminded himself. And for the first time in a long time, he missed Brenda. One thing he had to say about her, she would have known what I was going through in here. Look what she had done for her father whenever he went to prison. Ashamed as she was, she never missed a visiting day, sent her father a package of goodies every week, and put spending money in his prison account every month. Now, where was Morty's comfort? Angela hadn't shown up, and he sure didn't expect Tony to leave his fancy prep school. Where was anyone who wasn't looking for a handout or a favor? "So why did you come, Shelby?" he asked her, tired of her whining. "I mean, if it's so much to go through, why did you come?"

Shelby's tears stopped immediately. Her drawl lengthened out again. "Morton, we have to talk. You have no idea what this is doing to me. All your money is tied up by the feds, and

Ah don't have a red cent. You've *got* to do something. Ah still have my social responsibilities. *And* a business to run. You were going to underwrite my business until it began to pay its own way, remember?"

She touched at her eyes once again, but to Morty it seemed only as a way of punctuating her statement.

"What happened to the twenty-five thousand dollars Leo deposited in your checking account?" Morty asked, letting his irritation show.

"Morton, how far do you think twenty-five thousand dollars goes? There were clothes and bills and some paintings Ah had to pay for. What with odds and ends, it's gone."

A signal blared, marking the end of the visiting period. Getting up to walk back to his cell with the other prisoners, Morty suddenly knew for certain what he had only suspected most of his life. He was alone. The sensation was like a deep hole drilled in his stomach, a hole that would never be filled. He looked at Shelby. He sighed. "Talk to Leo Gilman. He'll set you up."

But Gilman had only bad news.

"Look, Mort. Something's up. They don't want to go to bail."

"What? Are you crazy? What do they base it on?"

"Well, they seem to believe that you have significant secret assets abroad."

"What are you talking about?" Okay, so he had cheated— well, played—with his taxes, but he had *declared* the money he had put in Europe. Nothing illegal about it.

"It seems they searched your place. I couldn't stop them— they had a warrant."

"Well, so what?"

"Well, they found something."

Morty searched his mind frantically. "What? What?" he shrieked.

"A key. A key to a safety deposit box. A Zurich bank. Another account, one you didn't declare." Leo shook his head. "Morty, I told you over and over, you gotta be straight with me. I can't work in the dark, Mort."

What the hell was going on? He had no Zurich safety deposit box. Someone was trying to frame him, maybe. He thought of the money he had in the numbered account in Switzerland, but Leo wasn't talking about that. It wasn't illegal, although that was why he was being detained here, because of his significant holdings abroad. No bail because of it. Okay, but what was this crap about a Zurich safety deposit box?

"But there is no safety deposit box!" Morty cried "There isn't."

When Miguel De Los Santos walked into the interview room at the Federal House of Detention, Morty Cushman did not look formidable to him. The man sat, a short fat guy in a blue jumpsuit, sunken into himself, his head in his hands. Miguel knew he was taking a chance, but if the boys over at Internal Revenue cooperated, and if his calls to that sleazy Gilman had worked, he might be able to pull this off.

"Hello," Miguel said.

Cushman looked up. "You from the IRS? If you are, I want my attorney here."

"No. No. I'm not from the IRS," Miguel assured him. "But I *am* with the government and I'm here to help." The guy was sweating. He was a pile of jelly. Miguel smiled.

"Very funny. What's the deal?"

"Exactly. It's time for deals, Morty. That's why I'm here. Because you are going to do time. The question is, how much and what kind? The IRS has got you by the *cojónes*."

"Fuck you!" Morty said, but Miguel could see he was listening.

"Offshore assets, undeclared cash in safety deposits, lots of tax evasion. So now, you have a choice to make. Hard time, or soft. Allendale is very pleasant. You'll lose weight. Play some tennis. Get a tan. Or we can send you to a nasty place, where you'll be keeping house for someone not as laid-back as Big Mo."

"Who the fuck *are* you?"

"I'm Miguel De Los Santos, and I'm from the SEC. I'd like to ask you a few questions about your stock offering, and if you cooperate, Morty, then I'll talk to my friends at the IRS. As a witness against Gil Griffin you might be given a break. Mr. Cushman, it's time to play 'Let's Make a Deal.'"

5

Marriage à la Merde

Chris shook hands with both his father and with Leslie, the bride. He muttered some congratulations, then moved off the receiving line and grabbed a glass of champagne. After one sip he put it down; it left a bitter taste in his mouth.

He looked around Leslie's loft as the guests continued to make their way along the line. It felt strange to be at his father's wedding today, in his father's new home, so different from the Greenwich house he grew up in. And so different from his parents' apartment—his mother's, he corrected himself—on Gracie Square.

What a crowd, he thought. There was that Rosen guy, Leslie's brother, who'd already put the make on Karen. Jesus, was that guy a slime bucket! And the rest of the crew didn't look much better.

Chris looked at Leslie and tried to smile. He just couldn't understand his father. It wasn't just loyalty to his mom—this woman seemed so cold. Last night, at the bachelor party, Aaron had seemed morose. After a couple of drinks, he had pulled Chris aside and told him he was afraid he might be making a mistake. "Well, then, postpone the wedding, Dad."

Chris had told him. "Oh. I can't do that. Leslie would kill me. She'd lose too much face—we both would."

It seemed a bad reason to go ahead with a marriage. And he'd heard other stuff that made him question his father's judgment. There was a rumor at the office that his father was being investigated by the police or something, and another one that he'd stolen some company funds. Chris didn't know what to believe.

Well, he knew he hated this event. It wasn't what a wedding should be. Neither Leslie nor his dad looked happy, and the guests, well, he didn't even know them. His grandparents weren't here. His dad hadn't invited a single person from the office, not even Jerry. Chris wasn't even sure Karen was welcome, but he wouldn't have come without her.

Chris took Karen's hand and inched toward the front door, then turned around, got his father's attention over the heads of the other well-wishers, and waved. He pointed to his watch, then went through the door.

By the time he dropped Karen off at her place and arrived at Ottomanelli's, Chris had almost managed to push his father's wedding from his mind. He was genuinely glad to see Annie when she came in a few minutes later.

"Good choice, Mom, although I'm a little overdressed for a pizza parlor, aren't I?" he asked, looking down at his dinner jacket.

"Well, you said you felt like a good hamburger, and this is the best in town. And I can have a pizza, so we're both happy."

Chris's beer and Annie's diet Coke arrived. "I have some good news, Mom," he said after a sip of beer. Putting the glass down, he looked into his mother's eyes. "Karen and I are going to be married."

Annie smiled broadly at him. "I'm very happy for you both."

"Mom, please don't be nice. I know she's a lot older and well . . . I want your approval, your *real* approval."

He watched his mother for a brief moment before she spoke.

"Well, you're not going to get it. Nor my disapproval. This is between you and Karen, Chris. It has nothing to do with me—or anyone else. I only want you to be happy; anyway, age is not a concern unless you're thinking about having children." She put her cool hand on his cheek. "You are happy, aren't you, Chris?"

"Oh, yes, I love her. She's great, Mom."

"I know it." Annie smiled, then added, "But no one would know it by the expression on your face."

"You know, Mom, I came directly from Dad's wedding."

"And it was so wonderful that it inspired you and Karen?"

"It was gruesome. Before the ceremony—I guess because Alex couldn't make it—all of a sudden I was given 'favored son' status. You know, like how Dad does it with Alex. 'Chris did this, Chris can do that, Chris is going to do. . . . ' It was embarrassing." He looked down at the hamburger the waitress had placed before him and picked up a french fry.

"But he's proud of you, Chris. You know how happy he is to have you with him at the agency."

"It's so out of character for him. It's like he's buttering me up for something." Chris took a bite of his rare burger. "Something's going on at the agency. I mean, he's changed. He's not popular with the rest of the staff like he used to be. He acts as if he's the only one pulling the weight of the business. As if no one else is even competent. He's the only one that knows anything. He's spending way too much money trying to get new business. I don't know. Maybe it's just his involvement with Leslie, but he's become a prima donna." Chris thought perhaps Annie winced at Leslie's name, but he wasn't certain.

"Can't he be reined in, Chris? It seems to me the agency is doing excellent business if Aaron got himself in check."

"It would be. With a stronger administrator. Or maybe without Dad." Chris wiped his mouth with the paper napkin and threw it on the plate. "People are choosing up sides. And I can't take his, Mom."

"You have to be on your own side first, Chris. Do what is right, even if it hurts him."

"I've heard rumors. About Sylvie's trust fund and some kind of investigation. Are they true, Mom? Did Dad steal from the company?"

"I can't say for sure, but I doubt it. Not steal. Your father did get into some kind of stock difficulty and borrowed money from Sylvie's trust, but he's paying it back."

"Mom . . ." Chris didn't want to involve his mother, but he needed to talk. "Something bad is going to happen at the agency. I just know it." He paused, then continued, "Dad is going to be humiliated."

"Maybe. But it's not your problem. It's Aaron's."

Aaron entered the boardroom at Paradise/Loest feeling suave and confident. He wore a navy blue French rayon shirt with a pattern of white mice. The tie was of the same fabric, but cats replaced the mice. His navy slacks had three pleats and a chalk stripe. And this morning he had splurged on a nifty white, hand-knit English sweater that looked as if graffiti had been scrawled over it, though the pattern had actually been painstakingly knit and purled into the cardigan. He felt young and hip again. Reborn. He'd walked confidently down the hall to the boardroom and taken his seat across from the basketball hoop mounted on the wall, at the end of the conference table.

Aaron counted on his ability to rise to the occasion, in

spite of any dogshit he might have stepped in. He smiled at the assembled group and winked at his son Chris. Then, as he greeted the junior partners, he flashed them a broad thumbs-up grin and looked like a man who had already won his victory. All a lot younger than Aaron, the staff were what he considered yuppies. Chris sat next to Karen, as he always did. They were pals. He'd even brought her to the wedding. For a moment it occurred to Aaron that there might be something between them. There was that undefinable something between them in the air. Then he dismissed the thought. Karen was almost ten years older than Chris. He'd once thought of dating her himself. Chris would be way out of his league with her.

Next to Karen was Dave Stein, the comptroller, his only failure. The guy had no vision at all. A pencil counter. He was the only one that Aaron could possibly see as potential trouble.

Dave and Jerry went out for drinks sometimes and seemed to have some kind of mutual understanding. Now they both looked at Aaron as if they knew something he didn't. Jerry sat beside Dave, on Aaron's left.

"So, how goes it?" Aaron smiled at the seven. They were extremely competent and professional, and, he thought, very hard-hearted about business and money. But they liked him. He had hired them and brought them along. This was one reason he was sure they'd all back him up.

Drew Pettit, vice president and senior art director, was on Aaron's left. He was a handsome thirty-one-year-old workaholic whom Aaron had brought in six years ago as a layout and paste-up person. Drew was ambitious and Aaron envisioned bringing him in as a senior partner as soon as Jerry's ass was out of there. Who knew, Drew might even be slotted for the top spot if Aaron himself wanted to ease off in another ten years. Much as he loved Chris, he wouldn't hand the spot over to him. Chris would have to compete for it.

Next to Drew was Julie Thurow, the first woman to be a partner of Paradise/Loest. An incredible amount of Madison Avenue experience, and a lot cheaper than men with the same background. But no real excitement there.

Then Phil Connell, a stocky, athletic guy who seemed to Aaron to have no visible sense of humor, but he came up with absolutely dead-on copy that made for effective print campaigns.

Jerry cleared his throat and Aaron spoke quickly to head him off.

"Okay. You all know the reason I've called this meeting. As I stated in my memo last week, we have, to speak plainly, some management difficulties that need to be ironed out.

"When this agency was founded, back when the eighties were young, it was as an equal partnership. Frankly, I feel that for a long time now it hasn't been that. I know it is not only *my* impression that I have carried the bulk of the burden of management for as long as . . . well, for as long as some of you have been here." He glanced quickly at Jerry.

"I feel that the organization as it's now structured is obsolete." Aaron paused and looked around the room. He was more nervous than he had thought he would be. Strangely, he couldn't catch anyone's eye, not even Chris's. But he did notice some signs that he interpreted as favorable. Dave Stein was looking at the opposite wall and nodding his head up and down very slowly. Maybe the pencil counter would fall into line. If that was the case, it was going to be a landslide. Jerry was looking down, defeated already, Aaron thought.

"Of our twelve major money-making accounts, I've brought in nine. Karen, of course, brought in Planet, and Drew and Julie brought in the other two." Aaron went on, "I feel that I have assembled a dynamite staff, and as I see it, Paradise/Loest has a great future, a really great future. But we can't have a troubled management. And we have that now."

Again, Dave Stein nodded. Okay, Dave. Aaron smiled and flashed them all a grin.

"Jerry, I don't think you can disagree with me. It's painful, I know, but I think the time has come for us to part ways. I would like to buy you out." He paused. Complete silence reigned. Well, of course. Partnerships were tricky to break up. Maybe he'd been too abrupt. "Sorry, Jerry. No hard feelings." His son flashed him a look. Maybe I should have prepared Chris for this, he suddenly thought. No, he told himself, let him learn how business is done.

Aaron looked up at Jerry and smiled again. Then the fucker smiled back.

"I agree with you, Aaron, about the management problem," Jerry began. "Somehow, Aaron, I think you and I parted ways a long time ago. I'd have to agree with that. We haven't been able to pull off a united effort for years. But I don't see myself leaving. In fact, I'm buying *you* out."

Aaron was astonished. "Get serious, Jerry. I *am* the firm. If you'll excuse the pun, you'd just be Loest without me. And you haven't brought a major account in here in years."

"Well," Jerry said, "I was going to make a couple of announcements at this meeting. One of them is that during the last two months I've negotiated for three very big accounts and I've gotten them." He looked at Drew, Julie, and the rest. "With a lot of help from my colleagues, of course."

Aaron sat motionless, frozen in shock. Three new accounts! In the last two months! It took years to bring in major accounts. Yes, and schmoozing and lots of work. Jerry was famous for having spent two years on Snapple only to lose the bastard. How could Jerry have done it? Without Aaron's even knowing about this? Impossible. It must be a desperate lie. "What are they?" he snarled.

"Van Gelder International Bank, Bloogee Industries, and Benadrey Cosmetics." Jerry had stood up as he spoke and walked to the door. With his hand on the door handle, he continued, "And my guess is that the combined annual billing is worth over twenty-five million dollars."

"The only way we're going to be profitable, Aaron, is if we cut expenses as well as bring in accounts," Dave Stein said. "I'd like to mention that your new business costs, including a suite at the Carlyle for most of last year, ate up the profits."

"Jesus Christ, Dave. Don't tell me how to spend my money."

"*Our* money," Jerry reminded him. He paused, and at last looked genuinely uncomfortable. "It's not just the money, Aaron. When we started, we agreed we wanted to be more than client ass-kissers like most of the guys in advertising. Frankly . . ." He stopped.

"When have I kissed ass?" Aaron demanded hotly.

"Frankly, Herb Brubaker's butt still has your lipstick blots," said Julie.

Christ, was that feminist bitch still holding a grudge?

"It would be best to let *us* buy *you* out," Jerry added.

"Yeah, well, where are you getting the money to do it?" Aaron asked. Jesus, he wasn't going to roll over for peanuts, and that's all these guys had.

"From Cushman," Jerry said.

"Cushman?" Aaron said, incredulous. "*Morty Cushman* is loaning you the money to buy me out?" And *not* giving me back the money he promised? Aaron added silently.

"Not *Morty* Cushman," Jerry said. "*Brenda* Cushman."

Jerry now opened the door to the outer room and said, "Won't you come in now?" Brenda walked into the room and, without looking around, sat in the seat indicated by Jerry. Jerry stood beside her, his hand on the back of her chair, and said to everyone assembled, "I'd like to introduce you to the Cushman who is going to help us straighten out our problems, Ms. Brenda Cushman."

The other partners, except for Aaron, broke into cheers. Dazed, Aaron stared at Brenda, trying to interpret the bland look on her face.

"Drew, Julie, Phil, thanks for helping to ensure that the partnership will be in the black for a long time to come," Jerry said.

Turning his attention to Aaron, he said, "I'm ready to buy you out."

Aaron sat back in his chair, stunned. Brenda Cushman, Morty's ex-wife, Annie's friend, just sat there, looking at him; then she grinned like the Cheshire cat. Aaron looked around the table at the other partners. They all had their eyes on Jerry and were ignoring Aaron. What had happened? It felt unreal. Aaron out and Jerry in! How could they do this? After he'd hired them, given them a chance, given them their head.

Aaron felt an actual pain in his chest. How could they? Why would they? Over the silly La Doll incident? Over his expenses? Because Jerry had given them the spotlight? Because they'd helped bring in the bacon? Aaron knew how exciting it was to pitch, how exhilarating to win an account. He had always pitched the new business. And he knew how much fun it was to take potshots at your boss. So, these little fuckers had been doing all this behind his back. Jesus Christ!

"You can't make it without me," he told them.

"I'd like to remind you," Dave said, "that for some time I've been concerned about the expenditures for some of the work we do. For example, last year alone, the four hundred thousand we spent on speculative new accounts that we ultimately lost would have increased bonuses by almost a hundred percent. I feel, Aaron, you've been reaching too far, spending too much, and not targeting enough. Brenda Cushman agrees and will be in charge of monitoring new business expenditures. Then there was the loss of Federated Funds. But there were no cutbacks to match it." Dave took a breath. "Lastly, we are going to have to relocate by the end of next year or pay double the rent, reducing profits even further. And, I might add, it appears that the Madman account is in turmoil. We still have no written authorization for the new campaign work we've done. I hope we don't end up eating it."

"Knowing Morty, you probably will," Brenda cracked.

Aaron glared at her, at Dave, then at Jerry, who looked back mildly.

"Sorry, Aaron. No hard feelings," he said.

"No hard feelings? *Are you crazy?*"

Aaron stood up and started for his office. As he passed Chris's chair, he paused and made a slight indication for Chris to walk out before him. Obviously, his career here was over. But unbelievably, Chris turned his head away and faced Jerry. *Et tu, Brute,* Aaron thought, and continued out the door. There was nothing he could think of to say right now. He needed to be alone. No one spoke to him. At least they were letting him cope with his humiliation in private.

As he walked down the long hall to his office, he made a move to loosen his tie, but found that he already had. He felt constriction in his throat and pressure in his chest. Ah, the final indignity: a fatal heart attack in his own hallway. Fuck them—no way. He'd be damned if he'd let them inherit the key-man insurance.

He finally reached his office, collapsed into the chair in front of the desk, got the bottle of Chivas out of the lower drawer, and poured himself a drink. All the little bastards had turned on him. It was unbelievable. He'd hired them—all of them, even Chris—nurtured them, made them what they fucking were. Christ, it was unbelievable. And then, to have his betrayal witnessed by Brenda Cushman, Annie's friend! He stopped for a moment. Could Annie have had anything to do with this? he wondered.

He shook his head. Christ, he was getting paranoid! Annie couldn't even balance her checkbook, he reminded himself. But he hoped she'd never hear of his humiliation. He was shocked to find that tears were stinging his eyes. Look what those bastards have done to me, he thought. I haven't cried since I was sixteen. He wiped at his eyes with the scratchy fabric of his new, ridiculous sweater sleeve.

6

Babes in Boyland

Annie was thrilled by Elise's offer of a trip to Japan: after all, when would she ever get the opportunity to fly via private jet and be introduced to Japan by Bob Bloogee's "man in Kyoto."

"Now, Tanaki is a difficult man," Bob explained once the steward had helped them settle into their glove-leather easy chairs and had served them a glass of Veuve Clicquot Ponsardin (though Elise didn't drink hers, Annie noticed).

"Why should he be difficult? We're doing him a big favor. We're warning him of a hostile takeover in time for him to stop it," Brenda pointed out.

"Ah. Yes. Well, in the States that might have a predictable response. But in Japan . . . well, it's different." Bob looked around the luxurious interior of the plane as if the rubbed teak or the velvety carpet held an explanation. Apparently they didn't, for he sighed before he continued.

"I've known Tanaki for almost twenty years. We've done half a dozen deals together. But the Japanese are a very private people. He's never invited me to his home or said a personal word. I've never met his family. He's old-fashioned Japanese. That's why he located Maibeibi headquarters in Kyoto. No airport, no subway, but it's the most Japanese of cities."

"Why should all this affect his reaction to the takeover news? Isn't business business?" Elise asked.

"Well, not exactly." Uncle Bob paused again. "Do you know the story of the forty-seven samurai?" Brenda and Elise shook their heads, but Annie knew it. In the 1700s, Kira Yoshinaka, a royal retainer, insulted Asano Naganoni, Lord of Ako. Asano drew his sword to retaliate, a major sin because they were on the grounds of the imperial castle. Asano, for his transgression, was expected to commit seppuku, ritual suicide, and he did.

"You mean the guy offed himself when all he'd done was try to defend himself?" Brenda asked.

"Honor demanded it," Uncle Bob explained. "It protected his family. But that left his samurai without a leader. And their loyalty to their lord was so strong that they plotted for months on how to kill Kira, while they pretended to accept the situation. At last they found their chance, killed Kira, cut off his head, and placed it on Asano's grave."

"Yech!" Brenda exclaimed.

"Well, that didn't end it. The forty-seven samurai were now all *ronin*, leaderless knights, and honor demanded their own suicide. So they did it."

"What? All forty-seven of them?"

"All of them. It was an incredible gesture. There is a temple built to their honor in Tokyo."

"Ridiculous!" snorted Brenda. "Only men would pull that shit."

"Their memories are still worshiped," Uncle Bob pointed out mildly.

"Well, but what has that to do with Tanaki and the takeover?" Elise asked sensibly.

"Oh, yes. Well. Tanaki is a particular devotee of the forty-seven *ronin*. Many traditional Japanese are. He supports performances of Kabuki when they play 'Chushingura,' their story. And he makes retreats to the Sengakuji temple where they are buried. When he hears that some of his stockholders have been disloyal, he will lose face. He may be upset."

"Upset enough to off himself?" Brenda asked.

"Well, not that extreme, but perhaps enough to retire, to step down. And then Gil will step right in. So this has to be done . . . well . . . in the right way."

"Will it make it more difficult to have us at the meeting?" Annie asked. She knew that women were given a very small business role in corporate Japan. They were called "office flowers" and often expected to quit when they married or turned thirty.

"Oh, surely you won't attend the meeting. No. We'll all meet Tanaki for a dinner, a sort of banquet that he'll host, and then I and my man in Kyoto will meet with him alone, the following day."

"Forget it," said Elise.

"Excuse me . . . ?" Uncle Bob paused.

"We aren't going all this way to be window dressing," Elise said. "This is, after all, our caper."

"Not window dressing, but perhaps not really beneficial to . . ."

"Because we're women? Ridiculous, Uncle Bob. This is the twentieth century."

"Not in Kyoto." Bob Bloogee sighed.

By the time they arrived at Osaka International airport, Annie was exhausted from excitement, and from the endless flight, despite all the comforts that the private plane provided. She was grateful to Mr. Wanabe, Uncle Bob's "man in Kyoto," when he ushered them through customs and had a

Rolls-Royce waiting for them, but the ride to Kyoto was still long and tiresome.

The Tawaraya Ryokan, the traditional inn, came as a revelation. Mrs. Sato, the owner, met them at the gate, bowing low to Mr. Wanabe, then to all of them. Her family, he explained, had owned the Tawaraya for eleven generations. There were only nineteen rooms, and each was austerely magnificent as well as incredibly expensive.

Annie's exquisite room was matted with tatami and had a wall of glass that opened to a wooden veranda strewn with cushions. There was very little furniture: a beautiful antique chest, a dark, low lacquer table, and a gilt screen with painted irises. The emptiness was set off by the beautiful vase in the wall niche, the *tokonoma,* filled with blooming quince, and the garden was a fabulous green, the mossy stone lantern already lit with a flickering light. There was a mesmerizing tranquillity to the place. A knock on the door interrupted her trance of admiration.

"Hey, someone stole your bed, too," Brenda exclaimed as she walked into the room.

"Oh, Brenda, there are no beds. The maids will lay out a futon on the floor for us."

"I knew that. Boy, you must think I'm really ignorant. Look, they gave me a free kimono." Brenda help up a cotton robe.

"No, kimonos are much more formal; that's just a *yukata*. It's to wear to the bath. Shall we?" Annie invited, slipping into hers.

"What? Take a bath *together?*"

"Everyone does."

"Forget about it!" Brenda laughed. "What do you think I am, some kind of pervert?"

. . .

Dinner at the inn was magnificent. Even Brenda loved it, though she was unimpressed with the last course—plain white rice. Then Bob, Elise, and Brenda were ready for bed—"or futon, we should say," Brenda reminded them.

Annie, though exhausted, was too excited to try to sleep. "Do you think it would be safe to take a little walk?"

"Safe as houses," Uncle Bob assured her. "There's no street crime here, and you won't get lost because Kyoto is laid out on a grid, like New York."

Annie ventured out, a little hesitantly at first. But the night was soft, the moon was out, and every view intrigued her. Buddhist temples knelt beside Shinto shrines crowded next to teahouses and bars. Private houses seemed each to be protected behind a wooden gate. Cobblestones glistened wetly under her feet. It seemed so exotic, so Asian, yet she felt so deeply at home.

She got as far as the bridge that spanned the Kamo River, the boundary of the Pontocko district, where the famous geisha reigned. Annie stood on the bridge and watched the reflection of lighted windows and lanterns on the water. Why haven't I come here before? she asked herself. I have always been fascinated by Japan. Why did I wait so long? Why is my stay so short?

She was swept, all at once, with a sense of recognition. She should stay in this place. Here, it seemed, there was order, beauty, and peace. Buddhism, bonsai, and kimono. She felt so "right" here. She had to return to Japan.

At that moment, almost as a gift to reward her for her new promise, a woman in full traditional dress appeared at a gate, her kimono glowing in the moonlight. By her long sleeves and elaborate hairdo Annie recognized her as a *maiko*, a geisha in training. The young girl glided by her, silent as the river below. What a strange and wonderful place, Annie thought. And in this moment of peace, she thought, I *can* write. She knew that now. And with this awareness, satisfied and at peace, she returned to the inn and her futon.

They spent the next day sight-seeing and shopping. The Imperial Palace, a teahouse for lunch, and then buying pearls in the afternoon.

"And now, ladies, I think it's time to get down to business. Tonight we meet Tanaki," Bob Bloogee reminded them. "He's holding a banquet for us."

"Black tie?" Elise asked.

Uncle Bob smiled. "Well, formal Japanese style. It will be a geisha dinner. Mr. Tanaki has sponsored many."

Annie's eyes glowed.

That night they readied themselves for Gion, the oldest and most revered geisha district in Japan. Annie dressed carefully, in a subdued dark blue suit. Ready early, she joined Brenda, who was still dressing.

"So, are they prostitutes or what?" Brenda asked as she struggled into a black dress.

"Certainly not," Annie told her. "They're artists. That's what *geisha* means. They're dancers and musicians, and they're professional conversationalists."

"Yeah, yeah. Just like actress-slash-models back in New York," Brenda said cynically.

"No, Brenda. It's an incredible honor to be invited to Gion. Foreigners rarely get to go, and women almost never. An evening will cost over a thousand dollars a geisha. They were the geisha of the imperial court."

"Right. Tell me they only plunked their guitars for the princes of the blood."

"*Samisens*, not guitars. No, they did grant the pillow privilege, but only if they wanted to. They were the first working women of Japan, Brenda."

"Working girls, it sounds like."

"They set up a kind of union back in the sixteenth century. They were the only women of substance who didn't have to marry. And they never had pimps. They had—still have—sisterhoods, with older geisha sponsoring young ones."

"Well, I say they sing like cats and wear too much makeup. Anyway, what makes *you* such an expert?" Brenda asked.

"I don't know. I've always been drawn to what the Japanese call 'the water business.' Geisha managed to pull off a lot of things without ever being either too pushy or sordid."

"Still, women here are really downtrodden," Elise said as she joined them. "Uncle Bob told me he's never met Tanaki's wife. That all businessmen entertain without their wives; that younger men go to bar girls and that older businessmen have geisha to help with their entertaining. What a country!"

"Oh, I don't know. At least here there is a convention that people observe. Men don't just walk out on women. And women do rule in the home. Most Japanese men hand over their paychecks to their wives," Annie reminded them.

Elise shrugged. Since she'd never had financial problems, it didn't seem like much to her, Annie supposed. "Well, let's get going. Uncle Bob and Tanaki await us."

Gion was a reserved-looking group of streets where discreet gates obscured lovely gardens. There were no neon lights, no signs of bars. The teahouse opened from its courtyard to a large room. Mr. Tanaki, his assistant Mr. Atawa, and several other men were already assembled. Bob Bloogee was led to the seat of honor, the *tokonoma* at his back. Annie knelt beside Mr. Wanabe on one side and Mr. Atawa on the other. But it was Tanaki who drew her attention.

He was old—perhaps in his early seventies, perhaps older. It was hard to tell. But he had what the Japanese call *iki*—the Asian equivalent of *chic*. His suit, a dark blue silk, was perfectly cut, as was his hair, a thick white thatch. His French cuffs were immaculate, the gold links that held them incised with a family crest or sign of some kind. On his left pinky he wore a small signet ring.

Perhaps he felt her eyes on him, for he looked up at her then. His own, deep brown, hooded, appraised her for a moment.

Why, he's sexy, she thought with surprise, and had no more time to think as the banquet began. It started with the *maiko* and geisha filing in, the *maiko* resplendent in brightly colored kimono and obi, the geisha's more reserved, more subtle. Smoothly, they moved to a place behind each guest and began to pour from the sake bottle each carried.

Annie looked over to Elise. Drinking, even to excess, was expected at a banquet such as this. But Elise deftly turned her tiny sake cup upside down on the table. The geisha looked at her for only a moment, then smiled and bowed her head. Annie sighed.

Next came the first course, always a raw dish, to be followed, Annie knew, by a vinegared, a boiled, a roasted, a baked, and so on. "Do you care for our food?" Mr. Atawa asked in perfect Oxford-accented English.

"Very much." Unlike the others, who seemed at a loss with one another, they talked about his job as a translator and assistant to Mr. Tanaki and of the performance soon to come.

"The *maiko* will retire and one of the geisha will dance while others play. Then Okiko, a very famous geisha, will sing *kouta*. Those are our ballads. Like haiku, but a bit longer. Do you think you'll care for them?"

Annie was sure she would, especially with Mr. Atawa's deft

simultaneous translation. One was about a geisha's loyalty, another about leaving Kyoto. They were short, and Brenda rolled her eyes at the dissonance, but Annie found the lyrics breathtaking and evocative. As Mr. Atawa translated, Annie's eyes shone. She looked across the table to see Mr. Tanaki once again watching her. She looked away and blushed.

What a strange country, she thought. Where courtesans are immortalized, even worshiped, but wives must remain anonymous. Where loyalty is an absolute, but men such as Tanaki split their time between family and geisha. She shook her head in wonder and looked up to see Mr. Tanaki's eyes on her again.

The following morning they were ushered into Tanaki's office, which was large but sparsely furnished—a shoji screen divided the space into a traditional Japanese area and a westernized one with a rosewood desk, an antique leather-topped table, and eight chairs. Both Mr. Atawa and Mr. Tanaki rose and bowed as they came in.

Mr. Wanabe presented the gifts they had brought, traditional for any visit, and Tanaki ceremonially presented his offerings.

"Please thank Mr. Tanaki for the wonderful opportunity to share the banquet last night," Annie requested of Mr. Atawa.

Tanaki asked something of Atawa. "Did you enjoy the music?" he translated.

"Yes, particularly the kouta by Izumi," Annie said. Tanaki bowed.

They moved to the chairs, though Annie wished they could have sat Japanese style. She felt Tanaki would be more comfortable that way, and after all, everything depended on his temperature.

After some pleasantries, Bob Bloogee cleared his throat.

"Mr. Tanaki. We come with some news. It seems that Maibeibi is being hunted. You have become a Wall Street target."

Mr. Atawa looked shocked for a moment, then translated. Tanaki shook his head and murmured.

"Many are hunted, few are brought down."

"Well, in this case, there is cause for concern. Mr. Gil Griffin of Federated Funds Douglas Witter has bought up blocks of stock, some bank holdings, and those of pension funds. He's promised very good returns . . ."

Atawa was translating simultaneously, then he turned to them. "Mr. Tanaki believes the majority shareholders will stand with him. If not, he is no longer necessary here."

"That's a gamble we prefer you not take, Mr. Tanaki," Elise said. "We have reason to dislike Mr. Griffin and his methods. We think your interest would best be served, as would ours, if you take more active steps."

Tanaki spoke to Atawa sharply. Mr. Wanabe cleared his throat. Annie watched the silk curtain descend. She knew the decision was made.

"Let me outline the proposition we have," Elise continued, oblivious. She told them how Bloogee Industries was willing to buy the money-losing Maibeibi Shipyards right now, scotching Gil's cash-raising plan, and how Bloogee would then sell the Portland Cement Works, which Maibeibi could use in their huge development project in Oregon.

Annie watched as Tanaki simply waited. It was all over. He had made his decision. Just as the geisha were being replaced by bar hostesses, traditions were ending. In the global economy that had followed Japan's economic miracle, there was no room for emotional decisions.

Annie sighed. Her eyes wandered around the room. Little of the man was visible in this office. There were a few plaques, a picture of Tanaki with Gerald Ford taken on that president's trip to Japan. And next to it was a picture of Tanaki and his family. A wife, quite a bit younger than he, but still middle-aged. Three daughters in their twenties. And a son. A son. Annie looked more closely. Staring at her from the silver frame was the unmistakable face of a Japanese teenager with Down's syndrome.

After she had shown him her wallet-sized picture of Sylvie, Tanaki had stopped the meeting and taken her out onto the terrace. He left Atawa behind, with directions to take the others to tour the moss garden. Then they stood in silence for what seemed like a long time. Then he turned to her. "You are unusual woman. Most unusual. I am right?" Tanaki spoke elegant, if accented, English.

Annie, completely surprised, nodded, then shook her head. "I don't know."

"You know," he told her, and then smiled, but his eyes stayed sad. "How old is your girl?"

"Almost eighteen. And your son?"

"Hiroshi is fifteen."

Annie wondered if the boy was a disappointment to his father. After all, it was the son who was expected to carry on the family and the business. But somehow in this extraordinary encounter with this extraordinary man, she thought not.

"He is an old soul, Hiroshi," Tanaki said. Then he was silent for a while. He turned, at last, back to Annie. "You are married?"

"Not anymore."

"Your husband is dead?"

"No. No. He . . . he left."

"Ah. American men. Very weak. I watch them. They have no sense of family, of what is . . ." He paused searching for the English word. "They look only at today, like children. Today's woman. Today's profits. Today's investment. And when woman, profit, investment, is older, it is over. They are not fathers. They were not good fathers to Detroit." He shook his head. "And Japanese men are following. They will be like Gil Griffin in ten years."

Annie nodded, shocked by such openness from the man, a stranger and a Japanese. "You know Gil Griffin, then?"

"I know many Gil Griffins," he said. "Let us talk of more important things. You like Kyoto?"

"Oh, very, very much. It is like a dream to me. Somehow, it feels as if I have always known and loved it."

"You are Christian, Mrs. Paradise?"

Annie nodded, though she was far from sure.

"Then, unlike Buddhists, you do not believe you may have lived here before."

"No, but I wish I had. It is so perfect, such a right way to live."

Tanaki shook his head. "All of that is ending, though. It is the old Japan, dying. This economic miracle has been no miracle at all for most of the people. Just hard work, much pressure. All of the ugliness of the West. And soon all the old beauty will be no more."

"It may change, but it doesn't have to die."

"It will. I will be replaced. The empty souls will take over."

"No, Mr. Tanaki. Please."

The man turned to her and cocked his head, appraising for a moment. "Perhaps, Mrs. Paradise, you would like to see the Imperial Palace Katsura?"

"Oh, yes," she breathed.

He nodded. "Then you and I will go tomorrow."

. . .

Annie knew that a privilege was being extended to her—a privilege and an unusual opportunity. It took a special permit for anyone, much less a foreign woman, to view the villa of Hideyoshi, the sixteenth-century ruler.

"Tanaki's got a crush on you," Brenda warned. "Watch out—he'll jump you in the teahouse."

"Brenda, don't be absurd!" Elise told her. "Annie, it's very difficult to get into Katsura—it's considered by most experts to be *the* ultimate Japanese achievement in architecture and gardens. Kobori Enshu, the designer of the garden, insisted there be no limit on cost or on time, and no interference."

"Sounds like a government job," Brenda commented.

"Hardly. The gardens are designed so that wherever you stand seems the best view, and there are four teahouses—one for each season."

"Is it perfection?" Annie asked.

"I don't know," Elise admitted. "I've never seen it."

Brenda whistled and turned to Annie. "Now I'm sure he's got the hots for you. Look, couldn't you warm him up and convince him my idea is good—trade off the shipyards and stay the boss?" Both Elise and Annie stared at Brenda until she shrugged in defeat.

"Be sure to see the murals by the Kano school of painters," Elise said. "They're supposed to be spectacular."

And they were. Katsura, with its breathtaking frozen perfection, wasn't cold or too formal—at least not to Annie. "The perfection, the simplicity, frees you," she said to Mr. Tanaki as he stood outside one of the structures and they looked out at the gardens. "It allows the spirit to rest, rest completely," she said with wonder.

"All done for Hideyoshi. So much beauty, possible only

because of his wealth." Tanaki turned to Annie. "He was a general and became dictator. He was a violent man."

"Hard to believe," she said, looking around her. The pine needles were swept up, each pebble seemed placed; in fact she was sure they had been. They stood together in silence. After a time, she began to walk and Tanaki followed her, silently.

Elise had been right. Wherever she and Tanaki moved in the garden, one could view ultimate beauty. Annie felt something deep inside her move, or break free. Something about this marriage of mankind and nature was so right, so perfect. Paradise.

There, on the gentle green rise, she at once knew something more about the world. Like all spiritual events, it was wordless, transcendent, indescribable. For a moment, a timeless moment, each thing, each molecule, was perfectly in place, in time, and she with it. A depthless feeling of joy mixed with sadness pierced her, moved her. She was flooded with gratitude. And she knew she would never forget it. She turned to Tanaki. "Thank you," she whispered.

His only response was a bow.

They eventually walked through the other two parts of the villa, and Annie dutifully looked at the paintings.

"They have been renovated—no, you say *restored*. For the first time in five hundred and seventy years."

"Very beautiful," Annie said.

"I, too, prefer the garden." Tanaki smiled. Outdoors, he turned to her. "It is time for luncheon. Will you dine with me?"

She nodded, but when she did, he only led her deeper into the gardens. They continued the walk, Annie holding her enlightenment inside her like a fragile thing. She hoped that nothing would spoil the mood. They came then to a wooden teahouse, set beside the water.

"Please," Tanaki said, and she removed her pumps and stepped up the two steps to the matted floor. She knelt beside him in the teahouse, transfixed by the views. The perfection and peace continued, increased by the beauty that was doubled by the pond's reflection.

"We shall lunch," Tanaki said, and a screen slipped open. A kimono-robed woman smiled and bowed. "*Kyobento*. Picnic lunch, Kyoto style," Tanaki told Annie.

"We may eat here?" She was delighted, and shocked.

"It is an indulgence. You see, I paid for the restorations." The woman handed Annie a lacquer box, black and shining with a pattern of iris on the cover. Tanaki took one, too. He opened the top lid, slid it under the box, and revealed the rice, fish, salad, and pickled vegetables of Kyoto cuisine.

They ate together, at first in silence. Annie sighed. "This is all so special. It has changed me."

"Ah, yes. Beauty transforms." Tanaki also sighed. "Your psychologist Maslow did experiments on beauty. Do you know?"

She shook her head.

"He and a colleague made three rooms: one beautiful, one plain, one ugly. They asked participants to judge pictures of faces. In the beautiful room, their judgments were positive, but in both the ugly and the plain rooms the same pictures were seen negatively." He sighed. "That is very bad news for me. It means that plain is not good enough. All must have beauty to see beauty. And there is only one Katsura." He turned again to Annie. "Tell me again about this Sylvan Glades. What does it look like?"

Annie described the school, the community and grounds, and Dr. Gancher. "It is expensive, and that makes it exclusive," she admitted, "but with more money . . ."

"I would like to visit this school. Perhaps bring some doctors from Tokyo to see it. And . . ." He paused. "Perhaps bring my son to see it, too."

Annie nodded. "I think Hiroshi might like it. My daughter does."

Tanaki looked at her. "Mrs. Paradise, do you think I should fight Mr. Griffin?"

"Yes, but I don't believe you should fight him your way."

"Not let the stockholders decide? Show their disapproval?"

"No. A good father must sometimes lead his children. Give the stockholders immediate treats, and long-term benefits. Sell the shipyards, buy the cement plants. Gain profits, stop losses, stop Gil Griffin. And Bloogee Industries can make the shipyards work."

"And if they cannot?"

"Nothing lasts forever, Mr. Tanaki. No matter what we would like. And some burdens are too heavy to carry alone."

He looked away from her, over the railing of the teahouse, past the rocks, past the lake and the pine trees. "Yes," he said. "You are right."

The initial contracts—letters of intent, really—had been drawn up quickly and signed. By the following day they were all assembled around Tanaki's low table on flat cushions doing the final-contract read through. Then Mr. Atawa was called away. He, in turn, called out Mr. Tanaki, who then gestured to Bob Bloogee. The women looked at one another and shrugged.

"More boys' stuff," Brenda surmised, and shrugged again. "You think we can get out of here soon? My knees are killing me."

But before they could answer her, Bob Bloogee returned and knelt beside Elise. "Dear, I have some bad news. It's your mother."

"Helena is sick?"

"It's worse than that, I'm afraid. Elise, your mother is dead."

They packed and were ready to leave Kyoto in less than an hour. Walking out to the car, Annie watched as Brenda supported Elise on one side, Bob Bloogee lending support on the other. For Annie, too, it was painful to leave. It wasn't the sweetness of their victory that she wanted to savor. Something else had been given to her here, something planted, and the tiny sprout needed nurturing and care, the way the gardens at Katsura had been tended. New York was not a place to cultivate one's garden, Annie realized. Taking her seat beside Elise, she thought of the *kouta* by Izumi that she had heard at the banquet just two days before:

> *My lonely departure*
> *From Kyoto*
> *Hiding tears,*
> *At the train window.*
> *Oh, please, please.*
> *Someone give me*
> *A cup of tea.*

7

Good Night, Lady

Elise stood in the doorway of the main viewing room at Campbell's Funeral Home and looked around. Every detail had been planned by Helena, saving Elise from the horror of last-minute funeral decisions. At least she didn't have to try to imagine what her mother would have wanted. No need for that, Elise thought. Everything was being done exactly as Mother had planned, right down to the luncheon at Mother's apartment after the cemetery. Elise knew that her mother had taken care of her one last time, and despite feeling so lost and sad, she was able to smile. Thank you, Mother, she thought.

Elise longed for courage, for something to help her get through this ordeal. Her loss and grief was mixed with tremendous self-pity. She craved a drink, she had to admit, and again remembered the pact she and Brenda had made at Thanksgiving. In Japan, when she had gotten the news of her mother's death, her first thought had been to have a drink. The reaction, the desperation of it, frightened her. It wasn't until that moment that she realized how dependent on alcohol she really was. And with it came her renewed resolve not to drink. No matter what. But this was hard.

She sighed and stepped forward. It was time to be her

mother's daughter. She took her place on the line, shaking hands and nodding mechanically. Lally Snow, Gunilla Goldberg, some people she didn't know, then an older woman, Mrs. Sonderberg, Mother's friend. Annie, of course. And Brenda, who gave her hand a tight squeeze. Dr. Brennan, the Van Gelders, several dozen others. It would be a good showing. Despite Helena's long illness, people had not forgotten her. Elise was grateful for that.

She saw him then as he walked into the room, his eyes looking about as he moved. Larry came toward her. He stood before her for a moment, his arms open slightly, inviting but not intruding. She hesitated for the briefest second, then took two steps to him and felt herself enfolded. The lightness of his hands on her back caused a deep, low moan to escape her lips. Then in the next breath, she was crying.

At first, the depth of her sorrow frightened her. Suddenly she knew what the fear was about. Her life stretched before her with no one standing guard against her own mortality. There was no one now between her and eternity, she thought, and clung more tightly to Larry's broad chest.

She let her sobs subside, then accepted the handkerchief he offered. "What do you want me to do, Elise? What do you need?"

"Just stay near me, Larry. I need you." She dabbed at her eyes again, then took his hand in hers and returned to her place on the receiving line, Larry by her side. It seemed as if a veil had been lifted, a mystery solved. Not only had her mother stood guard over her mortality, she thought, but Helena had also stood guard over Elise's morality.

Now there was no one to judge, no one to pull her back, no one to remind her not to be ridiculous. It's my life, she kept thinking, over and over. How do I want to live the rest of the time I've been given? She thought of Uncle Bob's words: *Don't waste the second half of your life.*

I thought I was doing the right thing when I married Bill. But the rules have changed, Mother. A younger man would not have been appropriate in your time, but it is now, Elise thought. Why is it okay for men to love and be loved by younger women? Why can't I love and be loved by a younger man? And I am, Mother, I know it. He loves me. Maybe not forever. He might even disappoint me. But right now, I know he loves me, and I love him, and *that* I won't let go of, no matter how ridiculous anyone thinks I may be.

Annie watched Elise sink into the down cushions of the sofa in Helena's living room and kick off her shoes.

"Whew, my feet are killing me," Brenda said as she kneaded her own stockinged feet.

"Wait a minute, Brenda," Annie said with a smile. "That's Elise's line. You weren't on your feet all day today."

"Oh, that's right. I'm just so used to *kvetching*, I fell right into it," Brenda agreed. "How are you holding up, kiddo?" she asked Elise, her voice filled with concern.

Brenda amazes me, Annie thought. She couldn't have been kinder to Elise. After Larry left, in fact, Brenda seemed to consider Elise her personal charge.

"I could use a drink," Elise said.

"And I want a piece of chocolate cake," Brenda said. "What else is new?"

"I'm not going to have a drink." Elise sighed.

Brenda grimaced. "I guess that means I'm not going to have any cake."

"I'm so proud of you both," Annie said. "With all you two

have been through, you both have been real troupers about keeping your deal."

Now Elise grimaced. "But brother, did I want a drink today." She shook her head and looked at Brenda. "It's not easy, is it, kid?"

Brenda shook her head slowly. "No, it's not. But, at least I've lost some weight."

Annie noted Elise was pensive for a moment. "And I got some clarity." She paused for a moment, as if considering whether to speak freely or not, then continued, "Today, at Campbell's, when Larry put his arms around me, I knew, beyond a shadow of a doubt, that I love him. And that he loves me."

Annie watched Elise first look at Brenda, then turn in her direction.

"And he's written a screenplay. It's wonderful, really wonderful. It's all about a woman's loneliness and fear. It's brilliant, really. It should be produced. It must be produced. But I've been hesitant to produce it . . . and star in it. Mother's advice was to never, never, put up my own money for a movie I'm in. But"—she looked at her friends and smiled—"Mother wasn't always right. So, I'm going to do it."

Annie thought of Miguel, and how her dates with him were becoming more and more important. When she'd got back from Japan early, she was surprised to find how happy she was when Miguel phoned almost the moment he heard she got in. Maybe Elise has something, too, she thought.

"Good, Elise," Annie thought. "At the risk of sounding like a cliché, life is too short."

Annie noticed how tired Elise seemed. "I better get going, ladies. Where are you staying tonight, Elise?"

"I'm going to stay here so I can get an early start packing things in the morning. I'm afraid if I go home, I won't be able to ever come back."

Brenda was surprised. "But you'll be here by yourself tonight, won't you? I heard you send the servants home." Brenda shook her head. "I'm staying with you, Elise." She paused. "Unless you *want* to be alone."

"Oh, no, Brenda. Thanks. I *don't* want to be alone."

"I could stay, too, Elise. Want me to?" Annie asked.

"Let's have a pajama party, girls," Elise said, smiling.

Aaron sat, biting a pencil, leaning at the granite-topped counter in the SoHo loft he shared with Leslie. He looked down and reread the sentence he had just written. *Therefore, with my resignation, I expect the removal of my name from the Paradise/Loest Agency.* He shook his head, took the pencil from between his lips, and erased *with* and replaced it with *effective from the date of.* He read it again, shook his head, and sighed. Then the intercom buzzer sounded.

It was Chris, downstairs. He buzzed him in. He'd expected Chris to show up eventually, apologize, and tell him he'd either quit or been fired. When Chris's call had finally come, it had been a relief, since all his other predictions had been dead wrong.

Right after the fiasco, when he spoke to Drew and accused him of disloyalty, Drew had laughed and pointed out that Aaron had started it by bringing Chris into the firm. Then Karen had resigned, but not because of the Jerry takeover but because she was pregnant—pregnant by Chris! Julie hadn't taken his calls at all, and, mortified, Aaron had decided not to contact any of the other bastards. Only his formal resignation was left.

He went into the bathroom, looked at himself in the mirror, and moaned at the drawn face peering back. He splashed it with cold water, knowing that wouldn't take the place of a good night's sleep and a shave, then walked to the door at the sound of Chris's knock. The kid was probably hysterical over the pregnancy. He'd need advice.

"Dad, we have to talk," Chris said as he walked into Aaron's living room and slumped onto the sofa. Aaron had been looking forward to this visit since Chris's telephone call, but now, seeing Chris's expression, he was concerned. Was this another wrong prediction?

"What's up, Chris?" Aaron asked. "I haven't seen you since the partners' meeting."

Chris shrugged. "Not much. Except I'm moving in with Karen, we're having a baby."

Aaron almost smiled. The kid was that naive. "Whoa, Chris. Let's not rush into this. You know, Chris, she's been around the block a couple of times."

"What's that supposed to mean?"

"Well, just look before you leap. Don't take on a responsibility that isn't yours."

Chris was silent for a moment. He probably needed time to let it sink in. But when he did speak his voice was angry. "Don't say that. I *know* the baby's mine. We didn't plan it for now, but I want Karen, and I want the baby." He stood and strode over to the window, looking out on a brick wall. He cleared his throat, his back to Aaron.

"Well, what will you do for money? Where will you work?"

"Dad, Karen supports my decision to stay on at the agency and work with Jerry, learning the business. Jerry *is* the best director of commercials in the industry, and he's willing to teach me." Chris turned from the window and faced his father. "I love the business. I'm staying at the agency."

Aaron could hardly believe it. "Chris, Jerry manipulated me out, for chrissakes, it's as simple as that. You're going to go on working with the man who did that to me?" He leaned over and clasped Chris's shoulder, though the kid looked away.

Chris shrugged his father's hand off without looking at him. "He just did to you what you were going to do to him, Dad. And only because you forced his hand. Don't play 'white knight' with me." Now Chris turned his gaze to his father, then he turned away again, looking at the floor. "When you and Mom broke up, I didn't take sides, although I felt deeply for Mom and her loneliness. You had Leslie. Mom had no one. But I didn't judge you."

Chris's eyes glistened, but he turned to look at his father despite the brimming tears. "I tried so hard to keep you on a pedestal because I wanted you to love me. I've always wanted that. But then I heard about what you did with Sylvie's trust fund, and I couldn't ignore the facts any longer. Like how you conduct business, trying to push Jerry out. How you were treating Mom, and not even visiting Sylvie."

Aaron felt Chris's eyes burn into him but could not look away, like watching the aftermath of a terrible accident on the side of the road.

"She wasn't perfect enough. Neither was Mom. Neither was I. I saw that. And I saw how it was Alex that you always boasted about to people. He *is* perfect, the poor bastard. Perfectly miserable. But he's your number one son. Do you know, when I first came to work at the agency, people were surprised to hear that Aaron Paradise had *two* sons? Most people thought he only had one, 'the doctor.'"

"Let me explain," Aaron said weakly. "I didn't mean to hurt you . . . you or anyone."

"I'm sure you didn't *mean* to hurt anyone. But you *did*. You hurt me and Mom and Sylvie and Jerry and Karen, and just about everyone else you used. You could never see yourself as you really are." Chris uttered a brief, harsh-sounding chuckle, then continued, "You know, I've learned a lot at the agency, and I'm grateful for that. But I've noticed something about people. Jerry thinks he's funny, but he's not. And Karen thinks she's tough, but she's not. I've always thought I was dumb, but I'm not." Chris hesitated, then said slowly, "Almost no one sees himself clearly, Dad. You, for instance, think you're a nice guy."

Aaron felt the tide of his rage rise. "Wait until you see even more clearly. You're nothing but a little peon that Jerry's using right now to undermine me. See how fast you're dropped, once my name is off the door."

"Dad, as long as I'm there, the firm will still be Paradise/Loest."

Aaron felt as if he had been slapped. The tide turned, washing away anger and leaving desolation.

"You drop people when they don't measure up to your expectations. You don't just love them in spite of their flaws."

Chris got up, walked across the room, and turned back. "So, Dad, I came to tell you this: I don't need you to love me anymore. And I don't need to love you. I may love you—I don't know yet—but I don't *need* to."

Aaron watched his son walk out the door. As it shut behind Chris, Aaron finally put his head down on the arm of the sofa and then, after what seemed a long, long time, began to cry.

8

Couples

It had been a very hard day. Annie looked up from her desk in the large, sunny kitchen and rested her eyes by staring out the window at Gracie Square. Today, she had not been working on the manuscript, which was growing, slowly, slowly, since her return from Japan weeks ago. Instead she'd been doing what she thought of as her math homework.

She figured she could get almost a million for the apartment. Maybe a bit more. Then, if she sold off the furnishings—some of the things her father had left her were quite good—she might raise as much as another $150,000 or a bit more. Invested conservatively, she could safely count on its bringing in $100,000 a year. That would pay for Sylvie's school and leave a little bit over. With prudent management, it could take care of Sylvie for the rest of her life.

Where Annie would live and how she would take care of herself was not so clear. She could sell Nana's cottage, but she hated to do that—it wouldn't bring much anyhow, and she'd always hoped to leave it to the boys. She still had a little cash—enough to rent a modest apartment for a year or so. She could get a studio apartment for about a thousand a month. Then what?

The image of herself, divorced, living in a boxlike room

and trying to make it on a few hundred a week frightened her. She could move somewhere less expensive, but where? Everyone she knew was here. She had lived in New York all her adult life.

Of course, Aaron would be getting quite a payout for his share of the agency, although all the particulars weren't worked out. And some of that money would flow back to Sylvie. Annie had to smile. By selling Bill's antiques to Brenda, Elise had managed to revenge herself on Bill, jump-start Brenda's career, and get some of Sylvie's tuition paid. All in a single shot.

But Aaron had told her he needed funds to start his own firm, and Annie had decided never to depend on him again. She alone would ensure that Sylvie would be cared for.

She pushed herself away from the desk, got up, and began to wander through the apartment. It was a clear day, but the bright sky did nothing to cheer her. Living in a dark room, giving up this light, this view, this comfort, was an awful thought. That was why she had put off thinking about her finances for so long. But it was clear that she had to *do* something.

She wouldn't take money from Elise, nor would she accept anything from Mr. Tanaki, though she was delighted that he was thinking of endowing Sylvan Glades and had, to that end, underwritten Dr. Gancher's visit to Japan to consider establishing another school there. Lastly, she had had to give up on Aaron and his promises to repay the trust. No, she'd just have to do something on her own.

The silken rug caressed her bare feet, the dark shine of the mahogany dining table glinted. There'd be no room in a new place for a dining table. She walked through the living room to the conservatory. The bonsai, her favorite, the maple, seemed to nod at her as she walked by. They had been her friends, her witnesses, as she had grown up here, as she had faced her reality. She gently stroked a small, red leaf. They couldn't survive without a greenhouse. No more bonsai.

She walked out onto the terrace. A light breeze ruffled her hair. Tears filled her eyes. I should be grateful, she told herself, that I have all this to sell. So few people do. I'll be able to see all three of my children happy, healthy, and taken care of. I'm not going to starve, and I have good friends, and I may even have some talent. I'm in charge of my life, and I'm taking the steps I need to. A nice man seems to like me, and I like him. That's more than most people have. I should be grateful.

But she wasn't. At the moment she was selfish and she was miserable, and she sat down on the terrace bench and wept.

That evening, Annie and Miguel went out to dinner, to a Cuban-Chinese restaurant on Columbus and Ninety-fourth Street, farther uptown than the yuppies and trendy West Siders usually got. Her depression from earlier in the day gradually lifted as they drank some inexpensive wine and Miguel made her laugh. He told her about his progress with Morty Cushman—he thought he had a good chance to get him before a grand jury—and that he could build a strong case against Gil Griffin. It wouldn't solve her problems, but it certainly cheered her. As her father had said, only the strong get justice. She made up her mind that she would be strong.

After dinner, they walked down Columbus and stopped at the Museum Cafe for a nightcap. Annie rarely got over to the West Side. It seemed younger, more frenetic, more ethnically diverse than her quiet neighborhood. Maybe she could find a place to live over here. But being here alone, she had to admit, she would feel anxious. Now though, she was not alone. She was delightfully coupled with this charming man. She felt a part of the Friday-night bustle as they walked the avenue, arm in arm.

When Miguel led her along the cobblestone path by the planetarium, she knew what was coming. And she was glad.

"Are you cold?" he asked, feeling her shiver. "Shall I take you home?"

"I don't want to go home. It makes me too sad right now."

"I know." He looked at her sympathetically. "My place makes me sad, too." He paused. "I would like to make love to you."

"I know. I want you to."

"But I wouldn't want to take you back to my place. It isn't my home. It's only where I sleep. It wouldn't be right."

She smiled at him. She thought back to the hassle sex had become with Aaron, and how it had led her to Dr. Rosen. Nervous, yet also confident, she thought, somehow, she wouldn't have a problem with Miguel. It's because I'm not outraged with him, she thought. It was that simple.

For a long, long time she'd been so angry with Aaron that she couldn't for a moment have let herself go. If I had, she thought, I might have tried to kill him. He had been truly dreadful to her, and for so long she had refused to see it. She paused for a moment, thought, and then she smiled. She looked at Miguel, then took his hand and led him to the corner. She put out her hand to flag down a cab.

"I know where we can go," she said quickly, as if inspired.

"Driver," she told the cabbie, "please take us to the Carlyle."

They stood very close to each other in the elevator, the key to Room 705 dangling loosely in Annie's hand, just rubbing against Miguel's thigh. Her hands were cold, as always, but she felt the heat that seemed to come in waves from his body. Wordlessly they walked down the hall. Easily, she fit the key into the lock and opened the door.

"Miguel," she said as they entered the room, "I'm nervous."

"So am I."

"I don't do this every day."

"Neither do I."

"I haven't slept with anyone except my husband since I was married."

"Neither have I. I mean, not your husband. My wife."

"Really?" Somehow, it seemed to Annie that men always had partners. Knowing Miguel hadn't didn't make her any less nervous now. I guess, she thought to herself with surprise, I still expect men to take care of this part. She remembered how easy Aaron had made it for her in Boston. So easy and so wrong.

Now, she took a step toward Miguel, taking his warm hand in her own cold one and gently pulling him to the side of the bed.

"You're so cold!" he exclaimed.

"Warm me," she told him.

He smiled and lifted both of her hands to his face. "This is Paradise," he said, nibbling her ear.

"Annie Paradise?"

"St. Michael in Paradise."

"Not yet, but soon."

He bent his head and kissed her palms, his breath so warm, so deliciously tickling her. Then his mouth was on hers, soft, pressing her down onto the bed.

Brenda lay on her back in the wide white bed, her hand on her stomach. It was definitely flatter. She could feel a bump on either side of her rounded tummy. When she had discovered the first knob, she'd become frightened: in her family lumps equaled cancer. But when she felt around for a few minutes and found the second one, she'd laughed out loud—despite her scare she had to admit it was funny, not recognizing your own hipbone.

She turned her head to look at Diana, sleeping beside her. Brenda smiled. It was sweet how childlike Diana's face became when she slept. Devoid of makeup, her straw-colored hair tousled, she looked like a farm girl. Brenda could hardly believe that this brilliant woman, this funny, successful, savvy broad, actually loved her, and loved her just as she was.

And lately she'd been better and better, Brenda had to admit. It wasn't just the weight. It seemed to Brenda that for the first time she felt confident enough to say what she felt and not just make wisecracks. The best part was that Diana listened and never seemed to think Brenda was nuts or unreasonable.

She pulled the sheet up over Diana's shoulder and tucked it in. Brenda was happy. She had enough money, she had a new job, good friends, she had her self-respect hack, and she was loved. How long can this last? she wondered, and then grimaced to herself. Cynicism was the old Brenda, and now she recognized it as a sign of her despair. As long as this lasts, it lasts, she told herself. Some people never get it at all. I'm one of the very lucky ones.

Okay, so who else would call themselves lucky to wake up a middle-aged, divorced, fat lesbian? Brenda asked herself. Well, maybe not fat anymore, she admitted. Maybe just chubby. But definitely the other three. Lesbian. She was trying hard to get used to the word, to the idea. Lesbian, queer, dyke, femme, diesel, gay, whatever. Brenda Cushman, girl queer. She turned again to look at Diana. If loving Diana made her a lesbian, then she was proud of it. Because loving Diana was a great thing to do.

And Anthony and Angela seemed to like Diana, too.

She wasn't sure what they suspected, but so far she'd laid low on the sex issue. In fact, she was laying low with the kids in general. Just yesterday Anthony had called *her*. and Angela complained that she wasn't getting to see her mother often enough. Brenda had to laugh at the turnaround. Well, maybe she *had* been a little overinvolved before.

Now she was too busy to intrude too much on their lives. Work at Paradise/Loest was fascinating, and she really felt as if she was contributing. And Diana was enthusiastic about everything, from a new restaurant to a great book to an emerging stand-up comic. And the sex! Even now, awake alone in the dark, Brenda had to blush. She had never realized that sex could be like this, so in tune, so sensuous, and yet so romantic. Brenda shook her head. If she was a deviant, a queer, whatever, so she was. It had been there since she was a very young girl. This was who she was and she was never going to give herself up again. Her only prayer was that Diana would keep loving her. Because love, however it came, was always such a miracle.

Gil stretched out in the wide, comfortable first-class seat. As always, he had bought two tickets so that he wouldn't be troubled by someone next to him during the eighteen-hour flight from Tokyo to Kennedy. Even in first class, you could be stuck with any kind of moron these days. But more important, this way no one would see his godawful fear of flying. Not even Kingston. Especially Kingston, who might spread it round the office.

A flight attendant offered him a blanket. These oriental women were charming, absolutely born to serve. Gil took two of the blankets, told her he had a bit of flu and wanted to sleep it off. Then he took two Seconals, washed down by a sip of champagne. Takeoffs were the worst. He'd get through that and then conk out.

He thought of his meetings this last week and grimaced. The trip, supposed to last six days, had stretched out into more than three weeks. Oriental men weren't charming at all. They were obstreperous little monkeys, but in the end he had managed it. And against hellish odds. The Japanese banks initially were hesitant to partner up with an American on the verge of taking over one of their own, despite the huge rewards. He presented his proposals, how he'd buy out Maibeibi, sell off several of the divisions, how they'd recoup all their investment off that and still own the central, profitable core. It was a classic case of having your cake and eating it, too. In the end, they'd caved in to avarice, just as, again and again, he had seen their American cousins do.

The only thing that troubled him was the damn lost file. Mary had sworn she'd put everything in the portfolio he'd taken with him, but some of the data was missing. *He* certainly hadn't mislaid it, he knew that. But when he'd left her, she had not been thinking well. And if she was angry, and she had been, she might have done anything with it, out of spite.

He shifted uncomfortably in his seat. It wasn't only the takeoff that was making him squirm. Perhaps the three weeks had been a good thing from that point of view. Time to forgive, to forget. He regretted the incident. He was determined not to fall into a hateful pattern the way he had with Cynthia. It was stupid. He wasn't the kind of man who hit women. He turned to look at the briefcase beside him. In it he had an exquisite opera-length pearl necklace, triple strand, a Christmas gift and peace offering to Mary. He was sorry and he longed for the comfort of Mary's body. He loved her. This incident, unfortunate as it was, would blow over. He'd taken care of the Japanese, he'd take care of Mary, and then he'd make his move with Maibeibi. Kingston had already put in the buy order. They were ripe as a cherry for picking, and he was determined to have his way. Then he'd be the undisputed king of the hill. No one had pulled off a coup like this. It made the others look like pikers. And it wasn't just the money. It was the prestige. He'd be recognized by everyone for this.

Meanwhile, Mary lay alone in the big canopied bed of the Fifth Avenue apartment. It was almost five A.M. New York time, but Mary wasn't sleeping. Beside her, the ice pack that she had used to reduce the discoloration of her eyes was still lying across the Porthault pillowcase. *Just me and my icepack,* she thought grimly. The swelling had taken almost two weeks to heal, but somehow she didn't want to give up the relic. The humiliation of showing up at work, of going to the benefit committee meeting, of sitting with Gunilla Goldberg and Bette Bloogee, her eye swollen shut! It had discolored first to an angry purple, then a green; then, after more than a week, an ugly yellow. Even now, alone in bed, she felt the pain of it. Everyone staring, then quickly averting their eyes.

The benefit was only two weeks away, and she couldn't imagine how she would attend. For years and years she had plotted, worked her ass off, sucked up to so many idiots, struggled to get into the center of things, into the elite world of wealth and power and talent and achievement. She wasn't especially beautiful, and she had no unique talent. So she'd just plugged away, hoping the right opportunity would come along. And now, now that she was nearly there, this had to happen.

What would she do? Leave Gil and try to make it on her own? She wasn't so stupid as to try it—she knew that for now she was here on sufferance. Gunilla, Anne Paradise, Lally Snow, Bette Bloogee, all of them would simply wait and watch her staying power. It would take a few years, at least, to solidify her position. But how could she stand to stay with Gil? How could she?

She still couldn't believe that Gil had hit her, that he had had the nerve, the complete lack of respect. Even Bobby, for all his faults and with all his macho foolishness, even Bobby had never dared to hit her. Mary lay there, on the hundred-thousand-dollar, rice-pattern-carved, four-poster Sheraton bed in the apartment that had cost close to a million dollars a room, and she realized that she had never felt so impoverished. And hurt. So badly hurt. How could a man who loved her do this? She couldn't sleep, and she couldn't think of what to do. She tried to imagine packing and leaving, but her practical side would never allow that. Oh, no. Not after all you've been through. You're notorious now. Who would hire you? No Excuses jeans? But if she stayed, she'd have to reconcile with Gil. Go to the Fantasie FunFaire with him. Appear in public with him, work with him, live with him, sleep with him.

"Never," she said aloud, shifting in the big, empty bed. She'd never let him inside her again. How could she stay, yet how could she go? Again and again, in the weeks since he'd left for Japan, she had gone over and over this. No way to stay, no way to go.

Quietly she cried. But the tears still hurt her bruised eye. Oh, if only she could cuddle up to someone, warm herself against Bobby's back, be held, be comforted. She'd like to be with him right now. Just for a little while. If only she could have an orgasm, a release, she could sleep. She had to get some sleep. Slowly, she let her hand creep down between her legs and thought of Bobby. His hands were enormous, his legs were so long. And his dick! She felt a little shiver pass over her. It had been difficult to get excited about that part of Gil after Bobby. Now she wouldn't have to try. "Bobby," she whispered as her fingers slipped inside the moistness his image had caused. "Oh, Bobby."

Duarto woke suddenly and didn't have to open his eyes to know Asa wasn't in bed next to him. Now that Duarto had gotten used to it—and surprisingly quickly—it was almost a sixth sense that woke him tonight, telling him that he was alone. It was different, this aloneness. Different from all those nights he had been sleeping alone since Richard died. It was different because, lately, he was falling asleep with Asa beside him, almost every night.

There had been no declaration of undying love, no decision to move in together. In fact, there had been no decision at all. Each day they approached as a new day. Duarto took nothing for granted, nor, it seemed to him, did Asa. Each day seemed to lead to another day, another date. It had evolved.

Without a decision, Asa spent more and more time at Duarto's apartment just off Fifth Avenue at Tenth Street. Slowly, Duarto began to make room for Asa's clothes in a closet, then Asa would come by with groceries and cook dinner, then Duarto found himself giving Asa his extra key. Asa still kept his apartment, but it seemed ridiculous to be paying rent for a place he *never* used anymore.

Duarto looked up at the ceiling, unable to make out the trompe l'oeil blue sky and white clouds he had painted there. If Asa was in the bathroom, he was there a long time. Duarto sat up, suddenly afraid. No light leaked out under the bathroom door. "Asa?" he called out. When he got no response, Duarto jumped out of bed and walked onto the balcony overlooking the living room in his studio duplex. "Asa?" he called out again in the darkness.

Duarto heard a sound, then was able to make out Asa, sitting on the sofa looking out onto the street through the two-story-high window, his figure now becoming distinct in the light from the streetlamp.

"Asa," Duarto said as he came down the stairs and walked over to him.

Asa sat forward, his elbows on his bare knees, his face in his hands. He was crying. Duarto went up to him and touched Asa's shoulder, but didn't say anything. He wanted Asa to know he was there.

After a moment, Asa's sobs began to subside, and he spoke. "Oh, God, Duarto, I have something terrible to tell you. You're going to hate me."

Duarto felt his knees tremble, and he sank down on the floor on his buttocks before his legs gave out. He didn't want to ask. He wanted this to be a dream, but he knew it wasn't. Asa's skin was warm under his touch. He couldn't bear the thought of what Asa had to tell him. He knew. After Richard, after all those men he knew who were dead, nothing had to be said.

Nor did Duarto want the words spoken, as if giving them sounds would give them life. He couldn't go through this again. Asa couldn't expect him to. After all the care he had given the dying, after all the loss, why now, why more?

But he also knew he couldn't *not* care about, and care for, this man. Asa had become central to his life. He tried to swallow the anger he suddenly felt at Asa. Why didn't you tell me earlier, you bastard? Before I fell in love with you? Before I made a commitment?

Then he shuddered. Oh, Jesus, if he's sick, we haven't been having safe sex. He told me he was negative, and celibate for five years. God, God, don't let him be a liar. Please, I'll take care of him if he's sick. Just don't let him have lied to me.

"Asa, I don't theenk I can ever hate chou, What's wrong? Have you lied to me about sometheeng? Tell me, Asa." Asa shook his head, and Duarto pushed on. He had to hear it all, right now. "Tell me the truth now, Asa."

Asa gulped his sobs, then, his voice a whisper, said, "I'm in trouble, Duarto. I sold out to Gil Griffin. I'm in trouble with the SEC, they're investigating Gil for stock fraud. They'll get me, too. I wrote a column for money. Gil paid me." Asa began to cry again. "Don't hate me, Duarto. Please."

Duarto stood up, feeling giddy with joy. "Thees is what you cry about, Asa? The SEC?"

Asa nodded his head. "I could be arrested."

Duarto leaned his head back and bayed like a wolf at the moon, then rolled over on the carpet and began to laugh. Asa lifted his head, shock showing on his face. "Duarto, are you crazy? What are you laughing at?"

"You're alive, and I'm alive," he said, then came over to Asa and put his arms around him. "I thought you were going to tell me you were seeck, that you had . . ."

"What? No, I'm not sick. I'm in perfect health. But, Duarto, don't you see how serious this is? I'm in big trouble."

"No," Duarto shouted. "You are not een trouble. Lyeeng een a hospital bed with tubes in your arms, that's trouble. The SEC? That's only a *problem*. A legal problem. That's why the devil made lawyers." He hugged Asa. "Now come back to bed. Everytheeng weel be okay."

"Oh, Larry," Elise was whispering at that moment. He was inside her again, moving so very slowly, coming so very deeply inside her. They had gone to bed, exhausted after the day of work, and slept for five hours.

Since the day after the funeral, she and Larry had been inseparable. And it was marvelous. He made her laugh, he held her when she cried, he pampered her when she wasn't busy pampering him. Now he had awakened her. Only a young man would do it. A young man in love. She felt alive, awake, refreshed. Five-fifteen in the morning was fine with her. There was no more confusing Greenwich time, no blurriness. She hadn't had a drink since her bargain with Brenda, though she'd come close. But now work and love were making her happy. Happy and sober. She looked up at his face, and he smiled at her, so sweetly, and stopped moving long enough to lean down and cover her forehead with kisses.

"Darling, beautiful Elise. I love you so much."

Once again, as usual, Elise felt tears spring to her eyes. Once again, Larry paused, but by now he had accepted the fact that her happiness made her cry, and he wasn't disconcerted. For her part, she tried hard not to be disconcerted by the comparison of her skin against his, her experience, her money, her age, against his. "Not yours against mine," he had said. "Yours combining with mine."

And so, she was making the film. That was decided. Their talents combining.

She had never had so much fun working with anyone. Not even with Truffaut. They did combine well, and Elise was delighted to find out how much she still knew about moviemaking, and how much Larry depended on her. She'd broken her mother's rule: she was bankrolling the production. Maybe it was a mistake. Maybe Larry was a mistake. But she also knew his eye was good, and his vision sure. The film would be small, tight, perfect. As long as her performance held up, it couldn't fail to be a succès d'estime. But Elise was hoping for more. Much more.

Now she held her arms out and surrounded Larry's shoulders, hugging him tightly against her. He moaned. She moved her hands down his broad back, into the hollow before the swell of his buttocks, and then over them, clutching them, pushing him more deeply into her. "So good," he murmured into her ear. Still, he hung back. She had already come once, earlier, but he moved his hand to just above where he entered her and began to stroke her again. It was almost too much, too sensitive. She shivered, just the tiniest movement, but he stopped immediately. "No?" he asked.

She smiled at him. "Could we stop a minute?"

Larry's eyebrows raised. "Are you all right?"

"Of course, darling. It's just that I'm so happy. The first day of casting went well, didn't it?"

He smiled, relieved. "Isn't that a cause for celebration? And I've got something here for you." He moved her hand down to his hard-on. She closed her hand gently around him. This was good, so good, but she simply had to talk.

"Larry, I want you to know that no matter what happens, no matter if the film fails, even if I become a laughingstock, or if you wake up one day and have to leave me because I'm an old crone, I want you to know that no one has ever made me so happy, or been so kind."

"And you've made me happy. And you've made Mr. Happy happy. And that makes you happy. Happy all the time."

"Why does a man name his penis?" Elise asked with a smile, looking down at Mr. Happy.

"Well, what am I supposed to call it, 'Hey, you'?"

Elise laughed. "Sometimes you are incredibly stupid."

"Thank you. All just a part of the Larry Cochran service, ma'am. And speaking of servicing . . ."

He was inside her again, now kissing her mouth, his tongue echoing his long, slow strokes. Elise held herself tight around him. She knew this man, his kindness, his talent, even his silliness. God, she loved him so much!

"Never talk about leaving me," he said. "Never leave me.

Please. Never leave me." His voice was deep, a moaning whisper. "Promise," he begged.

"Never," she promised. "Never."

Bill watched as Phoebe snorted the last line of coke off the glass coffee table. Copies of *ArtNews* and *Rolling Stone,* an old paint rag, and the remains of last night's Chinese takeout littered the table's surface. She had been excited when she called him last evening at work, excited and a bit incoherent, but when he got down to the loft, she had been almost comatose. Then, after mumbling to him for several hours, she had risen at midnight. Since then, she'd been almost manic. They'd hit every bar and club in SoHo and come back, at last, to the loft. Christ, it was almost dawn. She said she was snorting just a line or two to wake herself up. Then they were going off to her studio so he could see her new work.

He was worried. For weeks now she'd been more and more agitated about her work, but also more and more secretive about just what it was. "It's a breakthrough. A real breakthrough. I think that with Leslie's help I've finally torn away that bullshit separation that media puts between art and life. I mean it. This is important."

Bill hoped so, because he was nervous. Phoebe was still adamant about the rehab, and he had to take her side, but now he wasn't sure that this permission therapy was working. He wondered sometimes what that Rosen woman was up to. There was no question that Phoebe had become stranger and stranger: the drugs, the sex, the moods—they all seemed to be spinning out of control and he was spinning, too. Phoebe's family had cut off all communication and had already started an action to assign a conservator. And money was tight. Elise had spitefully sold off his collections for a dollar, and he could do nothing legally because of the wording of the divorce settlement he had so quickly signed. Phoebe, the job, his finances, were all too much. Yet he loved her. He could never give her up. She needed him.

But lately, since she'd started this permission therapy with Dr. Rosen, she'd only wanted anal sex. Bill had been delighted, at least at first. It was so forbidden, so very, very sexy, and when Phoebe stripped and leaned across the bed, her knees on the floor, begging him for it, he'd been thrilled to oblige. He'd been hard as a pipe. Phoebe had said something about reenactments, about primal scenes. All well and good, but it was starting to wear on him. The problem was, it was *all* she wanted, when she wanted sex at all. It was, well, he didn't know. Obsessive, maybe.

Now, Phoebe rose from the table, her body as thin as a whippet's. She looked over at Bill, and with a sinking feeling in his stomach and a quickening at his crotch, he recognized that fevered grin. Phoebe continued to stare at him, almost as if she were in a trance, then, slowly, began to pull up her skin-tight, tiger-striped, spandex dress. She pulled it as high as her waist, exposing her shaved labia, her thin legs, her sharply jutting pelvic bones. She turned her body but continued to stare at him over her shoulder. Slowly, slowly, she began to bend over, using the low coffee table to support herself. Then she moved her hands to her buttocks and separated her cheeks.

"Do me, Daddy. Do me there."

Mesmerized, his cock hard against his leg. Bill moved toward her. He bent over her, putting his arms around her. "No!" she hissed, jerking herself away. "Don't touch me. Just do me."

"Phoebe, I—"

"No talking," she hissed. "*Do* me."

"Please, Phoebe. Please." He felt his cock straining to be released. "Please talk to me. Let's lie down. Let me hold you."

Something was wrong. Something was very wrong. To his surprise, Bill felt his eyes tearing. The hell with that. He'd give her what she wanted.

"Just *do* me," Phoebe hissed again, and so he did.

Aaron woke up, the dream still more real than the form of his wife, lying stiffly in the darkness beside him. It was the bird again, the bird that swooped down and picked him up in its sharp talons, soaring high, only to drop him, plummeting through the air. He awoke before he hit the ground.

He stilled his panting, turned to look at Leslie, and wondered just how long she was going to keep up the freeze. After the trust fund losses she had shut him out for weeks. Now, with his plan to take over the firm in shambles, she had again put up the wall.

Aaron felt her warm form near him in the bed. Christ, things couldn't get too much worse than they were now, could they? He had fucked up his career, his daughter's future, his new marriage, and his relationship with his ex-wife all in a matter of months. What the fuck was wrong with him? Was he a loser?

Aaron began to sweat. Christ, he *wasn't* a loser. Losers were people over thirty who rode the bus, who wore off-the-rack suits, who had to rent dinner jackets and called them tuxedos. Losers had thighs that rubbed together when they walked. They lived in suburbs and boroughs. They were the bridge-and-tunnel crowd. They picked up their own dry cleaning. They couldn't get into Nell's. Christ, they'd never *heard* of Nell's. They had receding chins, receding hairlines, protruding bellies. They borrowed money from HFC. He wasn't like that. He had made something of his life. His son was in medical school. He'd created Paradise/Loest from nothing. He wasn't a loser.

He turned to Leslie, rubbing his hand down her narrow back. Surprisingly, she moaned and turned toward him, though she kept her eyes closed. Her breasts, so beautifully large and rounded in contrast to her small frame, were pressed against the top of her blue silk teddy, her left nipple just peeking over the top of the lace. Gently, cautiously, he ran his hand down, down, into the deep cleft of her cleavage; then he buried his head there.

Oh, to be, safely, on her breast. Aaron felt he could lie there forever. It wasn't sex he wanted. It was warmth, it was comfort, acceptance.

But Leslie was moving her hands to his thighs, then to his crotch. Then she jumped back as if scorched.

"What the hell does that mean?" she asked, obviously fully awake and staring at his limp member.

"I don't know. You're the sex therapist." He was empty of desire for her; empty as an oyster shell picked clean of its cargo. And he knew in a moment of clarity that he'd never feel desire for her again.

"And *you* are an impotent bastard," she spat.

"Just perfect for a castrating bitch." He rolled over.

He looked at the clock: 5:33. Predawn. The hour of the wolf. Aaron knew he'd never get back to sleep. He wondered for a moment if her rage at him was so deep that she felt it in her sleep. Whatever, there was no comfort there. Oh, well, he thought, it had been a disaster, he had to admit that. In the dark, Aaron almost smiled at the irony. It wasn't until he had married a sex therapist that he couldn't get it up.

Morty Cushman lay in the earliest light of dawn, watching the prison window lighten. Around him he heard the snores and the other, more threatening noises. He tried not to identify them, but they were unmistakable. Deep-throated moans, sex-talk in harsh whispers, the long "Oh, God" of someone's climax. Morty was disgusted and very frightened. He knew the universal truths, that men confined without women became sexually aggressive with other, less powerful men, and that sex was a marketable commodity in prison. He knew it, but he somehow never really believed it. Never wanted to believe it, least of all now.

But realizing that someone was paying for something terrified him. If his TVs and ghetto blasters ran out, he knew he would have to buy safety some other way. He remembered the crack the trustee had made about having dentures and was grateful for his electronics. But what would he do when they ran out? He tried not to think about that now. From below him, in the lower bunk, the rattling snores continued in a steady tattoo. Thank God for that. Big Mo was asleep. Morty himself hadn't slept at all.

He'd cut the deal with De Los Santos. Now it was certain he'd do time. But not much. Not if he testified against Gil. And he would. He'd sing like a bird to get out of this hell.

So the wake-up bell would sound and then breakfast, which he wouldn't be able to eat. Morty wasn't sleeping or eating well here in prison. And as far as sex was concerned, Morty didn't even want to think about it.

9

Is You Ain't Maibeibi?

Since her return from Japan, Annie had felt reborn, suffused with new energy. Mr. Tanaki, his wife, and their son were coming to New York and going to visit Sylvan Glades. Dr. Gancher's visit had been a success, and Tanaki was planning a community like it north of Kyoto.

I've done good, she thought. And filled with new power, she got an idea. A naughty idea. A wonderful idea. Icing on the Gil Griffin cake.

"You're not going without me," Brenda insisted as she sprawled across the sofa at Elise's office. "What will you do if you get into trouble?"

"What will *you* do if I get into trouble?" Annie asked. She slipped off her pumps and replaced them with sensible boots because of the slush outside. She appreciated Brenda's loyalty, but she regretted that she'd told her about her plan, now that Brenda was being so unreasonable. "You two have done so much about Gil. I haven't. I have no money to put in Maibeibi. And I feel I *have* to do something."

"Are you kidding? You made the Maibeibi thing happen. If it weren't for you, Tanaki would have let Gil step on him."

"Well, I'm doing this myself. Don't be a nag."

"Don't be a martyr. You're not going by yourself. We don't

—

do that anymore. You, me, and Elise. We work as a team. Anyway, you *need* me. I'm used to fighting dirty. You haven't figured out all the strategic requirements."

"Brenda, this is only an act of vandalism, not a war."

"Not if we do it right. Anyway, Elise would kill us if we went without her. Plus, since her mother died, all she does is work on her movie. She's gone from alcoholic to workaholic. She needs a distraction."

Annie sighed. "All right, all right. But I'm not responsible if something goes wrong. And you watch, that's all. I do it, and if anything happens, *I* take the blame."

"Okay, okay!" Brenda chortled. "So what's the timing?"

"Tomorrow afternoon. I know that Miguel De Los Santos is seeing Gil then."

"Great. That ought to screw up his day."

Brenda's voice changed. "So how are things between you two?" she asked, obviously more than a little curious.

"What do you mean?"

"Oh, don't play coy with me. All those lunches and dinners. Don't tell me that you're only discussing business." Brenda paused. "So, you're dating?"

Annie shook her head. "No, not really. We're just seeing each other."

"So you're 'seeing' a Puerto Rican?"

"So? Brenda, don't tell me you're prejudiced. How could you?"

"I was raised by Jews and Italians, the most prejudiced people on earth. But hey"—she made an airy-fairy movement—"I've risen above." She paused again. "So you approve of Diana?"

Annie took Brenda's hand. "If you're happy, I'm happy," she said in her best Jewish-mother accent. "So about tomorrow: we need paint remover. I can get that. And some shirt cardboard. Have you got rubber gloves?"

Brenda nodded. "How will we get in?"

"Just walk in, I guess."

"You see, you do need me! They'll never let us *walk* in. And if they do, they'll watch us."

"You're right." Annie stopped and thought for a moment. "I'd be too nervous to drive. And I'm not sure I could do a quick getaway."

"We need a driver."

"Hudson," Annie said. "But I wouldn't want to get him into any trouble. Maybe it's best not to get him involved. I mean, we *could* get arrested."

"Nah, in New York you can only get arrested for homicide and tax evasion." She hooted, thinking of Morty.

"Be serious, Brenda. Gil Griffin is still a force to be reckoned with." Annie remembered Stuart's warning and shivered.

"Then let's get Elise to drive the silver cloud. Christ, no one scares her. And let's face it, Annie. She'd murder us if we left her out of this caper."

Gil Griffin sat, coolly surveying this worm, this annoying piece of shit from the SEC who had the gall to stare right back at him. "Of course, Mr. Delasantis."

"De Los Santos," the worm corrected.

"Yes, of course. Well, we are prepared, of course, to cooperate in any way we can with your investigation, short of disclosing anything that would be proprietary. That has always been our policy." It sounded as glib and insincere as it was meant to. "We've been strict in our compliance with SEC regulations and will continue to be."

"Have you?"

Gil stopped for a moment and looked again at the Puerto Rican bug before him and wished he could crush the man under his shoe. The insolence! The audacity of this spic! It was unbelievable. But best not to let his annoyance show. Let the lowlife drive Stuart Swann round the bend. Gil ignored De Los Santos's question.

"If you need any help, our compliance officer, Mr. Swann, will answer any questions you have. Now, if you'll excuse me, I—"

"No. I'm afraid I have some questions for *you*."

Only he didn't look afraid. He looked . . . Gil searched for the word. He looked feral. Gil was enough of a hunter to recognize the look of someone who thought he was close to a kill.

"Really? What do you wish to know that can come only from me, Mr. De Los Santos?"

"Well, firstly, I wondered about one particular account: Aaron and Anne Paradise in trust for Sylvie Paradise."

Gil felt his stomach tighten, but made sure no sign of concern showed on his face. So that was what this was about. Fuck that little cunt. She must have gone to these pencil pushers. Well, she'd better be ready to have old Aaron's face smeared in the gutter and herself look like the fool she was. He shrugged. "It doesn't ring a bell. But we do have over three hundred thousand trading accounts. Who is the broker? You would have to talk to him." He paused. "Why? Do you think there's been any irregularity?"

"No, I don't think it."

Gil waited, but De Los Santos was silent. Gil looked at him, and he kept looking back. Interesting. Gil had to admit this one was more than the usual hack. One of his first laws of business was never to underestimate the opposition. Always a fatal error.

"What *do* you think, Mr. De Los Santos?"

"I think I'm going to bring you down."

Gil sat for a moment, the silence of his office almost ring-ing in his ears. This was absolutely unbelievable. The man must be crazy.

"Really?"

"Really."

Gil surveyed De Los Santos. Ill-fitting suit, frayed cuff. Cheap shoes. But the eyes. They were as dark as his own were pale, but they shared his intensity. De Los Santos's eyes were the eyes of a fanatic, an assassin. For a moment, the hairs on the back of Gil's neck stood up. Then he smiled. Too bad this worm had chosen the wrong victim.

"Ever played squash, Mr. De Los Santos?"

He saw him hesitate, confused. Fine, just fine.

"Yes, in college."

"Would you care for a game now?"

De Los Santos, nonplussed, paused. Then he shrugged, nodded.

Gil picked up the phone. "Mrs. Rodgers, call Boseman and cancel our squash game. But keep the reservation for the court. I'll be going on down there shortly. And have Max bring my dinner jacket and things to the locker room. I'll be leaving for the Metropolitan directly afterwards." He hung up and looked back at De Los Santos. "Shall we adjourn to the playing fields of Eton?"

Miguel stood, in borrowed Nike sneakers, on the smooth blond wood of the squash court. He'd been very good back in college, but he hadn't played in some time. He remembered the rules, of course, such as they were. Hit the ball so that it didn't bounce between the wall and the line, then return any-thing the motherfucker slung at you. Of course, there weren't a lot of squash players in his neighborhood. Miguel had gone back to handball to keep in shape.

He was sweating already, but it was nervous perspiration, not the clean sweat of activity. Griffin looked cool. His equipment, his game, his turf. Well, Miguel had played four or five tough sets of handball this past weekend, at the playground on 116th Street, and the competition there was fierce enough. Plus, he was younger than Griffin, he told himself, and angrier, too. This was the man who had hurt Annie, a man who'd ruined his own wife, cheated common people, a man with no remorse. Miguel shifted the racquet familiarly in his hand. Now he wished he could smash the ball directly with his hand, the way he'd like to hit Griffin, the arrogant *pendejo*.

Above the court, a glass window-wall allowed observers to watch the match. Only one man stood there now, elegantly attired for sport, as Griffin was, in a polo shirt and shorts. Miguel had accepted borrowed shorts but was wearing his own undershirt.

He would dress as his *muchachos* at the handball courts did. Fuck these *gringos*.

Griffin bent over, stretched, and turned back to Miguel. "Ready?" he asked. Silently, Miguel nodded. Griffin lifted his racquet and served.

The ball came slamming out of nowhere, past his ear, then behind him, almost too quick for him to have his racquet up. Almost, but not quite, and he returned it, though without finesse or strategy. Wham. It was sent back, high, and off the back wall. Miguel twisted, jumped, and slammed, once again returning it, but once again having no time for strategy.

The ball was harder to hit than in handball, even with the racquet extending his reach. And it was far harder to place. Wham. The ball rocketed off the walls, the noise ricocheting with almost as much force as the ball itself. Miguel had forgotten about the noise. In the boxlike court, the noise was thunderous. And each time Miguel hit the ball, Griffin returned it with renewed force and a scream of effort as he controlled the orbit of the sphere. Miguel hated the noise.

He was already breathing hard and covered with sweat. Little matter. He would not let this *jefe* win. He must focus.

Wham! It came at him, but Miguel had time to concentrate. It wasn't thinking: it was the absence of thought, other than the pinpoint of awareness. Wham! Ball, racquet, opponent, movement. Now. Slam it there. He did. Now. At him again. Wham! Twist, jump for it. Swing. He was fast. Concentrate. Get the *pendejo*.

Wham! Past him. He tried, diving for it. Too late. Missed it. What was the score? No matter. Just hit him. Hit him. Wham! And again. And again.

Gil jumped, missed, and fell heavily on one foot. Miguel heard him curse, then mutter. What had he said? Was it only "shit" or had Miguel heard "spic"? Had the bastard dared?

Miguel served, slamming the ball with all his strength. Wham! And wham! Miguel was rage, movement, power. He would not lose this game.

Gil Griffin limped out of his elevator and through the lobby to the lift that took him down to the garage. He looked elegant, cool as ever in his Bijan dinner jacket, but his legs were actually shaking, and he couldn't tell if it was from anger or exhaustion or both. His ankle throbbed, the pain maddening, but he could tell it was only a slight sprain. He would ignore it. Just as he had to ignore Miguel's level gaze after the match, and ignore the snickers in the locker room.

It had been a stupid mistake to play the man. Like a trial attorney asking a witness a question that he himself didn't have the answer to. And like an attorney at a trial, bungling in front of an audience. He had only taken a single glance up to the observation window, but he had seen a dozen faces, at least. Swann, DiNardo, Boseman. They must have paged people to watch him go down in flames. Well, it was his own goddamn fault.

He stepped, wincing, into the spotless, well-lit garage and moved past the guard's office without acknowledging the man's hat tip. Christ, he wished the goddamned party weren't this evening. It was the last thing he needed. Now, he simply longed for the silence and power of his baby, his E. But as he approached the Jaguar, he stopped. It was unbelievable. Someone had left a soda can, or something worse, right in the center of the hood. Jesus Christ. There were eleven layers of hand-rubbed lacquer finish on that car, each one lovingly, expertly applied, and some asshole piece of shit had left their garbage on the hood. Unbelievable!

He felt new energy, fueled by rage, well up in him. Christ! They paid God knows how many hundreds of thousands of dollars a month for high-tech security systems down here, for those deadbeat security bastards to keep out vagrants, madmen with a grudge, terrorists, and the homeless, and this still happened. The entire city was a cesspool and nothing was safe.

With a yell to the old black guard, he ran across the cement floor to the Jaguar and grabbed the can off the hood. As he lifted it, the cardboard that had been placed across the bottom of it was pushed aside by the heavy, glutinous contents, which poured out onto the hood, dripping, moving slowly, like lava, all across the car. Without thinking, he threw away the can, violently casting it off, and heard it clatter somewhere behind him. Cupping his hands, he scooped up some of the goo and pushed it off the hood, leaving an immense smear. Horrified, he watched as the finish on the car began to bubble, the deep,

deep red paint curdling up, sizzling and blistering like bacon in a pan. "Jesus Christ!" he shouted, and redoubled his efforts, but then he felt the stinging as his hands began to tingle, then burn, with a hellish ferocity. They were on fire! "Christ!" he screamed, and rubbed them down the front of his dinner jacket, but the burning continued, intensified.

"Acid!" he screamed to the guard. "They've got me with acid!"

"It's paint remover, sir," the guard said, carefully holding the retrieved can by the top edge. "I'll have it checked out, though."

"But it's burning! It's eating into me," Gil screamed. He began to hop with the pain of it, but when he came down on his sprained foot, he screamed again. "Help me!" he yelled. "Help me!"

"I'll call for aid. Meanwhile, try this." He brought a red fire bucket filled with scummy water over. Gil plunged his arms in, up to the elbow. Thank God! Some of the pain stopped. Perhaps it wasn't acid. Cautiously, he rubbed one hand against the other, removing the stuff under the water. It hurt, but it was better.

"If I wipe you down with a rag, it might help," the guard offered, pulling out an old chamois.

"Don't touch me with that filthy thing, you stupid nigger," Gil yelled at him as he held his hands out helplessly and looked down at his ruined dinner jacket. Then he looked over to his car. The paint remover was still merrily bubbling on the Jaguar. Holy Christ, the car was being destroyed before his eyes.

Gil turned away and vomited into the fire bucket.

"Oh, my God!" Annie whispered as she, Brenda, and Elise crouched on the back seat of Elise's sedan, peering out the rear window.

—

499

"Don't go all compassionate on us now," Brenda whispered fiercely. "That's the man who robbed your daughter."

"But his hands are burned," Annie said, thinking of her patients at the burn center. "I never meant to burn his hands."

"Those hands are the hands that beat Cynthia." Elise added grimly.

"It's not serious. It just stings," Brenda whispered. "Look, the son of a bitch just threw the rag at the guy that was helping him. What's that all about?" She jabbed Annie. "Crack open the window. I want to hear this."

Annie and the others could hear Gil's screams of rage plainly now. After a minute, Brenda started to laugh.

"He's going to get the guard fired," Brenda said to her friends, as if translating. "The guard is a tub of shit. A cocksucking, shiftless, black, motherfucking—"

"Stop, Brenda, we can hear," Elise said, beginning to laugh also. "Oh, my word, I never heard such language!"

Gil was raving. The guard had picked up the thrown rag and was standing with both hands on his hips.

"Get me help, you asshole."

"Get your own fucking help," the guard said, and throwing his hat on the pavement, began to walk away. "This nigger's just quit. He don't like working for scumbags."

The three women fell over each other, the tears streaming down their faces.

"He should never have called the guy 'shiftless,'" Brenda said.

10

Bette and Bob's Bash

It was another New York society ball, and as always, a limousine drove up to River House so that one social-ite could pick up another. It was more ecological. Larry Cochran visibly squirmed as he waited for the driver to get around the car to open their door. Then he helped Elise out of the car. It was the first time they'd be appearing in New York society together, and he, at least, was nervous. But Elise looked more serene, more beautiful than ever. She was dressed in the special costume that she, Brenda, and Annie had cooked up for the three of them, and she looked adorable.

Larry followed her into the building, then up to the Bloogees' penthouse. A butler opened the door and led them through a huge entry hall to a vast room where the walls were covered in a gold-brocade fabric. Over the enormous marble fireplace was a painting that looked a lot like a Holbein to Larry. That wasn't all. There was an enormous Turner, a breathtaking sunset on the Grand Canal. And what looked like a Paolo. Impossible. There were only half a dozen of those in the world. Hey, but who knows? This is the richest guy in America, he reminded himself. Maybe there are three more in the kitchen.

The room was filled with antique gilded furniture, the

tables covered with *objets* and vases of magnificent flowers. Larry had found it a little difficult to adjust to Elise's Park Avenue place, but this made hers look like the Joad farm. "Quite some place he has here."

"Yes, it is, isn't it?"

"It kind of shows what God could do if he had the money."

"Larry! You didn't say that. Alexander Woollcott did!"

"Elise," Larry said in an exaggeratedly patient voice. "Alexander Woollcott has been dead for years. I did say it, just now."

Elise made a face, but before she could say anything more pungent, Bette entered. She was breathtakingly lovely, dressed in a magnificent white chiffon gown, her shining auburn hair falling down her back, braided with white flowers. Bob Bloogee, dressed as a jester, followed in her wake. He was beaming.

"Ya ready ta go?" Bette asked them brightly. "Gee, Elise, ya look beautiful." She pronounced it "beeue-tee-ful."

"Doesn't she?" Larry asked.

"Indeed," Bob Bloogee agreed, smiling paternally.

But Elise, for all her good looks and good manners, stood transfixed, staring at Bette. "Bette, you are quite the loveliest girl I've ever seen!" Elise declared. In all her time in Hollywood, her work in European films, she had never seen anyone as perfect, as luminous as this. She paused. "But what are you costumed as?"

"A virgin," Bette said, and laughed.

It was another New York society ball, complete with beards. Brenda arrived with Duarto. They would meet their lovers here, in the museum rotunda. Asa was escorting Diana. Brenda was dressed in a quasi-baseball uniform, with a cap initialed FWC and her name embroidered on the jacket pocket.

"But what *ees* theese costume, Slugger?" Duarto asked. He was one of the minority of men in costume, dressed as a nun.

Brenda turned and proudly displayed the back of her jacket. *The First Wives Club* it said in Yankee-like red satin script. Below it, the international symbol for *No*, a red circle with a bar across it, blocked off a trophy. Below that was emblazoned the motto *Hell hath no fury*.

"Most unusual," Duarto commented.

"Look who's talking. A nun with a mustache!"

"All the nuns *I* knew had them," Duarto declared, and Brenda laughed. "I theenk you lose more weight, Slugger?" he asked, looking her up and down.

"Four more pounds. Don't I look divine?" Brenda did a little twirl. Her uniform pants fit snugly across her behind.

"Chou do!"

"Wait till my teammates get here." Brenda smiled. "We're all going public."

"I don't doubt eet. But really, I think chou are not so angry as chou used to be. Fat women wear ugly clothes because they are angry. This looks cute."

"Thank you, Dr. Freud. I have news for you. Fat women do *everything* they do because they are angry. But they don't usually get to *act* angry. It makes all the difference. Hey, here comes Diana. Now *she* looks good in black."

Diana, also dressed in rustling serge as a nun, walked briskly up to Brenda and Duarto. At her side, a full seven inches shorter than Diana, was Asa, dressed as a monk. Despite their shared clerical theme, they made an odd couple. Duarto smiled at Asa, seeing him truly at ease for the first time since they had met. Asa had learned today that he would not be prosecuted for his part in the Morty stock deal with Gil Griffin. Through Miguel De Los Santos's efforts, the DA had accepted Asa's plea bargain in return for his agreement to stand as a witness against Gil. Of course, Asa would never work on Wall Street again, but with Brenda leaving his business, Duarto had plenty of room for Asa to join him.

The foursome paired off comfortably into boy-boy, girl-girl couples, and harmony descended upon them, until an attractive waiter waltzed by. Duarto eyed him, then caught Asa eyeing him back.

"Forgive me, Father, for I have sinned," he confessed, and knelt for Asa's blessing.

It was another New York society ball. The black-jacketed waiters continued to circulate with trays of beautiful and tasty hors d'oeuvres, and the wine continued to be poured into stemmed crystal and sipped by elegant people who continued to murmur devilish little secrets and slanderous gossip and occasionally, to throw their heads back and laugh elegant laughs showing their well-cared-for teeth.

Annie and Miguel arrived, she costumed in the First Wives' team uniform. He was in chain mail, a white plume hanging from his helmet, a small dragon curled around his lance. They joined Brenda, Duarto, and the others in the foyer.

"It's all so beautifully done," Miguel De Los Santos said to Annie, looking up to the balcony above the rotunda, where a quartet was at that moment playing Mozart. "I'm impressed."

"It's just another New York society ball. What did you expect?" Annie teased. "Nudes on platters?"

Miguel laughed. "No, I mean that it's not at all *over*done. It's very tasteful. Opulent, but tasteful."

"We usually manage to be wretched without excess," Annie agreed. "Though I think you'll find dinner will probably err on that side. Lally can't control her urge to feed."

"Tell me about this crowd, Annie," he said affectionately,

taking her arm. "I'm ready to hear more about them than how they made their money."

"Okay, but I can't promise to leave out how they spend it."

"Go ahead."

"Well, that man with the thick, white hair over there—first American to climb all the major peaks of the Alps. Still climbs. He's seventy-seven. His wife's standing next to him, the one with the bun on her head. She spends six months of every year working with orangutans in Borneo." Annie smiled at Miguel. "They're nice people, and her work with the animals has produced some important scientific data.

"Now the short man talking to the tall one, the one dressed as a matador, he and two partners have opened the four hottest bars and restaurants in the city. They were the ones to introduce high-style Tex-Mex to the city."

"Almost as important a development as the Salk vaccine." Miguel smiled.

"They live together, work together, and maybe sleep together. Everyone calls them the Three Mesquiteers."

Miguel laughed, sipped his wine, and continued to look around. "I wonder how much Lila Acheson Wallace left for these flowers," he mused, eyeing the six-foot-tall arrangements of rubrum lilies, white roses, and allium, always kept fresh through her endowment. Then Annie noticed a tanned, blond woman in the crowd. "Look; do you see Shelby, Brenda?" Annie asked.

Shelby Cushman was wearing a green velvet hoop skirt complete with upholstery tassels. Her long blond hair was netted in a thick brown snood.

"Holy shit, it's the Tara *portières*! The bitch thinks she's Scarlett O'Hara!" sniped Asa.

"She does look awfully good for a woman whose husband's been in the slammer for weeks," Brenda admitted. "Of course, I always looked better when Morty was away."

Kevin Lear, the movie star, drifted by, accompanied by his new fiancée, the star of his latest film. Annie wondered, for a brief moment, what had happened to the last fiancée. Wives were no longer the latest in disposable, she guessed. So were fiancées. Lear, as always, looked handsome, his skin glowing with health. "Well, I know who *he* is at least," Miguel said, then looked past him and added, "Ah . . . the lineup is complete at last," as Elise, also wearing a First Wives Club jacket and uniform, appeared with Larry at her side. Larry was dressed as an umpire.

"Hello." She smiled at them, clutching Larry's arm. Behind them, Bob and Bette Bloogee waltzed up to join the group. Introductions and greetings rang out.

"So," said Bob, looking at the three teammates, "you're out of the closet."

"God, is it that obvious?" asked Brenda, eyeing Diana. Everyone laughed.

"Who's the tall, skinny one in the bizarre outfit?" Diana asked Brenda. She discreetly indicated a young woman, pale as death, dressed in a truly strange costume of chains and pieces of stuffed toy animals.

"That's Phoebe Van Gelder—Elise's ex-husband's current, if you can follow that," Brenda answered. "Boy, the Cromwell Reed partners are really going to *love* that getup."

"You mean that old guy with her is her husband? God, what a weird couple!"

"Look who's talking!" Brenda laughed and took Diana's hand to lead her in to dinner.

The Hall of the Temple of Dendur was stunning. The Egyptian temple itself stood on an enormous flat marble island and was lit dramatically, here and there, with spotlights, giving it an unreal, mysterious look. This left the rest of the vast room in comparative darkness, but for the hundreds of tiny candles flickering on the eighty or so tables. The candles illuminated the simple white orchids that seemed to float above them. Because it was another New York society ball, there had been fierce competition for the desirable tables. Women, and more than one man, had besieged Elise and Bette about the seating. The dozen or so key spots, the prime real estate, were on the island beside the Temple. The Wives had one of these. Behind them there was an area left open for dancing, and behind it was Peter Duchin and his orchestra.

"They have been around forever," Duarto quipped. "They played at my bar mitzvah," he added as the Club and their guests took their seats at their table.

"They played at my coming-out party," Elise rejoined, laughing. "Or was that *Eddie* Duchin?"

"Don't believe a word of it," Brenda said to Larry as they took their seats. "I can see you're gullible."

"No, I'm just open to experience. And I'm enjoying this one. But I must say I'm always a little disappointed at these affairs. Not that I attend them frequently—ahem—but seriously, the 'beautiful people'? This is an outright lie. Most of the women look so drawn."

He sucked in his cheeks and pulled his jaw way down. "So severe," he mugged in a throaty Park Avenue drawl, just as Lally Snow waltzed by.

Elise looked around at the crowd and laughed. He was right, of course. It was a look that so many of these women cultivated. Proud, superior, disdainful. And painfully thin. "Tom Wolfe called them social X rays," she said.

"Now, *you* look nothing like that," Larry told her. "You look like a real woman."

"I think that means I should lose some weight." Elise laughed. She nudged Larry. "There's Annie's ex, and his new wife," she whispered.

Both Aaron and Leslie were wearing dinner jackets, black ties, and sashes. "She looks like Patton," Larry observed.

Elise giggled. "What about Mary Griffin?" she asked, looking past him.

"What about her?"

"How does she look?"

Larry turned to look at the blond young woman beside the hawklike Gil. They were standing with the Bloogees, Sherman McCoy, and Sol and Gunilla Goldberg, a coven of the rich and powerful. Elise had already told Larry that Sol was cheating on Gunilla, and also that Gil had smacked Mary around. Now Larry shook his head in disbelief. The external image and the internal truth were hard to integrate. Mary, costumed as a milkmaid, wore a gingham dress, with a low neckline and winglike puffs of white organza at the shoulders. Her hair was glossy blond.

"She's very attractive," Larry appraised. "But my dear," he said, looking back at Elise, "she ain't got your bones. Like I said"—his voice dropped diplomatically as he leaned close to her—"you're the only really beautiful woman here."

It was another New York society ball. After a little more buzz and chatter, the twelve hundred guests were finally in their seats and ready for the first course: soup. The guests began to eat. . . .

"I hate consommé madrilene!" Phoebe Van Gelder protested, much too loudly, two tables away. Uncle Wade and Julia, her mother, exchanged worried glances.

The guests danced . . .

"You *do* want to dance, don't you, Annie?"

"Of course, Miguel! Right now!" She had loved to dance with Aaron. "But what will you do with your lance?" Miguel looked at her, laughed, and leaned it against his chair. Then he took Annie's hand and led her to the dance floor. She felt his arm encircle her waist and she leaned her body toward him, settling in comfortably.

"Why, you dance superbly," she praised him. "Where did you learn?"

"Not at Mrs. Stafford's," Miguel laughed.

Together they moved as one across the floor. When they returned to the table, Duarto was standing at their chair, listening to Gil Griffin's complaints about the apartment. Gil, his eyes intense, his face beaklike, turned for a moment, registered Annie with a cold grimace of dislike, and then Miguel, who was moving his dragon-entwined lance away from his seat. Gil's tight jaw tightened further in recognition and, perhaps, fear?

"Pretty small dragon," Gil sneered. "Is that the best you can do, Saint Michael?"

"All dragons are small once they have the fire knocked out of them," Miguel told him.

"Yes. And he has *such* a beeg lance," Duarto lisped. Then came the second course . . .

"Shrimp!" Brenda exclaimed. "The most beautiful shrimp I've ever seen!" Then she shrugged. "Just bring me a half of cantaloupe," she told the waiter. "And make sure it isn't an orange potato. I want a ripe one."

She looked up to see Shelby floating across the floor. "The nerve of that bitch, coming as Scarlett," she muttered.

Diana smiled. "It does take a certain arrogance, coupled with a lack of imagination." She thought for a moment, reached into the hidden pocket of her habit, and drew out a pencil and notepad. *Dear Scarlett*, she wrote. *I know your Rhett is in jail, and that your business is jeopardized. But don't worry, you can always go professional in your true calling. If you do, you are welcome to work for me.* Then she signed it, *Belle Wattling.*

"Oh, my God!" Brenda laughed. "Diana, you're even meaner than me!"

"Mean enough to send it," said Diana, and flagging a waiter, sent the note on its way. "My only concern is that she won't get the allusion."

The guests indulged in toasts and observations . . .

"So, now that you're assembled, may I lift my glass to the First Wives Club," Bob Bloogee proposed.

"Hear, hear."

Annie turned to her program and smiled. A whole page of it had *First Wives Club* written on the top and the No Trophy emblem emblazoned across it, compliments of Bloogee Industries.

"An expensive tribute." Annie laughed as she passed it around the table.

"A good cause." Bob smiled.

"Whattzamatter? Aaron and the new wife won't dance? He used to be the one who never sat down," Brenda observed to Duarto, sotto voce.

"Look at her closely," Duarto said. "Chee is one of those beeches that make a man pay and pay and pay. Chee weel grow fat while he grows theen."

It was another New York society ball, including insults . . .

Stuart Swann, on his way over to say hello to Annie, watched, with some confusion, as Mary Griffin approached him from the opposite side of the room, smiling and waving. Why was she so happy to see him? Had something changed? He smiled back and raised his hand to greet her. But Mary's face didn't acknowledge him as she moved toward the First Wives Club table, where she greeted Elise and Annie and Bette. "I heard that Gil had some input for Duarto." Mary smiled. "You know, I hope you can forgive him if he was abrupt. The pressure of the business—"

"We don't like to talk business at these events," Bob Bloogee said. "But some people have always mixed business and pleasure." Mary colored. Stuart watched her as she tried to be warm and charming, her blush heightening the effect of the fabulous pearl necklace that she wore, incongruously, with the milkmaid getup.

Stuart was mortified. Had anyone seen the snub? "That's it," he said to himself. "That's it." He'd been ready for a long, long time. Ready and like a bomb, ticking toward an explosion. He strode out of the enormous room.

It was another New York society ball, with lime sorbet to clean the palate . . .

"Can't we leave soon?" Miguel whispered to Annie.

"Aren't you hungry?"

"Only for you."

It was another New York society ball, with intrigues and gossip . . .

"Who's that?" asked Brenda, nudging Bob Bloogee and gesturing with her chin at a woman in black wearing what looked like a thousand carats of diamonds.

"The ex–Mrs. DeVere."

"The diamond-mine DeVere?" Brenda asked.

"The same."

"Jeez," said Bette. "What a chandelier."

"They're fakes," Bob told her. "They're the paste copy

of the gems she had, but remember, she's the *ex*–Mrs. DeVere."

"Yeah, so what? Don't they have community property in South Africa, at least if you're white?"

"More a type of equitable distribution: he kept the diamond mine, she got the shaft."

"Do you see Jon Rosen, the good-looking one over there?" Gunilla Goldberg asked Khymer Mallison.

"Sure, the one with the two women leaning on him. The weird one and Morty Cushman's wife."

"Yes, well, he looks positively exhausted. They are both waiting to devour him and Bill Atchison is being ignored. It's hilarious."

"Ignored *and* cuckolded, I hear."

"Yes." Since Morty Cushman's unfortunate fall from grace, Gunilla had done some abandoning of her own. She had warned Shelby that during this awkward time she had to be above reproach, but the little silly was making a spectacle of herself with the Rosen person. Not only a Jew, but an intellectual, with no money to speak of. Some Rhett Butler! Well, Shelby would never make it now. She was seated at a dark table in the corner. Gunilla had washed her hands of her.

Also relegated to Shelby's undesirable table were Aaron and his wife. Dr. Leslie Rosen Paradise spoke in a voice that would have killed love had there been any left to kill, but very quietly, so only Aaron could hear. "I am outraged, Aaron, at being seated here. It is conspicuous ostracism. Anne must be behind this. I knew she was passive-aggressive, but really, I expected a bit more class. I did not marry you to be insulted."

Aaron reached for his wineglass. Hell, he thought, it keeps on coming. He looked at Leslie in despair. If it would have done any good, he would have told her that their marriage was over, that he knew they had little regard for each other left, and that the best thing they could do now was just shut up. But she was too angry. Why the hell was *she* that angry? It was *he* whose life was ruined.

The music swelled. Even here, in his frigid corner, it was a warm invitation to move, to sway. But Leslie didn't dance. All at once, a desolation, a wave of loneliness and need, swept through Aaron. He thought of Chris, of Jerry, of Sylvie, of Annie. He longed for Annie. He longed to hold her, to feel her responsiveness in his arms. He longed to hear her laughter.

It was an irresistible impulse. He would find Annie and ask her to dance. Annie would be amused by his costume, though he hadn't gotten a smile out of Leslie. He was wearing his dinner jacket, but on one foot he had put on a yellow sock and a swim fin. He had come as What Is Wrong with This Picture?

Leslie was in a high bitch of a mood. Annie would laugh at his costume. He rose, as if drawn to her like a dowser to water. He mumbled an excuse to Leslie and walked out from the shadows to the island where couples swayed together. She would be sitting there, he knew. And after just a few moments, his radar picked her out. She was in a strange outfit, something he couldn't quite figure out, but she was smiling, and she was sitting with all her friends: Brenda, Elise, and people whom he didn't know. They were all talking and laughing gaily. He stood, watching them. He knew that much as he desired her, he hadn't the courage to break into that circle. Why, Elise Atchison and Brenda Cushman had helped destroy him. If only Annie would look up. If only she would sense him and come to him, feel his need.

But as he watched, she turned to the guy dressed as Sir Galahad who was sitting beside her. He continued to watch as the stranger led her to the dance floor and put his arms around the woman Aaron loved.

Well, he could cut in. He knew how to do that, and she'd never refuse him. He slipped off the swim fin, placed it over his arm, and walked onto the dance floor. He made his way through the Marie Antoinettes and devils, finally reaching Annie, dancing with her knight. He tapped the guy on the shoulder.

As if in a nightmare, he turned to look into the face of Miguel De Los Santos. He pulled his arm back as if the chain mail were red-hot. How did she . . . he . . . how did they . . .

"How? How . . . ?"

The two of them stood there, their arms entwined, and simply looked at him.

As Annie and Miguel walked back to their table, Stuart Swann nearly collided with them. He was walking unsteadily, too rapidly for the time and place. Annie guessed he must be drunk. He spoke to her.

"Watch this now, Annie," he hissed. He seemed beside himself with excitement. "Watch this."

What on earth is he up to? Annie thought. She looked after him and saw him sit down and turn toward the Goldberg table, his eyes glued intently on Gil Griffin. Annie followed his gaze and saw an attendant approach Gil with an envelope. Gil raised one of his bandaged hands in a gallant gesture to the rest of the table as if to excuse himself and, with some difficulty, opened the envelope. Annie felt a stab of guilt, then noticed that, to judge by Gil's exaggerated movements, he, too, had had a good deal to drink. She glanced back at Stuart. His face was tense, excited, and malignant. She shuddered and turned away.

Suddenly, she heard a loud shout from Gil's table. She

turned, as did many of the guests, to see. Gil stood over a cowering Mary, his arms outstretched. In his right hand he held a piece of paper, which he was waving up and down.

"You unbelievable bitch," he was yelling. "What the fuck have you done? You traitor! You dirty whore! You traitor!"

Now Mary Griffin was looking up at him. Her face was pale and her eyes were wide. She had leaned away from him at his first shout, but now sat paralyzed while he stood over her threateningly.

"You traitor!" he yelled again, and began to raise his hand over his head. Suddenly, Mary slipped sideways out of her chair, turned, and began to walk quickly away. Gil overturned his own chair and went after her. He grabbed her arm and shoved the paper into her face.

"You filthy little lying slut." His face was distorted with rage and his voice sent chills down Annie's spine. This is what it must have been like for Cynthia, she thought. Annie turned her head. Several men had risen in readiness to intercede, but the rest of the Hall of the Temple of Dendur was silent and still.

"My God, it's all being recorded," Elise said, breaking the silence with a loud whisper. "Look at the reporters." At the side of the room, the press was busily clicking and whirring away.

"Stay here," Larry said to Elise, rising. "I'll see what I can do."

"What do you have to say about this?" Gil now yelled, slapping Mary with the paper. She began walking away again, out of the light, across the bridge to the island that led to the exit.

Sol Goldberg waddled over to Gil and began earnestly talking to him. He tried to hold Gil's arm to detain him, but Gil shook him off. The major drama apparently over, the crowd began to buzz and stir.

Annie watched as Stuart Swann went up to one of the reporters, handed him a piece of paper, and spoke to him briefly. Then he walked over to Annie.

"This is what made Gil go berserk," Stuart said quickly, shoving a sheet of paper into Annie's hand. He then hurried away.

Annie unfolded the paper and looked at the photo upon it. Oh, this was vile, this was low. Annie stuffed the photocopy of Mary's first wedding picture into her bag, showing it to no one. She knew, though, how bigoted Gil was. It made her sick that Stuart Swann had caused this hideous scene; had caused Mary to be physically assaulted; made her sick that Gil was this demented; made her feel shame for knowing him. She thought that she must destroy the copy quickly, before anyone else saw it.

Just then, Gil broke away from Sol and began to run down the corridor of the Egyptian galleries. Sol moved after him, and so did some others. "I think I'd better go, too," Miguel told Annie, looking at her livid face. "Will you be all right?" She nodded mutely.

In the rotunda, Gil had just caught up with Mary, running now with hysterical energy. When he reached her, he tried to stop her, but she pulled away from him. In a rage, he snatched at her, grabbing her pearl necklace. Mary kept going, though her neck snapped back as Gil yanked on the pearls. For one long moment they stood, almost balanced, a strange pas de deux. Then she lunged away, and the necklace snapped. The hundreds of huge pearls scattered, bouncing over the marble floor.

Now Sol, Miguel, and the other men reached the rotunda. But Mary was out the door, on the stairs outside. It was cold, with a wet wind whipping down Eighty-first Street. The steps of the Museum were treacherous with ice. Still in furious pursuit, Gil reached for her, grabbing her hand and swinging her around. Cameras flashed in the darkness. Mary screamed. He was about to strike her when she lost her balance and began to plunge down the stairs. Gil, feeling her loss of footing, released her hand.

She fell forward, then rolled, then tumbled. At last she came to a stop at the bottom of the wide marble stairs. She was barefoot. She lay facedown, still.

II

Cromwell Reed It and Weep

The night of the ball had been the coup de grace for Bill. Before leaving home, Phoebe hadn't let him see her getting into her costume until she was completely dressed, then presented herself to him with an exaggerated "Tada." She had on thigh-high black leather boots with little fluffy stuffed bunnies pinned to the toes. She wore a chain vest over a black leather bra and had miniature stuffed teddy bears pinned randomly all over the vest. Black leather Mickey Mouse ears topped off the costume; the total look was lost on him, and she refused to explain it. "Art needs no explanation, darling. Now be a good daddy and lay out a couple of lines of sugar for your little girl."

He made a face. "It's just to keep the edge on, darling," she explained. He knew she was beyond the point of needing just an edge, but tonight he tried not to see it. Sitting at the table with all the Cromwell Reed people and Phoebe's mother, Julia Van Gelder, was excruciating, trying to control Phoebe's drug use and behavior in the presence of her disapproving mother and his partners and their wives, especially Celia Reed. When Phoebe began quoting Proust and inadvertently slipped into Mark Twain, he quickly led her away to the dance floor. She broke away from him, however, when she saw Jon

Rosen. Together they hurried off to the secrecy of an alcove. Bill turned away disconsolately. He knew he was in for a long night. Jon Rosen used almost as much cocaine as Phoebe.

Bill glanced over to his table and saw that all there had their eyes on Phoebe, measuring her degree of inappropriateness with an imaginary thermometer. Celia Reed had just said something through very pinched lips to Julia Van Gelder, and Julia picked up her purse and headed for the ladies' room. As she passed Bill, she snarled through clenched teeth, her lips not moving, "Get her under control or get her out of here. Do you understand me?" She didn't wait for an answer.

Bill intercepted Phoebe as she made her way back to the table and took hold of her arm forcefully. "Ow, does Daddy want to get rough? I'm dressed for it tonight," she said in a baby voice.

Anything to get her out of here. "Why don't we leave and you can show me the work that you've been keeping so secret at your studio?"

Needing no more urging, she grabbed Bill with one hand and a bottle of champagne with the other.

Phoebe was very excited; she had always said that Bill would be the first to see her finished work before it went to the gallery for the showing. As they got to her door, she stopped and said, "Close your eyes, it's a surprise."

As the door was opened, Bill's first sensation was an odor, a bad smell. Eyes still closed, he heard the studio spots being lit one by one, then the popping of a champagne cork. As he took his first sip, he opened his eyes, surveyed the room, and sputtered the unswallowed champagne down his shirtfront.

He tried to make sense of the brightly lit works, but couldn't shake the belief—the hope—that what he was seeing was some kind of a joke. But the odor was very real. It was worse than a stable. He stifled the urge to gag.

"Bill," Phoebe cooed, not able to interpret his physical reaction because of the drugs and alcohol. "*This* is my *greatest* work!" Bill's nausea increased as his eyes moved from one display to the next, noting the titles.

In individual Plexiglas cases sat mounds of excrement. Enough to have come from every sentient being on the planet, he first thought. With great effort, he isolated some of the descriptive labels: *From Shorty Jackson, Death Row, Sing Sing Prison;* a woman who had skied with the Pope attested to the authenticity of another specimen; monkey ca-ca; doggie-do, a major dump from someone at the Pentagon, and—the chef d'oeuvre—Phoebe's own. Mounds of it. Heaps of it. Oh, Jesus. Oh dear, sweet Jesus Christ.

Bill slumped against the wall for support, perspiration beading on his forehead. He closed his eyes to shut out the sight, but couldn't escape the smells. Phoebe was chattering on, unaware of Bill's repugnance. "Art is creation in its simplest form," Phoebe was saying. As drunk as Bill had been on leaving the ball, he became immediately sober and felt as if he were seeing life as it really was for the first time. Phoebe had gone over the edge. His love, his soul mate, was losing her mind. He couldn't let this happen; he needed her. It took all his powers of control to gently lead her back downstairs to the car and home.

Phoebe's entrance into the apartment on their return home seemed to give her new energy. She ran from room to room calling for her dog. She hadn't had a dog since childhood, he knew, but he let her run herself down, hoping that she would exhaust herself into sleep. He needed quiet, he needed to think.

Phoebe finally sat on his lap and asked him to read her a story. He agreed and she presented him with the *Story of O* and curled up into him like a little girl who was being read

Where the Wild Things Are. Bill knew he had no choice. He began to read to his little girl, her head resting lightly on his shoulder.

It took until six o'clock in the morning, but Phoebe was at last finally asleep, thanks to the Valium he found stashed in her bedside drawer. Bill, exhausted, did a line of coke and called Dr. Rosen at her home. After being reasonably assured that she was awake enough to understand, he told her of his discovery of Phoebe's latest art medium and self-expression. Leslie seemed not the least surprised. Or concerned.

"Bill, Phoebe has to express her unconscious in her art. This is a wonderful breakthrough for her. She's finally getting in touch with a very traumatic period of her life."

"For chrissake, Leslie." Bill had no patience for this psychobabble now. "She's doing cocaine, Valium, and vodka like a kid locked in a candy store. She's babbling, making a spectacle. She's killing herself."

"That's only a symptom of a deeper underlying disorder, Bill. There's a very important issue at play here." She paused. "Since you're almost her husband, I think you should know what it is that Phoebe is struggling with." Again she paused, this time to find the right words. "Phoebe had been anally violated repeatedly as a young child by her maternal grandfather."

Bill flopped into a chair. His stomach heaved. Those scenes, those debauched anal scenes between them. Whose part had he been playing?

"What? What are you telling me? Malcolm Phipps, the steel tycoon, was fucking his little grandchild up the ass in a household of at least twenty people in residence? That's crazy."

"It's the truth, Bill. I'm sorry to have to break it to you this way. But it is the truth. And it's very important now that you give her permission to act out, to express herself in any way she chooses. Without validation, she could indeed decompensate. There could be a major paranoid incident. I know how she behaved at the party last night, but that's just anger, a sign of her growth, not her decline."

"Growth? Are you fucking crazy? I just told you what she's using as art materials. And you saw her getup and her behavior at the party last night. You're going to tell me that this is all a sign of her *growth*?"

He caught his breath, his rage growing in spite of his attempts at control. "What the fuck is she growing into, can you tell me? *I'll* tell *you*. A flaming, drug-addicted nut case, that's what. And I think *you're* the one that's crazy. Go fuck yourself!" and he slammed down the phone.

Now, totally alone, he was unable to cope with the enormity of the situation. He was losing her. He was losing Phoebe, he thought, and he couldn't bear it.

Coldly, because it was necessary, Bill began to dial for an ambulance. Maybe this was the wrong thing to do, maybe it was a betrayal, but he simply could not cope.

Bill was not sure of very much anymore, but of two things he was certain: Phoebe was totally wacko, and in spite of it, he was still completely and utterly obsessed with her.

Bill sat at the desk in his law office, his fingers combing compulsively through his hair. Before him sat a styrofoam cup of cold coffee, slowly leaking on the blotter of his Mark Cross desk pad.

Phoebe was gone. And she would be away for a very long time. The psychiatrists at the private hospital in Hartford had assured him that Phoebe had now crossed the line into schizophrenia. The most that could be hoped for was a degree of stabilization, then perhaps some degree of reality through a regimen of drugs that would also, as their side effects, make her uncommunicative and very passive.

And there was the problem of money. Well, not really a problem. Since the Van Gelders had cut him off from access to Phoebe's trust fund by assigning a conservator, he had only his income from the law firm to rely on. Well, he could make do for a while. It would mean cutting back a little, but then again, he had developed his client billing and creative book-keeping to an art form.

His eyes scanned the office, his head hardly turning. The damage done by Elise's whirlwind outrage had been minimized: the broken antique Imari had been repaired, but their value and beauty greatly diminished; he had replaced the bent golf clubs; his antique hand-carved duck decoys had been expertly restored by a master of the art in Maine. It was a crime that Elise had sold off his collections for nothing, for spite, but he'd survive. Even after that debacle, he had been able to recoup, pick up the pieces, put that incident behind him. Well, he could do it again.

Bill's head snapped up as the intercom startled him out of his reverie. It was the senior partner, chairman of the executive committee. "Bill, I'd like you to come to my office right away."

Bill hung up and pulled out the small vial of cocaine he kept in his watch pocket for these emergencies. After a couple of lines, he threw some cold water on his face, combed his hair, grabbed his jacket, and rushed out the door and down the hall. Now what? he thought.

Don Reed motioned to a chair as Bill entered the room.

"Bill, there's a pall hanging over you like a shroud, and it's affecting the partnership."

Bill started to speak, but Don motioned him silent.

"Elise Elliot—your ex-wife—has pulled all her business

from Cromwell Reed, her considerably lucrative business. This firm has been handling her family's legal work for generations. And the family of your current—um, what-have-you—well, the Van Gelders have also threatened to pull their considerable business from the firm; again, after several generations of a relationship." Don paused and leaned his elbows on his desk.

"And Elise's uncle, Bob Bloogee, and Bloogee Industries, has also, after a longtime relationship, left us. So you can see, Bill, not only are you not bringing in any new business, but you appear to be directly responsible for the loss of millions—*millions*—of dollars of billings to this partnership each year."

Bill felt the sweat begin to dampen his armpits.

"Let me be brutally frank," Don said. "The executive committee has decided to let you go. You don't have a place in the partnership any longer. And we're hoping that you will do the gentlemanly thing and simply accept the decision."

Bill felt his chest heave, then he jumped up, the cocaine surging through him, turning his surprise into rage. "The *gentlemanly* thing? Accept getting fucked by my partners? Where is a fifty-seven-year-old ex-partner supposed to find work? What am I supposed to do now? Just 'take it like a gentleman,' shake hands, and say goodbye?"

This was more than he could bear. Anger rose in him, an irresistible wave. Someone had to be blamed for this, but who? Someone had to be punished. He'd kill this fat bastard. How many years had he listened to his stupid jokes, put up with the scraps from his table?

"Well, fuck you and the other 'gentlemen.' I'll sue your ass. You can't dump me just because I've had a few family problems. So you put me on trial for this?"

Bill noticed Don Reed sigh, as if pained. "The SEC has been around, Bill. They're looking for some information on

Morty the Madman stock. And you know how idealistic
young attorneys can be—and how scared. They're singing
like canaries, and you will most likely be subpoenaed. Which
means that this firm is—*I* am—in for some very close federal
scrutiny." Don clenched his teeth. "And we don't like that,
Bill. We don't like that *at all*."

Don Reed shifted upright in his chair. "So this isn't a trial,
Bill. Think of this as more of an execution. To top it all off,
we've also discovered your extensive cheating on your client
billing sheets. We consider that stealing from the partnership.
You can imagine how that last piece of news went over with the
executive committee. Married to one of the richest women in
the world, and he's stealing from his partners and clients. You've
lost your sense of subtlety, Bill, your sense of proportion."

Don lifted a cigar from the humidor and lit it, while Bill
sat watching as if from outside himself.

"So, I wouldn't talk anymore about suing if I were you,"
Don continued. "In fact, you should consider yourself lucky
that you're not being prosecuted for your crimes. Not yet, anyway."

"You cocksuckers," Bill whispered, rose unsteadily, and
headed for the door, now eager to get out of the room and the
building, his face linen-white.

But he was tired. It's no use, he thought. I can't go on.
Phoebe, my job, all gone. What am I going to do? How can I
go on without her? He had never felt this way for anyone. Now
he couldn't imagine what it was like not to want Phoebe. And
he couldn't fight the Van Gelders, the Don Reeds, alone.

Don Reed followed him, his face a mask of malevolent
anger. "Please vacate your office immediately. There are two
security guards waiting outside to watch you pack your personal belongings *only*, and a moving man with cartons is in
your office right now beginning the packing."

Bill slammed the door behind him, but it was hardly enough to express the desperation and isolation that had enveloped him. How did this all happen? How did he lose everything? Phoebe, job, money, position—everything? All gone.

Where do I find another wealthy woman, he thought, now that I have *nothing* to offer?

12

Shark Meet

At about the same time that Bill Atchison was being ushered out of Cromwell Reed, another partners' minyan stood in the carpeted corridor outside Gil Griffin's office. "He's lost control," one of the senior partners said, his voice trembling. "He's lost control."

"No, he's just lost it," said Stuart Swann, very matter-of-fact.

"I'm telling you, the same thing happened with Mitsui, and I made a horse's ass out of myself," Dwight McMurdo, another senior partner, asserted. "You're all overreacting. The man's a genius; he knows exactly what he's doing. First he set up the market on Mitsui and sold short. Now he's got everyone all crazy over Maibeibi. I tell you, he knows what he's about." Dwight spoke as if he had the inside track.

"But the price dropped eleven points last night, and then another five this morning, and it's only a quarter after nine in the morning!" the other partner whined anxiously. "What the fuck's going on?"

"Do you realize that he has almost seven hundred million dollars of our money tied up in this?" Robert Jamison, the oldest partner in the firm, asked. "And that was at the earlier, higher cost per share." His voice and hands shook, but as they often did, it wasn't clear whether he was more nervous than usual.

"Anyway, where is the fair-haired boy?"

"He might be a bit late today," Stuart Swann predicted with a smirk. "He had a big weekend."

"He's never been late before," cried McMurdo.

"He's never been in jail before!" said Stuart Swann.

The tabloids were intolerable. They lay crumpled in a pile beside him on the seat of the limousine. He looked up over the driver's shoulder and clenched his teeth. The traffic was brutal and this man couldn't drive. He looked down at his red, aching hands. Gil wouldn't be driving for a while, and not in the Jag. He winced. Someone had done a terrible thing to his baby. And to him. In fact, a lot of people had done terrible things to him; Mary was only the worst of the betrayers.

His glance fell on the *Post* headline, and he winced again. TRADER YELLS 'TRAITOR,' BEATS WIFE, it said. There were pictures, too. Mary running from him on the stairs of the museum. Him with his fist cocked, ready to belt her. SOCIETY BASH, read the *Daily News*, with a close-up of the two of them. But the worst was the wedding picture of her and that ape.

How had they gotten hold of that photograph so quickly when he himself had been so blissfully, so stupidly, unaware of it? How could Mary betray him in such a way, the disgusting, lying bitch? A shudder of revulsion passed over him. Her skin and his. Her breasts against that animal's chest, her silky hair against his kinky nigger mop. His hands on her, in her. His . . . God, it sickened him.

He didn't regret hitting her, not for a moment. In fact, he wished now that he could beat her within an inch of her life. Kill her, even. The thought cheered him for a moment. His fist smashing that lying mouth, his hands choking the breath out of her body, the whore. No, he didn't regret hitting her that time, before Japan. Now he wished he'd hit her harder.

But he did regret doing it publicly, making himself a laughingstock. All of his enemies—Steinberg, Bloogee, even Stuart Swann—would revel in this. They would rise up against him, a horde of smirking, smiling faces. At any meeting, any one of the bastards might sit there and gloat over the incident, secretly sneering while they blandly talked about new issues or ROIs.

Gil felt as if he might be sick. He choked back the sour taste that rose in his throat and tried to calm himself. *If I think about that, I'll never make it through the day. And I've got to. I've got to make it.* After all, she was only another cunt. Another useless woman. Tricked out differently, but as deceptive, as hopeless as all the other women he had known. His mother, who mouthed words of love and then let his stepfather beat him; his first wife, who couldn't choose between him and others, always straddling the line, wanting her family and babies and him, too. And now this one, the worst. Well, he'd let his lawyers handle all the rest of this.

But so far they had failed him, too. Two nights ago, detained by the police after the ball, when he had been allowed one phone call, he had called Cromwell Reed and, at two-thirty in the morning, had been unable to reach anyone. Not even Bill Atchison, that ninny. He had had to spend five hours sitting in that filthy cage at the Nineteenth Precinct until, at seven, some sniveling associate had been roused by his message on the tape. And the incompetent had taken more than an hour to bail him out. Christ, he must have paid that firm over $6 million last year alone, and that was the kind of response that he got? He'd talk to Don Reed about that.

Apparently Mary was in the hospital. Broken ribs, smashed nose. So what? He had not hit her there on the steps of the museum, only let go of her, and if the bitch hadn't stumbled, he doubted that she'd even be bruised. But the police, of course, were making the most of it, talking about attempted homicide if she died. The mini-lawyer from Cromwell Reed had said it had been a bit difficult to get him bail.

Well, he had gotten out, gone back to the apartment, recuperated, had the locks changed, put ointment on his chafed, burned hands, and dictated a memo to Mrs. Rodgers that could be released as a statement through their PR firm. Now, Monday morning, despite everything, Gil was ready to go into the office and complete the Maibeibi deal, the biggest of his life, the most important Wall Street coup since the Nabisco/Reynolds multi-billion-dollar merger. In the way he alone could, he compartmentalized, putting Mary and all the events of the weekend behind him. That was then, this is now, he said to himself, and wondered for a moment where he used to hear that phrase.

"I'll only do it if I can be in the club, too." insisted Bob Bloogee as Elise, Brenda, and Annie sat with him at a window table in the restaurant of the Regency Hotel. It was a magnificent room for breakfast, the walls painted with murals of castles, lakes, the woods, the soft fairytale blues and greens contrasting with the dark suits and serious mien of the heavy hitters who habitually breakfasted there. This was the place for New York power breakfasts, and at sixteen bucks for coffee and a croissant, Brenda wondered how even Zeckendorf and Rohatyn could afford it.

"Uncle Bob, come on. Don't be silly. How can you be a First Wife?" Elise asked reasonably. "You aren't a woman, and you've been married four times. Anyway, the Club isn't really a club. It's more a state of mind."

"Exactly my point," agreed Uncle Bob, beaming at them.

"I like your spirit, and I share it. Bette and I had a wonderful time with you at the ball. You all were superb in Japan. And I've enjoyed helping you. Gil was disgusting at the party. Bette wanted to knock his block off. I hate raw deals. I don't give anyone a raw deal, and when I get one, I take steps. And I like to think I'm often just like you ladies. Paladins. Righters of wrongs."

"Nah, she's a writer of novels," said Brenda, indicating Annie. "Not that she'll show us anything," she grumbled.

Annie, ignoring Brenda, smiled at Uncle Bob. "I think I see a way we can get around this impasse. Why don't we make you an honorary member in Cynthia Griffin's place, with the privilege of attending a meeting each year? And all social functions. After all, without your help there would be no justice for Cynthia."

"There you go, Annie, pissing me off, being perfect again," Brenda said. "So I second the motion. You third it, Elise?"

"There is no thirding. But yes, I agree." She smiled at her uncle. "As president of the First Wives Club, I welcome you." She extended her hand.

"Who died and left you president?" Brenda asked.

"Will we get justice today?" Annie asked Uncle Bob. "Will the whole Maibeibi thing work?"

"Ladies, I think I can safely promise you major bloodletting." Uncle Bob smiled wickedly.

Annie waved a thick file before them. "Let's boogie!" she cried, taking Brenda's arm.

In his limousine, still stuck in traffic, Gil Griffin's red, chafed hands held up the *Journal*, his eyes going over and over the numbers in disbelief. What the fuck was going on with Maibeibi? *Why* would it have dropped so much? Why would it? Gil had been prepared for a precipitous rise when word of the takeover got out and had bought an enormous number of shares to take advantage of the camp followers' impact. But this was out of left field.

Well, he wasn't going to be frightened. He was too experienced for that. There was no telling what was going on with those crazy bastards on the Exchange. He had nothing to fear. After all, the company was basically sound. Sound as a bell. And selling off the real estate and the shipyards would give everyone a windfall. He already held a strong enough position to announce his intention and stem the tide. But first, perhaps, take advantage of this. Perhaps buy a few more shares at this price. Then let the word out. Use this blip in the market as a bonus.

Gil nearly smiled. The difference between himself and other men was that he could take opposition and turn it into opportunity. He would do that now. But Christ, there wasn't even a phone in the car. He so rarely used it that he hadn't had one installed, though he had told Mary to look into it. Incompetent bitch. He pushed the thought of her from his mind. Well, he'd be at the office in just a few moments now.

George, his driver, pulled into the underground garage of 125 Wall and glided up to the lift, passing the empty spot where the now-ruined red Jaguar had stood. Gil averted his eyes as one might from the scene of a bloody accident. He longed for his car. I'll have Mrs. Rodgers check today on when it'll be ready, he thought. And she can get a phone in the limo, too, while she's at it. Now it was time to make some big moves.

When Gil Griffin walked through the lobby toward his elevator, he steeled himself. He would be impervious to anything, everything. Nothing but his work mattered. It never had. His mistake had been to think otherwise. He had always known that he wasn't like other men: he saw more, did more, commanded more. The weekend's unseemly social reversal simply confirmed his difference.

As he stepped off the elevator on the executive floor, he squared his shoulders and walked as briskly as ever. Mrs. Rodgers, waiting for him, hustled along, just as usual. If she felt anything, if she had read anything—and he supposed she had—she was smart enough to keep it to herself. Brusquely, he told her to check on the Jag, install a car phone, told her to cancel the rest of his morning meetings, and to get hold of Scopper, who would now handle his wife's special projects. She nodded, took notes, and stopped when he did to consult the Quotron.

Christ, Maibeibi had dropped further! Not a rout yet, but fifteen points. He went through everything again in his mind: their current cash position, the products, the facilities, the capitalization, everything. There was no reason for this fall. Well, he'd move ahead more quickly, before all the market sheep got scared. He'd make his press announcement today. God knows, everyone would show up—he was newsworthy after Saturday night. And the act would have a certain bravado.

He stopped at Kingston's office. The kid jumped up, ready to start jabbering. "Buy another six million of Maibeibi. Then another four." Gil stopped. Kingston, his eyes big, only sat down again and nodded.

"I'm holding a press conference downstairs at noon," Gil told Mrs. Rodgers. "Call corporate communications and let Lederer know. I've already briefed him. Hold other calls." He strode to the door of his office, flung it open. There was a woman there, sitting in a wing chair, her back to Gil. He turned to Nancy Rodgers, his anger apparent.

Her eyes opened wide. "Mrs. Paradise *said* you had an appointment with her, one that you made last night. She *said* your wife sent her."

"Yes, I told Mrs. Rodgers that. Don't blame her." Anne was sitting calmly, her hands in her lap, her legs crossed. "I wanted to have a little talk." Turning to Mrs. Rodgers, she added, "I'm sorry for the deception. You may go now."

She acted as if she owned the place!

"Is it all right, Mr. Griffin?" Mrs. Rodgers asked.

"Certainly," Gil said, shutting the door in her face, then striding across the room. Gil had seen Anne at the ball with Miguel De Los Santos, and at that moment he had decided she might have too much power to snub completely. But he wasn't about to be cowed either. "I've got a busy day, Anne. If this is about the party incident, you can take me off the committee. Whatever. My apologies."

"This isn't about the committee, Mr. Griffin. Not at all. No doubt you'll be blackballed for a while, and then your money will buy you onto other committees. Providing you still have the money."

Anne spoke in a pleasant voice, so Gil wasn't sure why what she said sounded so ominous. Well, she was a nobody. And it appeared that she'd gone native, socializing with that Puerto Rican. Find out what the bitch wants and get her out. "What can I do for you?"

"Mr. Griffin, I don't think you like women. Am I right?"

Gil snorted. Christ, he had no time for amateur psychology now. And what the fuck business was it of hers? He started to say the empty words that had been prepared for his public statement. "Listen, the incident the other night was a terrible mistake—"

"Oh, that isn't true. You hit your wife before this, and you beat Cynthia as well," Anne said pleasantly enough. "We know that."

"'We'? I know no such thing, and I resent—"

"'We' is me and my friends. Cynthia's friends. And we

don't like the way you've behaved." She looked at her watch, then stood. Stunned, Gil thought, well, at least the crazy cunt is leaving. But though Anne turned and walked to the door, she paused there. "My friends," she said, and opened the door. In walked two other bitches, and Bob Bloogee. It took him a moment to place the women: Morty Cushman's ex-wife and Elise Atchison.

"What the hell—"

"Your party's over, Gil," said Anne.

"We're here because of Cynthia," Elise said.

"You're going to be s-oo-rrrrrr-y!" the Cushman bitch added.

"Whatever you think you're doing, I want the four of you out of here in less than a minute. Otherwise I'll have security eject you."

"Ooooh, now I'm really scared," said the Cushman woman.

"Listen to me, you crazy bitches," he hissed. "I don't know what you think you're up to, but three embittered hags and a midget don't dictate to me."

"We're not dictating, Mr. Griffin," said Bob Bloogee.

"Not dictating, we're singing." The Cushman bitch began to hum. "'Yes, sir, that's Maibeibi. No, sir, don't mean maybe. Yes, sir, that's Maibeibi now.'"

"Your Japanese deal has just gone down the toilet, Mr. Griffin," Anne said.

Gil felt his stomach knot in fear. "What are you talking about?" he asked in a low voice.

"How much of it do you own now? About twenty-eight percent? Maybe even thirty? And what did you pay for it?" Anne Paradise asked. "Well, you may think you control the company, Gil, but Tanaki has already sold the shipyards to Bloogee Industries. We've made sure of that." She waved the contract by its corner. "In fact, you may find the value of your shares will plummet even more, once *that* piece of news gets out.

"Maibeibi is a very paternalistic company," Anne continued, "and Tanaki a very paternalistic CEO. When Tanaki understood that your takeover of his company meant that the shipyards would be immediately sold off so you could essentially get the rest of the company for free, he felt bound by loyalty to his employees. He couldn't let their company be diminished in such a way."

"I'll offer him more for it," Gil said. "Your deal won't hold."

"We think it will. Because Bob Bloogee sold Tanaki the Portland Cement plant that they need to get into the U.S. market. That agreement has also been signed," Anne said, indicating the contract Bob was now dangling from his fingers.

"Who the fuck do you think you are?" Gil began to scream. "I'll negotiate a deal with Tanaki—"

"Hardly likely. He's an honorable man," Annie said. "And it will hardly be relevant after today. You'll be trying to scrape this deal off your shoes for a long time to come. If you're still on Wall Street, that is."

Remembering the last time she was in this office and how Gil had treated her and her daughter's problem, Annie felt good. This was right and just, she thought. She laughed. "My goodness, Gil. Talk about stepping in it," she said, and turned up her nose at the imaginary smell.

Annie saw that Gil's face was as gray as his hair. For a moment she almost felt sympathy for him—after all, he was on the edge of the abyss—but then she remembered the words of her father: *Only the weak seek revenge, but only the strong command justice.*

"How does it feel to lose seven hundred million dollars in a single morning? Of your partners' money?" Anne Paradise asked.

"Why have you done this?" he asked, his voice a whisper.

"Ask Cynthia."

Gil's hands were shaking. For a moment he considered jumping over the desk and grabbing any one of them. But then they rose as one and without another word, turned and walked out of the room.

Was it true? he wondered. It couldn't be. He'd be ruined. He'd lose it all. His coup would turn into a fiasco. His partners . . . Holy shit, the bastards would throw him out. Jesus Christ, they'd crucify him.

Mrs. Rodgers came in. "The press conference has been arranged, but Mr. Lederer needs to speak to you first. And Mr. McMurdo and the other senior partners have been calling. They want to see you immediately, they said, in the boardroom. And there's another visitor. *He* says *he* must see you now." Mrs. Rodgers paused and smiled. She's enjoying this, Gil thought. She doesn't know what's going on, but she smells blood—my blood—and she's enjoying it.

"Has everyone gone crazy?" Gil nearly screeched. "I can't see *anyone* now."

"Oh, I think you'd better see me," said Miguel De Los Santos as he walked into the room. "You're going to have to see me about a lot of things."

Mrs. Rodgers closed the door quietly behind her as she left, the small smile still on her lips.

Gil, frozen for a moment like a diver before his plunge begins, thought of Napoleon's comment after the retreat from Moscow: *From the sublime to the ridiculous there is only one step.*

13

Paradise Lost

nnie. It's Aaron."

Somehow, she wasn't surprised. Still, she felt her stomach tighten, even if it was only for a moment. She took a deep breath, tried to loosen her grip on the phone.

"Hello."

"Listen, about Saturday night . . . at the party . . ."

"Yes?" His voice, the voice she knew so well, was subdued.

"Annie, please meet me for lunch today. I have to see you," he burst out.

"I can't, Aaron. I have a busy afternoon." Now, after her final, successful confrontation with Gil, she had only a few more things to do. She felt good. She'd taken charge of her life. She'd gotten justice for Cynthia. Today, she was seeing two different real estate brokers to talk about selling the apartment, and then she was driving out to Amagansett, to see agents out there. But why did she have to tell Aaron she was busy? Why couldn't she simply say no and put down the phone? She was in no mood to hear him whine about Miguel or Jerry or Chris or anyone else who was victimizing him.

"Please, Annie," he coaxed. "It's important. We could make it quick."

Aaron scanned the crowd nervously, looking for Annie's face among the nannies, out with kids, the joggers, the homeless, and the other flotsam and jetsam of a mild winter's day in Central Park. Since he had seen Annie Saturday at the ball, he had done some hard thinking. He didn't know what her connection was to the Santos guy, but he didn't blame her for telling the guy the truth. He saw his mistakes now clearly. And his need for her had grown and grown.

He was early, and although he was nervous, he felt good, lifted out of the lethargy that had dragged him down. He had told Leslie he needed some air and simply walked out the door. He was taking an action. I know what I want, and I can still get it, he thought.

Annie's slim form and brisk movements attracted his eye. There she was.

"Hello, Annie."

"Hi, Aaron."

"You look great, Annie. That color becomes you."

Annie laughed. "'Pink is the enemy of chic.' I read that last week. But thank you." She smiled.

Aaron smiled, too. What a relief to be with Annie! He took her by the arm and walked her out of the park thoroughfare they were standing in.

"Do you really want to eat here?" Aaron asked, looking doubtfully at the zoo restaurant.

"There's really not much choice," she admitted, scanning the scant menu. "But it's such a mild day, and the food is supposed to be better than at the old zoo cafeteria. Remember how we used to take the boys there? Are you hungry?"

"A little," Aaron lied.

"I just want tea and yogurt. And I would like to eat out on the terrace, if that's okay with you. It's not too cold. Then I really have to run."

"Fine," Aaron answered. "It *is* rather charming."

He opened the door and held it while Annie entered. As she did, she brushed very close to him and he became suddenly aware of the scent of her perfume. It nearly felled him. In a single moment it was all before him, the life that they had had together, the harmony, the ease, the friendship, the support, the love. He leaned against the doorframe to steady himself. He felt weak and on the verge of tears. Pulling himself together as best he could, he walked up beside her and looked at her to see if she had noticed his weakness. She had not.

Aaron took coffee and a sandwich. Then he and Annie, with her tea and yogurt, made their way out to the terrace that lined the walkway to the zoo.

"So, now you have to pay to get into the zoo," Aaron observed.

"Yes, and of course, the whole zoo is fenced off. Not like it used to be. You can't even walk through to go to the Wollman rink."

"I don't like it. It's not at all gracious," Aaron muttered. Christ, he thought. I hate this small talk. It's so fucking awkward.

"They did it for the animals' security, I believe," Annie went on. "But it's part of a general trend. People abuse assets and, therefore, lose them."

Aaron felt so sensitive that for a moment he thought that the remark was an indirect comment on him. He looked at Annie, but her face was serene—there was no malice. In fact, she looked to him like water to a thirsty man. He restrained himself no longer. His voice broke as he spoke. "Annie, I've got serious problems."

"I gathered that from your phone call," Annie replied calmly.

"Annie, things have gone from bad to worse. I'm in unbelievable trouble."

"I'm sorry, Aaron. Like what things?" There was a touch of concern in her voice, but only a touch.

"Well, you know that I always intended to get back Sylvie's money. And now with the sale of my partnership, I will," he hastened to assure her. "But even before that I really had a plan for the company which would have given me more earnings. I was going to borrow from Morty, and if it had gone right, I would have had enough to replace what I lost. But . . ." Aaron leaned over and covered his face with his hands. "I cheated. Morty gave me a tip. I used it when I shouldn't have." He didn't dare to look up, didn't dare to see her. "And Chris is angry with me. He says he's not sure if he loves me. He says I almost ruined him and Alex."

He sat for a moment, gathering his courage, and at last looked at her. The improvement in his looks that had come from his walk to the zoo and his new focus was gone now. His nose was red from the cold. It was Aaron, defeated, who spoke.

"And believe it or not, I regret now that I was going to try to force Jerry out. I realize that I like the guy. I need him. I behaved badly with him, with Morty. And with Chris. I need Chris. I need them all."

He turned his eyes back down to his untouched sandwich.

"Now there's that guy from the SEC who's called. I guess I'm in trouble. But haven't I been punished enough?"

Annie sighed and Aaron turned back to her. He sounded pathetic; he knew it. This wasn't going as he had planned. He'd better get back on track.

"I'm sorry, Annie. I shouldn't be burdening you with this." Then he looked at her with a gaze expressing as much sincerity as he had at his disposal. "Look. I don't how know how else to say it. It was a mistake to leave you. I see that now."

Annie sipped her tea.

He waited for a reaction. There was none. "What do you think of that? That I think it was a mistake?"

Annie was slow to answer. "Well, if you think it was a mistake, then, for you, maybe it was."

"But what about *you*, what do *you* think?"

"Do *I* think you made a mistake? At the time of the divorce I did. But then, when you married what's-her-name, I thought you were crazy." She looked at him. "I gather your marriage is in trouble, too."

Aaron was embarrassed and couldn't answer at once. "We have no deep understanding," he finally said, hoarsely.

"Ah."

"And I don't think we ever could. We have different values."

Annie made a little noise; was it a sort of snort? It irritated Aaron. At last, he sensed her detachment; he looked at her accusingly. "I get the feeling you don't care about what I'm telling you."

"Oh, I care, Aaron, somewhat. But you're married to someone else. I'd be crazy to stay emotionally involved with you." She paused. "But we were very close for a very long time, so, I still care . . . somewhat."

Aaron felt the affront but couldn't afford to take offense. Jesus, he told himself, you can't afford this pride. Please, please, let her see how you feel. Let her see how you need her, how you want her again. Once more he pulled himself together, focused all his energy, and took her hand. He knew she was his last hope.

He took a deep breath. "Do you think we could possibly get back together?"

Annie laughed slightly and rolled her eyes at him.

Aaron was confused but felt warmed by her laughter. His head was throbbing and he'd take any kind of relief. He smiled at her. "You think I'm crazy to want to try again?"

"Yes, Aaron. I'm sorry but I'm afraid I do. Do you think I could ever take you seriously? You're in trouble up to your ears, your wife isn't supportive—that's obvious—and you come running to good old Annie to make things better for you. You expect me to roll over like a dog, as if my life has just been on hold. I should just fall in with your plans. At least until they change. Aaron, do you know you're insulting me?"

"Insulting you? I'm asking to marry you! I think you're an angel. I'm willing to humble myself to get you back. I love you, Annie."

Annie became serious. "Give me a break, Aaron. You're a man who crumbles in adversity. You were a good enough dad to two easy, healthy boys, but even then you always favored the brighter boy. And you collapsed when faced with a handicapped daughter. Work was great when it came easy. Marriage, too. But when it gets tough—and it always does, Aaron—you bail out. You talk as if you haven't realized that I have a life of my own—plans of my own. Well . . . I do have plans. I'm not available."

Aaron felt as if he had been kicked in the stomach, or perhaps somewhere lower. For a moment it seemed as if the terrace actually shook under his feet. He gripped the edge of the white metal table. He thought of that De Los Santos character. Was there something going on there? Something more than professional? He was desperate now.

"Annie, how can you be so heartless? I'm in such trouble.

You're all I have. I love you! Doesn't our marriage mean anything to you?"

"Aaron"—Annie looked at him incredulously—"*we're* not married."

"Oh, God." Aaron cringed. "Don't remind me!" He put his hands over his eyes. "What am I going to do?"

Annie looked at him steadily and spoke to him in a way she never had before. "I guess you'll have to deal with your problems. Solve them. You *do* realize that *you* created this situation—you're not a victim."

Aaron took his hands away from his eyes. He could hardly believe she had used that phrase. She sounded like Leslie! He glanced back at her again to see if she was making some kind of macabre joke. No, she was serious. He felt the last shreds of his world crumbling. And he felt insulted. Well, if it wasn't too late, he'd rescue his dignity.

"So, you expect your knight in shining armor to save you?" he sneered.

"I don't need to be saved. Or rather, I did, but I saved myself."

"I have nothing else to say then," he said stiffly.

Annie was silent for a few minutes. She felt, deep inside her, even now, the longing not to go, the urge, despite everything, still to cling, to continue the drama. But the other part of her, the real Annie, was ready to leave. And I can stand the tear now, the tearing that felt so intolerable once. Now there is scar tissue. I had to take it when my mother left me, and when Aaron left me before, and when Sylvie left. Now I know I'll survive. It's he who doesn't know that now.

She spoke gently to him. "I guess I'll go then, Aaron." She looked at him, his handsome face surprised, a look that said, *This can't be happening.*

"But Annie. I'm so lonely."

"Don't worry. You'll get used to it," Annie said, and she left him.

Annie walked toward the zoo entrance. She paid the admission fee, went through the turnstile, and entered. She hadn't seen the new zoo.

It was much improved, but it was still only a prison for animals. Moving through the glass-enclosed habitat of the waterfowls, she felt sad. The ducks were swimming around in what at first looked like a large outdoor space, but upon closer observation, she realized a trompe l'oeil backdrop gave the appearance of expansiveness, and a mirror doubled the view. She doubted it fooled the birds.

She stood before the tricked-out cage and for a moment wished that things were different. If only Aaron hadn't left her. They had been happy. In the coldness, the falseness, of the fast-paced New York life, they had made a family. She wished, oh, how she wished, that they could go back to the way it had been. But that past wasn't real and she saw more clearly now. She saw the real edges of the cage it had been.

The sadness of the plight of the trapped animals was lifted by her sudden realization: I don't love Aaron. And I don't even want him anymore. We all live in cages, she thought. Loving Aaron was a cage, and the large penthouse apartment, filled with such sad memories, was another.

I'm luckier than the ducks, she thought. I can walk away.

She continued to walk through the zoo. She came to the polar bears. For a moment she felt sorry for her ex-husband. But Aaron doesn't love me, she thought. He's just like these caged animals now. They don't look dangerous, but they are. Like the wild beasts in the zoo, if allowed back into her life, the moment that he didn't get what he wanted from her, the moment he no longer needed her nurturing or felt deprived of it, he would attack and destroy her. Or leave her. As he had already done.

She walked outside, past the monkey enclosure, toward the exit of the zoo. She was filled with that profound feeling she had had in Katsura. I have my friends, she thought, my writing, and if eventually only a small studio apartment, it will be larger in some ways than any place I have ever lived before.

"I'm free!" she said, and left the zoo, entering the real world.

The Wives

Getting It Together

Paths

Gunilla Goldberg extended her arm, bending back her wrist and twisting her hand in the characteristic movement of a newly manicured woman. The talons that tipped each finger were now a uniform two inches long, and all were colored an even, glossy carmine. In New York, for approximately six dollars a finger, your nails could be coated with a thin layer of silk, sealed with glue, and thereby maintained at perfection at all times. "What do you think?" she asked Khymer Mallison, who sat at the table beside Gunilla's, her own hand being ministered to.

"Nice," Khymer told her absently, though she felt the color made Gunilla's skin sallow.

Gunilla shook her head. "Too hard. I knew I should have gone with the Bridal Path Pink." She looked up at the anxious Eastern European woman across the table from her. "Take this off. I prefer the pink."

Malla hid her sigh. Three coats *and* a top coat before the *strenka* changed her mind. And Malla knew from experience that Mrs. Goldberg wouldn't tip enough to make up for the lost time. She forced a smile, picked up a cotton swab, immersed it in remover, and dragged it over Gunilla's index finger, making a bloody clot of the polish.

"You know who I saw the *autre jour?*" Gunilla asked. Khymer turned, mildly interested. "That Mary Griffin. The one who Gil Griffin beat up before he went to jail."

"Really?" Khymer asked. "Where did you see her? I thought she'd disappeared."

"Well, I was discussing a fund-raiser at the Morgan Library—you know, it's in that dreary neighborhood where Altman's was—and I broke a nail. I needed a quick fix, so I went into one of those Korean places." Both women shuddered. The Korean manicure shops that had sprung up all over Manhattan catered to working women, not the Khymers and Gunillas of the world. "Butchers, of course. They wanted to *cut* my cuticle! Well, anyway, I looked up, and there was Mary Griffin, sitting as close to me as you are, getting a pedicure."

"Did you talk to her?"

"*Bien sûr.* They had nothing to read but four-month-old *Vogue* and *Cosmo* magazines. She was more interesting than *that*, though not much, the poor thing."

"I thought she had left the city. What's she doing?"

"Oh, working for some insurance company in a totally dreary job, and living in Turtle Bay. It was embarrassing, really. But *c'est la guerre.*"

Yes, Gunilla thought, if you don't keep fighting, you could slip down the greased pole and wind up in Turtle Bay. But she'd been on the top, and she would be again. She wondered if things were going well between Ted Turner and Jane Fonda. Well, even if they were, she didn't mind. She'd find *someone*. And Jane had almost made it chic for a mogul to date someone his own age.

"Whatever happened to that *other* blonde?" Khymer was asking. "You know, Shelby Cushman?" Khymer was taking a dig at Gunilla. Another of Gunilla's little social plans that had gone awry.

Gunilla sighed. "Oh, she filed for divorce from her husband before he went off to Allendale, and then she got dumped by Jon Rosen and went home to Savannah or wherever it was. Of course, the Symingtons were wretched. But I hear she finished the divorce and is off hunting in Dallas. She might do well

there." She gave Malla a bright smile of thanks as the manicurist began applying the new polish. "Are you going to the
Van Gelders' party next week?" she asked casually.

Khymer smiled. "Yes. You, too?" She knew that Gunilla
hadn't been invited. Since Sol had left her for that Sally Wor-
thing, Gunilla's social life had slowed down quite a bit. "I hear
they're announcing their daughter's engagement. You know,
the weird one with the funny name."

"Phoebe," Gunilla told her in a voice that sounded tired.

"Yeah. I heard that she's quit art and gone into acting.
She's going to marry that movie star she met in the rehab
hospital."

"Kevin Lear. Yes. It's the *only* way to meet men nowadays,"
Gunilla said bitterly. "Liz Taylor did it. It's that or prison. Let's
see: Morty Cushman, Gil Griffin, Ivan Boesky, Milken, and
Steve Brettan. No wonder there's such a shortage of men."

Khymer laughed. "*I* haven't noticed," she said bitchily.

"You will, dear. You will." Gunilla wondered just how
well the Mallison marriage was going. Khymer's husband has
always seemed to like me, she thought. Perhaps . . .

Just then, Annie Paradise walked by them. "Hello, Annie,"
Gunilla said. "It's been simply ages."

Annie stopped and smiled. "Yes. Well, I've been sort of off
the social circuit."

"I understand," Gunilla said.

Annie walked into the bare foyer of her now almost empty
apartment, being careful not to smear her manicure. She
hadn't had one in months, both because of all the typing she
was doing and because of the money they cost. But now things
would be a bit easier. The penthouse had sold, not quickly, but
at a good price. She crossed the living room, echoing not only
with memories but with the sound of her footsteps against

the shiny parquet, snapping back off the vast glass windows. Without the muffle of furniture and curtains, the room was an echo chamber, and without the ability to close off the view it became too close, too invasive, too hard.

It was her last night in the apartment, in New York. All that was left was her old mattress, not worth storing, and a cracked lamp from Sylvie's room, plus a few odds and ends that she was leaving behind. Well, she was really leaving all of it behind, she thought.

It hadn't been so difficult to say good-bye to Sylvie this time. Annie wondered if it was because Sylvie seemed so content or because Annie's own life was so much more full. She thought back to the moment of insight she had had in Japan. It had stayed with her and sustained her.

Sylvie and Hiroshi had already become friends; their lack of a common language seemed unproblematic. Hiroshi had brought Sylvie one of the lovely Kyoto dolls that were so justly famous, and Sylvie seemed to love him and it equally. She was a happy girl.

Annie entered the bedroom where her suitcase was lying opened on the mattress. She had only to add the new dress, an extravagance, but one she could justify. After all, Elise had sent her the tickets to Nice, a first-class round-trip, and her note said there was a room waiting for her at the Hôtel de Paris in Cannes.

Annie would be taking the nine A.M. Pan Am flight tomorrow morning. This would be her last evening in New York and in the apartment she had so dearly loved. All the furniture had gone into storage, the bonsai were distributed to friends and the hospital, her clothes already packed and shipped. And tonight Annie was having a farewell dinner with Miguel at Le Refuge. All she had to do was dress and pack her new gown and the ever-growing manuscript. Then she'd be ready.

But as she began to fold the dress, she was tempted to try it on once more.

She slipped it over her head. It was simple, but made of the most luxurious silk jersey. Round-necked, with long, tight sleeves that were meant to be wrinkled and clingy, it had a clinging bodice that then, almost magically, spread to the floor in a bias cut so beautifully done that one couldn't trace where the fullness started—it was like an inverted blossom. And it was crimson, a true flame color. So unlike her, in her usual safe oysters and creams and pinks. Annie smiled at the reflection she made in the bathroom mirror. With her mother's earclips, she'd look very nice indeed. She wouldn't shame Elise.

Miguel picked her up at seven. She let him into the empty place, and he walked through the rooms to the window wall.

"Very nice," he said, looking out over the river.

"Once it was." Changing the subject, she asked, "You're certain that you can't come to France?"

He shook his head. "Elise invited me, but there's just so much work right now. You understand, don't you?"

Annie nodded. Since the Gil Griffin conviction, there had been talk of Miguel for DA or maybe even mayor. She smiled.

He turned to her. "You know, Annie, my divorce is final in another month. I haven't asked you about your plans beyond your trip to Japan."

"And I appreciate it. I really do. Japan is something I want to do on my own. It's my gift to myself, and I think it's the first thing I've done just for me. Mr. Tanaki's offer is too good to refuse. I'll have a little house, and a tutor, and a Buddhist teacher. Let me finish the revisions to the book, and then I'll come back, and then let's see." She paused, searching his face. "Is that all right?" She took his hand. He held hers tightly. "When I come back, since I won't have a place here to live, maybe I can stay with you for a night or two?"

"It's a distinct possibility." Miguel laughed. Gently he reached up and stroked her cheek.

When Annie got off the flight in Nice, she had only her carry-on bag, and it made customs and immigration easy, if any French bureaucracy could ever be called that. But as she walked out of the swinging doors to the rest of the Nice airport, she immediately saw her name—her maiden name—held up by a uniformed driver. At her nod, he hurried to her and took her bag. "Mademoiselle MacDuggan? I 'ave been looking for you," he confirmed in charmingly accented English. "Mademoiselle Elliot asked me to take you to the villa right away. It is okay?"

"Villa?" she asked, and he nodded.

"There 'as been, 'ow you say, a change?"

The drive, along the winding coast road, was breathtaking. Annie realized, with a pang of regret, that she hadn't been to the south of France for more than a decade—since her tenth-anniversary trip with Aaron. What had she been waiting for?

Well, that's all over now, she thought, comforting herself. I'll keep to my path, and I'll try not to confuse my dream of anyone with who they really are. Aaron is over, Sylvie is taken care of, the boys are fine, and I am alone. For now. She thought of Miguel and hoped she'd go to him out of strength, not weakness. She stared out at the beautiful Mediterranean. I have never felt better, she thought, patting the bag at her side.

"Annie, darling, you've arrived! Was your flight ghastly?" Elise greeted her with a warm hug at the door. Larry kissed her and offered to take her bags, but Annie kept the small one beside her.

"I'm sorry about the change of plans, but since the first, unofficial showing, it's been a nightmare. The press and the distributors won't leave us alone." Elise laughed. "Where were they last winter? All you have to do is make a phenomenally successful film and then they won't leave you alone. The hotel was a mob scene, so we took this place instead. I hope you'll like it."

Annie looked at the enormous white room that opened to a terrace, pool, and a more distant view of the Côte d'Azur.

"What's not to like?" asked Brenda, coming in from the terrace. "Surprise, surprise!"

"Brenda! You lying dog! You said you and Diana couldn't get away."

"Well, if you're stupid enough to believe that I'd give up a free trip to Cannes and seeing my buddy here win the Film Festival, just to keep everyone honest at Paradise/Loest and to attend a Gay Pride Day march in Poughkeepsie, you deserve to be lied to." She, too, hugged Annie warmly. "Come on out to the veranda and join the party."

"So, we do get to do this all together!" Annie exclaimed. The other two nodded, guilty. "You sneaks!"

"And not just First Wives. Honorary members as well," said Bob Bloogee, walking in from the veranda with Bette beside him.

"Yo, Annie!" she called.

"I think this calls for a drink," said Larry, carrying in both a bottle of champagne and San Pellegrino water. He gave each of the guests their choice. Then, from off the buffet, he raised a slice of bread. "A toast!" he exclaimed, and they all laughed.

Later, after a superb dinner and more than a couple of bottles of assorted beverages had been drunk, Elise, Annie, and

Brenda sat together in the salon, the lights dim. The next morning they'd be up early for the screening, but they felt, all three of them, reluctant to let the evening end.

"Well, fellow club members. I think we've succeeded in doing what we set out to do," Elise said with satisfaction.

"Yes. Morty is broke, Gil's lost his status, Bill's been neutered, and Aaron's abandoned. Not bad for beginners, huh?" Brenda asked.

"Hell hath no fury . . . ," Elise murmured.

"I think it's time for a new slogan, though," Annie suggested. "Since it *is* over when it's over"—her two friends looked at her expectantly—"how about, 'Living well is the best revenge'?"

"The proposal is on the floor and seconded," Elise said approvingly.

"Passed unanimously," added Brenda. "First Wives Club meeting now adjourned."

They sat for a while in companionable silence.

"So, you're off to Japan and Miguel is out of the picture?" Brenda asked. "Permanently?"

"No. Only for now. He's wonderful—he's a really good man—but I'm not sure that a man is what I need most right now."

"Tell me about it," Brenda said, laughing.

"Oh, Annie, won't you be lonely in Japan, all by yourself?" Elise took her hand. "I'm so very happy with Larry. I wish that you—"

"I won't be alone. Mr. Tanaki and his family will host me. I'll be fine. Wish me spiritual growth. Wish that I could finish the second draft of my book."

"Second draft? What about the first?"

"Done," said Annie proudly.

"Why, talk about sneaks!" Brenda cried. "Did you really? What a good little girl you are."

"Well, not as good as I used to be, I hope."

"But how thrilling. May I read it?" Elise asked.

"More importantly, did you dedicate it to me?" Brenda asked.

Elise snorted. Then she switched into Elise in action. "You know, I am in contact with a lot of agents. . . . We're hot right now." She paused, thinking. "Swifty Lazar maybe. Or Mort Janklow."

"Thanks, but they're not for me. Anyway, I already have taken care of it. Amy and Al at Writers House have been wonderful."

"Annie, you finished the book and got *two* agents and didn't tell us a thing? You still can't be trusted."

"Well, you and Diana were busy renovating your apartment, and Elise and Larry were doing their movie. I had to keep busy *somehow*, didn't I?" Annie smiled. "Anyway, I wanted to wait until I found out if the book was an embarrassment or not." She paused for a moment. "My agents are very encouraging. They say it might even be commercial."

"Annie! How great. So, what's the secret masterpiece about?" Brenda asked.

"Oh, you know," Annie said slyly, looking at her two dear friends. "The same old, same old." And she lifted the *First Wives Club* manuscript out of her bag and put it down between them on the flat, shining surface of the table.